Abby smiled, and wit... she was going, stepped into the hall. She collided with a granite wall of flesh and stumbled backward.

Something warm, strong, yet gentle secured her arm.

"Oh. I'm sorry, I wasn't watching where I was—" Words escaped her the instant her eyes landed on the sculptured face of the handsome man gazing down at her, still holding her arm.

He looked every bit as startled as she was. "Are you all right, miss?"

"I'm—I'm fine. Thank you." She straightened. Only mere inches from him, her eyes never drifted from his.

"I'm sorry for staring, but you have very unusual eyes. They're quite beautiful."

Those same eyes twinkled. "Thank you." The stranger said it like he meant it, but his closed-lipped smile didn't stretch very far. "Could you please tell me where I might find Miss Abigail Bowen?"

"I'm Abby."

Surprise flounced across his face, and his attention drifted over her again, starting with her feet and ending at her hair.

"You're...Miss Bowen?"

Debra Ullrick
and
Janet Dean

The Unintended Groom
&
The Bride Wore Spurs

LOVE INSPIRED
INSPIRATIONAL ROMANCE

LOVE INSPIRED®
INSPIRATIONAL ROMANCE

ISBN-13: 978-1-335-44878-1

Recycling programs for this product may not exist in your area.

The Unintended Groom & The Bride Wore Spurs

For questions and comments about the quality of this book, please contact us at CustomerService@Harlequin.com.

Love Inspired
22 Adelaide St. West, 40th Floor
Toronto, Ontario M5H 4E3, Canada
www.Harlequin.com

Printed in U.S.A.

CONTENTS

Debra Ullrick is an award-winning author who is happily married to her husband of over thirty-five years. For more than twenty-five years, she and her husband and their only daughter lived and worked on cattle ranches in the Colorado mountains. The last ranch Debra lived on was also where a famous movie star and her screenwriter husband chose to purchase property. She now lives in the flatlands, where she's dealing with cultural whiplash. Debra loves animals, classic cars, mud-bog racing and monster trucks.

Debra loves hearing from her readers. You can contact her through her website, debraullrick.com.

Books by Debra Ullrick

Love Inspired Historical

Visit the Author Profile page
at Harlequin.com for more titles.

THE UNINTENDED GROOM

Debra Ullrick

And we know that all things work together for good to them that love God, to them who are the called according to his purpose.
—*Romans* 8:28

To God be the glory. Without His help, and the help of my dear friend and author extraordinaire Staci Stallings—God blessed me abundantly by sending her into my life—my stories would never get written.

And to my husband and best friend, who throughout our thirty-eight years of marriage consistently told me that whenever a problem arose, God would take care of it. Sweet hubby, you were right. God always did and still does. So thank you, darlin', for being my example of faith and trust in a loving Savior.

I love you so very much and always will. You're the other half of my heart and soul.

(MEGA HUGS AND KISSES)

Your forever devoted wife,

Deb

Chapter One

~≈~

Hot Mineral Springs,
Colorado 1888

"What do you mean, I can't?" Abby Bowen fought to keep from slamming her hands on her hips and glaring down at the rotund man seated in front of her.

"I'm sorry, miss," the mayor and head chairman of Hot Mineral Springs, Mr. Prinker, said as his checks flushed.

"Why didn't you tell me this before I bought the place?" She clenched her teeth as hot anger boiled inside her. There was no excuse for this. None whatsoever.

"We didn't know what your intentions were for the building. We assumed you wanted to open a dress shop or a restaurant or even a luxurious mineral spa for women. We already have one for men, you know." He grabbed the lapels of his jacket and puffed out his chest like a zealous rooster who was full of himself. "Any one of those would have been allowed. However, we—" he glanced around the large rectangle table at each of the seven town committee members "—cannot allow a single woman to open a theater. Why, something of that nature would be quite scandalous and ruin our town's fine upstanding reputation. Not to say your own, young lady." He shook his forefinger at her.

Abby wanted to latch onto his meaty finger and shove it up his bulbous red nose. But that attitude would get her nowhere, much less please the Lord. She quelled her anger as she searched for another option. Why some townspeople thought women who ran a theater were of questionable repute, she didn't understand. In other towns, people did it all the time, and it was not considered a scandal.

"It's too bad that your name is not *Mr.* Bowen," Mr. Prinker said as if in deep thought. "For if it was, we might consider your proposal. However, as it stands, we will have to refuse the license required by our town to open such an establishment."

Such an establishment? What did that mean? Whatever it meant, she didn't care. She just wanted to make sure she understood him correctly. "Let me see if I get this straight. Are you saying if I was a *man,* I would be able to obtain this license?"

"In a manner of speaking, that's precisely what I'm saying. However—" he rubbed his double chin for the longest moment of her life "—there is one other alternative."

"And what, pray tell, is that?" Abby didn't even try to keep the sarcasm from her voice. She'd about had enough of these men and their preposterous accusations.

"If you were to take on a male business partner, a gentleman with an outstanding reputation, then we would consider allowing you to open your theater. Isn't that right, gentlemen?"

They all nodded their heads.

What?! Surely these buffoons weren't serious. Were they? Abby gazed at each man to see if they indeed were. Their stoic faces confirmed her assessment. She shook her head at the utterly and completely outlandish idea. "So you're saying, *if* I obtain a *male*—" she emphasized the word male with abhorrence "—business partner, then you will allow me to open my theater? Correct?"

"Yes, ma'am. We feel it's the only proper way. I am certain, ma'am, that you will find there are many upstanding men in our community who would be more than willing to help you with your business adventure. Including any one of us here in this room." The mayor's horse teeth overtook his supercilious grin.

Oh, how she wanted to reach over and whip that arrogant smirk right off his thin lips. Humpft. As if she needed their help running a business. There wasn't one person in this room with whom she'd ever consider doing business with. They all looked shiftier and greedier than a gang of bank robbers.

"Excuse me a moment, gentlemen." She all but choked on that last word. These men were no gentlemen.

"Of course." Mr. Prinker's smile couldn't get any phonier than it was right now.

Abby stepped outside the room and slipped around the corner so she could be alone a few minutes. She paced up and down the sparkling-clean hallway, wringing her gloved hands. With each step she took on the polished hardwood floor, her button-up shoes echoed, her pink silk bustle gown swished and the pink plume on her hat danced.

She couldn't believe this whole ludicrous thing was even happening. After spending the last year and a half going to plays and even participating in a few, she knew what she wanted to do with her life. That desire had only escalated when her ex-fiancé, David Blakely, had broken their engagement—the very day she had told him she could never bear children. After that, every time she'd seen him with his wife, the woman he had married two weeks after he had ended their engagement almost one year ago, and their newborn son, the dagger of rejection plunged deeper into her heart. That's when she had plotted her escape from the Idaho Territory. Eventually, as she worked on her new life, the pain had gone away, and her focus turned completely to fulfilling her dream, a dream that was about to die before it even got started. All because of a room full of portentous, dishonest, stodgy old men.

And if she were honest with herself, her own stupidity, as well.

Why hadn't she listened to her brothers? Haydon, Michael and Jess had warned her about buying a building without seeing it first. But no, she had assured them the ad stated the mansion at the edge of town was previously owned by a prominent family, so therefore, it had to have been well taken care of. They weren't convinced. But she refused to let that stop her. Her stubborn exuberant way took charge as did her dream of life outside the confines of her family. Thus, she let them know she had prayed about the whole thing and was confident in her decision to go ahead with her plans.

The theater was third in her line of dreams, but it was all she had left to dream about. So using the money her father had left her, money he had intended for her and her siblings to use to fulfill their dreams, she'd gone ahead and purchased the place sight unseen. What a mistake that turned out to be.

The very day she arrived in Hot Mineral Springs, Colorado, she quickly discovered her brothers had been right. No maintenance had been done on the home since the owner had moved back east years ago. Because of the mansion's abandoned condition, there was no way for her to sell the place and get her money back so that she could move somewhere else. Someplace where she would be allowed to open up her business.

Abby stopped pacing. For a brief moment she closed her eyes and sighed. No, like it or not, she was stuck with the place.

She flicked her thumbnail with her teeth as she tried to come up with a plan, but nothing came to mind.

Oh, if only she could have opened her dinner theater back home in Paradise Haven, but she couldn't. They already had one, and the town wasn't big enough for two. Not only that, she had to move away.

She just had to.

Being at home constantly reminded her of the two things she wanted most out of life but could never have—children of her own and the love of her life, David. What she needed to do now was to expunge the past and its painful memories. She'd start now by forcing her mind to take a turn in another direction, to figure out a way to make her business adventure work. Operating a theater would not only keep her busy, but it would give her life meaning. Something she desperately needed.

With a new resolve, Abby determined it would be a hot day in a shed full of ice before she would allow anyone to throw away her opportunity for happiness and fulfillment. No one, not even these men, would steal those things from her. There had to be a way to fulfill her dream.

There just had to.

It was in the next moment Abby remembered that it was God who had led her here. And it would be God who would solve the obstacles before her. She sent up a quick prayer for wisdom, and within seconds a plan formulated in her mind. It was a drastic one, but it just might work. Knowing it would be strictly for business purposes, she would place an advertisement for a business partner. A male one. She rolled her eyes at that one. But she'd do it. That would fix these pompous men's wagons fine enough.

Satisfied and feeling somewhat pleased with her scheme, she headed back into the boardroom. Abby put on her best acting face and eyed each man with a sweet smile. "Gentlemen, I've decided to do what you have asked. I will take on a *gentleman* business partner."

Their faces lit up and greed ravished their eager eyes.

"But—" she held up her hand "—it won't be with anyone here. Good day, sirs." With those words, she whirled on her heels and breezed out of the conference room, leaving each man with his mouth hanging wide open.

Now all she needed to do was make haste and find a gentleman who would be willing to become her partner. Was there such a man? One who would agree to the terms she'd already started formulating in her mind?

Outside, the light breeze brought with it the smell of sulfur from the hot mineral springs. She'd been here two months now and she still hadn't gotten used to the rotten-egg odor. To think that people actually bathed in that smelly water made her shudder. How revolting.

She'd been amazed to learn that Indians believed the waters to be sacred. That they relaxed in the natural hot mineral pools here, believing it healed their minds, bodies and souls.

To think that the mayor actually thought she would want to open a women's spa utilizing that water. Did women actually bathe in that stinky stuff, too? She wrinkled her nose, then hiked a shoulder. If they indeed did, she might have to consider opening a spa. Something she would have to discuss with her business partner. Or would she? Could she do one on her own and the other with him? Whoever he was.

The very idea of having a partner, someone who would have a say in how things were run, was about as pleasant as the thought of a million spiders crawling all over her. Over the past two years, she planned exactly how she wanted to run her dinner theater. What it would be like. What meals would be served. What plays would be staged. What furniture and place settings she would use. All of it. Down to the very last detail. Would her new business partner, if she found one, try to change those plans? What was she thinking? She shook her head at her own silliness. Of course he wouldn't. She wouldn't let him.

Maybe the man would agree to split the business

60/40. That way she would have controlling interest of how things were run. Mr. Barker, her new stepfather back in Paradise Haven, whose business-savvy mind she'd questioned almost daily over the past year and a half all the way up until the day of her departure, had taught her that. But… She sighed. Where would she find such a man who would be willing to do that? She didn't know, but God did. Her lips curled upward with the knowledge that God was in control and that He would work it all out.

Abby gazed up at the clear, blue sky and sent up her prayer request. When she finished, she thanked God for the answer. After all, that's what living by faith was all about. Trusting Him for the answer before it ever came. Two scriptures popped into her mind. Hebrews 11:1 *Now faith is the substance of things hoped for, the evidence of things not seen.* And Philippians 4:6 *Be careful for nothing; but in every thing by prayer and supplication with thanksgiving let your requests be made known unto God.*

Confident she had done that very thing, her attention slid downward toward the tall mountains surrounding the eighty-five-hundred-feet-above-sea-level town. The high altitude had taken some time getting used to. At first, breathing the thin air had been difficult, and she had gotten a lot of headaches. Drinking more water seemed to help. Eventually, she had gotten used to the thinner air, and the headaches were gone. Because of that, she now loved living in these majestic mountains. Mountains unlike any she'd ever seen back home in Paradise Haven in the Idaho Territory.

Back there, the land was much different from here

with its rolling hills, bunch grass, tall wheat and rich volcanic ash soil. Here there were large hay meadows, oodles and oodles of sagebrush and high mountains covered with aspen, blue spruce and ponderosa pine trees. Hidden in those breathtaking mountains were running brooks of crystal clear water, concealed waterfalls, wildflowers, caves, bears, mountain lions, bobcats, foxes, coyotes and lots of lots of deer and elk. Her favorite things in this remote mountain town were the hummingbirds, the tiny striped ground squirrels and the itty-bitty chipmunks. Each brightened her day with their cute antics.

The desire to stay in this beautiful town snuggled cozily into her. Only one way to make that happen, though. She'd better get to it. And now. Anxious to get home so she could word her advertisement carefully, and post it as soon as possible, she picked up her pace, sending up yet another prayer. "God, send me the right man. And make it quick."

Harrison Kingsley sat at his deceased father's massive mahogany desk and re-read Abigail Bowen's advertisement for the fifteenth time.

Wanted: Business Partner.

Prosperous business opportunity for the right gentleman. Guaranteed full return on investment within three months, including interest. If interested, please contact newspaper for more information.

At first he'd thought the ad had been some kind of prank, but his gut told him it wasn't. Years ago, he'd learned to follow his gut instincts and to trust in them, so three weeks ago he had contacted the paper. They informed him all correspondences would be made through them.

Within a week of responding to the advertisement, he'd received his first reply and was shocked to discover the advertisement had been written by a woman, a woman who had asked many questions about his life. Such as, how old he was, what he did for a living, where he was from, why he was interested in becoming a business partner and many more. Harrison answered each one honestly, and even asked some of his own. The hardest one to answer was, "Why are you willing to invest?"

Need. That's why. He glanced at the legal paper lying on his desk mere inches from his fingers. With a heavy sigh, he picked up his father's will and re-read the final stipulation, the very one he had memorized by now.

Notwithstanding anything contained herein, in order for my son, Harrison James Kingsley, to receive his full inheritance as set forth above, he must first prove that he is capable of operating my businesses. As proof of such capability, Harrison must start his own business, which business may be in any manner of industry or trade but which (a) must be located in a community other than Boston and specifically in a community in which he is unknown to the other residents, and (b) must show a profit of at least 1,000 dollars before his twenty-fifth birthday. If he fails to satisfy the foregoing requirements on or before his twenty-fifth birthday, all my assets will be divided equally between the following charities...

Anger bubbled up inside Harrison as it did every time he read that section of his father's will. He tossed the paper onto the desk, pinched his eyes shut and pressed the bridge of his nose with his fingertips and thumb. How could his father do this to him? Give him so little time to accomplish this? Did his father really hate him that much? Or was he still punishing him for the death of his mother? Harrison didn't know. But what he did know was that his father still controlled him, even from the grave.

Harrison Kingsley, Sr. had controlled and manipulated him since his birth. Every minute of Harrison's day had been planned by his father, who ordered the staff to see to it that his strict regimen was followed to the letter. Not only had he been told what to wear, where to go, when to go, who to see, but also whom he was to marry.

It was there Harrison had drawn the line. On the day of his twenty-first birthday, he eloped and married the love of his life, Allison. When his father found out, he was livid and stripped Harrison of any and all income. To this day, Harrison had no idea how his father had managed it, but no one would even consider hiring him for fear of his father's vengeance.

Harrison had even thought about moving out west in hopes of gaining employment there, but he'd had no money to support them along the way. The final determining factor came when his wife developed complications and was confined to her bed during the remainder of her pregnancy. No other choice remained but to once again succumb to his father's strict rule of thumb.

Soon after his sons were weaned from their mother's milk, Allison disappeared, leaving a note saying she no longer loved him. Harrison's heart had been ripped from him that day and his only consolation was his sons.

Days after his father's death, Harrison received a parcel that contained two letters. One from Allison, and one from a Mrs. Lan informing him that Allison had been killed in a buggy accident, and that the woman had been asked if anything ever happened to Allison, to send the letter to Harrison.

Allison's letter stated how she'd never stopped loving him, and that his father had forced her to leave by threatening to withdraw all financial support from them. When that hadn't worked, he'd threatened to send the boys to boarding school. Allison knew how Harrison despised the idea of sending his sons to boarding school and how powerless he was against his father. She loved him and the twins too much to let that happen, so she'd left. Harrison felt the pain of that decision even now. What kind of father did something like that to his son, anyway?

He'd always known his father resented him and blamed him for his wife's death. But to go to those extremes? To strip him of the wife he loved and his innocent children of a mother's love? That was low, even for his father.

Determination rose up inside of Harrison like a geyser. His boys had suffered enough at the hands of their grandfather. He'd be hanged if he'd let them lose their inheritance, too. Therefore, he decided he would do whatever it took to make sure that didn't happen. His father thought he'd defeated him even in his death. Well, he'd show him.

His gaze slid to the will sitting in front of him.

His only hope in fulfilling the detestable stipulation his father had thrust on him in such short notice was the one line from Miss Bowen's advertisement, *"Guaranteed full return on investment within three months, including interest."*

He gaped at the envelope staring back at him, wondering if its contents would seal his fate or secure his future. Perhaps it was a good sign that this one had been mailed directly to him instead of going through the newspaper. He read the return address.

Miss Abigail Bowen
777 Grant Street
Hot Mineral Springs, Colorado.

Just where Hot Mineral Springs was in Colorado, he didn't know. Didn't matter. Going out west to see the rugged Rocky Mountains he'd heard so much about from his friends and their travels was something he'd always wanted to do. Now he just might get that chance.

He pressed his hand to his aching, nervous gut, and drew in a deep breath, blowing it out long and slow as he broke the seal off the envelope, and slipped the letter from its pouch.

Dear Mr. Kingsley,
From what you have said in your posts regarding the stipulation in your father's will, it sounds like this business arrangement would be as advantageous for you as it would be for me. Therefore, after much consideration, I have decided to offer you the first chance at this opportunity.
Please let me know what you decide as soon as

possible so I can let the other gentlemen who responded to my advertisement know your decision. Thank you.
Sincerely,
Abigail Bowen

Harrison paused and gazed at nothing in particular in the large office decorated only with the finest of furnishings. This whole arrangement was almost too good to be true. Either that or it was just crazy enough to work.

The way he saw it, this was his only chance to get the inheritance he needed to secure his twins' future. And since no other prospect had presented itself, he had no other choice but to give Miss Bowen's dinner theater prospect, something she had mentioned in one of her previous letters, a try. What money he had saved from working for his father wouldn't go far if he didn't find a way to secure at least his position in his father's businesses, if not the outright inheritance.

It would also enable him to fulfill his lifelong goal to right the wrongs his father had done to the fine people in Boston, and to restore the Kingsley name to what it had once been.

The discovery of his father's true legacy still pained him greatly. It was after the death of his mother that his father had changed so drastically. He'd become a bitter, angry, vindictive man with no scruples when it came to business. Every time Harrison thought of the things his father had done, how he had cheated those poor people out of their businesses and their homes, his stomach churned with sorrow and disgust. Like now.

The only way to take care of those matters would be to take Miss Bowen up on her offer, and then come back to take over the helm and set things right.

Rather than take the risk of his post to Miss Bowen getting lost in the mail and her taking on another partner, he decided to go a faster route. He would send a telegram and head out west immediately.

He quickly penned a short telegraph message and reached over and pulled the string, ringing for his butler.

Forsyth stepped into his office and stopped in front of the expansive desk, his posture stiff as a wooden plank, his black suit and white shirt pressed to perfection, his white gloves immaculate. "What may I do for you, sir?"

"Have Staimes pack my clothes. Tell him we'll be going out of town for a couple of months or so. Let Miss Elderberry know, too, so she can pack for her and the boys. I'll need you to take care of things here while I'm gone." Harrison handed his trusted butler, who never revealed or spoke of Harrison's affairs with anyone, a folded slip of paper. "Send this telegram out immediately and purchase tickets on the next train heading to Hot Mineral Springs, Colorado."

"Yes, Mr. Kingsley. Will that be all, sir?"

"Yes."

"Very well. I will take care of this immediately."

"I know you will. Thank you, Forsyth."

"You're quite welcome." With that, the aging man who'd served his father well, and now him, turned and left the room.

The leather chair creaked as Harrison settled his back into its softness. His gaze dropped to the letter, her letter, still lying on his desk. A peace he hadn't felt in a long time settled inside him. He had a gut feeling this arrangement would indeed fulfill the nonsensical stipulations in his father's will along with everything else, too.

He could be back in Boston in three months with a new future for himself and his family, a future filled with hope that he himself had never known.

"Abby, this telegram is for you." Colette Denis walked into the room of Abby's three-story mansion, holding a slip of yellow paper. Abby was so grateful Colette and her two sisters had decided to come with her to Hot Mineral Springs. Since her mother's remarriage, the Denis sisters' maid services were no longer needed back in Paradise Haven. Mother refused to let them go, though, until Abby had come up with a plan to take them with her. She needed their services and the sisters had no family in Paradise Haven so they were more than happy to move with her and to work for her.

Abby dropped the washcloth she was using to wipe down the windowsills and bookshelves in her office into the bucket of soapy water. She dried her hands on the only dry spot left on her apron and took the telegram from Colette. "Thank you, Colette." She slid the paper into the pocket of her skirt. "Did you remember to stop by the mercantile and post my ad for a carpenter on their bulletin board?" Colette had a tendency to get distracted and forget what she was doing. Abby did, too, so she could relate to the girl who had a good heart but a somewhat scattered brain.

"*Oui.* Well, at least I tried to, anyway."

"What do you mean, you tried?" Abby's lips pursed into a frown, and she pushed back the wet strands of hair plastered on her cheeks.

"When I went to tack it onto the corkboard, I could not reach the only empty place. This nice man offered to help, so I gave it to him. But when he looked at the ad, he asked if he could keep it." Colette wrung her hands and her green eyes shaped like an almond shell drifted over to Abby, then cut to the floor.

"Is something wrong, Colette?"

Colette glanced at Abby, then back at the ground again. "I—I am so sorry, *mademoiselle,* but he is here."

"Who's here? The man who kept my post?"

"No, *mademoiselle.* Mr. Kingsley."

"Mr. Kingsley?" Abby frowned, then her eyes bounced open at the recognition of the name. "Mr. Kingsley is here? Now?"

"*Oui.* I am sorry." Remorse crackled through Colette's voice. "That telegram came several days back, but I forget to give it to you. When I went to wash my dress just now, I found it." Colette rattled on, intermingling French with English.

Abby heard nothing more as she looked down at her soaked apron and the simple blue dress she wore to do chores in. She caught Colette's gaze glossed over with unshed tears. Her heart went out to the poor girl who tried so hard, but always seemed to fall short. She looped arms with Colette and headed toward the door. "Don't you go crying now, you hear? I know you didn't mean to forget. Nothing in this life is worth fretting over. Everything will work out the way it's supposed to. God has a plan. Even in this." Abby encouraged her, sincerely hoping she could take some of her own advice. What was she going to do? He was here!

Well, she couldn't let that bother her. He was here, so she might as well go ahead and make the best of it. She just hoped and prayed he wasn't one of those snobbish businessmen like the city council members were, one who would surely look down his nose at her attire and might even judge her for it. Nothing in his letters indicated he was. But even if he was, she decided as they headed to the door, that was his problem, not hers.

Realizing she still had a hold of Colette's arm, Abby let it go, but her attention stayed riveted on the sixteen-year-old girl, looking for any sign that she felt better. The frown on the young girl's heart-shaped face disappeared, and Abby was glad to see it. "Are you all right now?"

A moment and Colette nodded.

"Good." Abby smiled, and without looking where she was going, she stepped into the hallway and turned right. Her body collided into a granite wall of flesh and stumbled backward.

Something warm, strong, yet gentle secured her arm.

"Oh. I'm sorry, I wasn't watching where I was—" Words escaped her the instant her eyes landed on the sculptured face of the handsome man gazing down at her, still holding her arm.

He looked every bit as startled as she was. "Are you all right, miss?"

"I'm—I'm fine. Thank you." She straightened. Only mere inches from him, her eyes never drifted from his. Something was different about his eyes. Abby looked at one, then the other. One was minutely wider, and the other looked like it hadn't quite awakened yet because the outer half of his eyelid rested against his eyelashes a little heavier than the other one did.

That wasn't what was different about them, though.

Abby placed her fingertip on her lip. It was something else. Then she spotted it. Her mouth formed into an O. Both eyes were grayish-blue except the right one. A third of the lower iris was hazel. The amber color started small at his pupil, but spread out, ending with the same grayish-blue as the rest of his eye. She had never seen anything like that before. "I'm sorry for staring, but you have very unusual eyes. They're quite beautiful."

Those same eyes, surrounded by long but straight medium brown eyelashes, twinkled. "Thank you." He said it like he meant it, but his closed-lipped smile didn't stretch very far. Far enough, though, to reveal a crescent-moon line on one side of his half-full lips and a quarter-crescent moon on the other. "Could you please tell me where I might find Miss Abigail Bowen?"

"Abigail? Oh. Oh. Yes. I'm Abby." She waved her hand at her momentary lapse into forgetfulness because no one ever called her Abigail. Except her mother, and that was only when Abby was in trouble.

Surprise flounced across his face, and his attention drifted over her again, starting with her feet and ending at her hair. "You're Miss Bowen?" One of his eyebrows peaked.

Hey. She knew she looked a mess, but the man didn't need to be so blatantly rude with his disapproving perusal of her. Abby pushed her shoulders back and stood as tall as her five-foot-six-inch frame would allow. "Yes, sir, I am."

Once again, his gaze roamed over her.

This time, she wouldn't let it steal her joy or her peace.

If he didn't approve of what he saw, again, that was his problem, not hers. But in all fairness, the man did have a good reason to be shocked. He probably wasn't expecting to see her looking like a scullery maid, especially since from his perspective, she should have been waiting to meet him for the first time. "Please forgive my appearance. Because of an oversight, I didn't get word of your arrival until a moment ago, so you caught me in the middle of cleaning."

"So I see." A chuckle vibrated through his low, brassy voice. "Well, Miss Bowen. I'm Harrison Kingsley." He reached for her hand.

Abby quickly tucked both her hands behind her back. "Trust me, Mr. Kingsley. You do *not* want to touch these hands. They've been in soapy water all morning and probably feel pricklier than pig bristles." And the rest of her, she was certain looked even worse. Oh, well, couldn't be helped. She had a lot to do. If his time was as valuable to him as hers was to her, rather than keep him waiting while she cleaned up, she decided to go ahead and get right down to business. "Colette, would you make some tea and bring it to the parlor?"

"Oui, mademoiselle." Colette curtsied.

"Thank you." Abby spoke to Colette's retreating back before she turned and faced Mr. Kingsley. What a fine specimen of a man he was. Like one of the heroes in the dime novels she often read. Only she hoped he wasn't as stuffy as some of the heroes in those books seemed to be.

She couldn't help but wonder, if instead of the dark blue three-piece suit Mr. Kingsley had on, what would he look like in a blue plaid shirt, denim blue jeans, Hyer boots and a black Stetson? No. Nix the cowboy hat. It would cover up that lovely head of medium brown hair. Abby liked the way he parted it—not on the side, not in the center, but in between the two, and straight in line with the inside of his right eyebrow.

She pried her attention from his broad-shouldered frame. "Shall we?" Abby swayed her upward palm toward the direction of the parlor. At his nod, she headed that way, tucking the loose strands of hair back into place as she went.

Having someone as handsome and fine-looking as Mr. Kingsley for a business partner was going to be a lot harder than she had anticipated. She'd always been a sucker for a handsome face. Probably due to all those romance novels she'd read. A handsome face didn't guarantee happiness, though, as she had discovered with David. The most important elements in any human being were their hearts and their souls.

While that was definitely true, a quick glance at the gorgeous man standing in front of her, and she knew because of the romantic nature in her, she would have to work very hard at keeping her focus on business, or she might very well risk opening up her heart. Having done that once before, she refused to do it again. Therefore, her hopeless romantic notions would have to stay locked deep inside her heart, tucked away safely, even from herself. No. Make that *especially* from herself.

Chapter Two

Harrison's footsteps thumped on the old hardwood floor that was in need of a good polishing, ricocheting off the walls of the large mansion as he followed Miss Bowen to the parlor. The place was almost barren. There wasn't much furniture and the walls were empty.

As they made their way toward the parlor, he marveled that the woman hadn't even offered to go and clean up first. The little beauty was an unpretentious woman, and he liked that. Back in Boston he was surrounded by ostentatious women. The type of women he would rather avoid.

His possible new business partner wasn't anything like them, or what he had expected. He'd expected a woman of sophistication. Pious and haughty like his ex-fiancée, Prudence Whitsburg. Not a veritable maid who smelled of cleaning soap and dust.

Yellow strands of hair had come loose from her bun. Some of them clung to her damp, yet slender neck. Black smudges brushed across her lightly freckled nose and above her delicately arched eyebrows. Yet none of that deterred her beauty from shining through. Her sapphire eyes smiled even when her lips didn't, and long medium brown eyelashes surrounded them. Her bottom lip was slightly fuller than the upper one, and when she smiled, straight white teeth sparkled back at him.

They reached the parlor door and stepped inside. Harrison held back his shock. The only pieces of furniture in the expansive room were a worn-out, faded, blue settee, a matching wing-back chair in the same shape as the settee, a scratched and marred coffee table and a small, round table with a blue globe oil lamp sitting on a white-and-blue doily.

His attention went to the massive fireplace. Several framed photographs lined the mantel, along with two oil lamps, one on each end. Other than that, the room was almost empty. Nothing hung on these walls, either. He didn't know if this was where she planned on opening her business or not. They hadn't gotten that far. But if it was, it was going to take a lot of money to fix this place up. More than he had right now. And that made him more nervous than he wanted to admit, even to himself.

"Mr. Kingsley, won't you be seated?" Miss Bowen's voice reverberated throughout the empty room and thankfully yanked his attention away from where his taxing thoughts were heading.

She motioned for him to sit. When he reached the chair, he noticed how clean it was. How clean the whole room was. Even the bare windows sparkled. He sat down and was amazed at how comfortable the aged chair actually was.

Miss Bowen sat across from him on the settee, facing him.

The young girl who she'd told to get tea entered the room. She set a tray with a teapot, two cups and saucers, and a plate of cookies with some sort of filling in the centers on the coffee table in front of them. She went right to work pouring the tea into the cups and serving it along with two cookies on the side.

"Thank you, Colette."

The girl turned.

"Don't leave just yet, Colette."

Colette faced them, nodded and waited.

Abby looked over at him and asked, "Mr. Kingsley, would you like to join us for dinner this evening?"

He saw no reason not to. "I would like that. Thank you."

She smiled and turned her attention back to her maid. "Would you tell Veronique we'll be having a guest join us for dinner this evening?"

"Oui, mademoiselle." With a quick curtsy, Colette left the room.

Miss Bowen faced him and sighed. "I still can't get used to her calling me *mademoiselle.* I finally gave up trying to get her not to. It sounds so formal. But it's much better than what she used to call me."

"Oh? What was that?"

"Miss Abigail. That just sounds so stuffy to me." She wrinkled her cute nose and shook her head. "And so gratingly formal and impersonal. Especially when she and her sisters are more like family to me than hired help."

Harrison understood exactly what she meant. They had that in common. He oftentimes asked Forsyth the same thing. After all, the man was more like a father to him than a butler. But Forsyth refused, and so Harrison had finally given up, as well. "You said that she and her sisters were like family to you. Do you have any family, Miss Bowen?"

After taking a sip of her tea, she placed the cup onto the saucer and rested it on her lap. "Yes. My father died a long time ago, but my mother recently remarried. I have three older brothers and an older sister, who are all married. Several nieces and nephews, too." She looked away. The moment was brief, but long enough for him to understand that something she'd said had bothered her. He'd seen it in her eyes. What it was, he didn't know. Nonetheless, whatever had caused that momentary look of sadness was none of his concern. He was here on business. Not to get involved in her personal life.

"What about you?" Abby asked him.

"There's just me and my two sons."

"Sons? Oh." She took a sip of tea, seeming to take in the news with excitement, worry or concern. He wasn't sure which. "How old are they?"

"Josiah and Graham will be four August twenty-ninth."

"Twins?"

"Yes."

"My brother Michael has twins, too. A boy and a girl." Affection softened the blue in her eyes before they glazed over with a faraway look mingled with pain, and the room grew quiet.

He wondered if she was thinking about her family and missing them. And if that would be a problem. Would she walk away from the business to go back to her home? Wherever home was for her. "Where are you from, Miss Bowen?" So much for not getting involved in her personal life.

She blinked, then looked at him as if she remembered he was in the room. "What? Oh. Sorry. Yes, you asked me where I'm from. Paradise Haven. In the Idaho Territory. And you?" She shook her head and waved her hand. "Never mind. I already know that. You're from Boston, Massachusetts. I don't know where my mind is." She steadied her teacup and wiggled in her seat, then sat up straighter.

Was she always this scatterbrained, or was it home she was missing? He doubted it was the latter because she hadn't looked exactly prepared for his arrival, either. Worry etched inside him, wondering what he had gotten himself into. Well, they hadn't agreed on anything or signed any papers yet. So he could still get out of this deal if he so chose, but his gut twisted, wondering what he'd do next if this plan failed.

"Mr. Kingsley." She paused and looked him in the eye. "Would you mind if I called you by your first name? All this formality isn't for me."

"Oh, by all means, please, call me Harrison. And may I call you Abigail?"

"No." She shook her head and frowned.

Taken back by her blunt answer, he moved backward.

"Please call me Abby. Like I said, Abigail sounds so stuffy." She wrinkled that petite nose of hers again, and he was certain those close-knit freckles had kissed each other when she did. "One thing you will discover about me, Harrison, is I am not a woman who believes in pomposity and strict formality when there is a real person on the inside just waiting to be met. When one is so reserved and refined, you never get to know the heart of that person, and what makes them who they really are. That's a real travesty as far as I'm concerned."

Harrison wanted to remind her that she had come across like that when she signed Abigail in her letters to him, but he didn't.

"After I sent my letter to you and had signed it Abigail, I wanted to snatch it back. I still have no idea why I did it. Anyway—" she waved her hand and shook her head again "—shall we get down to business? After all, that's why you're here." She smiled.

Harrison returned her smile with one of his own. He had a hard time keeping up with her bouncing from one subject to the next, but he found this down-to-earth woman to be quite an enigma. He was going to enjoy being her business partner. And that made him more nervous than a hunted fox. Better to plunge forward with business than to let his thoughts go down a road he didn't want to travel. "Do you have plans on how you want to run this business?"

"Of course I do." She drained her tea.

By the look on her face, he could tell that he'd offended her. "I was certain you did, but I thought I would ask." He sent her a smile, and that of-course-I-do look disappeared. "What building were you planning on using?"

"This one."

Just as he feared. His gaze slipped around the room and ended at her.

"I haven't purchased furnishings yet. After I hire a crew of carpenters to restore the place, then I will. Just so you know, because this will also be my home, I will be funding the total cost of remodeling the building. The kitchen is quite large so I won't need to do anything to it, but the rest of the place, well…" She sighed and raised a dainty shoulder. "As you can see, it needs a good cleaning, which we've already started, along with numerous repairs. I am certain that once all of that is completed, this place will make a fine dinner theater." The conviction of that shone in her blue eyes.

"I'm sure it will. Do you have a layout planned for the theater already?"

"Yes. I do. It's in my office. I'll run and get it. Be right back." She pushed herself off the settee and fled the room.

Harrison blew out a long breath, grateful one of his fears had been put to rest and that he didn't have to come up with a large sum of money to fix up the place or for the theater. He only hoped the money he did have to fork over would be a small amount.

Abby's footsteps echoed outside the doorway, announcing her arrival. Harrison tugged on his sleeve cuffs and straightened the lapels on his jacket. He rose when she stepped inside the parlor, hands loaded with several rolled-up papers. Before he could even take one step toward relieving Abby of her burden, the woman had scurried over to him, sat down on the settee and unrolled them, pulling out and flattening the first one.

Harrison shook his head, marveling at the little bundle of energy. He lowered himself next to her, careful not to sit too close, but close enough to see the drawings.

"This is where the theater will be. The stage will go here…." She leaned over and pointed to the areas she referred to. "The chairs here. Sixty to start with, at least.

Then as the business grows, more can be added. There will be chairs up in here in the balcony, as well. Maybe even a few dining tables and chairs, too. I haven't decided on that particular yet. Anyway—" she waved her hand as if remembering what she was doing "—here in the room next to the theater is where the dining tables and chairs will be. Guests will dine there before they head into the theater to watch the plays." She continued to explain the intricate floor plans to him.

Harrison was impressed. A lot of thought had gone into designing this place.

When she finished, she sat up straight and turned those smiling eyes up at him. Those eyes sparkled with the dream. This thing obviously meant a lot to her. One thing Harrison had discovered if someone was willing to put the hard work it took to make a business come to fruition and put their whole heart and soul into it like she was, its chances of being a success were quite good. Somehow, after seeing her plans and witnessing how she lit up with the dream, that dream now mattered to him, too. And not just because of his inheritance and plans, either.

Abby rerolled the papers. Before things went any further, she needed to tell him something that had been pricking at her conscience from the very beginning of this whole thing. She sat up straight and turned her attention onto him. "Before we go any further, Harrison, I feel I must be honest with you about something. The only reason I'm taking on a partner is because the town committee will not grant me the license I need to open my dinner theater. The only way they will even consider it is if I take on a gentleman partner." She huffed.

"Can you believe it? I mean really. What difference does that make? I still can't believe they even suggested such a thing. As if I'm not capable of running my own business. I'm just as smart as any man. My stepfather, who is a brilliant business man, taught me…" She prattled on and on until she remembered she was talking to a potential business partner. "Sorry. As you can tell, I'm quite frustrated over this whole situation."

"I can see that," Harrison said with an amused chuckle. "Now, it is my turn to tell you something, Miss Bowen."

Her stomach tensed, wondering what he was about to say. Was he going to back out of this deal before it ever got started? "What's that?" She held her breath waiting for his answer.

"Once we get this business up and running and I get my investment back, plus interest as you stated in your ad—" his eyes twinkled along with his half grin "—then I plan on heading back to Boston to claim my inheritance and to run my father's businesses."

Abby's stomach relaxed. "Just as I had hoped."

He frowned.

"Oh." She waved her hand. "No offense to you personally. It's just that I was hoping things would turn out this way, and they have. Like I said, the only reason I took on a partner was because of the license. I really didn't want nor need one. So as soon as we, if you're interested, get this theater up and running, I will no longer need a partner. After all, the town didn't say how long I had to have one, now, did they?" She smiled.

"That plan may backfire on you, Abby."

"What do you mean?" She frowned.

"They could revoke your license."

"They can?" She hadn't thought of that. "Surely they wouldn't. Would they?"

"Yes, then can, and from what you've told me about them, I suspect they would, too. So here's what I propose."

Propose? She gulped.

"Even though I will be leaving, I am willing to remain your partner. A silent one, in name only, if you will. And I will only take a dollar a month from you."

"That's hardly a partnership."

"This would not be an equal-share partnership. The way I see it, you are helping me a vast amount more than I am you. I want to reciprocate by helping you, too, by remaining your partner in order for you to keep your license. You will be able to run the business the way you want without any interference from me. That way we both come out of this arrangement with exactly what we want—nothing more, nothing less."

"Do you think the town will object to you not being here?"

"I don't see how they can. You will still have a partner. I would even be willing to come back for let's say—" he rubbed his chin "—once a month for six months."

"You would do that?"

"Yes. I would. I am convinced that when they see the revenue your business will bring this town, and see what an amazing cultural place it will be, they will no longer care about such matters in time, anyway."

"You really think so?"

"I do. Or I wouldn't have said so."

Abby's insides danced with the fact that everything was going to work out the way she'd always hoped it would.

Harrison couldn't believe his good fortune. This was working out better than he had imagined. Only one question he needed to ask before he made this deal. "Do you have a dollar figure in mind of what you will need from me?"

"Yes. Five hundred dollars."

That was it? He thought he would have to put up thousands and live on an even stricter budget than he was right now over the next three months. Relief poured over him, but he didn't allow his face to show it. She didn't need to know about his dire financial situation, and five hundred was definitely doable.

Right then, he determined that even though he would get his money back and then some, he would help her as much as he could to make her business a success. Not that she needed his help or anything, but he wanted to make sure her endeavor came to fruition.

"So what do you think?" Abby asked. "Are you in?"

Harrison turned his attention onto her and smiled at the expectant look in her eyes. "Only one question first. I hate to ask, but I need to know how you can guarantee a profit so quickly."

"Oh, that." She waved her hand as if she were brushing away his comment. "The reason I can is because even if the business doesn't make a profit right away, the investor will. I am going to give them fifteen hundred dollars once we get the place up and running."

Harrison swallowed his shock. Not only would he get the amount his father's will stipulated, but his initial investment, as well. This was almost too good to be true. Maybe it was. Suspicion crawled over him. "Why would you do that?"

"Because. The investor or business partner, whichever you prefer, will be helping me to make my dream come true, so I want to make it worth their time. Your time. That is, if you're interested."

This woman wanted her dream. And she wanted it badly. He had a feeling she would do whatever it took to fulfill that dream, too, including giving the large sum she had guaranteed just for the trouble of helping her out. Before he'd left Boston, he'd had a background check done on her and knew she was good for the money. The woman came from wealth and her own bank account was hefty. The way he saw it, he had nothing to lose, and everything to gain. Not only would he get what he wanted, he would be helping her to get what she wanted. A mutual benefit arrangement. Those were the best kind of business deals. "I'm interested. Count me in."

She clutched her hands together with a smack and tucked them to her chest. Her smile lit up her whole face. "Excellent. Thank you!" She tossed her arms around him, gave him a firm hug and released him just as quickly. Her exuberance was contagious. He found himself wanting to hug her in return, but he didn't dare. "You won't regret this, Harrison, I promise."

He had a feeling that promise would hold true. Normally he would have had a contract drawn up, but that would only delay things. Knowing how much this meant to her, his gut told him she would hold to her end of the bargain, so he wouldn't bother with a contract this time.

They continued to talk about what needed to be done, the expenses, her plans, his thoughts and the whole general situation. An hour later, he looked at his watch. Three o'clock in the afternoon. "Well, I should go now." Harrison stood. "What time would you like me to come this evening?"

"Five-thirty. Dinner will be served at six."

"Very well." They walked side by side to the front door. There, he grabbed his fedora off the hat rack and held it in his hands, then shifted his focus onto her smiling face. "I will see you at five-thirty, then."

"Looking forward to it." They stood there for a moment looking at each other.

"Until this evening." With those words, he opened the door and stepped outside. Outside where the detestable smell of sulfur lingered in the air. But that vile stench didn't detract from his fine mood. For the first time in years, hope glimmered inside him. At the bottom of the steps, he stopped and looked up at the bright June sun. Forsyth would say God had arranged this whole thing because He loved Harrison so much. But Harrison didn't believe in a loving God. How could he? His life had clearly proven otherwise.

Chapter Three

Standing in front of the free-standing mirror, Abby perused her appearance. The sides of her hair were pulled back and held with pearl combs and a dark blue ribbon. Tiny curls framed her face, and the rest of her hair hung loosely down her back. Her white, tufted-cotton bustle gown with the dark blue lace and ribbons and midlength sleeves would be cool, but not too cool for a warm evening in the Colorado Rocky Mountains. But just in case it wasn't, she snatched up her knit shawl, then skipped downstairs to see if Veronique had everything ready.

The words to "Amazing Grace" sung by either Colette or Zoé, whose singing voices were very similar, floated through the massive room as she made her way into the formal dining room. "Hi, Zoé."

Zoé, the middle sister to Veronique and Colette, turned from placing a silver chafing dish on the mahogany serving table and smiled. "Good evening, Abby," she said in the same strong accent all of the sisters spoke with. Her soft gray eyes were the first thing a person noticed about Zoé. While the color was soft, because of the way her eyes were shaped, they appeared hard as if she were angry all the time, which she wasn't.

Abby looked at the long table set for two. Her mother's silver candelabra stood tall in the middle. Silver pedestal dishes set on each side piled high with fresh fruit and French pastries. Wedgewood bone china and crystal glasses sparkled like bright sunshine raining down on a clear mountain brook here in Colorado. Silverware…polished to perfection. "This looks great, Zoé."

The eighteen-year-old girl's face lit up. "You think so?"

"Yes. I sure do."

"Zoé," Veronique hollered from the other side of the swinging door.

Wisps of chestnut-blond hair swayed when Zoé yanked her attention in that direction. "I will be right there." She curtsied and scurried into the kitchen.

Abby followed. Fresh bread, beef and pine aromas from the wood stove met her nostrils.

Veronique stood in front of the massive cook stove, wearing the same blue-and-white uniform as Zoé, stirring something in one of the copper pans sitting on the stove with a wire whisk. Without looking, Veronique told Zoé to grab the pastry-wrapped cinnamon apples out of the oven.

Colette sat at the table, slicing and peeling carrots. She, too, wore a matching uniform.

Abby wasn't too keen putting on fancy dinners, but she had better get used to them for when she opened her dinner theater. "Something sure smells good, Veronique." Abby raised the lid on one of the pans, leaned over and breathed deeply. "Umm. What is that?" She pointed to the dish.

"It is *filet de boeuf charlemagne*," Veronique explained without taking her eyes off the pan she was stirring.

"Trans-la-tion…?" Abby drew out the word and let her sentence hang, waiting for Veronique to interpret what she'd said into English.

"Beef tenderloin Charlemagne."

"Huh?" Abby frowned.

"Simply put, it is beef fillet steaks with mushrooms. What I am making now is a *béarnaise* sauce. I hope you like it."

"I'm sure I will. I haven't eaten anything of yours yet that wasn't absolutely delicious."

Veronique flashed a quick smile Abby's way before putting her attention back onto the saucepan.

Abby glanced up at the kitchen clock. Five-twenty. "Well, I'll get out of your way. Mr. Kingsley will be arriving in a few minutes."

Veronique nodded as she placed the copper lid on the pan she'd been stirring. She removed it from the heat, tossed a pot holder onto the breadboard counter then set the pan down.

Abby had just turned to leave when she noticed a tray of strawberry and apple tarts. With a quick glance back at Veronique, like a little kid sneaking an early dessert, she snatched a strawberry tart off the plate and tossed it into her mouth.

Through the dining room and into the main room of the mansion she went, munching happily on the delicious treat.

A knock came at the door. Abby chewed fast and swallowed. Colette, Zoé and Veronique were busy, so she hollered, "I'll get it." Her heels tapped along the floor as she made her way to the front door. She swung it open and blinked. There stood Harrison holding a small boy in each arm.

"I'm sorry, Abby, that this notice is so late, but a few minutes ago, the boys' nanny and my valet came down sick. Must've been something they ate this afternoon because my sons aren't sick. The food they ate wasn't the same as what Miss Elderberry and Staimes ate. I don't know anyone in town, and I won't leave my boys with a perfect stranger. So, I'm here to let you know that I won't be able to make it to dinner this evening. I'm sorry." Remorse wrinkled his handsome face.

Abby glanced at the two boys. A fresh ache filled her heart, but she refused to let it get her down or to dwell on what could never be. Instead, she sent the boys and their father her most inviting smile and quickly swung the French doors open. "Don't be silly. There's no need for you not to stay. Besides, there's more than enough food. I'll just have Zoé set two more places and find something for the boys to sit on. It'll be just fine." Now she just had to convince herself of that by reminding herself that God had a plan, as vexing as that could be sometimes. She leaned toward the boys, eyeing each one with a smile. "And who might you boys be?"

Neither of them said a word; they just tucked their tiny shoulders closer into their father's chest and eyed her warily.

"This one here—" Harrison nodded toward the child

on his right "—is Graham. And this one—" he nodded at the child on his left "—is Josiah."

"Hello, Josiah and Graham. Welcome to my home. Won't you come in?" she said to the twins who resembled their father in much, much younger versions. They even had Harrison's light brown hair and grayish-blue eyes. Except neither of their eyes had a portion of hazel coloring like their father's did.

"Can you say hello to the nice lady?" Instead of saying hello, they buried their faces into their father's shoulder.

"It's okay," she mouthed, and waved him in with her hand. She moved out of the way, and Harrison stepped inside. "Are you sure about this, Miss Bowen? We really hate to impose."

She wasn't sure of anything, but she'd make herself be. "It's Abby, and of course I'm sure or I wouldn't have said so. Listen, why don't you take the boys into the parlor, and I'll inform Veronique there will be extra guests this evening? I'll be right back." Abby whirled around and headed toward the kitchen. Those adorable boys in their skirts and knee socks resurrected the pain shoved deep down in Abby's heart and soul. The one she rarely allowed to surface into her actual consciousness lest it rob her of her happiness completely. "Lord, help me get through this evening."

Harrison lowered himself onto the settee in the parlor, and settled a son on each leg. When Staimes and Miss Elderberry came up sick at the last minute, Harrison's own stomach had taken ill. Not from food sickness, but with worry. He feared upsetting Miss Bowen by ruining her dinner plans, but he didn't. Women of his society back home in Boston wouldn't have been so gracious. They would have shunned him for days, and some indefinitely over something like this.

He would have hated it if Abby would have shut the door in his face. And even though it couldn't be helped, he wouldn't have blamed her. After all, a lot of hard work and hours of preparation went into making a meal, not to mention the food that would have gone to waste if he hadn't been able to come.

Relief skimmed over him the instant Abby had smiled and opened her doors to him and the twins, and his stomach stopped hurting. He no longer had to worry about how she would be with the children.

Harrison's lips curled, knowing he wouldn't have to miss dinner with the twins. He and his sons almost always ate breakfast and dinner together, unlike most of his friends who sent their children away to boarding school or left them with a nanny twenty-four hours a day. That wasn't for him or his boys. No, he never wanted his children to feel like he had growing up— unwanted and unloved.

Just then, Abby breezed into the room, holding a medium-size box with toys sticking out of the top. "I found these in the attic. I was going to send them to my nephews, but I'm sure Josiah and Graham would enjoy playing with them." She set the box on the coffee table in front of his sons.

Their eyes widened, but at first they did not move. Finally, he slid them both to the floor and nudged them in that direction. They slipped from his protection, and with their heads together, they gazed into the box.

"Go ahead. You can play with them." They looked up at her, then at him as if seeking his approval. He nodded.

Each one quickly snatched a toy, and together, they headed over and sat down on the floor near the fireplace. They had each selected a section of train, and when Harrison brought the box over to them, they began removing the rest of the toys from the container.

Knowing they were occupied and having fun, Harrison came back and placed his attention on Abby. "Thank you for that. And thank you for understanding about the ruined dinner plans. I really hated to do that to you."

Abby waved him away. "It's nothing. Really. And you didn't ruin a thing."

"By the way, I meant to tell you, you look very nice this evening."

"You mean compared to earlier?" An amused smirk curled her lips.

"Oh. I see how that sounded. My apologies. I didn't mean it that way. I just meant you look very nice." She did, too. Dressed in a striking white dress that showed off her trim figure, and with her shining hair hanging freely down her back, she looked stunning. Even her hands looked nice. Her long graceful fingers weren't red like they had been earlier.

"I had it first, Siah!"

Harrison's attention darted toward his boys.

"No. I did!" Josiah yanked it from his brother's hands.

"Boys. That's enough." He stood and headed toward them, but he was too late.

Josiah snatched the toy in question, raised it and

whacked Graham, hitting him squarely in the head. The wail that ensued could surely be heard in Boston.

Harrison picked up his screeching son and held him close, patting his back and speaking soothing words to him.

Abby was at his side in an instant, worry etched on her face. She dropped to her knees and started talking to Josiah. Harrison couldn't hear what she was saying because Graham's cries still filled his ears.

Minutes passed before Graham's tears finally let up. Harrison leaned him back to check the top of his head. A small amount of blood streamed through his hair. "Abby, do you have a washcloth I can use?" Oh, how he hated having to ask, hated having to bother her with this. She was going to think he was far more trouble than he was worth.

She stood, holding a tear-soaked Josiah in her arms. "I sure do. I'll be right back. If it's okay with your father, would you like to go with me, Josiah?"

He wiped his eyes and slowly nodded, then looked over at Harrison. Remorse and trepidation filled his son's eyes. "You may go with her. But before you do, you need to say you're sorry to your brother. It is never okay to hit someone else. Do you understand that?"

Josiah nodded. "Saw-ree, Gam."

Graham wouldn't look at him. Instead, he buried his face into Harrison's collar.

"Graham, what do you say to your brother?" Harrison asked.

The boy did nothing.

"No. Come on. It's time to make up. Give your brother a hug." He put him on the floor.

Abby lowered Josiah, as well.

Graham shook his head.

"Very well, then, Graham. You will not be allowed to play with Miss Abby's toys any longer."

Graham turned wide eyes up at him, then rushed to his brother and hugged him long and hard. Pretty soon they were giggling. His sons sat down on the floor again next to the toys.

"That didn't take long." He turned to Abby, who was smiling up at him.

"You sure handled that nicely."

Her words made him feel proud. His biggest fear was failing as a father. "Thank you."

They smiled at each other.

"I'll run and get that washcloth now."

"Thank you."

Harrison watched his sons as Abby exited. He sighed. Great first impression they were making.

Abby entered the room a few minutes later holding a bowl and a clean cloth. While Harrison and Abby cleaned his small wound, Graham squirmed and fretted, acting as though they were torturing him or something. When it was all over, he settled back onto the floor and started playing as if nothing had happened.

"*Mademoiselle,* dinner is ready."

The woman standing only a few yards from him was tall with chestnut-blond hair and grayish-green eyes, who spoke with a French accent very much like Colette had earlier.

"Harrison, this is Zoé, Colette's sister. Oh. I forgot to introduce you to Colette earlier. I was, um, a bit disheveled." Abby's soothing laughter reminded him of the musical sound of a sparrow songbird back home in Boston. "Anyway, Zoé, this is Mr. Harrison Kingsley."

"It is a pleasure to meet you, sir." She curtsied.

"Nice to meet you, too," he said. Even though he wasn't used to people in his society introducing him to their help, he liked it. He liked the informality a lot. Back home it sure wouldn't be acceptable. But, then again, he wasn't back home. He was here. A quick glance at Abby, and he was glad he was, too.

"Shall we head into the dining room?" Abby asked.

His heart plummeted to his perfectly shined shoes. Abby had no idea what she was getting herself into when she'd invited his boys to dinner. He should have warned her before accepting her generous offer.

Abby's arm rested on top of Harrison's. "It'll be okay. I have several nephews and nieces. I know how they can be."

Harrison let out a long breath of relief. It was nice not having to worry about someone wanting to whisk his rambunctious sons off to another room. Or even worse, a boardinghouse, like Prudence had wanted to send them to once they were married. Over his dead body would he have ever allowed her or anyone else to send his boys away.

Good thing this whole arrangement with Abby was strictly business because with her kind heart and gentle way with his boys, he could easily fall for her. And he was never going to let that happen again. He'd been duped once before by a pretty face and a sweet disposition toward his children. Prudence had always acted like she loved children. Loved his sons. Even though he hadn't loved Prudence, something she was very much aware of, it was because of her love for his sons that he had asked her to marry him. He hoped love would eventually follow. However, he soon discovered that her fondness toward them had been nothing but a ruse to marry a man who could keep her in the style she was accustomed to.

He'd never forget the day when Prudence had roughly handled his boys and said intolerable and cruel things to them. Of course, she didn't know Harrison had been nearby. Thankfully, he had been. He had immediately put an end to her abuse as well as their relationship, and sent her away for good that very day.

Thus, Harrison needed to remind himself often that Abby was a business partner and nothing else. One look at her smiling blue eyes and sweet face, though, and he knew keeping it strictly business was going to be a challenge.

The early morning sunrise peeked through the curtain in Abby's sparsely furnished bedroom. Snuggled under the red-and-white quilt Mother had sent along with her, Abby rubbed the sleep from her eyes.

Her thoughts drifted to the calamitous dinner from the night before.

Poor Harrison had been so mortified.

Not her; she laughed the whole time—inwardly of course.

The near-four-year-olds' antics had more than tickled her, even when they'd tossed glazed carrots at one another and a piece had landed in her hair. And even when they'd dumped mashed potatoes and gravy onto the floor, or when they'd spilled their milk all over the white linen tablecloth.

The whole thing had been hilarious to her, but not to Harrison, who had profusely apologized, repeatedly. She had assured him none of it had bothered her, that nothing in this world was worth getting fidgety over, and that they were just things that could be washed.

Other than those few incidences, everything had gone quite well. Dinner conversation flowed freely until the boys had fallen asleep with the sides of their faces resting in their dessert.

She and Harrison cleaned them up before he left with the promise of arriving early the next morning.

Speaking of arriving early, Abby tossed her quilt off and went to the window and pulled the curtain back. Dark clouds drifted toward the direction of town bringing with them a Rocky Mountain rainstorm. Didn't matter. She wouldn't let anything stop her from today's mission.

While she donned her peach satin bustle gown and plumed hat, she couldn't help but think about Harrison's boys again. The longing to have her own children chopped away at her heart. Why did she think moving away from her beloved nieces and nephews would solve her problem? At the time, it sure made sense. Of course, back then she didn't know that the town committee wouldn't let her start her business without a male partner.

And back then, she didn't know that the man God had placed in her life would have two adorable little boys who would capture her heart with a single look, either.

Abby closed her eyes and sighed.

What was she going to do?

Ever since Doctor Berg, who she'd only gone to see because she had missed several of her monthly cycles in a row, had told her she had womb death, her life had never been the same. The drying up of her womb, something most women started in their forties, meant she would never bear children. Hearing that diagnosis had crushed any hopes she had of being a mother. That dreadful day she had fled from his office and cried until her heart felt numb with grief. Grief for the children she would never carry. That same day, when she told her fiancé, David, about it, he immediately broke off their engagement, telling her how important it was to not just him, but any man to have offspring of his own. Watching him strolling around town with another woman on his arm and later, holding his baby, had been much too painful for her to endure.

Same thing with her siblings. While she was extremely delighted for her brothers and sisters, seeing them happily married with children reminded her daily of what she herself would never experience—a loving husband and a house filled with children.

It was because of all that she decided to open a dinner theater far away from Paradise Haven. She loved how when she was on stage acting, or sitting in the audience watching, she was transported into another world.

A world of happily ever afters.

A world she could participate in, instead of standing on the sidelines and being an observer only.

Of course, none of it was reality, but still, it helped take her mind off the pain of her reality.

Thinking about reality, she needed to hustle her body downstairs. Harrison would be there any minute to pick her up.

At the bottom of the winding staircase, Abby saw Veronique heading toward the front door.

Harrison must already be here.

"Good morning, *Monsieur* Kingsley. Won't you come in?" Veronique stepped aside to let him in. "May I take your *chapeau,* sir?" He handed his fedora to Veronique, who hung it on the hat rack.

"Thank you. Veronique, isn't it?"

"Yes, sir."

His gaze shifted from Veronique and onto Abby as she strolled toward him.

Veronique slipped away.

The closer Abby got to him, the more she realized no one should be allowed to be that handsome. It wasn't fair to women who were trying to not notice that fact. Women, like herself, who had to disengage her emotions in order to guard her heart where the male species was concerned. Still, she couldn't help admire how nice he looked.

Dressed in a finely tailored, dark gray suit with a light gray waistcoat, white satin shirt and a dark gray neckerchief, he made an intimidating presence. Just what was needed when going up against the committee board.

"Good morning," she said with a bright and chipper pitch to her voice.

"Good morning to you. You look very nice."

"So do you."

"Thank you, ma'am. Well, are you ready for this?"

"Am I ever." She couldn't wait to see the mayor's face or the committee members' faces, whichever of them would be there this morning, when she walked in with Harrison.

Abby started to wrap her shawl around her shoulders, but Harrison finished the task for her. She grabbed an umbrella, and Harrison offered her his arm. She looped her arm through his, and as they headed out the door, he snatched his hat off the hook and set it on that lovely head of hair of his.

Cool morning air greeted them as they stepped outside.

Abby's attention went to the sky. Judging by the black ominous clouds, she knew it would be only a matter of minutes before a downpour of rain came gushing down on them. "We'd better hurry."

Harrison followed her gaze. "You're right."

Down the steps they scampered. Abby paused at the buggy sitting in front of her house. "You didn't need to do that. It's only a short walk to the town hall."

"I know. And yes, I did. Can't have a fine lady such as yourself walking now, can I?"

"I do it all the time." She shrugged.

"Well, not today." His half smile showed up. He extended his hand, palm up.

Abby laid her hand in his and immediately noticed how liquid warmth spread up her arm and throughout her chest. She'd never experienced anything like that before, and she had no clue what it meant, either. But it was a very nice feeling just the same.

"Abby?"

Abby blinked, then looked at him. "Yes?" He gave a

light tug on her hand. "Oh. Forgive me." She raised her skirt above her shoes and stepped up into the buggy, then tucked her skirt inside.

Harrison went around to the other side and sat next to her. His wide shoulders came close to touching hers. He picked up the lines and clicked them. The buggy lurched forward, yanking her backward a tad.

"How are your valet and nanny feeling this morning?" she asked.

"Much better." His gaze trailed to her hat. "You're not hiding the carrot my son tossed at you under that hat, are you?"

Abby laughed. "No."

"I don't know how my nanny does it. The boys can sure be rambunctious."

"Don't I know it. If you think your boys are rowdy, you should see my nephews. Your sweet sons are mild compared to them."

His brow spiked.

"Well, maybe not."

They both laughed.

Harrison stopped the buggy in front of the town hall just as a bolt of lightning pierced the sky and the thunder boomed immediately afterward. Abby screeched.

"We'd better get inside."

Yes, they'd better do just that. Hurry and get inside so she could get her license. A thought flicked through her brain that if for some reason she didn't get it, there would be even more thunderous rumbling going on and it wouldn't be from the storm, either. Especially after doing what they'd asked, obtaining a gentleman business partner, how could they possibly say no now?

She looked into Harrison's eyes as he helped her down. Make that a very handsome business partner. *Careful, Abby. Don't get too close to him. You'll only end up hurt if you do.*

Harrison forced himself to look away from Abby's piercing blue eyes. She was a beautiful lady who didn't flaunt her beauty.

A rare thing in this world. Or at least the world he came from, anyway.

Another snap of lightning zigzagged through the sky. It was only a matter of seconds before the rain came. Cupping Abby's elbow, Harrison led her up the steps and inside the extravagant building.

They walked up to a steely-looking lady seated behind an oak desk. "May I help you, sir?" No warmth or friendliness came through her voice.

"I'm here to see the mayor."

"And you are…?"

"Mr. Harrison Kingsley and this is—" he looked at Abby "—Miss Abigail Bowen."

"Yes. I know. We've met. How are you today, Abby?"

"Very well, and you, Miss Elsa?"

"Well, my shoulders are giving me fits again and my leg is acting up because of the weather, but that's to be expected. I ain't as young as I once was."

Harrison couldn't believe this was the same lady who came across so stern. Perhaps it was because of the pain she was in. He waited patiently while the ladies chattered on.

"We're here to get my business license," Abby finally finished.

"Business license?" The woman tilted her head, looking confused. "You don't need a license to run a business."

Harrison looked over at Abby, and Abby looked at him, wide-eyed. His frown started at his forehead and dropped all the way down to his heart. "What's going on here?"

She genuinely looked surprised. "I have no clue. All I know is I was told I had to have a license, and that they wouldn't give me one unless I took on a business partner. A male business partner." She looked as confused as he now felt.

"Well, we'll get to the bottom of this." He turned his focus onto Miss Elsa.

Miss Elsa's face turned the color of sheep's wool. "Abby, please don't tell the mayor I said anything. I can't afford to lose my job."

"Don't you worry about that, Miss Elsa. We won't say anything, will we, Harrison?" Abby's eyes pleaded with him for Miss Elsa's sake.

He didn't want to cost the elderly woman her job, but something fishy was going on here, and he was going to find out exactly what it was. He'd just have to figure out a way of doing it without saying anything. "We won't say anything. Will you please tell the mayor we're here?"

The color returned to the lady's face. "Yes, sir." She rose, paused and looked at him. "Thank you."

He gave her a quick nod.

The woman limped slowly toward the end of the hall.

Seeing her handicap, Harrison embedded it into his brain not to say anything about what the woman had said to them. He didn't want to cost anyone their job. Especially someone who could barely walk.

Miss Elsa returned. "The mayor will see you now."

"Thank you, Miss Elsa," Abby said with a smile.

Harrison and Abby followed Miss Elsa down the long hall. Portraits hung on either sides of the wall. "Who are these men?"

"That one's the mayor." She pointed to the largest portrait. "The others are the town committee members."

"I see." That painting of the mayor told Harrison a lot about the person he was about to encounter. He was full of himself. Harrison knew exactly how to handle someone like him. After all, he'd had a lot of practice at that endeavor.

Miss Elsa knocked on the door.

"Come in."

The woman opened the door and moved out of the way. "Get us something to drink," the short rotund man sitting behind the massive desk demanded of Miss Elsa without so much as a please anywhere in sight. No wonder the woman had looked so miserable when they'd first walked in. Anyone who had to work with someone like him, someone with no manners, would be miserable. He knew that firsthand working for his father. From what Miss Elsa said, she had no choice. She needed the job. Well, when they got their business up and running, he'd talk to Abby about hiring the older woman to help ease her misery.

The portly mayor didn't even stand when they entered the room. Harrison mentally shook his head. This was going to be an interesting meeting. But he loved a good challenge.

"Miss Bowen, good to see you again." The way he said it spoke volumes. He hadn't meant a single word of his greeting. This arrogant snob was phonier than fool's gold. His eyes ran up and down Harrison, a look meant to size him up and to intimidate him. Harrison wasn't the least bit fazed. He'd come across his type before.

"Mr. Prinker, may I introduce Mr. Harrison Kingsley? My new business partner." Abby's gaze stayed on Harrison, though he caught the smug look she gave the mayor just the same.

Mr. Prinker's thin lips separated, and his bushy brows rose toward the ceiling.

Harrison grinned inside and extended his hand. "Mr. Prinker."

The mayor just stared at the hand as if it were something that would devour him. He was right; Harrison just might cause the man some bodily harm if things were as he surmised they might be. Moreover, he knew he had the upper hand the moment the mayor showed the slightest sign of weakness. One always had to assess their opponent before going into battle. His father had taught him the art of combat well.

Mr. Prinker quickly masked his surprise, and his face turned stern. "There's been a change in plans, Miss Bowen. I was going to send a message to you this afternoon. We've decided not to grant you a license, after all." He sent Harrison a sly grin. The challenge was on.

Chapter Four

Abby's ire rose. Something that happened a lot since coming to this town. How dare this man try to stop her dream from coming true? Especially after dragging Harrison and his boys halfway across the country. "What do you mean you've changed your mind?" Her anger came through her voice loud and clear and she didn't care one whit that it did.

"Before you answer that…" Harrison glanced down at her, and she immediately caught his silent message to calm down. She'd try, but it wasn't going to be easy.

Harrison stared down at Mr. Prinker. His tall stature, broad shoulders and glare made for quite an intimidating figure. "You need to explain yourself, why you have changed your mind and why Miss Bowen even had to obtain a license in the first place."

Mayor Prinker's eyelids lowered toward his meaty hands, then his gaze came back up to Harrison. Gone was the haughtiness, replaced with uncertainty.

Abby hid her grin of satisfaction, knowing the man had met his match.

"The committee and I decided with Hot Mineral Springs growing as rapidly as it is, in order to make sure no unsavory businesses soil our upstanding town or bring trouble to our quiet community, we voted to implement the business license law. We feel a dinner theater will bring too much riffraff here."

"What?" Abby slammed her hands on her hips. "Just what kind of an establishment do you think I will be running?"

The mayor turned his eyes on her, then at Harrison, whose one eyebrow spiked and whose other eye narrowed menacingly at him. Swaying and tugging on his tie, the rotund man loosened it. Sweat drops formed on his balding forehead. He pulled a monogrammed handkerchief from his pocket and blotted his forehead with it.

"Explain yourself, sir." The authority in Harrison's voice snagged Abby's attention. He crossed his arms, and the glare he sent the mayor was even more pronounced. "Before you do, you need to apologize to Miss Bowen for insulting her with your misguided insinuation. Anyone with class can tell just by looking at her that she is a fine, upstanding person. I am not sure I can say the same for you, however."

"Now just you wait a minute." Mayor Prinker shot upward, his chair scraped across the wood floor. He slammed his palms flat on his desk and leaned toward Harrison. "I'll not sit here and listen to you insult my reputation."

Harrison's brow hiked again. "And yet isn't that exactly what you're doing to Miss Bowen?"

The mayor blinked and closed his eyes for a brief

moment, then plopped his bulky form back onto the black leather chair. "I see what you're saying." He looked up at Abby. "Please accept my sincere apology, Miss Bowen." He folded his hands together and lowered them onto the desktop in front of him. "However sorry I am, I still cannot issue you a license." The apology was sincere, not only in his voice, but his eyes, and Abby actually felt sorry for him.

"Mr. Prinker." She stepped forward. "I thank you for your apology, and I understand your concern. However, I assure you that my—" her attention swung to Harrison "—our establishment will only bring culture and even more refinement to your...to our lovely community."

His eyes slatted as if he didn't believe her.

Abby restrained herself from allowing her frustration to show. None of that would get him to trust her or get the license she needed. "I can assure you our theater will host only the finest of plays. Are you familiar with Jane Austen's work, Mr. Prinker?"

"Yes, I am."

"Well, then you know what wonderful works of art her novels are."

"I sure do." His chest puffed out.

"That there is nothing questionable in them to perform. Correct?"

The mayor nodded, and Abby noticed the slight curl of Harrison's lips.

"No alcoholic beverages will be allowed in our establishment, only the finest teas and beverages will be served. Our guests will dine in high fashion. They will savor six-course French cuisine meals prepared by my cook, Veronique, who hails from France." At that, the man all but drooled. Abby wanted to roll her eyes but didn't because she herself was on a roll. "They will then be escorted to the theater where they will sit in exquisite, plush-velvet chairs and watch plays put on by reputable people only." She gave that a minute to sink in before she proceeded.

"A theater such as the one we intend to create, like the one back home in Paradise Haven, did not bring in riffraff, nor did it cause the town or anyone else any trouble. On the contrary, actually. When word got around, society's very elite traveled from miles away to watch the productions. Those very people stayed in the town's hotels and increased the revenue of every establishment there."

Greed shrouded his eyes.

She refused to tell him that people who didn't have much came, as well. From the little bit she'd been around the mayor, he might deem them as riffraff or undesirables, which they weren't, of course. "I assure you, Mayor Prinker, just as the theater in Paradise Haven did not tolerate anyone who caused trouble, we will do the same."

The mayor sat back in his chair and raked his fingers across his double chin.

Abby looked over at Harrison. His smile of approval meant a lot to her.

Mayor Prinker rose and walked around his rich mahogany desk and stood within feet of her. "I need to discuss this new information with the other board members. I shall call a quick meeting in the boardroom. You and Mr. Kingsley can either wait here in my office, or you may come back later this afternoon."

"We'll wait here." Harrison spoke before she had a chance to.

"Very well. I shall be back in a few minutes. Have a seat and I will send Miss Elsa in with some tea."

"That won't be necessary. But thank you." No matter how thirsty she was at the moment, Abby didn't want the poor older woman to have to walk any more than she had to with her bad leg.

"Very well." With those words he stepped out of his office and disappeared from their sight.

Abby and Harrison sat down in chairs not nearly as nice as the mayor's.

"You handled that very well, Abigail."

She felt so good about things, she didn't even mind that Harrison had called her Abigail instead of Abby. "Thank you. So did you." She nibbled at her lip a moment. "Do you think they'll agree to give us the license now?"

"Judging by the greed in Mayor Prinker's eyes, I'd say that's a pretty good indicator that we'll get the license."

No sooner had the words come out of his mouth than Mayor Prinker came rushing through door, huffing and puffing. That had to be the shortest meeting in history.

"Miss Bowen, Mr. Kingsley." He breathlessly said their names as he scurried around to the other side of his desk and plopped down in his chair. He pressed his hand against his chest and drew in several streams of air. "I—I t-talked to the other members…" He panted out the words, then reached for his cup. Between breaths, he took several sips of his beverage. When his breathing neared normal, he spoke again, "We have decided to issue you a license, after all."

Abby wanted to jump up and down and hoop and holler, but in order to maintain a professional persona, she restrained herself.

"But—"

Uh-oh, here it comes. She should have known there would be a but in there somewhere. There always was with him.

He held up his hand, looking only at Abby. "Anytime either I or the committee members feel your establishment is harming our community, or it doesn't conform to the high standards we have set for our town, we will shut you down. And, the stipulation of maintaining a male business partner remains the same, or we will shut you down. Is that understood?" This time the mayor looked at Harrison.

"I foresee no problem with that," Harrison answered with a confidence she didn't feel.

Abby yanked her gaze in his direction, wishing she had the same assurance as he did as she had no intentions of maintaining a business partner, and he had no intentions of staying here. Unless…hmm. Unless he eventually became the silent business partner they had discussed the day before. She didn't know why that wouldn't work. After all, nothing was said about him having to remain here in town.

The whole thing was a huge risk. One she was willing to take. Convinced once the mayor and his cronies saw how much money the business brought to their town and just how classy the place was, she had a feeling they wouldn't care if her business partner lived here or elsewhere. Doubt niggled at her, but she paid it no mind. Nothing would douse her joy. Nothing.

Pride was the only way to describe how Harrison felt. The way his new business partner handled things just now amazed him. There was more to Abigail Bowen than a pretty face. It was a good thing he was indeed heading straight home. He'd been fooled once too often by a pretty face. He needed to be extremely careful just who he let into his heart. Not only for his sake, but his sons', as well.

He cupped Abby's elbow and led her outside the town hall building. Unlike when they'd first arrived for their meeting, nary a rain cloud could be seen, only miles of pale blue sky. Humidity and fresh air with a hint of sulphur filled his nostrils. Wagon ruts raked through the street reminding him of his sons' drawings.

At the edge of the boardwalk, Abby stopped. She closed her eyes and turned her face upward. The sun covered her youthful skin with its bright glow. She drew in several long breaths. What a lovely vision she was. Harrison watched her with fascination. She was a woman of means, yet there was something outdoorsy about her and completely refreshing from the women he had been raised around.

Her eyes, the same blueness as the sky, slowly opened. Beauty bathed her in all its glory. Only one other woman was as comely as she, his dear departed wife. He pinched his eyes shut to blot out the painful memories that routinely followed thoughts of his sweet Allison.

"Are you all right, Harrison?" Abby's hand settled on top of his arm.

His gaze drifted toward it. The gesture, meant to comfort him, sizzled his arm with her feminine awareness. A feeling he knew all too well. When he'd first met his wife, the same thing had happened to him back then, and he'd married her. Stunned at the correlation and its impact on him, he abruptly stepped to the side, allowing Abby's arm to separate from his. "I'm fine."

One look at her face and he knew he hadn't fooled her, her disbelieving frown told him as much. "Why don't we go and celebrate?" he asked to keep her from questioning him a second time. "Pie and coffee. My treat." He pulled his attention from her and settled it on the town before them. "Who here makes the best pies?"

Her sigh was audible as she pointed to a sign hanging several doors down from the hall. "Lucy's Diner. Her pies are exquisite. Almost as good as my mother's. Her pie crust is so flaky and light, it barely holds together."

"Sounds like my kind of pie. Shall we?" He offered her the crook of his arm. Big mistake that turned out to be. That same heat sizzled up his arm again, only this time he refused to let his mind dwell on it or its implications. Instead, he reminded himself that he was here for the sole purpose of securing his inheritance for not only his sons' sake, but for the sake of the unfortunate people back in Boston who his father had greatly wronged. A quick glance at Abby and he needed to add one more reason to the mix. After meeting Abby and seeing just how much she wanted this business to succeed, he wanted to do everything in his power to make her dream come to fruition, as well.

They strolled down the boardwalk, their footsteps echoing underneath them. When they reached the steps that separated one building from the other, Harrison glanced down at the muddy ground, then at her delicate gown, and contemplated what to do. If she was his wife, he would swing her into his arms and carry her across, but she wasn't. And yet, how could he do nothing and allow a lady to soil her garment. "If you will permit me, I would like to carry you across the mud."

Abby blinked as if he'd gone daft or something. "Thank you. But no. I can walk. I was raised on a farm. I'm used to mud. A lot of it." With those words, she hiked her skirt and tiptoed through the thick mire to the other side.

Harrison stared at her back. No Bostonian lady would have ever done that. In fact, they would have insisted Harrison call for a servant to carry them across or that he lay his coat down for them to walk on. Abby was nothing like those ladies. She was more like Allison in that way, too. Realizing what he was doing, he reprimanded himself for comparing Abby to his deceased wife.

They arrived at Lucy's Diner. Harrison opened the door for Abby. Apples and cinnamon filled the air.

Abby headed to a table by the window, and he followed, holding her chair out and waiting for her to be seated before he took the chair across from her. His gaze slid around the room at the informal, homey establishment. The sparkling-clean place was small but not cluttered. It was also void of patrons, which had him wondering why since according to Abby, it served the best pie in town.

"How fortunate we are that we missed the morning breakfast rush." Abby answered his unspoken question.

A petite, slender woman in a bright yellow dress with a stained apron over it bustled toward them. "Abby! It's so nice to see you again. Couldn't stay away, huh? You come back for some more of my strawberry-rhubarb pie? I made a fresh batch this morning. There's three pieces left. So if you want one, you'd better grab a slice before the next rush of customers comes barreling in. You want coffee with that pie, or tea? Oh, I'm sorry. I didn't even ask. Maybe you don't want strawberry-rhubarb today. I have two pecan pies coming out of the oven in a few minutes. You want a slice of that instead?" As if she finally realized Abby wasn't alone, the woman stopped her rapid-fire talking and her brown-eyed gaze fell to him.

"Oh, dear me. Forgive me, sir. Don't know where my manners are. Hello. I'm Lucy Cornwall. Owner of this here place." She grabbed his hand with her sticky one and pumped it vigorously with a grip as strong as any man's. A grasp that certainly didn't match her petite size.

"Lucy, this is Mr. Kingsley. My new business partner. We're here to celebrate."

"Oh." Her eyes lit up. "What you celebrating? Oh, wait." She shook her head. "You said he's your new business partner. This must mean that ornery old mayor and his little cronies gave you your license, then. Good. Cuz, if he didn't, I was fixin' to march down there and give that man a good tongue lashing, and let him know he'd get no more pie from me. That'd serve him right. Won't have to now. Okay, what'll you have?" She pulled a piece of paper and a nub of a pencil out of her apron pocket, chewed on the wood like a beaver gnawing on a log until more lead exposed itself, then she placed the dull point on the paper. Her friendly smile landed on him first, then Abby. "Now I'm ready."

The woman reminded him of a hurricane, long-winded and unpredictable. He glanced at Abby. She winked at him and smiled before turning her attention to Lucy. "I'll take the strawberry-rhubarb pie and tea."

Lucy scribbled it down and turned to him.

Harrison couldn't believe she needed to write their orders down. After all, the place was empty and it wasn't like she had a ton of orders. Didn't matter what she did or didn't do, it wasn't his place to decide how she did things. "I'll have the same. Only make mine coffee instead of tea."

"Yes, sir. I'll be right back with your orders." She whirled around and within seconds her tiny form disappeared behind a swinging door.

He shook his head.

"You get used to her."

"You do?"

Abby laughed. "Yes. You do. I promise. She's really a very sweet woman. One who would give you her last bread crumb. Lucy gives more food away than she has paying customers. I have no idea how she even stays in business. But she does. And people love her."

He settled his elbows on the arms of his chair and clasped his hands. "You come here often, then?"

Heat filled Abby's cheeks. "Yes. Once you taste Lucy's pie, you'll understand why. But don't tell Veronique."

"Your secret's safe with me." His lips curled upward.

The swinging door leading to and from the kitchen squeaked, and out came Lucy advancing toward their table like a locomotive trying to make its destination on time. How the woman moved so fast holding a tray loaded with two filled cups, a cream pitcher, a sugar bowl and two large slices of pie, Harrison didn't know. Not one drop had spilled, either.

"Here you go." She set their orders in front of them, chattering like a wound-up parrot as she did.

Harrison had a hard time keeping up with her and finally gave up—thankful Abby occupied the woman. Well, thankful wasn't quite the word. He wanted to visit with Abby without distractions, to talk about business so they could get the theater up and running as soon as possible. The sooner the better so he could get back home. In the next breath, the mayor's stipulations ran through his mind.

As soon as Lucy left to tend to the three customers that had just walked in, Harrison turned his focus onto Abby, who had just forked a bite of pie and settled it into her mouth. He waited until she swallowed, then asked, "What did you think about the mayor's stipulations?"

Abby took a drink of her tea and dabbed the corners of her mouth with her napkin. "What stipulations?"

"About maintaining a male business partner."

"Oh. That." She placed her napkin on her lap. "You and I already discussed that, remember?"

"I do. But what if he doesn't approve of my being a long-distance partner? Then what will you do?"

"I'm not sure. But what I am sure of is, God will take care of it. He's taken care of everything else up to this point, and He will finish what He started." Her smile swelled with confidence. She continued to eat her pie, sighing contentedly with each bite.

Harrison wondered how she could be so certain God would take care of it. God had never done anything for him. Course, it had been years since he had asked Him to, and God hadn't answered his prayer back then. Since then, he wanted nothing to do with God or church. In his experience, most people who prayed or went to church did it solely for show and for social reasons.

Every Sunday he and his father sat in the front row of the largest church in the city, listening to the minister go on and on about money and how much he needed for this project and that project. Father gave the greedy man what he needed. In front of the whole congregation filled with only society's elite—poor folks weren't allowed there—his father made a huge display of his donation.

Then all the way home and all day long, Harrison had to endure his father's complaints about the money he'd just donated and about how God never did anything for him, and how everything he owned he worked hard for. It ended with the same warning that God couldn't be depended on for anything. If He could be, then he wouldn't have to give his money and his wife wouldn't have died. That was the one thing Harrison and his father agreed on. Just why Abby thought she could depend on Him, Harrison had no idea, but in his curiosity, he wanted to find out. "What makes you so sure God will take care of this?"

"Because He always has." She took another bite of her pie, and a patch of red juice clung to her lower lip.

Without thinking, Harrison picked up his napkin, reached across the table and brushed her lip with it.

She stopped chewing, and stared at him.

Harrison yanked his hand back. "Forgive me. I'm so used to wiping my sons' mouths that I didn't stop to think about what I was doing. It's an automatic response, I suppose."

She relaxed her fixed stare, finished chewing and swallowed. "Trust me. I understand." Her eyes dimmed, and her gaze suddenly fell to his untouched pie. "Aren't you going to eat your pie?"

Confused about the sadness in her eyes and the abrupt change of subject, it took him a second before he realized what she had asked. His attention drizzled to his full plate, then over to her empty one. "Why? You want it?"

She licked her lips, a gesture that lit a spark inside him. He yanked his focus onto his plate and suddenly became very interested in his pie, devouring it within minutes.

"I guess that means yes." Her smiling eyes danced with amusement.

He couldn't help but smile, too. He sat back in his chair and patted his flat stomach. Something so uncharacteristic of him to do, but Abby brought out the playful side of him, just like his Allison had. *Stop comparing her with Allison.* He cleared his throat. "Sure was."

They finished their drinks, talking about the weather, the mountains and nothing else of consequence, and then they headed back to her place.

He pulled his buggy in front of her mansion and stopped. He jumped out and went around the side of the buggy to help her down. Their hands connected, and the spark flew into him again. This was going to be a long three months.

Abby ignored the heat that ran up her arm when Harrison's hand clutched hers. Soon as her feet touched the ground, the man yanked his hand from hers and stepped back. His abrupt action shocked her, but she shrugged it off. No time to worry about what had just happened; she had a business to build. And nothing, not even the charming, handsome Harrison Kingsley would stop her. She hoped. "Would you like to come inside?"

His brows pulled together.

"To discuss business. The sooner we get started, the sooner I—we—can open."

He removed his pocket fob watch and flipped the gold H K engraved cover open. After a quick glance at it, with a click he snapped the lid shut and nestled it back into his pocket. "I told my boys I'd take them to lunch today. It's still early. So yes, we can do that."

"Wonderful."

Up the mansion stairs they went.

Zoé met them at the door and took Abby's wrap and Harrison's *chapeau*. They made their way to the parlor.

Before sitting down next to him on the settee, she retrieved her writing tablet containing all her notes, along with a fountain pen. "Would you care for something to drink?"

"No, thank you. But if you do, please go ahead."

"I don't care for anything, either." She smiled at him and shifted her knees his direction, careful to not touch his. "First of all, we need to hire a carpenter. I had Colette put up an advertisement on the bulletin board, but someone took it from her. If we don't hear from whoever that was today, I thought we could put up another ad and ask around town to see if anyone knew of someone who could get the job done in the next couple of months." How strange it felt to keep saying *we*. It had always been *I* up until today. In an even stranger way, it sounded nice.

She never thought she would admit something like this to herself, but truth be told, she liked having a partner. Oh, not just any ol' partner, of course, but one particular strong-figure-of-a-man sitting next to her. Close enough in fact that she could detect the scent of lemon spice and something entirely masculine.

Something about the man awakened her senses to a new height and made her want to… *No. No romantic thoughts allowed, Abigail.* That's what she called herself when she needed a good talking to. She shook all thoughts of romance from her head and reminded herself that no man wanted a woman who couldn't bear children. Besides, Harrison would be leaving soon. And she'd do well to remember that, too.

"You all right, Abby?"

Her gaze darted to his. She waved her hand. "Oh. Yes. Yes. I'm fine. Now, where were we?"

"We were discussing—" Harrison stopped talking; his attention was toward the door of the parlor.

Abby shifted in the settee to see what he was looking at.

"Forgive me for intruding, *mademoiselle*. But there is a gentleman here to see you," Zoé said.

"Thank you, Zoé. Send him in, please."

"Very well." Zoé left.

Abby twisted back in her chair. "I wonder who that could be. Hopefully the mayor didn't change his mind again." Abby tugged on her lip with her fingertips.

"In here, if you would, please, sir."

Abby turned in time to see Zoé make a motioning gesture with her hand.

In stepped a man she'd never seen before.

She and Harrison stood at the same time.

"Miss Abby. This is Mr. Fletcher Martin." Zoé presented him to her.

The man strode over to Abby. He towered over her by at least a foot. "Ma'am." He extended his hand.

Abby accepted the gesture. Rough calluses met her hand when she did. With a sweep of her hand toward Harrison, Abby introduced him. "This is Mr. Kingsley. Harrison Kingsley."

"Pleasure to meet you, Mr. Kingsley," Mr. Martin said.

Two large, very masculine hands met in between them.

From the corner of her eye, Abby noticed Zoé standing by the door with her hands clasped in front of her, looking around uncomfortably. "Thank you, Zoé. You can go now." She sent her a smile, one filled with appreciation.

Zoé relaxed and smiled. She turned and left the room with a scurry in her step.

Abby shifted her focus back to the stranger. "What can I do for you, Mr. Martin?"

He removed a slip of paper very similar to the one she'd given Colette to post on the bulletin board from his shirt pocket and unfolded it. "I've come about your advertisement."

"Please, won't you sit down?" She motioned to the empty chair across from her, and then sat down. Harrison did also.

Mr. Martin lowered his tall, broad-shouldered frame into the chair across from them. Dark brown eyes trailed to her. Fletcher Martin was an extremely handsome man, but not as handsome as Harrison. He had many more edges to him, and most of them looked quite rugged.

She stopped in midthought. Why was she comparing him to Harrison? Ridiculous. That's what it was. Just plain ridiculous.

Drawing on her business persona to get her mind where it needed to be, she slogged forward. "Mr. Kingsley and I are looking for someone to not only repair this place—" her arms made a wide arc of the room "—but also someone to build a theater stage and props."

"I can do that."

Her insides danced with the prospect of having found a carpenter so soon.

"What kind of experience do you have, Mr. Martin?" Harrison asked.

Now why hadn't she thought to ask him that?

Mr. Martin looked at Abby, then at Harrison.

"Mr. Kingsley and I are business partners."

"Oh." He gave a quick nod. "I see." He reached inside his pocket again, pulled out another slip of paper and unfolded it. "Here's a list of references." He stood and handed the list to Harrison.

Something about that bugged her. She was in charge

here, not Harrison. Of course, Mr. Martin didn't know that. At that moment, she realized she'd better get used to it. They were partners, after all.

Harrison studied the paper as she sat with her hands in her lap patiently waiting while he did.

Finally, Harrison nodded. "That's quite an impressive list, Mr. Fletcher."

"Thank you, sir."

"Do you mind if we keep this? We'd like to check your work before we consider hiring you."

How sweet of him to include her.

In a million years, she never thought she would like someone taking over the charge of her business affairs, but something about the way Harrison did it was so attractive and so alluring and so like the heroes in her romance novels.

Stop thinking like that. She reset her gaze on the carpenter across the way, determined to keep her notions—romantic and otherwise—under wraps.

"Not at all." Mr. Martin stood. "If you would like to see some of my work, you can head over to the town hall. My crew and I built that building. We made most of the furniture in it, too."

"Oh. You make furniture?" Abby's interest and excitement piqued.

"Yes. We do." His attention gravitated from Harrison to her.

"What kind do you make? Do you have any pieces for sale?"

"Yes. I have a storehouse outside of town full of furniture."

Her eyes widened in hope and surprise. "You do?"

"Yes, ma'am. When things are slow, especially during the winter months here, we build furniture. Not to boast or anything, ma'am, but some of our items have shipped as far east as New York, even."

"Wonderful. I'd love to come see what you have. I need to fill this place with furniture. What you can't supply me with, I can have shipped from catalogs." She stopped and gazed over at Harrison. "That is, if it's all right with you."

He hadn't left her out, and she wasn't going to leave him out, either. Besides, she knew it hurt a man's pride to have to take orders from a woman or to not look like he was in charge, so she'd let him think he was. But she knew the truth. And that was all that mattered.

Chapter Five

Dressed in a simple cotton dress, Abby grabbed the blue wrap that matched it and waited by the front door for Harrison. Before he'd left the night before, they had agreed to go to the furniture place together. They'd also agreed if they liked Mr. Martin's work, they would hire him and his employees.

Harrison pulled his buggy in front of her house.

Abby swung the door open, scurried down the steps and met him just as he stepped out of the carriage. "Good morning." Her cheery attitude chirped through her voice.

"My, you're quite chipper this morning."

"I have reason to be. I can hardly wait to see what furniture Mr. Martin has in his storeroom. I'm so tired of looking at those sparsely filled rooms. I hope, hope, hope he has what we need."

Harrison helped her into the buggy and hurried over to the driver's side. With a flick of the reins, the black mare clomped forward. Harrison glanced over at her then back at the road. "I don't want to put a damper on your good spirits or anything, but I wouldn't count on him having enough chairs to fill the theater or enough tables and chairs for the dining area."

"Huh? Oh. I didn't mean that. I meant for the parlors, the seating area and the foyer. He won't carry what I have in mind for the dining area and theater, anyway."

"What do you have in mind?"

"I want royal blue, plush-velvet chairs for the theater and shield-back style Chippendale chairs with gold, padded seats and matching Chippendale tables for the dining area."

"Chippendale is extremely pricey furniture," he stated.

"Yes, I know."

"Do you also know how expensive they will be to ship out here?"

"Of course I do. You know, I may have been raised on a farm, Mr. Kingsley, but I'm no country bumpkin, and I understand business. My father was a successful New York City businessman. My brothers are successful businessmen. My stepfather owns several successful businesses, half of Paradise Haven, actually. And my mother, my brother Michael, and my brother Haydon all have Chippendale furniture in their homes. So I am very much aware of how much things cost." She hadn't meant it to sound so huffy, but his insinuations bothered her. Besides, she didn't know anyone of his means who would be concerned about the cost of things. Then again, maybe his wealth was tied up in his father's will. That would explain it.

"I didn't mean to insult you. I just wanted to make sure you knew how expensive it would be."

"I can assure you, I do. I've been planning this for a very long time now. I have several furniture catalogs, and I've checked on the prices of everything, including the cost of shipping the items I want. I would be foolish not to. The Bible makes it clear when it says, 'Consider the cost.' Well, I've done that for all of it. And I have more than enough funds to cover everything. My father saw to that before he passed away."

She narrowed her eyes. "Listen, if you're worried about me asking you for more money, I already told you that all you need to invest is five hundred dollars. The rest is at my expense. And I will keep my end of the agreement that within three months' time, you will get your original investment back, plus the profit I promised you. Even if there is no profit from the business, you will obtain one at my expense." She knew she sounded defensive, but after being judged by the town committee and now having Harrison questioning her business instincts, too, well, enough was enough. How doltish did they all think she was, anyway?

His hand settled on her arm. "Abby, I meant no offense. I didn't bring up the subject because I was concerned about having to invest more money. I was only watching out for your interests."

Her gaze slid to his bluish-gray eyes and the amber color settled at the bottom third of his right eye. Gorgeous was the only way to describe those orbs of his.

She knew she should look away. But she saw no harm in admiring his good looks and stunning eyes. After all, she knew there would never be anything more between them than a business relationship. Even still, that didn't mean she was dead. She admired a handsome man just as much as the next woman did. Only difference was, she had to be careful not to give him or any other gentleman the wrong idea, as she could never marry.

The reminder that she could never bear children came as it always did when she thought about marriage, but she refused to entertain it. Instead, she shifted her mind back onto business. "Thank you, Harrison. I appreciate your concern. It is my turn to apologize. I fear I have overreacted. My only excuse is, after what the town committee put me through, treating me like I, a mere woman, had no business running an establishment, well, I guess I'm a little sensitive about the whole thing."

"That's understandable. But I want you to know from what little I've witnessed, you have a great mind for business and for detail."

His words embraced her with sweetness and confidence. Knowing he had faith in her meant a lot.

He drove the buggy down the main road through Hot Mineral Springs. A quarter of a mile out of town, a large building with a sign *Martin's Furniture* came into view. Bubbles of excitement popped throughout her stomach as this was one more step in making her dream become a reality.

Harrison came around to her side of the buggy and helped her down. Cupping her elbow, he led her inside the building.

They stepped inside and Abby stopped. Her hands flew to her cheeks, and her mouth fell open. "Oh, my! I've never seen so much furniture in one place before!" Rows and rows of bedroom furniture, settees and sofas of various colors, kitchen tables, dining room chairs, dressers and much more lined the walls and filled the whole interior. There was furniture everywhere. And not just any furniture, either, but beautifully crafted pieces.

Her inspection ended at Mr. Martin, standing in the back of the store. As soon as he spotted them, he said something to one of the three men standing with him, then headed their way gazing at them with a smile on his face. "Nice to see you again, Miss Bowen."

Harrison noticed Mr. Martin's gaze lingered on Abby longer than necessary. He also noticed the attraction in the man's eyes. Not that he could blame him. Abby was an extremely beautiful woman. A man would have to be dead not to notice.

Mr. Martin extended his hand toward Harrison. "It's good to see you again, too." His smile was genuine, and he shook his hand as if he were a long-lost friend.

So far, everyone here in this small town treated Harrison the same as they did everyone else. Something Harrison found refreshing.

Back home, his father had been known as a ruthless businessman. While he hadn't done anything illegal, some of his business dealings were definitely unscrupulous. By association, Harrison had been thought to be like him, and, therefore, a lot of people treated him with the same disdain they had his father. Except for those who wanted something from him or his deceased wife. Allison had loved him for who he was, the real him. The others? Well, he was either resented or used—neither of which set very well with him.

He shook hands with Mr. Martin and offered him a

friendly smile, then looked around the room. "When you said you had a storehouse full of furniture, I expected to see a few pieces. Not this." He eyes took in the room as he spoke the last words. He studied the intricately carved dresser closest to him. "I've never seen such fine craftsmanship anywhere. What are you doing here? You need to move back east. You could make a fortune back there."

"Thank you for the compliment. But I have no plans to live anywhere else. I'm happy where I am."

Harrison could understand that. Hot Mineral Springs was a beautiful place filled with friendly people, except for the mayor and his cronies. Then again, if Harrison was being honest, he didn't blame them. All they were trying to do was protect their town and keep it safe and clean from undesirables.

Would they consider him an undesirable if they knew about his father and how he managed his affairs?

Harrison did what he always did when that thought came around. He reminded himself he was nothing like his father, and he would prove it when he got back home by righting as many wrongs as he could, and by earning the good folks of Boston's respect. "Well, if you ever change your mind, you let me know. I'd be glad to help you get set up and would even be interested in investing in your company. You could even move your operation into one of the Kingsley buildings."

"That's right nice of you. But like I said, I'm happy here." He smiled. "Now, what can I help you folks with?"

With a look, Harrison turned that question over to Abby.

Her already bright blue eyes sparkled even more. "Well, let's see." She ticked the items off her long, mental list.

That began a trek around and through the workshop as Mr. Martin showed her piece after piece. After she purchased what seemed like over half of the storehouse, she turned to Harrison and asked, "May I speak to you privately for a moment?"

He nodded. "If you will excuse us…"

"Of course." Mr. Martin grabbed his list and went to the back of the store where the other three men were working.

Abby led him out of earshot of the others and gazed up at him. "If this furniture is any indication of the type of work he does, I think we should hire him. What do you think?"

Harrison knew how hard it was for her to include him in her plans. She'd never wanted a business partner and resented the fact that she'd been forced to get one. From what he'd witnessed, she didn't need one. Still, he was pleased to be included in the decisions. "I agree. But before we do—"

"—we need to do a walk-through and show him exactly what needs to be done and find out how much he will charge to do the job." She finished his sentence.

"You read my mind." He smiled at her. "Do you want me to ask him, or do you want to do that?"

"You can ask him."

"Very well." They strolled back to where Fletcher was. "Mr. Martin, when would be a good time for you to come to the mansion again? We would like to show you everything that needs to be done and get an estimate from you as soon as possible."

"If you two are free now, I can follow you over there."

Harrison glanced down at Abby. Anticipation sparkled through her eyes, and she gave a quick nod.

"Yes. That'll be fine. We'll meet you there."

They turned to leave, but Abby stopped. "When's the soonest you can deliver my furniture?"

"My men can deliver it this afternoon if you'd like."

"That would be wonderful." She clasped her hands together. "Thank you, Mr. Martin. I shall finally have real furniture. What great joy!"

The carpenter's face registered the enthusiasm of her words, much to Harrison's displeasure.

"Please, call me Fletcher."

Her smile resembled summer sunshine. "And you may call me Abby."

For some odd reason, Harrison didn't like the informality between them. But Abby wasn't one much for formality. Besides, he had no claims on her.

"We'll see you back at the mansion." Harrison normally cupped her elbow, but this time, he looped her arm through his and led her outside. Did he do it on purpose? If so, what for? To give Fletcher the idea they were an item so he wouldn't pursue her. That wasn't fair to Abby. After all, he would be leaving, and she would be here. She deserved to find a nice man. He discreetly moved his hand to her elbow. If she noticed the change, she didn't say anything. Much to his relief.

On their way back to her place, her excitement bubbled over and so did her words. "I'm so happy. I never expected to find everything I needed right here in town.

Can you believe it? I mean, really, who would have thought such a thing? Well, with the exception of the theater furniture, that is. Oh, I wish Fletcher had time to make our chairs for us. Did you see the quality of his work?" Her gaze darted to his, but she didn't wait for his answer. Instead, she went on and on about Fletcher, the furniture, his talent and more.

All the accolades about Fletcher almost made Harrison jealous. Almost. But that was just plain ludicrous, and he knew it.

The three arrived at the mansion at the same time and headed inside.

They showed Fletcher through the house. In each room, he jotted down notes. Lots of them. While Harrison was no carpenter, he did know a bit about buildings. And this one needed a lot more repairs than even he originally thought. He wondered if Abby knew just how many repairs were needed. She said she'd counted the cost, but judging by the smile on her face, he had a feeling she didn't know just how much money this place was going to take to fix it up.

Somehow, he needed to warn her before they got the estimate. In the meantime, he could only hope he was wrong.

In the massive theater room, Abby told him about the stage and props she would need built, and Fletcher continued to jot down notes. His list grew, and so had Harrison's dread. What if she didn't have enough money to cover all the expenses this place needed? Would she still pay him as promised? While that was important to him, it was equally important that she succeed at making her dream come true. And once again he was determined to do whatever it took to help that dream become a reality.

When they finished the lengthy inside and outside tour, she ordered tea and cookies for them. Abby sat next to Harrison on the settee, and Fletcher sat in the chair across from them. She asked the man a million questions, ending with, "How soon can you get those figures to us?"

"Tomorrow morning."

"Will that work for you, Harrison?"

"Yes. That'll be fine."

Fletcher stood. "Well, I need to get going. Thank you for the tea and cookies. I'll bring my estimate by tomorrow morning. Around nine, if that's acceptable."

Abby looked up at Harrison. He nodded.

"See you at nine." Fletcher headed toward the parlor door.

Harrison started to follow him.

"You're not leaving now, too, are you?"

He stopped. "I was. Why? Did you need something?"

"Well, we still have business to discuss." She glanced at Fletcher, then back at him.

"Very well."

"I'll walk Fletcher out, and I'll be right back." Her warm, grateful smile made him glad he'd stayed.

What was it about her that had him wanting to please her?

Abby couldn't wait until she finished seeing Fletcher to the door so she could get back to Harrison. Back inside the parlor, Harrison stood at the window with his back to her. How regal he looked, a fine figure of a man to be sure. But she'd already established that earlier and many times in between. "Well, that was a productive morning, I think." She breezed over to where he stood.

Harrison turned toward her, and if she wasn't mistaken, unease dotted that gorgeous face of his.

She wondered what had him so concerned. She peered out the window in time to see Fletcher swing his tall frame onto his saddle and ride out of sight; nothing out of the ordinary there.

Should she ask him what the matter was or wait until he hopefully volunteered the information? The latter won. "That man sure does exquisite work. I can't wait to get my new furniture and get rid of this old stuff." The sway of her arm and her eyes took in the whole of the parlor, and she wrinkled her nose in disgust. The furniture had definitely seen better days.

"That he does." The furrow between his brows was still there.

"Is something the matter, Harrison?"

Troubled eyes shifted to hers.

Something was definitely wrong. Her stomach pinched with worry. "Please, tell me what's bothering you?"

He stared at her for a moment as if contemplating what to do.

She laid her hand on his arm. "Whatever it is, you can tell me," she assured him, then braced herself for whatever it was.

"This is very awkward, Abigail."

Abigail? Uh-oh. That wasn't good.

"I don't want to offend you or anything, but I need to ask you something."

"All right." She nodded.

"You said you had counted the cost and that you had plenty of money. That your father had seen to it." He swallowed, looked away then returned his focus to her. Each moment he didn't speak caused her stomach to pinch harder.

"And…"

"There's no easy way to say this, so I'll just come right out and say it."

Again she nodded, again she braced herself.

"Do you realize just how many repairs are needed on this place? And just how much money it's going to cost to fix those repairs?"

She tilted her head and frowned. "What do you mean?"

"Several of the windows and doors need replacing. The fireplaces are in need of repair, not to mention needing to be cleaned thoroughly. Plus, there are a few weakened and cracked walls that need fixing."

"Weakened and cracked walls?"

"Yes. I'm just hoping they're not from a foundation problem."

"Foundation problem?" She knew she was mimicking him, but she didn't understand what he was talking about. She hadn't seen any cracks in the walls or anything wrong with the building's structure. Of course, she was no carpenter, either.

"Part of the kitchen floor needs to be replaced, as well."

"It does? Why?"

"Because, when I stepped in front of the water pump, the floor caved some. It will only get worse, and you can't have someone falling through that and breaking a leg or getting hurt."

How come she'd never noticed any of those things before? Especially the kitchen floor. Her gaze brushed over Harrison's stout physique, then over her petite frame. Did the weight difference have anything to do with the floor giving? She made a mental note to ask Veronique if she had noticed the weakened floor. She wondered just how many more things she had missed. What if the repairs were numerous? More than she'd estimated? While she had plenty of money, she also knew she would need a vast amount to get everything set up and to run things for a time. She rolled her lip under with her top teeth. Might her dream crash at her feet before it ever got a chance to be realized?

"I can see I've upset you, Abby. I'm sorry. I shouldn't have said anything. Fletcher did a thorough inspection of the place. I'm confident that he noticed those things, and that he knows what he's doing, so why don't we just wait to see what he says and how much his bid is?"

She gazed up at him and nodded.

"Now, what did you want to discuss with me?"

"Excuse me?"

"You asked me to stay, to discuss business."

"Oh. Oh. Right. I wanted to show you the chairs and tables I'm going to order. I have the catalogs here." She strolled over to the coffee table, and he followed.

They sat down on the settee, and she turned the catalog to the earmarked page.

Harrison scooted closer to her. Leaning over, he peered down at it.

His nearness and aftershave swirled through her

senses, making it hard to concentrate on anything but him. Being a dreamer and a romantic most of her life, she had to forcefully turn her mind off his masculinity and on to the task at hand. "These are the chairs I had in mind for the theater." She pointed to a picture of them. "And these are the ones I had in mind for the dining room."

"Very nice. You have exquisite taste, Abby."

She turned her face toward him, and his was close enough to where she could see that half-moon color again. Something she found extremely attractive and very appealing. But before she started daydreaming again, she quickly thanked him, flipped to the next earmarked page, and pointed to the next item on her list. "This table is the one I've chosen for the dining room." As an afterthought she added, "That is if that's all right with you."

"It's very nice." His gaze alighted on hers. "You know, Abby, while I appreciate you running everything by me, you don't have to. Again, I know that you only have me here because of the town committee's stipulation. You already know what you want. You should just order it. After all, you'll be the one to have to look at it when I'm gone."

Gone. That one word drove through her, leaving its painful mark. Truth was, she rather liked having a partner, someone to run her ideas by. And not just any partner, either; she liked having *Harrison* as a partner.

After all, the man was easy to get along with and had a special way of easing her loneliness.

As he said, though, he would be leaving, best not to get too used to having him around. She closed the book and sat up straight. "You're right. I do have to look at it when you're gone. And I was forced to take on a partner. But I don't mind running things by you. Truth be known, I rather enjoy it. But if you don't care to know or to see what I'm doing, then…" She hiked a shoulder and left the sentence dangling for him to pick up.

"I do care. I want this place to succeed. For your sake as well as mine. I just don't want you to feel like you *have* to share everything with me is all."

"Oh, but I truly do want to. After all, two heads are better than one, right? Besides, I really am enjoying working with you."

"I'm glad you feel that way. I'm enjoying working with you, too." He smiled at her.

Her lips smiled back at him, as did her heart. Mixed emotions, both turbulent and sweet, scattered and rolled across her brain like fast-moving storm clouds.

If only she could have children.

And if only he wasn't leaving when this business deal ended.

And if only her heart didn't skip with happiness every time she was around him.

But… She sighed. The "if onlys" would always be there. So it was best if she saved her emotional fantasies of having this man around for the rest of her life for her daydreams because that's all any of it would ever be.

A fancy.

A dream.

And nothing more.

Chapter Six

"Mademoiselle." Veronique entered the study. "There is a gentleman here to see Mr. Kingsley. He says it is rather urgent."

Abby glanced up at Harrison.

"Excuse me." Harrison turned and exited the room.

Abby didn't know whether to follow him or not, so she opted to stay in the parlor and wait for him.

Minutes ticked by, the noise of a loud ruckus came from outside the room. She pushed herself off the chair and stepped out of the parlor. Her attention immediately flew to the sound of giggling boys near the front door, and to Harrison who was chasing one of his sons, and to a very distraught, yet distinguished gentleman running after the other.

An overturned potted plant lay sprawled across the floor. Harrison's sons dodged the men, giggling as they did, and kicked at the dirt, sending the mess flying across the floor.

Seeing that the disgruntled men needed help, Abby took pity on them, and bustled their way.

"Josiah! Graham! That's enough!" Harrison's loud voice, filled with anger and frustration, echoed off the walls in the large, near-empty room.

His twins stopped and turned wide eyes up at their father. Tears pooled in their gray-blue orbs, and loud wails followed.

Abby's heart broke seeing their little faces like that. How her arms ached to comfort them, but it wasn't her place to get involved like that; they weren't her children. But oh, how she wanted to.

Harrison dropped to his knee, giving no attention to the fact that he had just settled his expensive, tailor-made suit right smack in the middle of the moist plant soil. He pulled the boys into his arms and held them. When they stopped sobbing, he leaned back and peered into their faces. He brushed the moisture from their cheeks with the handkerchief he removed from his pocket, then returned it. "I'm sorry I yelled at you. But you mustn't run in the house. We need to find Miss Abby and ask her for a broom so you can clean up the mess you made."

The boys' blinking eyes widened. Their little gazes took in the mess on the floor. "But we don't know how to cwean the mess."

This time Abby stepped in. "I'll go and get a broom and a dustpan."

All three pair of eyes swung in her direction. Make that four counting the gentleman in the perfectly pressed suit.

Harrison rose, clasped his sons' hands, and held one at each side. "I'm sorry about the plant. I'll have my valet, Staimes, here—" he glanced over to the distinguished gentleman standing feet away from him, then back at her "—find another one and replace it."

Abby brushed her hand in a dismissing wave. "No, no. That won't be necessary. It's just a plant. No harm done." She smiled down at the boys. "I'll be right back with the broom, and then if your father doesn't mind, I'll show you how to clean up the mess. All right?" Her gaze slid to his.

He nodded and mouthed, "Thank you."

With a quick brisk to her walk, she made her way into the kitchen, grabbed a broom and a dustpan from the closet and hurried back to them.

After she finished patiently showing Josiah and Graham how to clean up the mess, she eyed each child. "You did a lovely job, boys."

Their faces beamed, and little chests puffed out.

"You sure did," Harrison added. "I'm proud of you two." He glanced over at his valet standing by the door, stiff as a statue. "Staimes, can you handle the boys for a few minutes?"

The valet's brows yanked upward, then dropped into a V. He glanced down at them, then back up at Harrison. Fear and desperation blinked through the man's eyes.

"It's only for a few minutes. You'll do fine."

Staimes didn't look convinced, but he gave a curt nod and stepped forward.

Harrison handed the children over to him, making sure the man had a hold of their hands before letting go. "Boys, do not let go of Staimes's hands. If you do, Daddy will have to discipline you. Do you understand?"

They lowered their eyes and nodded.

"Very well, then. I'll be right back." He looked at Abby. "I need to speak with you, if you will."

"Is everything all right?"

He led her to the far end of the main room, opposite of where the children were, and stopped. "I'm sorry, but I have to leave. Miss Elderberry, the boys' nanny, quit, and I have no one to watch my sons. I'm going to have to find a replacement nanny as soon as possible."

Abby struggled with what to do. She wanted to offer to let the children come with him, but being around them on a daily basis would be too hard. Knowing just how hard it would be for her, after much contemplation, she decided to instead offer to help him find a nanny. "If you'd like, I could help you." Then as an afterthought, she added, "Until you find one, I'll see if Zoé would mind watching them for you. She's very good with children."

"So was Miss Elderberry. But Staimes said she couldn't handle these two any longer, that they were just too rambunctious for her."

"How long was she with you?"

"Two months."

"Two months!"

"Yes. She stayed longer than the last nanny. Miss Rothman lasted only two weeks."

"Two weeks?" There she was parroting him again.

"Yes. Mrs. Fairchild, the one before Miss Rothman, stayed the longest, which was four months." He ran his hand over and under his chin. "I don't know what to do. I've tried every form of discipline, but they have so much energy. If they aren't fighting, they're destroying things." His focus shifted to where the plant had spilled.

"Don't you worry about that plant. As for the boys, do they get out much? I mean, do they have a place to burn off all that energy? And are they fed a lot of sweets?"

"No. None of the nannies took them out very often because they were just too much of a handful for them. As for the sweets, I don't know about them other than the desserts they had after dinner." His brows furrowed. "Come to think of it, Staimes did say that Miss Elderberry mentioned how bribing them with sweets hadn't worked, so…" He let his sentence hang.

"I could always tell when my nephews and nieces were given too much sugar. They'd talked a mile a minute and couldn't stand still for a minute. My brothers finally gave the boys chores to do, and their wives cut down the amount of sugar they consumed and started planning more activities for them during the day."

"What kind of activities?"

"Well, in the summer, they took them fishing and on long hikes where they explored some of the hidden caves on the ranch and studied different species of animals and rocks. Stuff like that. A lot of times, they just went for a long walk through the woods. In the winter, they'd play games or have treasure hunts in the house. A lot of times they were outside building snowmen, or going for sleigh rides."

"Weren't they worried about them getting sick being out in the cold so long?"

"No. In fact, I think children that play outside are healthier than ones who stay indoors all the time. We, my siblings and I, were always outside doing something. Whether it be chores or riding horses or playing in the dirt and snow. We went on a lot of picnics, too. A lot of times, Mother would sit on the bank while we played in the stream. Honestly, most of the time we worked. There was so much to do on the ranch that we all had assigned chores. I was so glad when they hired more hands to help. I hated cleaning the chicken coop."

"Somehow I can't picture you cleaning chicken coops."

"Oh, but I did. And much worse, too." She wrinkled her nose at the memory of mucking the pig barn and horse corrals.

"I don't live on a ranch and never have, so I'll have to see what else I can come up with for them to do. But first, I need to find a nanny. And right away, before they get into any more trouble."

As if on cue, a loud crash sounded at the opposite end of the room.

"Oh, no," Harrison groaned and quickly made haste toward his boys.

Abby followed.

Pooled in the middle of the floor was a shattered drinking glass amid a puddle of milk.

"I'm sorry, Mr. Kingsley. It was my fault. I dropped the glass." Staimes's words came out rushed.

Harrison's eyebrows spiked. "You're responsible for this mess?"

"Yes, sir. The maid brought the boys some milk and cookies. I was trembling so bad that they slipped out of my hand." The blushing look on the poor man's face was so comical that Abby couldn't help herself. She covered her mouth with her hand and tittered.

Harrison and Staimes gawked at her. That, too, was

comical, and she wanted to laugh even harder, but she quickly suppressed it so as to not stun the men even further. But on the inside, she was roaring.

Lunch had been a complete and utter disaster. Harrison wanted to find the nearest rock and crawl under it. Once again, Graham and Josiah had made a mess of things. He shouldn't have let Abby talk him into staying for the noon meal. Instead, he should have been out searching for another nanny.

Did they even have nannies in Hot Mineral Springs?

Before he decided to stay and help Abby arrange the furniture that would be delivered within the hour, Harrison had tried to talk Staimes into taking the boys for the afternoon, but his valet surprised him by threatening to quit. Harrison knew he wouldn't, but he also knew that's how frightened Staimes was of watching the children. The man wasn't much on taking on young wards. Besides, Staimes wasn't just his valet, but his only true friend.

He had to admit he'd been relieved when Abby had asked Zoé to watch them for a few hours. The woman was only too happy to, which gave Harrison some peace. Still, he wondered what they were doing right now and if they were minding the woman.

"Don't worry." Abby's hand settled on his arm. "Zoé loves children, and like I said, she's very good with them."

"How did you know what I was thinking?"

"It wasn't hard to figure out. You kept going to the window and looking outside."

"For all you know, I could have been watching for Fletcher."

"True, but you haven't stopped pacing since Zoé took them. And I seriously doubt that you have reason to be nervous about my furniture."

He smiled down at her. "You got me there."

"Would you feel better if I went and checked on them?"

"Would you?" He sent her his most hopeful look, and Abby grinned in return.

"I'll be right back." She scuttled out of the room.

As soon as she disappeared, he realized that he should've gone and checked on them himself instead of letting Abby do it. He hated to admit it, but as much as he loved his sons, sometimes they were even too rambunctious for him, and spending too much time around them made him nervous. What kind of father was he that his own sons made him edgy?

Minutes later, Abby returned.

Harrison turned anxious eyes on her and met her at the doorway. "Well?" His breathing halted while he waited for her answer.

"They're fine. They're having the time of their lives."

He released an audible sigh.

Abby giggled. A sound he enjoyed.

"What are they doing?"

"Playing in the mud."

"They're what?" His voice came out louder than he'd meant it to.

"Relax. Zoé found some old clothes up in the attic. They're wearing them and having a grand time playing out by the water pump. Don't worry. She'll clean them up before she brings them inside."

Relax? How could he? A Kingsley never played in the mud or dirt. Father would never stand for that. It was too low of a thing to do. But then again, his father wasn't here. And unlike him, his boys would enjoy their childhood, and do the things he'd never been allowed to do. Like play in the mud—something he had to go and see for himself. "Would you show me where they are?"

That brought out one second of uncertainty in her soft face. "Sure."

Side by side they stood at the back door. His heart smiled, hearing his children's laughter and seeing them having so much fun. In between bouts of adding another layer to what he assumed was a mud castle, a rather lopsided one at that, he watched his sons toss mud in the air and follow it with their eyes until it landed. The urge to join them was strong. But his deeply embedded upbringing prevented him from doing so. Besides, the furniture would be delivered any minute now.

He stepped back out of the doorway and looked at Abby.

Her smile was infectious, and so were the laughing blue eyes she turned up at him. "I told you they were having fun."

"That you did. That you did." He chuckled, and she joined him.

Together they headed back to the front part of the house.

Harrison hadn't felt this carefree or this good ever, and he had Abby to thank for that.

Abby. She was one special woman. A woman he

could easily attach himself to if he wasn't careful. Careful, he would be. In the meantime, however, he was no fool. He would enjoy every precious moment of the time he had with her before he had to head back to Boston and leave her behind. That thought caused a hitch in his chest. And that was not good. Not good at all.

The instant Abby saw Fletcher's wagons pull up in front of her house, her heart skipped, and she felt like a child at Christmastime. She always loved Christmas, watching her nieces and nephews opening their gifts and searching for hidden treasures that she and her siblings would hide all over her mother's house.

Abby rushed to the door and flung it open.

"You aren't anxious or anything, are you?" Humor brushed through Harrison's voice as he came and stood behind her.

She glanced back at him. "No. No. Not at all. Why do you ask?" She sent him a playful smirk.

"No reason." He sent her one back before he removed his jacket and hung it up. When he rolled up his shirt sleeves, she noticed the rock-solid muscle that had been hidden underneath them. She wondered what it would be like to be held and to be protected by those arms.

Stop it, she silently reprimanded herself. *You've been reading too many romance novels.* Harrison wasn't some knight riding up on his white steed to sweep her away and to defend her against the forces of evil. Then Mr. Prinker and the committee members faces popped into her mind. On second thought, maybe he was. She muffled a giggle.

"Miss Abigail Bowen, if you will let me by, I will

go and help them. That way you'll get your furniture much faster."

"Oh, indeed, I shall let you by, Mr. Harrison Kingsley," she said with a dramatic flare and using her imitation of a British accent. Abby stepped out of his way and let him by.

He met Fletcher just as he hopped down from the wagon he'd ridden in on.

Seeing Harrison and Fletcher side by side, she noticed they both had wide shoulders and trim waists. Fletcher's physique, however, was lankier than Harrison's.

Both had powerful arms. Very powerful arms, if the bulge in their muscles when they hoisted the dresser out of the wagon was any indication.

Both were very handsome. Harrison especially, whose grayish-blue eyes had that unique hazel half-moon, and whose hair resembled the color of pecans. Yum. She loved pecans.

Fletcher's eyes, on the other hand, were the color of molasses, and his hair, a ginger-blond.

Both were tall, Fletcher a bit taller than Harrison, too tall for her taste. She preferred Harrison's height.

With one on each end of the dresser, Harrison and Fletcher turned and headed toward her, ending her comparisons.

Movement behind them yanked her attention to it. A little girl, clutching her doll, followed them closely behind.

"Where do you want this, Abby?"

"Oh." She blinked and stepped out of their way. "Um. Uh. Follow me." She glanced back at the pretty little girl with the ebony hair and whose brown eyes were like her father's, and smiled.

"That's my daughter, Julie," Fletcher answered her unvoiced question.

One of Julie's shoulders rose, her eyelids lowered and her thumb went to her mouth.

"Hello, Julie. I'm Abby. It's nice to meet you."

The girl never looked up.

"Can you say hello to Miss Abby?"

Ebony curls swung with the shake of her head.

Fletcher shrugged his apology to Abby, then the two men moved forward.

Abby rushed ahead of them and on up the steps, glancing back down at the lovely child who continued to follow her father like a puppy.

Upstairs in her bedroom, they placed the dresser where she wanted it, and then headed back downstairs. Before the little girl could follow them outside, Abby called her. "Julie. Would you like some cookies and milk?"

Julie's eyes widened. She looked over at her father.

"Yes, you may."

"There are two little boys outside who I'm sure would like some, too. Shall we go see?"

The child gave a quick nod.

She quickly instructed Fletcher and Harrison where she wanted the pieces to go before extending her hand out to Julie.

Julie nestled her small hand into Abby's, both warming and saddening Abby's heart with the gesture. But Abby refused to feel sorry for herself and instead wanted to do her best to ease the shy girl's discomfort.

As they headed to the kitchen, she wondered where Julie's mother was. Without asking the child directly, she decided to inquire in a roundabout way. "That's a beautiful doll you have there. What's her name?"

No response.

Well, that didn't work. She'd try something else. "Does she look like your mama?"

Julie hiked a shoulder.

That didn't work, either. Abby wasn't about to give up, though. "Does your mama have pretty brown hair like your dolly does?"

Julie's only response, another hiked shoulder.

Not knowing what else to say to get the little girl to open up to her, Abby decided to drop the subject. She refused to ask the girl outright and risk upsetting her.

A few steps from the kitchen, Abby barely heard the little girl when she finally spoke, "My mama left us."

"What do you mean she left you?"

"She took sick and left us. Mama lives with Jesus now." Sorrow covered her face and warbled through her tiny voice.

Abby stopped and squatted until she was eye level with the child. "Oh, honey. I'm sorry your mama is gone. Do you remember her at all?"

Her curls bounced as she nodded her head. "She was pretty. Like you. Only her hair looked like mine. Papa says I look like her." Her eyes brightened and her tiny lips curled upward.

"Was she as sweet as you?"

"Uh-huh." Her head nodded slowly. "She used to make me cookies and give me milk."

"She did? Well, let's see if we have some cookies like your mama used to make, shall we?"

"Uh-huh," she said with a passel of exuberance.

Abby stood. Through the dining room window, she caught a glimpse of Harrison's boys, still playing and having a grand old time, something they needed desperately. Not wanting to interrupt that, and knowing Zoé would feed them when they were finished playing, she decided not to bother them.

Together, hand in hand, she and Julie walked into the kitchen. Cinnamon and apple, along with yeasty bread, floated in the air.

Bent over the open oven door, Veronique drew out a pan of cookies, turned around and screeched when she saw them. The pan of cookies nearly flew from her hand. "You gave me such a fright, *mademoiselle*."

Abby giggled. "I'm sorry, Veronique. I didn't mean to." She turned her attention on to Julie. "Julie, this is Miss Veronique Denis. Veronique, this is Miss Julie Martin."

"'Tis a pleasure to meet you." Veronique curtsied, and Julie tried to mimic her but it came out rather awkward.

"Nice to meet you, too, Miss Dee—" she paused, frowning "—Miss Dee-niece." She smiled, rather pleased with herself that she'd pronounced Veronique's last name correctly.

"Should we see if Miss Denis's cookies are anything like your mama's?"

Julie nodded, sending her curls bouncing yet again.

"What kind do we have today?"

"Oatmeal. With apple chunks and walnuts," Veronique replied.

Julie tugged on Abby's skirt and cupped her hand. Abby leaned down and the girl spoke in her ear, "She talks funny."

Abby whispered back into her ear loud enough so that Veronique could hear. "She sure does talk funny. That's because she's from France." Abby winked at Veronique, who tried to look upset but failed.

"Where's France?" Julie asked.

"It's way across the ocean. A long ways away from here."

"Oh," was all Julie said.

Abby grabbed two glasses and two plates from off the shelf and set them on the table while Veronique retrieved the milk from the cellar. After the glasses were filled with milk, she settled Julie on the sturdiest one of the kitchen chairs, and sat down to join her. "Veronique, would you like to join us?"

"No, thank you, *mademoiselle*. I have to finish the bread." She smiled at Abby and Julie and turned back to the wad of dough on the breadboard counter.

Julie slid from her chair and turned two chairs sideways. She climbed back on her chair and looked over at each one. "Bobby and Billy need cookies and milk, too."

Abby didn't mean to but she stared at the little girl. "Are Bobby and Billy your imaginary friends?"

Julie frowned. "No. You said two boys might like to join us. When I didn't see them, I thought you invited my brothers, Bobby and Billy."

Before she could stop them, Abby's eyes went wide. "You have brothers?"

She shook her head and the sadness was back. "Not anymore. They live with Jesus now, too."

Abby couldn't believe her ears. This little girl and her father had lost so much. She was surrounded by people who had endured more heartache than anyone should ever have to.

Abby's thoughts went to Harrison's sons. "Were your brothers twins?"

Julie's curls wiggled as she shook her head. "Bobby was ten and Billy was eight. I'm four." She held up four small fingers.

Same age as Harrison's sons.

"Bobby and Billy went fishin' when they weren't 'pose to. Papa said they fell in the pond and drownaded." Julie tilted her head. "What is drownaded?" Julie looked at Abby with expectant eyes.

Abby peered over at Veronique. Veronique turned the palms of her hands upward, pinched her lips and shook her head. With a look of empathy, she turned back to kneading her bread dough.

How on earth was Abby going to answer that one?

"Julie, are you being a good girl for Miss Abby?" Much to Abby's relief, Fletcher chose that moment to step inside the kitchen. Harrison was right behind him.

Harrison looked at the table and then at the empty chairs. "Where's Graham and Josiah?"

"Who's Jos—Jos. Who's Sigha and Grrahm?" Julie asked.

"My sons."

Julie looked over at Abby.

"They're the two boys I told you about, Julie. But they were having so much fun playing in the mud, I didn't have the heart to bother them," she said more for Harrison's sake than Julie's.

Julie wrinkled her nose. "I don't like mud." She looked over at the empty chairs and shook her tiny finger. "Billy. Bobby. Don't you go playin' in the mud, or you won't get any cookies."

"Billy? Bobby?" Fletcher's voice caught, his face paled. His gaze swung to Abby's, then back to his daughter.

Abby didn't know what to say or do. All she knew was she suddenly felt very uncomfortable. This was a conversation between father and daughter, not her, or anyone else. She sent Harrison a silent look to get her out of this situation.

"Abby, do you have time to show me how you want the parlor furniture situated?"

She pressed her palms on the table and rose quickly. "I'll be happy to." Abby glanced at Veronique, who worked her dough faster and harder than necessary. She tossed the huge lump into a bowl and covered it with the decorative, empty flour sack they'd washed and now used for a towel. With a quick glance at Abby, she rushed from the room.

Her focus slid to Julie, who seemed completely oblivious to the awkward atmosphere in the room. Julie took a drink of her milk and a bite of her cookie, swinging her legs crossed at the ankle as if all was right in the world.

Abby then turned her attention onto Fletcher. As if he understood her discomfort, he walked to the table and sat in the chair she'd just vacated. "Hurry up and finish your milk and cookies, sweetheart, so Papa can finish unloading the rest of the furniture."

That was the last words she heard as she and Harrison left the kitchen together. More upset than she'd been in a long time, she wondered how much more her heart could take, and why God was allowing so many children to cross her path. And not just any children, either, but motherless ones. Didn't He know how hard this was on her? And didn't He care? At that moment, the urge to scream at God, to kick something, to punch something, bombarded her until she thought her heart would burst from the overflow of pain attacking it. She brushed at a tear that had slipped out. *Why, God, why?*

"Are you all right, Abby?" Harrison asked from beside her.

She stiffened, remembering that she wasn't alone. She drew in a long breath and forced a smile onto her face before looking up at him. "I'm fine."

Harrison narrowed his eyes. "Sure you are. Care to talk about it?"

"Nothing to talk about," she answered with a fake lilt to her voice.

"If you say so."

She hadn't fooled him, but neither did she want to talk about it. David had made it perfectly clear that a woman who couldn't bear children wasn't a desirable woman, much less a human being.

While she knew that she and Harrison would never be anything more than business acquaintances, she didn't want him to know she was one of those undesirable women. It would change everything, and she rather liked that he treated her with respect. As if she were really someone. Since he would be leaving in a few months' time, he need never know the truth about her. She would enjoy the fantasy she had created in her mind just a little longer.

Chapter Seven

The way things had gone the day before, Harrison couldn't wait to get to Abby's house to see if she really was all right. All afternoon she had been quiet, subdued even. Every time he had inquired about it, she plastered on that same phony smile and acted as if everything was fine. Well, she hadn't fooled him. Not one little bit.

Unlike Boston, the June mornings here were nippy. One would think because of the high altitude and being that much closer to the sun that it would be warm, but that was not the case. Not that he'd experienced so far in the few days he'd been here.

He made his way down the winding, steep incline toward town. A chipmunk darted out in front of him, followed in hot pursuit by another. Birds sang in the pine and aspen trees that surrounded the road like tall pillars. Gnats swarmed the air just several yards ahead in front of him. All of this he found enchanting. This place was nothing like Boston.

The day before, he had rented a furnished, fourteen-room house up in the trees on the side of the mountain from a sweet elderly lady who was thrilled to know someone would be living in it, even if it was only for three months.

He'd been fortunate to hear from Lucy at her diner that Mrs. Morrison was looking to rent her place. Lucy had also informed him that the woman had taken a smaller house in town because with her age, it was just too hard in the winter to travel the half mile up the trees. Didn't seem that far to him. But then again, he wasn't an old woman living alone, either.

"Siah. That mine." Graham's voice shattered Harrison's thoughts. He yanked his gaze down at his sons sitting next to him in the buggy and at the carved Indian in question.

"Na-uh. It mine." Josiah yanked the wooden toy from Graham's hand.

"Josiah, give that back to Graham. You have the cowboy. You can't have them both. You boys need to learn to share."

"But I want Indian. Gam can have cowboy."

"Which one did you bring? The cowboy or the Indian?" he asked, not understanding why when they each had a cowboy and an Indian that they didn't bring both of them so they wouldn't fight.

Josiah dropped his head. "The Indian."

"Well, if that's what you brought, then you need to give Graham back his cowboy."

Josiah pursed his lips and his brows puckered.

"Now, Josiah."

The cowboy smacked against the palm of Graham's hand when Josiah grudgingly handed it over to him. He crossed his arms and protruded his lips in a pout. For a brief moment, Harrison closed his eyes and let out a sigh of frustration.

Both the cowboy and the Indian had been carved to straddle the wooden carved horses they'd brought with them. Did the difference between the Indian headdress and the cowboy hat matter that much to his boys? A toy was a toy as far as Harrison was concerned. Then again, he'd never had to share any of his. What little he'd had as a child, anyway.

Harrison swatted a horse fly that had plagued them persistently on their journey down the mountain to Abby's house.

He hated having to bring his sons to work. Over the past eight months or so, he'd had to do just that a few times because his nannies had resigned. Make that more like making a hasty retreat with only a moment's notice. All he could do now was hope that someone would answer the ad he and Staimes had placed on the bulletin boards all around town late yesterday afternoon. And answer it soon.

"Whoa." He brought the horse to a stop in front of Abby's mansion.

Josiah leaped off his seat and took a giant step.

Harrison grabbed a handful of the back of his shirt. "Where do you think you're going, young man? Sit down."

Indecision tumbled across Josiah's face.

"Now." Harrison used his sternest voice, and it worked. "You will be spending time with Miss Denis this morning. I want you to mind what she says. If I hear any report that either of you have misbehaved, you will be disciplined. Do you boys understand?"

They both nodded.

"Very well. Now, wait there until I come around and get you."

Harrison helped them down. Grasping their hands in his, the three of them walked up the steps to the front door. He raised the lion-head door knocker and tapped it thrice.

Seconds later, the door swung open. "Good morning." Abby's voice was bright and cheery and her smile appeared genuine, unlike the day before. Relieved to see her doing better, his own lips curled upward.

Her gaze went down to his boys. "How are Josiah and Graham doing this morning?" She squatted down and studied the toys in their hands. "What do we have here? A cowboy and an Indian? Oh, and horses, too. What are their names?"

"My horsey's name is Little Eagle and this is Big Feather." Josiah held up his wooden Indian. "Daddy helped name 'em." His son smiled up at him.

"My horsey is Bucky. And my cowboy—" he held up the cowboy for her to see "—is named Daddy." Graham tucked the cowboy to his chest, but his eyes were fixed on Harrison. "I name it Daddy 'cause I love my daddy."

Harrison's heart melted and swelled with love for his sons. There wasn't anything he wouldn't do for either one of them.

"Well, I think your father and you two boys did a fine job of naming them." She turned those smiling eyes of hers up at him, and theirs locked for a brief but meaningful moment. "Now, shall we go inside? Miss Denis has lots of fun activities planned for you this morning. Are you ready to have some fun?"

Their eyes brightened, and they both nodded.

"Very well, then. Shall we?" She rose and offered each of them a hand. Graham and Josiah slipped their hands into hers, and they preceded him inside. How well the twins looked with her. As if they were a family. That thought stopped him cold. They weren't a family. And never would be. She had her life here, and he had his back in Boston. Love, and especially marriage, were not on his agenda here.

The night before while lying in bed, as she had so many times in the past, Abby struggled with her feelings of unfairness about how she could never bear a child of her own. She confessed her anger and asked God's forgiveness for it and for her poor attitude concerning the whole thing. Josiah, Graham and Julie were all delightful children, and even though they were a painful reminder of what she could never have, right now they needed her, of that she was certain. So, putting her own feelings aside, she would be there for them as much as possible.

Making sure the boys were settled in with Zoé instead of going to the parlor as was their usual routine, Abby led Harrison to her office. The day before, before the furniture was delivered, Colette had cleaned it from top to bottom.

When she and Harrison stepped inside, she stopped and gazed up at him, wondering what he thought of the furnished room they would be sharing for three months. "Well, what do you think? It looks quite lovely with the new furniture, does it not?"

She followed his perusal of the room. The dark-

stained oak desk with the three squares of a lighter
shade of oak in the front and on each side outlined with
a gold, leafy vine design looked regal in the bright, airy
room. The three floor-to-ceiling, matching cabinets behind it and the matching bookshelf alongside the massive desk added to its appeal.

The sculptured oak chair with the black, padded-
leather seat and arm rests behind the desk reminded
her of Queen Anne furniture, as did the two chairs situated in front and off to the side of the desk. Only they
were padded with a burgundy and gold material that
resembled hundreds of miniature checker game boards.

A blue, gold and burgundy Victorian rug, one of
the few perfectly salvageable pieces that had been left
behind, the two new carved burgundy bench settees,
cream-colored sofa, two end tables and the coffee table
that matched the desk filled the other side of the office.

Knowing he'd finished viewing the whole room, she
looked up at him with eager anticipation.

"Very nice, Abby. I fear, however, that it makes my
office back home look quite shabby. I must say, you
have excellent, excellent taste in decor."

Abby beamed under his praise. "How very kind of
you to say so. Thank you." She clasped her hands together. "Well, would you like some coffee or tea while
we wait for Fletcher to arrive with our bid?"

"No, thank you. But if you do, please do not let me
stop you."

"I'm fine. I thought while we were waiting that we
could start putting together our order for the things we
will need for the business."

"Very well."

Abby grabbed everything she needed and motioned for Harrison to sit on the sofa. They went over everything they needed and had the list almost completed when Colette entered the room. "Excuse me, *mademoiselle,* but Mr. Martin is here to see you."

"Thank you, Colette. Send him in."

"*Oui,* Miss Abby."

Abby smiled at how formal Colette, Veronique and Zoé were in the presence of others. Even though she'd told them they didn't have to be, and that they were family, she had to admit, it made her feel as if they respected her—something she found quite nice.

Fletcher stepped into the room. "Morning." Was it just her or did she detect apprehension in his voice and on his face?

Harrison stood and the two men shook hands.

"I wonder if I might have a word with you before we begin," Fletcher asked Harrison.

That surprised Abby. What could the two men possibly have to talk about that didn't include her? Well, whatever it was, it was none of her business. Or was it? Did it have something to do with the Royal Grand Theater, the name she'd finally decided on? Whatever it was, if they wanted her to know, they'd tell her. No sense in getting fidgety over something that may or may not have anything to do with her or the business.

Harrison glanced down at her with a question on his face, too. Best not to read anything into that, either. "Excuse me, Abby. We'll be right back."

Abby rose. "No, you gentlemen stay here. I'll run and get us something to drink. It's warming up outside rather fast. Would either of you care for some cool tea?"

They both liked that idea, so she scurried out of the room, retrieved the tea from the cool cellar and headed back to the office. Two feet away from the door, she overheard, "I don't know how to break the news to her."

What news? She stood outside the door, waiting and listening to see if they would say more, but their voices were too low, so she stepped into the office and set the beverage tray on the coffee table. "Here you go, gentlemen." She handed each of them a glass. "Would either of you like sugar or lemon in your drink?" Both declined. After adding lemon and sugar to hers, she sat down beside Harrison. "Shall we get down to business? Do you have your bid ready?"

Fletcher and Harrison exchanged a look, a rather disturbing one at that.

"Something's not right. What's going on? What's wrong?" Her stomach twisted into knots while waiting for them to answer.

"I want you to know—"

"Allow me." Harrison cut Fletcher off.

Fletcher nodded.

"Remember when we talked about the repairs and the cost?"

She swallowed, wondering just how much they were going to be. While she had plenty of money, she still had a lot to buy, and she didn't want to spend it all on this place. After all, she needed money to live on until the business took off. "Yes."

"There is no easy way to say this, I'm afraid. The repair costs are massive."

She tilted her head, furrowing her forehead. "I don't... I didn't see that much that needed fixing."

"To the untrained eye, there isn't. I mean no offense by that. But unless you were a carpenter, you wouldn't notice certain things."

"Like what?"

"Here, let me show you." Harrison handed her Fletcher's itemized bid.

Abby's eyes trailed down the long list of repairs. With each one her eyes grew. By the time she got to the bottom figure, her eyes had all but popped out of her head. The amount was ten times the amount she'd calculated they would be, but that wasn't what bothered her. She stood, walked over to the window and draped her arms around her waist.

Behind her, she heard Fletcher say he'd be back later. Without saying goodbye to him, she stared out the window.

Concerned for Abby, Harrison stepped up alongside her. "Are you all right?"

She gazed up at him. "I'm fine."

His eyes narrowed.

"All right. I admit it was quite a shock."

"I know it's an exorbitant amount. One you probably weren't expecting. Perhaps I can help." How, he didn't know. Until he received his inheritance, his funds were limited, and he couldn't even take out a loan at his bank.

"It's not about the money, it's about the time. All those repairs are going to take much longer than I expected. It's just disappointing is all. But—" she turned her beautiful face upward toward him "—God will take care of it. He always does. As far as I can tell, Fletcher's figures are reasonable considering all that needs fixed around here. I think we should hire him. What do you think?"

The woman amazed him. She'd just had a huge blow and yet here she was as bubbly as ever saying God would take care of it. Well, he hoped for her sake that her God did. "I think you're right."

"Wonderful." She clasped her hands together. "Then let's not delay another minute. Let's go find him and see when he can get started. The sooner he does, the better. What should we have him start on first?" Not waiting for his answer, she continued. "The upstairs can wait. We need to have him work on getting the foundation fixed first. Then... Oh, why don't we wait and see what he says? Then afterward, if you don't have plans, would you and the boys like to have lunch with me?" He had never met a woman that could talk as fast as she could. Her excitement was contagious.

"Mademoiselle," he imitated the three French sisters, "lead the way."

Abby laughed, a sound as pleasing and soothing as a fine musical instrument.

Without thinking it through, he reached for her hand and looped it through his arm. The connection sent a warmness flowing through him. He gazed down at her, wondering if she felt it, too.

Their eyes met and locked.

Since his coming here, this was the first time he had a strong urge to pull her into his arms and kiss her. He wondered what it would be like to love this woman who was beautiful both inside and out. What it would be like to... She blinked, breaking the connection, along with his trail of thoughts. Good thing. He couldn't entertain what it was like to be married to her. Nothing good could come from that kind of surmising.

"Did anyone ever tell you that you have very unique eyes?"

It was his turn to blink. Where had that come from? And is that why she was staring at him? That it had nothing to do with the connection he'd felt? Why that idea disappointed him, he had no idea, but it did, nevertheless. Brushing it aside, he answered, "Yes. I've been told that before. Has anyone ever told you that you do?" *Watch it buddy, you're flirting with trouble.*

She tilted her head, and her perfectly shaped brows curled into an S. "Mine aren't unique."

"Oh, but they are. They're always smiling."

"Huh? What do you mean?"

"Even when you aren't smiling, you're eyes appear to be. They're very beautiful, you know?" *And so are you.* But that last part he didn't voice out loud. Best to keep that to himself, as it was too personal of a thing to say to a single woman, and could very easily be misconstrued as more than the simple compliment it was meant to be. "Shall we go?" He changed the subject.

Harrison arrived at Abby's minutes earlier than what had been discussed the day before. Zoé met him at the door, and after leaving his sons with her, he made his way into the parlor. He stepped into the room, and his heart jumped to his throat. There Abby was, standing precariously on a rickety ladder, leaning over the fireplace mantel at an angle, holding a huge picture.

"Abby, what are you doing? You're going to hurt yourself," he said, rushing toward her.

Abby jerked her head in his direction, and when she did, her body yanked with it. The ladder flew out from under her and the picture went crashing to the ground along with the ladder. Her arms shot out but not before her head whacked against the corner of the mantel. Harrison caught her right before she landed on the hearth. With her still in his arms, he asked, "What on earth were you doing up there on that thing?" His blood pounded hard into his ears.

"What do you mean, what was I doing? What did it look like I was doing? I was hanging a picture." Her blond hair covered one side of her face.

"That's a good way to get yourself hurt."

"I was doing just fine until you came in and scared me half to death," she puffed.

She had a point there. It was his fault she'd fallen. Still, one look at the rotten ladder and he knew it was only a matter of time before that thing collapsed.

Abby yanked her head with a quick jerk to the side and winced. She reached up and brushed the hair away from her face. Her fingertips patted at her forehead. When she pulled them back, they were coated with blood.

"You're bleeding."

"It appears that way, yes."

"Let me see that."

"No need. I'll be fine." She tried to get up, but he sat on the hearth and settled her onto his lap.

"Mr. Kingsley, this is highly improper." She arranged her purple day dress by tugging its skirt to where it hung farther over her ankles.

"Hang propriety. Right now I'm concerned about that

knot on your head and the blood dripping down your forehead." He pulled out his handkerchief and pressed it over the wound, making her wince away from it.

"You're ruining your monogrammed handkerchief. And, *I* care about my reputation even if you do not."

"What? Who said I didn't care about your reputation?"

She glanced at the way he held her nestled on his lap, then at the parlor door, then back at him again with one raised pointy eyebrow.

She was right. The way he was holding her could easily be misconstrued. "I see your point." He laid her hand over the handkerchief, quickly shifted her off his lap and stood.

He helped her up and led her over to the couch. "Sit."

Her small hand perched at her waist. "Sit? Excuse me? Do I look like a dog to you?"

"A dog? You? Well, if you are, you're a very cute one." He laughed, but she didn't join him. Realizing how that must've sounded, his laughter died in his throat. "I didn't mean to imply that you were a dog. I only meant…" Good-night, how did he get himself into these messes, anyway? "I mean you'd make a cute dog. Not that I think you look like one or anything. I just meant…" He clamped his mouth shut, deciding he'd better hush up before he buried himself even further into the hole he'd already dug for himself.

Her nostrils expanded, her lips twitched. "Gotcha!" Laughter bubbled out of her. "You should have seen the look on your face when you thought I was upset with you. I knew what you meant, but it was fun watching you try to talk your way out of it."

"Ha-ha. Very funny. I'm not amused." His lips compressed into a thin line, and he crossed his arms over his chest.

"Oh, don't be so stuffy. Lighten up," she said, giving a quick flip of her hand. "I'm just teasing you."

He continued to scowl at her.

"Look, I was only—"

"Gotcha!" He smiled and uncrossed his arms.

Her mouth fell open. Then as if she finally caught on, her lips curled in that cute way that made her eyes smile, too. "You got me a good one, and I deserved it, too."

When they stopped laughing, Harrison's eyes caught sight of the blood-soaked cloth.

"We'd better take care of that." He pointed to her forehead.

"Oh, right. I was having so much fun, I forgot about it."

He was, too. Fun was something he didn't experience much. It felt nice. Something he could get used to.

Abby enjoyed the easy camaraderie with Harrison. Who knew under that business suit lay a man with a sense of humor? An extremely attractive man at that.

He leaned over and removed the cloth from her forehead. Fingers light and gentle brushed the hair from around the wound. She peered up at him, his eyes intently glued to her forehead.

Her attention dropped to his chin, a firm, chiseled, neatly shaven one. A combination of bay rum, cinnamon, nutmeg, cloves and orange, a very enthralling aftershave fragrance on a very intoxicating man, floated around him.

Her eyes slid upward to his bottom lip, soft and not too full, but not thin, either. Her vision climbed to his upper lip. What would it feel like to be kissed by those perfectly shaped lips, and to feel the passion of the man behind that masculine mouth and tender heart?

Daydreams of what it would be like acted out in her mind like a romantic scene from a play, and she allowed them to

Harrison wrapped his arms around her, pulling her close, their hearts beat to the tune of a single drum. Her knees weakened as he dipped his head until his lips were but only a breath away from her own. His gorgeous eyes connected with hers, seeking permission to kiss her.

"May I?"

Abby's eyes darted open. "May you what?" She blinked.

"May I have permission to doctor your wound?"

To doctor my... Uh. Oh. Jolted back to reality, she relaxed, relieved that Harrison hadn't been privy to her romantic thoughts, because if he had, he would hightail it back to Boston quicker than a jackrabbit fleeing a fox. "Have you done much doctoring?"

His mouth and brow quirked sideways. "I have two sons. What do you think?"

Abby chuckled. "I think that I'm in very good hands. How bad is it, anyway?" Growing up on a ranch, she'd encountered many a cut and bruise. Some a whole lot worse than this one, and she had survived. Other than a throbbing headache, a bit of dizziness and a slightly blood-soaked handkerchief, how bad could this one be?

"It's not bad." The man had impeccable timing. As

if he could read her thoughts. Now that was a frightening thought. Especially with all the daydreams she had conjured up about him. "Just a little cut that doesn't need stitches or anything. But still, it does need to be cleaned and bandaged to keep infection out."

"I'll go and fetch my medicine bag." She started to rise, but his hand gently pressed down on her shoulder, forcing her in the gentlest of ways to be seated.

Their eyes met as they seemed to do so many times.

"Oh, forgive me. I didn't mean to interrupt anything."

Abby's gaze flew to the door.

Fletcher turned to leave.

"Don't go, Fletcher. You didn't interrupt anything."

Fletcher's eyes drifted to Harrison's hand still lingering on her shoulder.

She slouched her shoulder until Harrison's hand slipped away. "Oh. Yes. Well. You see. I hit my head on the mantel. I was just going to head to the kitchen to get my medicine bag, but Harrison stopped me. He insisted I stay put and that he go get it." She rushed out the words and glanced up at Harrison, who was looking at her as if to say, "Why are you explaining yourself to Fletcher?" Just why was she? Nothing was going on here. She had no reason to feel guilty. Well, all right, in a way she did because of her daydreams about the man. But no one knew about them except for her and God.

Flattening her hands on the sofa, she pushed herself up.

Pain pounded into her skull.

Stars twinkled in front of her.

Light pressure on her arm steered her back into a sitting position.

"Abby. Are you all right? You don't look very well."

"I'll run and fetch the doctor." That was Fletcher's voice she heard.

"No. No, that won't be necessary." The stars faded and light slowly replaced them. Harrison's face came into view first. Seeing his concern, she reassured him. "I'm fine. I just rose too quickly, is all."

"Fletcher. Go ahead and fetch a doctor for Miss Bowen."

Before Abby had a chance to stop him, Fletcher was gone. "Really. I'm fine." As if to prove it, she rose. Big mistake that turned out to be. The twinkling stars returned, then disappeared into the blackness that overtook her.

Chapter Eight

"Abby, Can you hear me?"

Abby turned her head toward the sound of Harrison's voice and slowly blinked her eyes open. "Harrison? What happened?"

"You fainted."

"I—I did?"

"Yes. Doctor Wilson is here to see you." Harrison moved from her view, and a handsome young man with blue-black hair and a thick matching mustache replaced him.

"I'm Doctor Wilson." He pulled a chair over in front of the sofa she lay on and sat down. "From what Mr. Kingsley here tells me, you hit your head pretty hard on that mantel. Is that correct?"

"Yes."

"Well, while you were out, I took a look at your cut. Harrison is right, it doesn't need stitches. I've already cleaned it and bandaged it. It appears you have a mild concussion. Therefore, I want you to rest today and to do nothing, especially anything strenuous."

Rest? Oh, no. There would be no resting for her. She had work to do. She shifted her legs off the settee and pushed herself into a sitting position. Her head throbbed and the blinking stars tried to return, but she drew in a long breath, forcing them into a hasty retreat. "Excuse me, Doctor, but I don't have time to rest. I have a business to tend to."

"*I* will tend to business. *You* will take care of yourself." Harrison's formidable tone had Abby's attention flouncing in his direction.

Excuse me? Who do you think you are ordering me about like that? You might be my business partner but you have no right to tell me what to do and to take over like that. She wanted to say the words out loud, but there was no way she would embarrass him in front of others, so she kept the thoughts to herself.

"Please, Abby?" He must have noticed the aggravation on her face. Noting his concern, her heart softened. He wasn't trying to be bossy; he was only troubled about her welfare.

Her frustration evaporated. "I'll try. But—" she held up her hand "—I'm not promising anything."

After leaving a few final instructions, the doctor left.

"Where's Fletcher?" she asked.

"He and his men are working on stabilizing the foundation."

"Oh. I see."

"As there is no immediate business to tend to right now, and as much as I hate to leave you, Abby, I must. I'll only be gone a short time, though. I have a couple of pressing errands to run, and then I'll be right back. In the meantime, however, I will leave strict instructions for no one to bother you if something does arise. I'll let them know where they can find me."

Reluctantly, she nodded.

He turned to go.

"Oh, before you leave." She sat up, wobbling with the effort. "I was wondering if you and the boys would like to come to church with me on Sunday. Then afterward, I thought we could have a picnic down by the river here in my backyard. Maybe the boys could do some fishing."

Harrison didn't answer right away. Had she been too forward? Did he read more into the invitation than what was there? "I thought I would invite Fletcher and Julie, too."

Still no answer.

"I'd love it if Staimes joined us. Colette, Veronique and Zoé will be there, too."

"I'm sure my valet would like that. And I'm sure the boys would enjoy it, too. Especially the fishing. Yes. Very well. We'll come." He sounded so formal about it all, but Abby decided not to dwell on that.

In fact, it was quite easy to push it out of her throbbing thoughts. "Wonderful. It's settled, then. You know where the church is, right? We drove by it on our way out to Fletcher's."

Harrison nodded as he spun his hat slowly in his hands. "I know where it is, but I'm afraid I won't be able to make it for services, so I'll just meet you here afterward."

"Oh. Okay." She wondered why he wouldn't make it to church but didn't ask. It was none of her business.

"Well, I'd better go. I hate to leave you, but this one

pressing matter cannot be delayed. Promise me you'll rest like the doctor said to, all right?"

"I won't make promises I can't or don't plan on keeping. But I promise I will try my best. Fair enough?"

He sighed, gave a short nod and left.

Abby tossed a couple of decorative pillows onto the settee and lowered herself onto its firm, yet soft, surface. She closed her eyes and tried to rest, but after forty minutes of shifting and trying to sleep, she gave up. Despite the fact her head still hurt, she decided to go see how Fletcher was coming along with the foundation. The sounds of work had been reverberating through the house most of the morning, so she knew they were, in fact, working hard.

Dry summer heat clothed her the second she stepped out the front door of her house. Rotten egg odor from the hot mineral springs hung in the air. She discovered she was getting used to the sulphur smell that was sometimes stronger than other times, so it didn't bother her nearly as badly as it used to.

One day, she'd take the time to go soak in the natural cave pool on her property to see what all the hoopla was over about bathing in the stinky water. Sure didn't make sense to her to bathe in something that directly afterward required a bath in order to remove the odorous water from a person's skin. What sense did that make?

She took a moment to stare at the magnificent mountain view across from her front door. One she never tired of. Hundreds of trees dotted it and the light blue sky outlining it made for a breathtaking backdrop.

Seconds later, she headed down the steps and rounded the corner. Knee-high weeds brushed against her skirt as she strolled through the perimeter of her yard. Unattended rose bushes created a fence barricade for the sorely neglected flower garden.

Potentilla and forsythia bushes smattered the yard. Along with white-and-yellow daisies, blue columbines, bluebells and another bright pink flower she couldn't identify. The tiered rock fountain was in need of a good scrubbing. She made a mental note to ask Fletcher if he knew of someone she could hire to rejuvenate the gardens. She would do it herself, but there was too much to do to get ready for the grand opening.

She went in search of Fletcher and found him and his men busy stacking rocks and bricks. Strong muscles flexed as Fletcher loaded his arms. Impressed with how much weight the man could carry, she watched him as he took them over to the pile with little effort. Before he caught her staring at him, she strolled over to him. "How are things coming along?"

Fletcher glanced over at her and smiled. He settled his burden, raised his hat and ran his sleeve over the sweat on his forehead. "It's a little too early to tell. But so far everything's going along pretty well."

"That's good to hear. Hey, I was wondering something. You wouldn't happen to know anyone around here with great gardening skills, would you? I need someone to turn this yard into the glorious garden I'm sure it once was."

Fletcher hooked his thumbs in his front pocket and looked around. "At one time, this place and this garden was the nicest one around these here parts." He rocked on the heels of his cowboy boots. "Sure was a shame to ride by and see it so run-down. But I'll tell you who can have it restored to its former glory in no time, and that would be Mr. Samuel Hilliard. He loves working in gardens. Matter of fact, he used to work for the folks that owned this place."

"Who does he work for now?"

"No one. Not much use for a gardener around here. He does odd jobs for folks around town just so he can stay living here. In fact, if I remember rightly, I heard he just finished a job and was looking for work. So he might be available."

Abby clasped her hands together against her chest. "Wonderful. How can I get a hold of him?"

"I can take you there during lunch if you'd like."

"Oh, yes. Yes. I would like that very much. Thank you." They stood there for a moment, neither saying a word. Finally, Abby spoke. "Would you and your men like something cold to drink?"

"That would be very nice. Thank you. I'm sure my men could stand a break. Lugging rocks and bricks is hard work."

With those arms, it shouldn't be too hard for him, but she wouldn't voice that. Hogwash rules of propriety prevented a woman from expressing those kinds of compliments. "Very well, I'll be right back."

"Wait. Harrison said you were supposed to be resting. Why don't you let me go and get it?"

"Nonsense. I can handle it."

"That's what Harrison said you'd say."

"Harrison said you'd say what?"

Abby whirled toward the sound of Harrison's voice and instantly regretted the fast shift. Her head swam in protest, but she would not let either of these men see her pain or the dizziness that was already lifting.

"That she could handle it," Fletcher answered with something between a grin and a grimace.

Harrison turned those stunning eyes of his on her. "You're supposed to be resting."

"I tried, but I couldn't sit still." Why was she answering to him about this, anyway?

Who was she kidding? She knew why she was. As much as she didn't want to, she liked having a man take charge and watch over her. She just better make sure she didn't get used to it was all. No harm in enjoying it while it lasted, though.

"That, I can believe. What were you doing that you weren't supposed to be doing?"

"I was just going to get these men something to drink, is all. I mean, really. That's not strenuous, and I'm more than capable of carrying a pitcher of fresh lemonade and four glasses. It's only a slight concussion, and the doctor said it only appeared that I had one. He wasn't even certain. Besides, if I didn't feel like I could do it, I wouldn't." That wasn't quite an accurate statement as she wasn't one to take things lying down. "I need something to keep me busy or I'll go mad. I thank you for your concern, but I'm going to go now and get those beverages."

Harrison caught up with her. "No. You won't. You go and sit down in the shade, and I'll go and get it."

A fleeting glance at the rickety bench that looked in worse shape than the ladder she'd fallen off earlier, and she wanted to laugh. Not used to taking orders, one glance at him, however, and she changed her mind.

Yet again. The man had a way of affecting her like that. "Oh, all right. But don't think I'm always going to give in this easily." She shot him a serious, albeit teasing, smile.

"Trust me, I don't." He sent her a teasing smile of his own. "I'll be back." With that, he ducked into the house.

Abby headed over to the shade, but not the spot Harrison had indicated. Without a doubt, if he saw just how poor of shape that bench was in, he would have never asked her to sit there. Of course, there was no way he could tell that from a distance.

Underneath the large cottonwood tree, she found a grassy spot and sat down, fanning her skirt out around her.

Fletcher headed toward her.

She gazed up at him, but the sun shining directly behind him made it difficult to see his face, so she cupped her hand to shield her eyes. "Harrison is getting your drinks."

Fletcher moved until the sunlight no longer blinded her. She lowered her hand and settled it onto her lap.

"He didn't need to do that. My men and I would be just fine filling our canteens down at the river. The water's nice and cold there."

"I haven't tried the water from there yet. I was afraid it would taste like sulphur."

"It doesn't. The springs and the river aren't anywhere close to each other."

"Whew. That's good to know. I'll have to give it a try sometime. Oh, by the way, I'm having a picnic Sunday after church down by the river. Would you and Julie like to come? Harrison and his sons and Veronique and

Zoé and Colette will be there, too. Oh, and Staimes, Harrison's valet."

Fletcher hooked his thumbs in his pocket again and for a time looked everywhere but at her. Moments passed and he finally turned his focus back onto her. "We'll come."

Was that disappointment she heard in his voice? "If you don't want to…"

"It isn't that. It's just…" He rubbed his finger over his bottom lip. "Thank you. We would love to come."

Although his tone wasn't completely convincing, it pleased her they would be there. "Wonderful. I'm glad you'll be joining us." That brought a smile to his face.

Abby loved doing things for people and this was just one small way she could do something special for those who were helping to make her dream become a reality. To make sure everyone enjoyed the day off, she'd hire Lucy, from Lucy's Diner, to supply the food. Abby loved big, outdoor get-togethers, something her family back in Paradise Haven did often.

Plus, she couldn't wait to spend more time with Harrison and his adorable sons. She knew she was opening herself up for more heartache by subjecting herself to being around the children, but she also knew children were a blessing, so therefore, she would enjoy them while she could. Before long, they would be gone. With the exception of Julie, perhaps. But even then, Fletcher would be gone, too, once the job was finished and so would Julie. She just hoped they didn't take her heart with them and leave her to pick up the pieces again.

Having never made lemonade before or anything else for that matter, Harrison was extremely grateful when Veronique insisted she prepare the drinks. Not only had she prepared the beverages, but she'd also added some delicious-looking French butter cookies to the tray, as well.

On his way to give Fletcher and his men their lemonade and cookies, something his servants would have done back home, Harrison searched for Abby. He spotted her sitting under a large tree with her purple dress fanned out around her, looking very regal. She was the type of woman who could fit in anywhere. There were times she appeared every whit the high-society lady, and other times a person wouldn't be able to differentiate her from the household staff. Either way, the lady was a breath-stealing vision of loveliness. One he could drink his fill of every day.

After he gave the men their drinks, he made his way over to Abby and handed her the already filled glass of lemonade with a slice of lemon hooked on the side of the glass.

"Thank you." She smiled up at him.

Good-night the woman was beautiful.

He held the tray in front of her. "Veronique sent along cookies, as well. French butter, she called them."

"Oh, how thoughtful of her." Abby peered at them like a small child would. She snatched two of them off the plate and took a rather large bite out of one.

Harrison marveled at how down to earth and genuine Abby was. The women in Boston would devour a woman like her. Good thing she didn't live there. He'd hate to see just exactly what the women there would do to her. They would probably strip her of her loveliness and her playfulness. Then again, maybe not. Abby was a woman who could hold her own.

He set the tray on the ground, lowered himself onto the hard, lumpy ground opposite of Abby and took a long pull of his drink. Sweet mingled with tart saturated his taste buds.

"Mercy. You must have been thirsty."

He looked at his nearly drained glass and chuckled. "I confess. I was. And *you* must have been hungry." Both of the cookies she'd taken were devoured in less than a minute.

"I must confess. I was." Her eyes twinkled as she imitated his response to her.

"Touché," he said, raising his glass to hers. They clinked them together before he drained the rest of his beverage.

Abby took several slow sips, and when she finished, she placed it on the tray and looked over at him. All of a sudden her blue eyes sparkled. "Oh. Guess what?" He had no time to take a guess as she hurried on. "I talked to Fletcher, and he knows a gentleman who does gardening. In fact, it's the same man who had taken care of this place for the previous owners."

Harrison scanned the weed infested, unkept yard that was definitely in need of much tending to.

"I said, 'had.'"

"Yes. I heard you. That's wonderful news. I'll find out where the man lives and take you there tomorrow. Today you need to rest."

"That's very sweet of you, but Fletcher offered to take me during his lunch break today." Her emphasizing the word "today" didn't get past Harrison. "I would love it if you would come with us."

The idea of her riding alone or spending time with Fletcher gnawed at Harrison's insides. "Are you sure you're up to it today? You're supposed to be resting."

"I won't lie, I do have a slight headache, but that's all it is, a slight one."

He thought about it for a couple of moments, debating on whether or not they should wait until tomorrow.

"Nothing's going to stop me from going, Harrison."

"I figured as much. I'll let Fletcher know."

Noontime arrived quickly.

Fletcher rode his horse alongside Abby's side of Harrison's buggy. All the way to the gardener's house, Harrison watched Fletcher from the corner of his eye. The man rarely took his eyes off Abby, and the two of them conversed as if they'd known each other forever, instead of only a few days.

This time there was no denying it; Harrison was jealous. He wanted Abby to himself. And yet seeing the futility of that, he stopped watching their interaction. Who was he to deny her a chance at happiness?

Ten minutes later, they arrived at a small, picturesque log cabin nestled near the side of the mountain. An array of purple, pink, blue, yellow, orange and red flowers, manicured shrubbery and blooming rose bushes that were all perfectly uniformed and organized surrounded the place, and not a weed in sight. The outside of the log house had been well taken care of, with no missing chinking or defects of any kind.

"Isn't his place lovely?" Abby sighed loud and long.

"It is quite impressive. The man does superb work."

Harrison tied off the lines, hopped out of the open-top buggy and headed to Abby's side to help her down, but was too late. Fletcher was already there assisting her, and Harrison thought his hand lingered on hers longer than necessary.

Abby perused the area, her lips tilted upward higher and higher with each turn she took. Awe and delight emanated from her. "Shall we go see if he's home?" She eyed both men with expectant eyes.

Up the path and onto the steps they went.

Strong stairs.

Sturdy railings.

Not one protruding nail.

Neat and swept clean, too.

Far as Harrison was concerned, the man was hired. But that decision wasn't up to him. It was Abby's to make.

Abby stopped feet away from the door. "Did you make those lovely rockers, Fletcher? They look like your handiwork."

"Yes, ma'am. I did. I gave them to Samuel for his fifty-fifth birthday."

"Oh. When was that?"

"In March of this year."

The door opened without squeaking, Harrison noted. A man no taller than Abby stepped into the light. "Fletcher, how good to see you." They shook hands, and the man's eyes shifted from Abby and to Harrison. "And who are these fine folks?"

"Mr. Hilliard, this is Miss Abby Bowen."

"Pleased to meet you, ma'am." The slightly balding

man gave a nod in her direction, then turned his focus over to Harrison.

"This is Mr. Harrison Kingsley."

Harrison stepped forward and shook the man's hand. Firm. Solid. Not a wimpy grip. The man was strong, that was for sure, and likely more than able to handle the job. "Pleasure to meet you, Mr. Hilliard."

"Samuel." He glanced at Abby and Harrison. "Mr. Hilliard makes me feel old."

"Very well, then. Samuel it is," Harrison agreed.

"To what do I owe this pleasure?" Samuel turned his question toward Fletcher.

"Miss Bowen bought the Glenworth place, and she's looking for a gardener. I thought you might be interested."

"Interested?" he all but bellowed. "How soon can I start? Today? How about right now?"

Abby's laughter and joy hovered through the air. "I have but one question for you first. Who did your yard?" At her teasing, knowing question, Harrison smiled.

Samuel puffed out his barrel chest, tugged on his red suspenders and ran his thumbs up and down the length of them. "Why, I did, ma'am."

"I knew that." Abby chuckled. "I was just teasing you." She turned questioning eyes up at Harrison, seeking his approval. That gesture pleased him immensely. A slight nod and the matter was settled.

"Samuel, Mr. Harrison and I would love it if you would come to work for us."

"Excellent! I'll run and get my horse." He bolted toward the steps and was halfway to the corral when Abby hollered, "Wait! We haven't even discussed your pay yet."

Samuel stopped and whirled toward them. "Who cares about that? I'm just thrilled to be able to restore the place to its former glory. It's bothered me for years to see it so neglected. But I'll have it looking great in no time." With that, he jogged his way to the corral, where a dark palomino horse stood in the shade of a perfectly erected lean-to, swishing her tail. Samuel swung open the gate, and the mare nickered and walked right up to him.

"Thank you so much, Fletcher."

Harrison turned to find Abby gazing up at Fletcher with gratitude. In that moment, Harrison wished he was the one who had found Samuel and not Fletcher. He wanted to be the one to put that smile on her face. *Good-night, Harrison. Stop this nonsense. You're leaving, remember?* Yes, he was, and was it ever going to be a challenge and take every bit of willpower he possessed to walk away from her when he did. She was a delight to be around. Her bubbly, upbeat, yet feisty personality was the type of woman he liked—immensely. But, alas, his businesses and his home were in Boston. Hers was here. And he didn't think anything would take her away from her dream. Not even him.

Neither could he give up his lifelong dream of righting the wrongs his father had done to the good people of Boston. Not one of them deserved the evil his father had done to them. The sooner he rectified things with them, the better he'd feel.

Soft pressure applied to his forearm cleared his mind of his daunting thoughts. He glanced down at Abby's hand, then at her face.

"I asked if you were ready to go."

Fletcher stood at the bottom of the steps, and Samuel sat atop his horse, waiting. "My apologies. For a moment there, my mind took a turn in another direction."

"Well, turn it back in the right direction, then. We're ready to leave." Mischief sparkled through her eyes as she said it low enough that only he had heard her.

"Very well, Miss *Abigail*. As you wish." Cupping her elbow, he led her down the stairs and handed her into the buggy.

They headed toward her place, bouncing and jostling along the bumpy road as they did. Halfway down from Samuel's place, Harrison pulled his horse to a stop.

Abby peered up at him with confused eyes. "What's wrong? Why did we stop?"

Harrison pressed his finger against his lips, signaling for her to be quiet, and pointed into the trees.

Abby followed the point of his finger. She squinted, looking hard through the trees.

He cupped her chin and turned it toward the direction of a deer and her fawn. Abby's eyes widened, and her mouth formed the word *oh*. They sat there for a few minutes, watching, until the deer yanked her head up, sniffed the air and darted off deep into the woods, her fawn leaping and hopping behind her.

"Oh, my, that was beautiful. Thank you."

"You're welcome," he said, thrilled that he was the one responsible for the pleasure and serenity that shone on her pretty face and striking eyes. Better him than Fletcher. Not one normally prone to thoughts like that, he mentally shook his head, and gave a click flick of the reins. Abby was getting under his skin and that wasn't good.

Chapter Nine

Three days later, Abby sat at the end of the long pew closest to the front door of the white clapboard church, wondering what was so important that Harrison couldn't come today. Nothing should take precedence over God. Nothing. But, she wasn't Harrison's judge. Whatever he did or didn't do was between him and God, not him, God and her.

After singing *Amazing Grace* and two other hymns, the congregation sat down. Reverend Andrew Wells stepped up to the podium. At forty-three, no wrinkles lined the minister's face, but he looked more like sixty or better due to his snow-white hair.

He gazed out at the congregation. Sun-darkened skin made his lime-green eyes and bright white teeth appear even brighter. Reverend Wells was a fine-looking man with a beautiful wife and five well-behaved children. All five had dark brown hair with red highlights like their mother, and their father's green eyes. "If you have your Bibles with you, I'd like you to open up to the book of first John four, verse eighteen." As it always did, his slow Southern speech reminded her of her sisters-in-law, Selina and Rainee, who were both from the South.

For the umpteenth time since leaving home, Abby wondered how they were doing. How everyone was doing. Especially her nieces and nephews. Had they grown since she'd last seen them? How she missed them and longed to see them, and yet a part of her was glad she wasn't there to see them. It was the same battle that always went around and around in her mind with no real lasting solution.

Children, whether it be her nephews and nieces or other people's children, were a constant reminder of what she couldn't have. Being around little ones always brought a fresh bout of raw pain no matter how hard she tried not to let it.

Light tapping on her arm stopped her train of thought. There stood Julie, looking at her with those innocent, big, brown eyes. Here stood a motherless girl who needed a woman's attention.

No matter where Abby went, there was no getting away from children. But oh, how she loved them. What she didn't love was the pain of being around them and the constant reminder. It wasn't their fault. She refused to be rude. *God, please take away this pain and let me enjoy this little girl, but help me not to fall in love with her so I don't get hurt.* "Hello, Julie," she whispered. "Would you like to sit with me?"

Julie turned and bent her head way back to gaze up at her father standing behind her. "Papa, can we sit with Miss Abby?" She whispered the question so low, Abby barely heard it.

Fletcher leaned over, and Julie repeated the question

into her father's ear. He glanced at Abby with the same question. She answered by standing enough to gather the skirt of her peach bustle gown and by scooting over.

Julie slid in next to her and then Fletcher. They looked like a family sitting there together. Abby shifted in her seat and squirmed. Not knowing how to deal with the uncomfortable awkwardness she felt at that thought, she dropped her gaze to her Bible and rummaged through the pages until she found the scripture reference the reverend had mentioned.

The rustling of pages throughout the congregation stopped, and the pastor's voice reached her ears. *"'There is no fear in love; but perfect love casteth out fear: because fear hath torment. He that feareth is not made perfect in love.'"*

He stepped from around to the side of the podium, rested his elbow on top of the angled surface and crossed his ankle. "Love is a risk. And yet if we never love, we never live. If we never open our hearts to love God or to let Him love us or to love mankind and to let them love us for fear of what they'll do to us, for fear of being hurt or rejected, we are losing out on the greatest gift God ever gave to mankind."

The word *rejection* plunged like a knife into Abby's soul. It was easy for Reverend Wells to talk about love and about letting yourself be loved. After all, he had an amazing wife who obviously loved him unconditionally along with five wonderful children. There was no way he could know or understand the heartache of loving and losing someone.

Well, she had.

Not only had she lost her fiancé, a man she'd once

loved dearly, she'd lost the means to bear a child, too. Equally, if not worse, she had lost her sense of value and worth as a woman. So yes, she feared rejection, feared love and even feared being loved. Who wouldn't after what she'd gone through with David? The only kind of love she wanted was one that existed in fantasies and dreams only. Those she could handle because they weren't real. They were just figments of her imagination. That was a safe place for them. And for her.

For the next twenty-five minutes Abby listened as the reverend continued talking about love and faith and trusting God no matter how things looked.

She couldn't wait for church to be over because his message was getting harder and harder to bear. How could she ever love again and risk getting hurt again? It took great restraint on her part not to get up and leave, not to mention fidget in her chair. All that talk about love and taking a risk did nothing but frustrate and anger her. Requiring the impossible is what her mind said it was.

Maybe she should have joined Harrison on his errand. That would surely have been more enjoyable than sitting here being judged for something she couldn't change.

The preacher finished his sermon with 1 Peter 5:7 *Casting all your care upon Him; for He careth for you.*

Now that she could do. Well, except for her lack of being able to bear children, that one she still struggled with giving over to God. She didn't understand why her, when she loved children like she did. She'd known other women who had a whole passel of them and they didn't even care for children. It didn't make a whit of sense to her, but then again, she wasn't God, nor would she try to figure Him out where this subject was concerned. Still, she couldn't help but wonder why, couldn't help but try and figure it out as she had so many times before.

Throughout the rest of the service, her thoughts bandied back and forth until she became dizzy with them. She couldn't wait to get to the picnic so maybe they would settle down.

Church finally ended, and with only a few words to Fletcher about meeting down by the river, Abby and the Denis sisters headed for home. The walk home was a pleasant one, in spite of the turmoil that had gone on inside of her at church.

She would not allow anything, especially that, to ruin her day. Instead, she chose to focus on how God had answered her prayer for nice sunshiny weather so they could enjoy their picnic without the threat of rain.

Back at the house, Abby changed her clothes into something lighter, a white cotton dress with life-size pink-and-violet roses and green leaves sprinkled throughout. She finished her attire with a white straw hat sporting a long ribbon that matched the material of her dress. Instead of tying the bow directly underneath her chin, she tied it loosely off to one side. Satisfied with her appearance reflecting back at her from her Louis XVI Giltwood looking glass, she snatched her white parasol out of the umbrella holder and headed downstairs.

Everyone was to meet down by the river, so when she neared the bottom of the staircase, she was surprised to see Harrison in the main entrance room standing there with his back to her.

Her heelless, soft leather shoes tapped lightly across the newly polished floor as she meandered toward him. "Good morning, Harrison."

He turned and his smile grew, melting her insides.

"Good morning to you, too." He met her halfway. "Aren't you a vision of loveliness?" He glanced down at his casual brown pants and then back over at her dress. "I fear I've underdressed. I thought we were picnicking today."

"We are."

His one brow curled into a sleeping S. "Aren't you afraid of getting your dress soiled?"

"Nope. When I go somewhere, I go to have fun. I don't worry about my clothing." She tilted her head. "Where are the boys? And why are you here at the house instead of down by the river?"

"I left Graham and Josiah down at the river with Zoé. Everyone else is down there except for you. So I came looking for you to make sure you were all right and that you weren't in any pain or anything from your fall the other day."

"As you see, I'm perfectly fine. Just late is all. How rude of me to be late to my own gathering. I mean, really, you'd think I would at least have started out sooner so I wouldn't be late. But no, I got sidetracked. That's what I get for daydreaming again." She spoke so fast, she had a hard time catching up with herself. Talking fast was a bad habit of hers. One she really needed to work on fixing.

"So, you're a daydreamer, huh?" He threaded her hand through his arm and tugged her toward the front door.

"Yes. It's one of my many failings."

"Many, huh?"

"Yes. Many."

"Well, I hate to differ with you, Miss Abigail Bowen, but I do not see where you have *many* failings, if any."

"That's because you don't know me very well."

"That's true, perhaps. But I think I'm a pretty good judge of character, and you, ma'am, are quite a character."

Shocked by his assessment, she yanked her gaze up to him and saw the teasing glint in his eyes. "And you, sir, have that right."

They smiled.

"So, how are you feeling? Does your head hurt anymore?"

"No. Not at all. That first night it did and most of the next day. But now, it barely hurts. In fact, I feel wonderful." She owned her speedy recovery to the fact that she loved picnics and loved spending time with her friends. Friends? Somehow the word *friend* didn't fit the way she felt about Harrison. Fear waltzed across her heart. Without being obvious, she unwound her hand from his arm. After today's message, she needed to be careful to not let her daydreams turn into real love. Dreaming about love and pretending they were in love was one thing, but to really allow herself to fall in love with him or anyone else was too risky. Rejection hurt way too much.

"Where are you, Abby?"

"Huh?" Her eyes collided with his. "Right here."

"You daydreaming again?"

"No." She shook her head. "Just thinking."

"Oh. What about?"

"About spending the day with my wonderful friends." She smiled up at him. That was partly the truth, anyway. And the only truth he needed to know. Of that she was certain.

For some odd reason, Harrison didn't like being considered as one of Abby's friends. He wanted to be more than that, a battle he'd been fighting ever since meeting her a mere week ago. It was a battle he was quickly losing. How could the woman have gotten under his skin in such a short time? He'd heard of love at first sight, but that was for saps. And he was quickly becoming one, so he needed to be more careful.

As they neared the river, he took in the small crowd of people Abby had invited. Underneath the canopy of trees sat Staimes, who appeared to be in deep conversation with Veronique, Colette, Samuel, Julie and Fletcher, whose eyes never once strayed from Abby.

Harrison cut a glance at Abby to see if she noticed Fletcher's obvious admiration toward her. But her face was turned in another direction, toward Zoé and his two sons squatted down at the edge of the water.

After seeing them in their play clothes the other day, he'd made a special trip to the general store and purchased garments for them designed specifically for outdoor fun. Today they were wearing blue denim pants instead of their knickers and knee-high socks.

"Miss Abby!" Julie leaped up from sitting beside her father. She rushed toward Abby and flung her tiny arms around Abby's legs.

"Miss Abby. Miss Abby." Graham and Josiah barreled toward her as fast as their little legs would carry them. Within seconds all three children's arms were draped around the petite woman.

Somehow, in spite of their arms around her, she managed to squat down and pull all of them into her embrace. A place he found he'd like to be.

"Are you having fun?" She eyed each one as she asked.

All three nodded gleefully.

"I'm so glad. Is anyone hungry?"

Again, all three nodded with the same enthusiasm as before. "Very well, then. Shall we get something to eat?" She stood. Each child vied for her hand. Harrison watched to see how she would deal with the situation.

"I'll race you to the food basket."

His admiration for her slipped up another notch. She had handled the situation very well.

The children whirled and bolted toward the picnic basket. Julie got there first, Josiah second, Graham third and then Abby.

"Ah-h-h. No fair. You all beat me. Does this mean I don't get anything to eat?" Abby sighed as if that thought were the most horrible thing in the world.

"You may eat, too, Miss Abby," Julie said, her manners were impeccable for one so young.

"And what do you boys say?" Her gaze touched on each one.

"Uh-huh," they both said at the same time, nodding.

"Oh, thank you all so much. I am so very honored to have the privilege to dine with you all on this fine day." She clasped her hands together with such flair and drama that the children's faces glimmered as if they had indeed done something wonderful. One by one she planted a kiss on top of their heads, then dropped to her knees in front of the basket, giving no heed whatsoever to the dirt-loaded ground soiling her dress. She raised the lid on the basket and made a huge display of studying its contents.

Pretty soon all three heads joined hers, peering into the basket just as intently as she was.

Harrison chuckled. The woman sure had a way with children. She loved them, and they obviously loved her.

"Now what do we have here? I'm certain there is something in here that children will like." She pulled a cloth off a sizeable platter to unveil several pieces of crispy brown chicken. Looking at each child, she asked, "Who here likes fried chicken?"

All three darted a hand upward.

"Oh, splendid. I'm so glad." Her head dipped and she peered into the basket again. "Hmm. Wonder what this could be?" Out came a round pan nestled onto the palm of her hand.

"I know. I know." Julie raised her hand.

"I know, too." Josiah wasn't about to be outdone.

"Me, too." Graham wasn't, either.

"Very well, then. On the count of three, all together, tell me what it is. One." Their eager faces stared at Abby. "Two." She dragged out the word. The children's mouths opened, ready to blurt out the answer. "Two and a half."

Giggles erupted.

"Two and three quarters."

The giggles increased. Seconds ticked by. Not one of the children took their eyes off Abby.

Suddenly she blurted, "Three!"

In unison, they yelled, "Pie!"

"Very good. Boy, you all are smart." She sat back on the heels of her feet. "Who here likes pie?"

Young voices mingled as they all said, "Me, me, me."

"I do, too. But—" she held up her finger "—if we want to have a slice of this here blackberry pie, we have to eat our lunch first. In order to do that, we have to wash our hands. We'd better hurry and go do that. Don't you agree?"

Three heads nodded vigorously before the whole lot of them whirled around and darted down to the river. Abby snatched up a towel and followed them closely. Down at the riverbank, she helped each one of them wash and dry their hands.

"She's something, isn't she?" Fletcher said from beside Harrison. "She sure has a way with children."

"That, she does." In fact, Harrison wished she could be the mother to his sons. Shock bolted from his gut and lodged into his throat.

Where had that thought come from?

When had she crept into his heart like that?

And even more important, how would he ever rip her out of it?

Was he falling for her? He searched his heart for the answer.

"Harrison, aren't you going to come join us?" Abby's voice pulled him from the reality he needed to escape.

He strode over to the spot where everyone was seated under the canopy of trees.

Food passed around the group and within minutes, everyone had their plates filled.

Abby looked over at him. "Harrison, would you like the honor of praying over our food today?"

Pray? His eyes widened before he could stop them. Him? He'd never prayed a day in his life. Well, that wasn't entirely true, but it had been years since he had.

"Our daddy don't pray," Josiah said before Harrison had a chance to answer her.

Harrison's gaze shifted to his son, then up to Abby. Her eyes were wide until he looked directly at her, then they quickly returned to normal. He had no idea what to do or say.

"Well, then why don't we ask Mr. Hilliard to pray today?" She sent an apologetic smile to Harrison for no doubt putting him in this uncomfortable situation before she turned her focus onto Samuel. "Would you do us the honors, Samuel?"

"Yes, ma'am. I'd be more than happy to."

They all bowed their heads except Harrison. He studied the top of Abby's head. It shouldn't bother him what Abby or anyone else thought because he wasn't a praying man. After all, it was no one's business but his own. Still, the thought of Abby thinking less of him bothered Harrison.

The short prayer ended.

Abby's attention wafted back over to him. He waited for the disappointment to come as it had with so many other religious people when they discovered he didn't share their faith. But it never came. Not one delightful thing in the whole world could compare to the smile she offered; it was one of complete acceptance. If ever there was a person he wanted acceptance from, it would be Abby.

* * *

Stunned by the news that Harrison didn't pray, Abby's heart went out to him and she felt guilty for asking him to pray in front of everyone. She tried to reassure him and to make him feel better by giving him her biggest, most accepting smile, but that wasn't enough as far as she was concerned. Of course, that's why he hadn't come to services. How could she have missed something so very obvious? She needed to figure out some way to somehow make it up to him.

"Abby, do you mind if I join you?"

Abby gazed up from her spot on the ground to find Fletcher standing over her. Four adults could fit comfortably on the blanket and she saw no reason why he couldn't join her. "That would be nice."

"This was a great idea. Thank you for including Julie and me." Fletcher lowered his lanky frame onto the blanket. He no sooner got settled, than Samuel stepped up. "Got room for one more? That is, if I'm not intruding or anything?" He looked from Fletcher to Abby.

"No, not at all. Please, won't you be seated?" Abby motioned to a spot on the blanket.

Samuel barely sat down when Harrison joined them.

Next thing Abby knew, Zoé, Veronique, Colette and the three children vacated their chairs, spread out a blanket next to theirs and joined the rest of them. Staimes remained in his chair until Veronique invited him to sit with them and patted the spot next to her. That must have been all the encouragement he needed because he joined them and sat in the spot closest to Veronique. Abby wished the two of them would find a future together. She'd never seen Veronique smile so much before. But that wasn't likely to happen as he would leave when Harrison did.

Oh, if only. Abby sighed.

Everyone took turns talking while intermediately eating Lucy's excellent fried chicken, her fluffy biscuits, cheese slices, hard-boiled eggs and the new potatoes smothered in butter and sprinkled with parsley. When the main course was finished and the blackberry, strawberry-rhubarb and apple pies were devoured, Abby was the first one to rise. Her attention shifted to the children. "Anyone ready to do some fishing?"

Josiah and Graham leaped up and made it to her side in an instant.

"Julie, don't you want to join us?"

Julie wrinkled her nose and shook her head.

"It'll be fun. I promise."

She shook her head again. "No, thank you. Fish smell funny and they're icky and slimy." The poor girl looked so repulsed that Abby didn't ask her again.

"Well, if you change your mind, we'll be right around that bend." She pointed to where the wide river disappeared around the corner.

"I'd like to join you, if you don't mind." Harrison stood. "I've never fished before, and I'd like to see what you do. Perhaps you could even teach me how to?"

Abby thought that a splendid idea. Anything to spend more time in Harrison's company. Not wanting to leave anyone out she eyed each person. "Anyone else want to join us?"

"I think I'll just rest here a spell. This is my favorite place on your property. Always was." Samuel leaned his back against the tree and stretched his legs straight out in front of him.

Colette settled on her side, braced herself on her elbow and rested her head in the palm of her hand. "I'm perfectly content to stay here myself."

Veronique and Zoé agreed.

"What about you, Fletcher? You want to come?" Abby watched as his gaze slid to his daughter seated next to him.

"No. I'd better stay here with Julie. Besides, I don't much care for fishing, either."

"Oh. All right. We'll see you all later, then." The four of them made their way to where the fishing supplies had been placed earlier that morning, including the coffee can of worms she'd dug up and placed in a cool spot.

Harrison took the fishing equipment from her, and the boys nestled their hands in hers. She led the way to the spot where Samuel had shown her the best fishing was. Josiah and Graham chattered the whole way there. Their excited voices had her feeling quite giddy.

They found the small clearing, and Abby went right to work showing Harrison and the boys how to bait their hooks and how to throw out their lines. Several times, Josiah's and Graham's lines got tangled. Finally, their lines were safely in the water. The current carried them up the river a fair piece. After giving them instructions on how to tell when they had a fish, she turned to help Harrison.

His casting was as bad as his sons', if not worse.

"Here, let me show you by guiding you through it." She placed her hand on top of his and froze. Their gazes collided, neither looked away. Some unique bond was transpiring between them.

"Daddy, you gotta throw it. Not hold it."

Abby was the first to break contact. She raised her hand, and instead of touching him again, she went through the motions on how to cast.

Harrison finally got his bait in the water instead of the trees behind them. Within minutes he had a bite. Like a Fourth of July firework display, his face lit up but quickly turned to panic. "What do I do? I got one!"

"Set the hook by giving a yank on the line."

He gave a sharp yank, and the pole came within inches of smacking her in the face.

Concentrating hard on the task before him, Harrison's hands cranked fast in small circles. The fish flopped and broke across the top of the water several times.

"See it in the water, boys?" Abby pointed to where the fish swam near the bank.

"Where? I don't see it?" Josiah squatted down and peered into the water. "I see it. I see it!"

"Where?" Graham looked at him.

Josiah grabbed his hand and pointed to it.

"I see it, too. I see it, too, Daddy." Graham jumped up and down.

"That's great, boys." His voice was filled with a case of the nerves. "Now please move back so your father can bring it onto the bank."

The twins slowly backed out of the way.

"Okay. Now. Whatever you do, Harrison, don't pick up your pole when the fish reaches the bank. Slide it in instead," she instructed.

He did as he was told and slid the fish over the river-bank and onto the dry ground yards away from the water.

The boys squealed and clapped their hands, their own poles all but forgotten now.

Abby watched Harrison. His face glowed with the same childlike expression as his sons had. He pressed his shoulders back, protruding his already broad chest. "This is the first fish I've ever caught. Thank you, Abby."

She smiled and nodded.

"I wanna catch a fishy now." Josiah hopped up and down.

"Me, too." Graham mimicked his brother by jumping up and down, too.

"All right, but let me get this one off the hook first, and then I'll help you boys, okay?"

They nodded.

"You don't mind touching them?" Harrison asked, sounding a little queasy.

"Nope. Been doing it ever since my sister-in-law Selina showed me how to fish."

Abby ran her finger under the fish gill on one side and her thumb under the other one until her finger and thumb touched. The fish flopped but there was no way it was going to get away from the grasp she had on it. She grabbed a rope and attached the fish to it. She tossed the fish into the water and anchored the rope with a heavy rock.

"You're a very impressive woman, Miss Abby Bowen."

She peered up at him. "Why? Because I can fish?"

"No. Not because you can fish. Well, not just because you can fish. You amaze me. Not only do you have a great business mind, you're a very elegant woman and yet you aren't afraid to get dirty or touch a fish. Most woman would never do that."

"Well, I'm not most women." She sent him a sassy smile.

"Thank goodness for that."

Abby frowned at the way he said that and wondered what he meant. Rather than ask, she tore her attention off him and put it onto the boys. After everyone caught at least two fish each, they headed back to the others.

"Well, how'd you do?" Samuel was the first to ask.

"We caught lots of fishies," Josiah answered.

Graham nodded.

The boys had to show everyone their catch, except for Julie; she didn't want to see them. Abby felt sorry for the little girl because she didn't like fishing and had been left out of the fun, so she decided to do something she might enjoy, too. "Julie, would you like to play hide-and-seek?"

Her little face brightened and swung toward her father's. "May I, Papa?"

"Yes, you may."

"I wanna play, too." Josiah spoke up first.

"Me, too," Graham added.

Zoé and Colette joined them, while Veronique closed her eyes. The six of them played hide-and-seek for over a half an hour.

Exhausted from the play and the heat, Zoé, Colette and the children lay down on the blanket Veronique and Staimes had abandoned. They were now seated in a couple of the chairs that had been brought down and were still chatting away. It was nice to see Veronique enjoying herself instead of working all the time.

Abby arrived at the blanket Fletcher and Harrison occupied in time to hear Harrison ask, "Will you be able to repair them?"

Her attention glided from one to the other as she sat down. "Repair what?"

Both men turned their attention onto her.

"Fletcher was just telling me that when he went on the roof to check the shingles he decided to check the chimneys while he was up there." Worry crowded Harrison's face.

"And…" Abby dragged out the word, waiting for one of them to respond.

"Abby," Fletcher spoke first. "Three of the chimneys are starting to collapse. Some of the rocks they used were sandstone and they've started to crumble. The chimneys will have to be rebuilt. It's going to take a while to rebuild them."

"How much time are we talking about?" She kept her focus on Fletcher while waiting for his answer.

"I'm not quite sure. I'll know more when I get started."

"Will you be able to get all of that done in the next three months?"

He cocked his mouth to one side. "Um. I'm not sure."

"Can you hire more help so that it can be done by then? Surely there are men in town who could use the work."

"There are. But—" his gaze dropped to his lap, and

he raised his hat and wiped his forehead off "—those repairs were not included in my original bid."

"That's no problem. Hire as many men as you need to get the job finished. And while we're speaking of jobs, I would love it if you could get the theater section finished as soon as possible. The chairs are supposed to arrive sometime within the next couple of weeks. And my…" Realizing she was leaving Harrison out and how that must look for him, her attention jumped to him. "*Our* actresses and actors will be arriving shortly after that. Since we need to start practicing right away, we'll need to have the stage and props done as soon as you can.

"So hire as many workers as you need to. Just please make sure of the men you hire that their quality of work is equal to that of yours. Plus, we prefer that you yourself build the stage and the props and everything to do with the theater and have your men work on the repairs." She hoped she wasn't being too presumptuous, so she looked to Harrison for his approval.

He sent her a discreet nod. She returned her focus back to Fletcher. "Will that work for you?" *Please say yes.* The idea of her grand opening being set back didn't bode too well with her. Then again, she stopped fidgeting, knowing everything would work out just fine because God would work everything out as He always did.

"I already planned on doing that. I'll hire more men tomorrow, and we'll get started on the theater right away."

"Wonderful." Abby clasped her hands and pressed them to her chest. "I can hardly wait to see what it's going to look like when you get finished." She closed her eyes and laid her head back. Contentment wrapped around her that her dream was quickly on its way to becoming a reality. Well, one of them, anyway. The other would remain a dream only.

Chapter Ten

Two hours later, the small party started to break up and go their separate ways. Staimes had asked if Harrison minded if he went back to the house with everyone else. Harrison smiled. He knew that everyone else had meant Veronique especially. It brought him great joy to see his valet relaxed and enjoying another's companionship.

Zoé had asked Harrison if she could take his sons with her because she had something she wanted to show them—a bug collection or something like that. Julie had been invited, too, but the little girl wrinkled her nose and shook her head. Harrison agreed with her. Why anyone would want to see bugs was beyond him, but his boys did, so he had let them go, knowing they were dead bugs mounted on boards. It amazed him a woman collected such a thing. Seemed all the women in Abby's household, including Abby, did things he wasn't used to seeing. Boston women didn't do those things. At least not the women in his society. Truth be known, he enjoyed these people's good society much more.

Harrison lingered behind in hopes of walking Abby

back to the house. He hadn't gotten over how the woman had responded to the news about her chimneys. Nothing about it fazed her and it should have. Therefore, he didn't think she truly understood the magnitude of just how much more it was going to cost her to fix those chimneys or to hire those extra men. To make sure she did, he wanted to discuss the matter with her, only he didn't want to do it in front of Fletcher or anyone else.

Minutes later, Fletcher and his daughter left. They were the last ones to leave the picnic area.

Harrison turned toward Abby and froze at the sight. A hummingbird hovered over her, pecking at the flowers in the ribbon around the crown of her hat. Abby sat statue still. They're eyes connected, then hers drifted upward to where the hummingbird still hovered before returning to his. Her disbelieving, exuberant smile and bright eyes reminded him of a child opening a birthday present.

Caught up in the captivating moment, he watched the fluorescent-orange bird, a rufous, the locals called it, test several more flowers before it flitted off.

"Did you see that? I can't believe it was that close to me." Abby clasped her hands in front of her and yanked them to her chest. "Aren't they the sweetest little things ever? That one was a rufous hummingbird. Odd how they look brown until you see them in the sun. Then the orange on their bodies and the red under their beak turns a brilliant fluorescent color, don't you think?" Again she gave him no time to answer as she started to rise immediately after her question.

Harrison rushed to help her up. Every time her hand settled in his, the warmth of her touch went straight to his heart and its effect resided there; this time was no different. Not wanting to feel the effects because of its implication, he let go of her hand.

"Thank you." She looked around. "Well, I suppose I ought to head to the house. I really hate to leave this place. I love the sound of the water lapping over the rocks. It's so soothing and comforting. Don't you agree?" She turned those smiling eyes up at him.

"I do." Not wanting their time to end and still needing to talk to her, he asked, "Would you like to sit a bit longer? There's something I'd like to talk with you about."

She tilted her head. "What about?"

"Let's go sit down over there." He pointed to a felled log near the wide river's edge.

They made their way there and sat down.

Abby crossed her knees in his direction and draped one hand loosely over the other.

"Earlier, when Fletcher mentioned the chimneys, you didn't seem the least bit upset about it. I just wanted to make sure you understand that the repairs are going to be quite costly. Not so much the rebuilding supplies, but the wages will be extreme as it will take many hours for the men to rebuild them."

"Oh. I see. Well, as we discussed earlier, you do not have to contribute any more funds. I will handle it."

Huh? This wasn't about him at all. "I wasn't thinking about me, Abby. I was thinking about you. I just wanted to make sure you understood just how much money this was going to take."

"That's very sweet of you. But don't you worry about that. Whatever it takes, I will pay. Nothing is going to stop me from my dream. Besides, God will take care of it."

There she was saying God would take care of it again. Was she really that naive? Didn't she know that God didn't care about people? Especially their problems? His heart ached that she believed all of that malarkey. He knew a man who trusted God to restore his business, and when God didn't come through, the man had become so bitter and angry that he not only lost his business but his wife and family, too. Harrison hoped the same thing didn't happen to Abby.

At one point in his life, Harrison himself had prayed. One time, he had asked God to heal his best friend's mother, and she had died, anyway. Another time he'd prayed, even pleaded with God that his father would love him. That prayer was never answered, either. The last time he'd prayed was when he'd asked God to bring his wife back to him. Look how that turned out. His twins were motherless. So as far as Harrison was concerned, God wouldn't take care of it as Abby seemed to think. Poor woman was delusional in her thinking. Didn't she know that if something needed done, a person had to take care of it themselves? Well, even if she didn't. He did. Therefore, he would do whatever he could to help her to make her dream come true. Even if it meant spending his last dime.

"Thank you for allowing me to teach you and your sons to fish. I had a great time." Abby's words pulled Harrison from his thoughts. The smile she sent his way was contagious.

"No. Thank *you*. I can't remember the last time I've had so much fun. Seeing my boys like that, squealing and jumping up and down when they caught their first fish. There's no greater joy. It made me wish I had several more little ones running around. Someday, if I ever find the right woman, my dream of filling my house with my own offspring will come true." Too bad Abby wasn't that woman. But she had her dreams and he had his, and the two didn't mesh.

Hearing Harrison's words about wanting a houseful of children, *if* he ever found the right woman, felt like a slap to her. His words hurt her more than she wanted them to. It was just another painful reminder that her ex-fiancé was right. Men wanted children of their own. And lots of them.

"Are you all right, Abby?"

No. But how could she tell him she wasn't? Then she would have to explain to him about her not being able to bear children. For some reason, she couldn't stomach the thought of him looking at her with the same disgust David and his friends had. "Yes, I'm fine, thank you." She plastered on a smile, one she didn't feel. "When you get back to Boston, I hope your dream of having a houseful of children comes true for you, and that you find the right woman for you there, as well."

"What about you? Do you want children?"

Did she want children? Yes! More than anything else in this world. Even more than her theater. But that wasn't ever going to happen and she didn't want Harrison to know that for the same reason she thought of only moments ago. *God, help me get out of this.*

"Forgive me, Abby. That was rather forward of me to ask such a personal question. Your private life is none of my business." He stood. "Speaking of children, I need to go rescue Zoé from mine." He smiled.

Abby relaxed. *Thank You, Lord.* "Yes. I need to get back, too. Tomorrow's going to be another long day." They headed toward her house.

"I meant to tell you, I found a nanny for the boys. That was the business I had to tend to yesterday. So I won't have to worry about bothering Zoé or having them underfoot while we conduct business."

So it was back to that again. Business. She had wondered what pressing business he had to tend to the other day, and now she knew. One would think she'd be happy knowing she wouldn't be around the little darlings so much and risk getting too attached to them. The emptiness that always accompanied their departure hurt. Even still, his news disappointed her. "I want you to know that Zoé didn't mind taking care of them. In fact, she enjoyed it. But I know how much it bothered you, so I'm so happy that you found someone. Has he or she met the twins yet?"

He rubbed his fingers across his wrinkled forehead. "No."

"Well, when she does, she will love them."

The worry lines on his forehead let up, but only slightly. "You think so? I told you the issue I've had with other nannies quitting."

"Well, if they don't, then they don't know what they're missing." She sure did.

"I hope you're right."

She did, too. For his sake as well as his sons'. They deserved no less.

They reached the gardens. Lilacs in full bloom

sweetened the air with soft, fragrant scents. A bumblebee hovered around her face. She swept it away with her hand, careful not to anger it so it wouldn't sting her. Many blooming flowers filled the garden, a temptation for any bee. Abby marveled at how much Samuel had gotten done already. One could actually see the blooms now instead of the tall weeds that hid the beautiful petals from view. While there was still a long way to go, just trimming the bushes and eliminating most of the weeds had already made a huge difference.

The sound of children's laughter floated on the breeze that brushed over them. How she loved the sound of children's laughter. It was music to her ears. "Sounds like someone is having fun."

"Either that or they're doing something they shouldn't be doing."

"Oh, I doubt that. Zoé knows how to handle children. She's very good with them."

"I didn't mean to imply that Zoé wasn't capable of handling them—I just know my boys."

That she could grin at.

They rounded the tall hedge that blocked their view of what was happening on the other side.

When they did, Harrison gasped, and Abby covered her smiling mouth with her hand.

The boys had a net on the outdoor table that they were trying to remove a giant bug from.

Stacked boxes of Zoé's bug collection and jars containing several insects and even a frog or two covered the majority of the table.

"Don't touch that!" Harrison's voice was filled with panic as he sprinted toward them.

Zoé and the twins turned wide eyes up at him and the insect took that opportunity to escape.

"That thing could bite you."

At the look of horror on Harrison's face, Abby couldn't help but giggle.

His frowning gaze turned and zeroed in on her.

It was meant to silence her, of that she was sure, but it didn't. All it succeeded in doing was making her laugh outright. Through that laughter she managed to say, "It's okay, Harrison. It's only a locust. They don't bite." She snatched up the net and hurried after the insect. A couple of tries later, she managed to capture the little beast. Unsnagging the insect's legs from the net, she held it up by its back legs for Harrison's inspection. "See?"

One glance of repulsion at the locust and he stared at her as if she was daft. Hadn't the man ever held a bug before? Probably not. After all, he was a city boy. She decided to show him some mercy, so she freed the insect, and then turned to Zoé. "Zoé, perhaps we should let them go now." She sent a knowing wink her friend's way. Zoé captured it immediately, so Abby continued, "Boys, you've got to watch them long enough. We wouldn't want them to die or anything now, would we? So why don't we set them free now?" Abby hoped her suggestion worked.

They pouted at first, but it only took seconds before they nodded.

One by one they opened the lids and dumped the living contents on the ground. Various species of insects scampered or flew off.

Only three toads remained.

"Do we gotta let these ones go?" Josiah asked, looking up at Abby and his father. "I like this one." He pointed to the largest toad inside the gallon jar. "Please? Can we keep them?"

"Please, can we?" Graham added.

"We'll take good care of them. We promise." He crossed his little fingers over his chest, and so did Graham.

Zoé and Abby both looked over at Harrison.

If it were up to Abby, seeing those blue puppy-dog eyes and hearing their pleading voices, she'd cave in and say yes. But it wasn't up to her to make that decision. It was Harrison's. He was the boys' parent. Not her.

Despite his horror, the lines around his eyes softened. "Only if they stay here."

The twins squealed. Apparently, he was a sucker for those cute little beseeching faces, as well.

"Wait. We didn't ask Miss Abby if it's okay."

Hopeful faces turned her way. No way would she say no to them. And yet she had to think of the frogs' welfare, too, and show the boys the lesson in that. "If we can figure out something to keep them alive, then I say yes. But if not, we have to let them go. Like I said before, we don't want them to die now, do we?"

They both shook their heads.

"Okay. Let's go look in the shed to see if there's something out there we can use." Abby took each boy's hand in hers and led them to the shed. Inside the building, she and the boys searched until she came across an old slatted, wooden crate with a lid. Upon inspection, she decided it would work. The slats were too narrow for the toads to escape.

She and the boys gathered grass and a medium-size rock and put them in the bottom of the crate. They used an old bowl she'd found in the shed, filled it with water, and settled it next to the rock. "Okay. You ready to release them?"

The twins nodded.

Abby removed the lid and reached her hand inside the jar.

"Are you going to touch those things?" Harrison asked from behind her.

Without removing her hand from inside the jar, she peered over her shoulder. "I am." Unfazed by the curling of his hiked eyebrows, she pulled the largest toad out. It legs dangled loosely.

"Did your sister-in-law teach you that, too?" The dismay on his face had her almost laughing again.

"Yes, she sure did. Selina taught all of us to enjoy God's creatures and how there was beauty and treasures just waiting to be found. That a person just had to look for them. And she was right. Take this toad, for example." She held it up to where everyone could see it. "To someone, this creature might be ugly, but to another who knows what to look for, it isn't. Look at the intricate markings on it. God took the time to make each one unique." To prove her point she retrieved the other one with her free hand and now held two of them in front of her.

She described their differences and even pointed out the differences in some species of bugs Zoé had preserved and had pinned onto boards.

Josiah and Graham's attention remained glued to what she showed them.

When she finished, even Harrison looked slightly impressed.

He squatted down until he was eye level with his boys. "You learned a valuable lesson today. Do you know what that was?"

"Yes. We want Abby for our mother."

Abby froze stiff as ice, afraid to look at Harrison. Instead, she busied herself by putting the frog back into the jar, and by sending Zoé a pleading look to get her out of this sticky situation.

"Well, *mademoiselle,*" Zoé said, striding right into the middle of the conversation with a knowing twinkle in her eye. "I've had enough fresh air for one day. I'm going to my room now to read that book you lent me."

Abby wanted to hug Zoé for annihilating a very uncomfortable situation. "Thank you, Zoé. I hope you enjoy *Emma* as much as I did."

"I'm sure I will." With those words, Zoé hugged each of the boys and picked up her bug collection boxes. Her skirt swayed like a bell as she scampered toward the house.

Abby kept her eyes on Zoé's retreating back, for fear of facing Harrison.

"I'm sorry, Abby." Harrison stood so close that his breath had brushed the hair around her ears when he spoke. She understood he needed to keep his voice down for the children's sake, but having him this close set her insides to squirming.

Oblivious to her discombobulated feelings, he continued, "I can see that my son made you uncomfortable."

Not as much as Harrison's nearness was.

"He did me, too," Harrison continued. "But he's just a child. He doesn't have any idea what he's saying."

Oh, yes, he did, and that was both scary and satisfying. Those thoughts would remain tucked inside her. She shrugged as if it was nothing. "Remember, I have nephews and nieces, so I'm used to them saying embarrassing things." Nothing quite as embarrassing as that, though. She discreetly stepped away from him.

Neither one said anything. Moments of silence passed. Finally, Harrison spoke. "Well. My sons have had a long day. I'm going to take them home."

"Ah-h-h. We don't wanna go home. We wanna stay with Miss Abby and Miss Denis," Josiah whined.

"That's not up to you to decide. I'm your father and I make the decisions. Is that clear?" Even though his tone sounded firm, the man's heart was as fluffy and soft as a baby duck.

"Yes, Daddy," Graham answered first.

Josiah nodded and scuffed the toe of his shoe in the dirt.

"Tell Miss Abby thank you for this wonderful day."

"Thank you, Miss Abby, for this wonderful day," they both said. Suddenly, before she could brace herself, the twins barreled into her legs.

Harrison's arm shot out to steady her, but he missed. She and his sons landed on the ground with a thud.

"Josiah! Graham! Apologize to Miss Abby this instant." He helped them to their feet, more yanking than helping. Then his hand took hold of hers, and her heart jumped inside her. The gorgeous man staring into her eyes affected her, and that wasn't good. Yet, she was powerless to stop it. The heart was a powerful, influential thing. Hers had gone and betrayed her by falling for another man. Not just any man, either. A man who had made it very clear that he hadn't met the right woman yet, and that he wanted a house filled with his offspring. It would do her good to remember that from now on. Her heart be hanged in this matter. She was in control. She sighed. If only that were true.

Chapter Eleven

Sitting on her front porch on one of the new outdoor chairs, sipping a cup of coffee, Abby watched the hummingbirds lick the nectar from her flowers. Delighted that everything else was going the way she had planned, a smile tugged at her lips.

With the extra men Fletcher had hired, the stage was now finished and a lot of the props were, too. Today the theater chairs and the carpet runners would be arriving by train. The table and chairs wouldn't arrive for a couple more weeks. Abby had tried to time it where everything didn't come at once, so it wouldn't be too hard for the hired men to have to deal with.

The sound of horse's hooves clomping on the hard ground pulled Abby's attention in that direction. It was Harrison. For two solid weeks now, after her heart betrayed her by falling for him, Abby had done her best to keep her mind off just how much she cared for Harrison, and onto business.

She missed the boys, too. She'd seen very little of them since they had a new nanny. That was a good thing. Right? Someone needed to tell her heart that. It kept forgetting, and she missed the little tykes something fierce. If she missed them this much now, what was it going to be like when they left for Boston and she never saw them again? Or Harrison? That thought thudded across her heart even more loudly.

Harrison raised his hand in greeting, and the familiar butterflies she got in her stomach every time she saw him returned. She reciprocated the wave as his buggy headed toward her house.

Harrison parked his carriage and joined her on the porch as he did every morning.

"Good morning. How are you this beautiful, sunny morning?" Abby asked.

"Very well. And I can tell just by looking at you that you're doing wonderful, as well."

My, how handsome he looked in his blue pants and light blue shirt. It was nice to see him in a more casual style of clothing. It meant he was getting used to the more laid-back style of country life. "Would you care for some coffee?"

Harrison pulled out a chair at her table and sat down. "I'd love some. I didn't have time to stop by Lucy's today. My nanny quit."

"What? Are you serious? Why?"

Harrison let out a long breath as his shoulders slumped forward. "Mrs. Glenn said they were too much for her."

Abby couldn't imagine what was wrong with the nannies he hired. There was nothing amiss with his sons. Yes, they had a lot of energy, but what boys didn't? And they were the sweetest boys ever.

"I'm afraid I won't be able to help you today. I'm going to have to find another nanny as soon as possible, or I'm going to end up losing my valet, too."

"I'm sure Zoé would be more than happy to watch them. She's been pining for them. And to be honest, I miss having them around, too."

He turned surprised eyes on her. "You do?"

"Well, yes, of course I do. I don't know what is wrong with those nannies. Josiah and Graham are adorable."

"I don't think it's the nannies."

Abby stared at Harrison. "How could you think that? Of course it's them," she blurted, surprised that he, their father, would even say such a thing.

"No. No, it isn't."

Abby's ire rose. She opened her mouth to give him a piece of her mind.

His next words stopped her. "It's yours."

"What? Mine? Well, of all the nerve! What do you mean it's my fault?"

"Just as I said. This time I think the boys purposely drove the nanny away. They kept talking about how much they missed you and Zoé. They'd been begging me to bring them with me so they could see you two. I think it was a concerted effort on their part to drive Mrs. Glenn to distraction because they think that will mean they will get to come back here."

Abby's anger melted away with those words, and she had to stifle the laugh, which didn't work at all. "Ahh. Those little darlings."

"Darlings? Hardly. Do you know what those little darlings did?"

She shook her head, anxious to hear.

"They caught a frog and put it in Mrs. Glenn's teacup. When she went to pour tea into her cup, she nearly fainted."

Abby pictured it and barely kept her giggle to herself.

"That's not all. They found a small garden snake sunning on the shale rocks near the front porch and put it in her bed. Staimes said he didn't know a woman could scream so loud."

Abby giggled.

"It's not funny."

Yes, it is.

"The final straw was when they caught several stink bugs and put them in her hair while she was sleeping. The stench had her heaving for quite some time."

Abby wanted to laugh again, but the truth was, she felt sorry for the poor woman. Stink bugs. How revolting. "How did someone so young come up with such ideas?"

"From you."

"Me?" she squeaked.

"Yes. You. Remember last Sunday when we went fishing again and you were telling me what your brothers used to do to you and how it made you want to run away from home because you couldn't stand it and feared what they would do next?"

Guilt made its way into her cheeks. "It is my fault. Oh, Harrison." She rested her hand on his forearm. "I'm so sorry. I had no idea that they were listening, or that they would use those things to get rid of their nanny."

"I know you didn't. Neither did I. As bad as those things were, that wasn't what caused her to leave. The final incident was the dead fish."

"Dead fish?" Abby swallowed. "So that's what happened to the missing fish last Sunday," she said more to herself than him. "Please tell me they didn't do what my brother Michael did to my sister, Leah?"

He slowly nodded his head. "I'm afraid they did."

Abby dropped her head back and groaned. She pressed her hand against her chest and blew out in a long breath before turning her attention back to Harrison. "I'm really sorry."

"Not as sorry as Mrs. Glenn was. I hope she can get the fish odor out of her clothes."

Abby tried not to giggle. After all, it wasn't funny what that poor woman had endured, but the giggle had a mind of its own and made its presence known. To her surprise, Harrison's own chuckle floated toward her.

Naughty as it was to find humor in the situation, the two of them ended up bubbling over with laughter.

When they finally stopped laughing, Abby wiped at her tears. Gathering her composure, she poured Harrison a cup of coffee and handed it to him along with a freshly baked, sugar-glazed cinnamon roll with walnuts.

He took a bite of the sweet treat and swallowed. "That cook of yours is amazing. These are the best cinnamon rolls I've ever tasted."

"I'm blessed that not only Veronique, but also her sisters, decided to join me."

"I'm sorry. I can't remember if you ever said, but how did you meet those three? Each one of those ladies is a rare find."

"That, they are. They used to work for my mother until she got married. Their services were no longer needed, but my mother didn't have the heart to let them go. My stepfather offered to find positions for them, but I asked if they didn't mind moving if I hired them. The Denis sisters were thrilled to come with me. One reason being, they weren't sure how they would enjoy working for a man like my stepfather."

"Oh. Why is that?" He sipped his coffee and then took another bite of his roll.

"He is a prominent man, who entertains some very prominent people. They felt uncomfortable in that high-society, social environment, so it worked out great for me. Here, they might have to deal with the elite, but they don't work for them. They work for me. And even though they do work for me, they are more like family to me, and I try to treat them that way, too."

"They're lucky to have you."

"No. I'm the lucky one. Make that the blessed one. They work hard and they're there for me whenever I need them as I hope I am for them. Speaking of work—" Abby set the teacup she'd been holding down on the table "—I can hardly wait. The chairs are arriving on the train this morning."

"With the nearest train depot six miles away, how many wagons did you have to hire to deliver the chairs here?"

"Oh, no." Her hand flew to the side of her head. "How could I have been so stupid?"

"What's the matter?" He frowned.

"I can't believe it."

"What?"

Embarrassed, she dropped her gaze to her lap. "I didn't think about that. I was so excited about ordering them, that I completely forgot about arranging for them to be delivered here. What am I going to do? How am I ever going to find someone this late to deliver them?" For the first time since starting her business adventure, panic took over and she felt completely inept as a businesswoman.

Seeing the distress racing across Abby's face, Harrison settled his hand on her arm. "Don't worry, Abby. I'll take care of it." He had no idea how, especially at such short notice, but he'd figure out something. He had to. He couldn't bear seeing her so upset. His mind searched for a solution until one came. "Fletcher has three wagons. I expect most of his men have wagons, too. Let me see if they'd be willing to take their wagons and go pick them up. Plus, I know the livery owner has two wagons. I can rent them for the day."

"Do you think they will? I'll pay them extra for their troubles."

"I don't see why they wouldn't. As soon as Fletcher gets here, I'll ask him. In the meantime, why don't we finish our coffee and rolls and enjoy the morning? By the way, I know it's not even seven o'clock yet. I hope you don't mind my showing up early. I would have never presumed to do such a thing, but I knew you would be sitting on the porch like usual, and I wanted to give you an early warning that I wouldn't be able to help today. I'll make the arrangements for the furniture and then I'd better get back home. Staimes can only handle the boys for a short time. They make him nervous."

"Oh. I forgot about that. Listen." She rested her arm on top of his, and that same warm feeling he always got when she touched him made its way into his chest again. "There's no need for you to find a nanny. Truly. Zoé will be more than happy to watch them, and I miss having them around."

"I can't ask you to do that. Besides, you need Zoé to help you with other things around here."

"Things are pretty well taken care of until we get closer to the grand opening. After that, you'll be leaving and Zoé will get back to her normal chores then."

The idea of his leaving didn't sound very appealing anymore. But leave he must. He'd made a vow to himself years ago, the very day he'd been told by a once close colleague of his father's, just how rotten his father had been to everyone who knew him after the death of Harrison's mother. Therefore, leaving was definitely a must.

Not only because it was the right thing to do, but he had to do it for his sons' sake. After all, he didn't want them growing up with that same marked dark cloud that had hung over his head. No, he wanted his sons to be able to hold their heads high in Boston or anywhere else without shame. Harrison was determined to make that happen, and he couldn't do it from here.

"It's settled, then. As soon as I finish breakfast, I'll ask Zoé if she minds. Which I know she won't."

He hated doing that, but the last time he looked for a nanny, he had trouble. There were very few single women in this town, and even fewer widowed ladies. Most all of them had their own households to take care of or they were too old to care for his young sons. No other choice remained. "Thank you, Abby. I appreciate this."

"You're welcome. And just so you know, I can drive one of the wagons."

"You can drive a wagon?"

"Yes. I've been driving one since I was little. My brothers made sure that my sister, Leah, and I learned how, just in case we ever needed to use one and they were too busy on the ranch to take us."

The woman never ceased to amaze him. "Tell me about your ranch."

"What do you want to know?"

"Whatever you want to tell me. For starters, do you miss it?"

"Yes and no. Yes, I miss my family, and the ranch is beautiful. No, I love being independent and not being smothered constantly by my overprotective brothers."

"I'm sure they meant well. If I had a sister, I would be overly protective of her, too."

"I'm sure you would." She chuckled.

"Tell me more." He took a bite of his half-eaten roll.

"Well, I'm not boasting now, mind you, but my family owns the largest ranch out there. We have many acres of wheat. There are apple, pear and plum tree groves galore on the place. My family used to raise pigs only until the train started coming through Paradise Haven. Now they raise cattle, too."

"Why only pigs?"

"Well, they were the only animals that could survive the rough winters there. They survived by eating camas bulbs. After the train came through, it was easier to get supplies and feed for the cattle. Now, enough about that. Tell me about Boston. What's it like?" She popped a bite of her roll into her mouth and tossed a chunk to a chipmunk that had made its way onto the porch.

"Downtown Boston is busy and noisy and there are buildings everywhere. One rarely has to have anything shipped in because of the huge variety of shops. It's highly populated and the people aren't nearly as friendly as they are here."

"You know—" Abby spoke as if she were almost speaking to herself and not him "—even though I was born in New York City, I was too young to remember it. Still, I could never live in a large city like Boston. While Paradise Haven has grown, it still has that small, hometown feel. Like here. After living here for the last few months, I could never see myself living anywhere else now. I just love it here."

Those words were the final clincher where he and Abby were concerned. She herself said she could never live in Boston. She was settled here; he was leaving. So for his remaining time here, he needed to protect his heart completely from allowing her into it. The finality of that saddened him.

They finished their breakfast listening to the blackbirds and tossing small chunks of their rolls to a persistent chipmunk, whose cheeks were puffed full now.

At the sound of harnesses rattling and horse's hooves clomping on the hard ground, the furry chipmunk scurried off, and the noise dulled the birds' singing.

Harrison rose and made his way down the steps. He met Fletcher just as he pulled in front of the mansion. "Good morning."

"Morning." Fletcher tied off the lines, set the brake and hopped down.

"I need to talk to you about something." Without looking, Harrison knew Abby was nearby; he could sense her, could smell the rose scent that normally surrounded her.

"Something wrong?" Fletcher asked.

"We've encountered a situation that we were wondering if you could help us out with."

"What's that?"

Harrison explained their dilemma.

"I'm sure my men would be more than happy to help. I know a few other men I could ask in town that would help, too."

Harrison hated that he couldn't be the one to solve Abby's dilemma and that Fletcher was. But what did he expect? He wasn't from around here, so he didn't know anyone, and Fletcher did. "Thank you. We need to pull out of here no later than eight so we can meet the train when it arrives. Will you take care of organizing it? Abby and I need to head on over to the livery to see about renting Mr. Barges's two wagons."

"That won't be necessary. I know enough men who can help that you won't need to."

"Very well, then. We'll see you in about an hour?"

Fletcher nodded, strode over to where his men were waiting by their horses and wagons, and started talking to them. Several heads looked their way and nodded.

Harrison turned to Abby. "Looks like you won't have to drive a wagon, after all."

"It wouldn't have bothered me. I'm used to it. In a way I was hoping I would have to so that I could go with the men."

"We can go in my buggy if you'd like."

"You wouldn't mind?"

"No, ma'am." His heart might take a beating, but seeing the smile on her face would be worth it.

Forty-five minutes later, after they got the boys and dropped them off with Zoé, a convoy of wagons lined up in front of Abby's. Fletcher let him know they were ready.

Harrison helped Abby into his buggy. When they pulled out, Harrison rode alongside Fletcher's lead wagon so Abby would not have to endure the trail dust the other wagons kicked up.

Conversation flowed freely. They arrived at the train station just minutes before the stack of smoke from the train's engine could be seen coming around the bend.

"I can hardly wait to see the chairs." She clapped. "Oh, no." Her joy quickly evaporated and she stopped clapping.

"What?" He looked around for the problem but saw none.

"We forgot to bring something to cover the furniture so it doesn't get dusty."

"No, we didn't." Harrison smiled. "When I asked Fletcher if he could help us, I also asked if he would have the men gather blankets and ropes to cover the pieces."

She placed her hand against her cheek and sighed. "Thank you, Harrison. You think of everything." She rewarded him with one of her beautiful smiles.

"I try." His lips curled.

After he and Abby inspected the shipment to make sure it was correct, and the chairs were being transferred to the wagons, Abby excused herself and headed into town. He hated her going unescorted, but she insisted she would be fine, and asked him if he would supervise the men.

Later on, when everything was loaded, Abby, along with three other young women, arrived carrying baskets. Several of the men eyed the females with appreciative glances. Within seconds, the younger single men rushed over to the ladies and took their burdens from them.

Before one of them could help Abby, Harrison beat them to it and relieved Abby of her heavy basket. "What do we have here?"

"Drinks. After that long ride here and with working in this here heat, I thought the men might want something to drink. I got them something to eat, too."

"How thoughtful of you to do that, Abby. Thank you."

She brushed away his compliment, and her gaze trailed to where the men were gathered. "It looks like they're enjoying the ham and cheese sandwiches. Shall we join them?"

"Yes, ma'am." He offered her his free arm. Just thinking about how thoughtful and sweet she was made him proud to know her and to have her for a business partner. Too bad their relationship had no hope of developing into something more. Like something more personal and permanent. If only there was a way to make it work. But once again, Harrison had to face the ugly truth and reality that it wouldn't.

Chapter Twelve

Shortly after sunrise the next morning, Abby rummaged through her dresses before picking out a pale peach one with white flowers and white leaves on it. Once she readied herself for the day, she skipped down the stairs and scurried into the large theater. Up the main aisle she strolled, running her hands over the plush fabric of one of the chairs as she did.

She made her way to the center of the stage and skimmed her gaze over the perfectly lined rows of royal blue chairs, and imagined herself performing in front of a packed house. Lines she'd memorized while performing Elizabeth Bennett from a theatrical version of Jane Austen's *Pride and Prejudice* passed through her lips with meaningful emotion. "'I do. I do like him. I love him. Indeed, he has no improper pride. He is perfectly amiable.'"

Harrison's face slipped into the front portal of her mind.

"Abby!" Zoé's frantic voice popped that image.

Zoé ran toward her, crying.

Abby darted off the stage and met her halfway down the aisle. "What's wrong?" Abby scanned her face.

"You must come quickly." Sobs tore from Zoé, and she grabbed Abby's hand and yanked her toward the door. Abby had to hurry to keep up with Zoé, lest she lose her footing.

"What is going on, Zoé?"

Zoé didn't answer and panic jumped into Abby's throat. Had something happened to one of Zoé's sisters? She had no idea, but she'd never seen Zoé this upset before, so she knew it had to be something dreadful.

When they entered the hall, Harrison and the town's sheriff stood in the main entrance room talking.

What was the sheriff doing here? A million questions dashed through Abby's mind, and she broke free from Zoé's grasp and rushed to them. "What's going on here?"

Harrison's attention brushed toward her, turned back to the sheriff, and then flew back to her. He strode over to her. "Have you seen Graham and Josiah?"

"Josiah and Graham? No. Why?" She looked at Zoé. Her face was blotchy, and tears pooled into her fear-filled eyes.

"We were hoping they came here."

"Came here? What's going on? Why would you think they would be here?" She fluttered a glance at the grandfather clock. It was too early in the morning for Zoé to have them as they weren't supposed to be here until eight o'clock, and it was only seven-fifteen now.

"When I woke up this morning, the boys were gone. We thought maybe they tried to find their way here." Harrison raked his hand through his disheveled hair and ran it across the back of his neck. Whisker stubbles dotted his normally shaved chin.

Suddenly it struck her what he'd just said. Josiah and Graham were missing. Fear threatened to rob her of her senses, but one look at the concern on Harrison's face and she knew she needed to be strong for him. "We need to pray." As soon as she said it, she remembered Harrison didn't pray, but she did.

Sheriff Long, Colette and Veronique joined them. They bowed their heads.

"God, the twins' disappearance is no surprise to You. You know exactly where they are. We're asking You to guide us to them. In the meantime, place a hedge of protection around them and keep them safe. Amen." Abby raised her head and her focus zoned in on the sheriff. "Sheriff Long, do you know anyone here who has a hunting dog?"

"I was thinking the same thing and was just about to say that Levi Huntley has a mutt that can hunt down just about anything or anyone. I'll run and fetch him and anyone else I can gather to search for the boys." Sheriff faced Harrison. "I think it's best if we start our search from up at your place."

"My place is…" Harrison started to tell the sheriff where he lived, but Sheriff Long held up his hand, saying he already knew where he lived because he made it his business to know the whereabouts of not only the citizens of Hot Mineral Springs, but newcomers and strangers, as well. "I'll meet you up there." With those words he strode toward the door, boots clomping hard and steady.

Abby turned her eyes up at Harrison. "I'm going with you."

"Thank you." He pulled her hand into his and held onto it.

Abby knew he meant nothing by it and that he just needed another human's comforting touch.

Keeping her hand in his, she turned to the Denis sisters. "Zoé, think of all the places you've taken the boys and then go look in those places to see if they're there. Colette, you go with her. And Veronique, could you throw together something for the men to eat and drink when we return?"

Veronique nodded and all three sisters left.

Hand in hand, Abby and Harrison hurried into the buggy and headed out of town. "When we get to the house, we'll need something of Josiah and Graham's. Something the dog can sniff to get their scent."

He nodded, saying nothing.

As they made their way up the winding road canopied by trees, Abby and Harrison scanned the trees.

Minutes later, Harrison's house came into view.

Staimes paced up one end of the deck and back down to the other. The instant he spotted them, he stopped pacing and ran down the steps to where they were just pulling up in front.

"Did you find them?" Staimes asked.

"No. I was hoping they were here." Defeat beat through Harrison's voice.

Abby could tell he was trying to be strong, but the disappearance of his sons was weighing heavily on him. It showed in his eyes and in the wrinkles around them.

She had to keep pressing down her own fears, lest

they overwhelm her sanity and ability to help him. She laid her hand on his arm, doing her best to be strong and confident. Neither of which she felt at the moment. "We'll find them. They've got to be around here somewhere."

Harrison clutched her hand and gave it a light squeeze. "I hope so."

By the time they got inside and retrieved an item that belonged to each boy, Sheriff Long and twenty-three men pulled into the yard. Without a dog.

Abby's heart sank. "Where's the dog?"

"Levi wasn't home. Mrs. Huntley said Levi had gone hunting and wouldn't be back until later this evening. I asked her to tell him when he got home, if we hadn't sent word to her yet that the boys had been found, to have him come here. We need to make sure someone stays here in case the boys show up. I think it should be you and Miss Abby," Sheriff Long told Harrison.

"No. I'm going with you. I can't just sit here while my boys are lost out there somewhere."

"I'll stay," Abby said, even though she really wanted to go with Harrison, to be there for him if he needed her.

Harrison faced her. "Thank you, Abby. I'd appreciate that."

The men gathered around and quickly discussed plans. Three shots were to be fired in a row if anyone found Josiah and Graham. Two shots if anyone spotted any signs of them.

In sets of twos, they all headed out in different directions. Some on horseback, others on foot.

Abby and Staimes stayed behind.

Unable to sit idly by and do nothing, Abby searched

every inch of the house, even though Staimes assured her they'd already done that at least twice.

Fifteen minutes later, at the sound of wagons coming up the road, Abby rushed down the stairs and flew out the door.

Fletcher and his men rode up on their mounts and wagons. Fletcher hopped down from the wagon and hurried over to her. "We just heard. How's Harrison holding up?" Being a father himself, she figured Fletcher had to know what Harrison was going through.

She herself could only imagine what Harrison must be feeling. Her own mind was tormented with negative what-ifs. But each time those thoughts came, she gave her fears and concerns over to the Lord. "He's taking it hard. He's trying to be strong, but I can tell this is really scaring him."

"If that was Julie out there, I'd be petrified."

She could only nod.

"Is there anything we can do?"

"The men have gone out to look for them."

"How long ago?"

"Fifteen minutes or so ago."

He raised his hat and ran the sleeve of his shirt over his forehead that wasn't even wet.

"I didn't even ask Harrison what happened. But I'm wondering if the boys were anxious to come to my place and perhaps headed down that way." The thought of the Colorado River dividing their places sent chills up and down Abby's spine. What if Josiah and Graham— No! She wouldn't even allow herself to think that way. She couldn't. She loved those boys as if they were her own. They had to come back, and they had to come back alive.

* * *

Harrison and Sheriff Long looked for any signs that the boys had been here, but there were none. Graham and Josiah must have slipped out of the house sometime before it rained during the night.

The thought of them out there all alone, in the dark, scared and cold, loaded his stomach with a boulder-size pit of helplessness and fear. His heart ached with a pain he'd only known twice before—once after he discovered his wife had left, and the other the day he had found out she had died. He hoped God had heard Abby's prayer because He certainly hadn't heard any of Harrison's over the years.

They beat back the pine-tree branches as they trekked their way through the thick woods. More than an hour had passed and there was still no sign of his sons.

Where could they have gone? One place kept coming to his mind.

"Sheriff." Harrison stopped. "I can't shake this feeling that my boys were headed to Abby's. Even though I already checked there, I think we should head that way."

The sheriff nodded. "Let's head that way, then."

They started walking toward Abby's place.

His mind trailed back to the day before and when they had gotten back from the train station. He and his sons had had dinner with Abby. Afterward, the four of them sat on the floor and built a cabin out of home-made wooden blocks. When they got tired of that, Abby picked out a children's book and read to them. He remembered her animated voice and the way she made the characters come to life, the excitement on his sons' faces as they listened with such intent, how they cried most of the way home, and how they said they loved Abby and wished she was their mother.

It was time for him to put his fears of remarrying aside. Instead of looking for another nanny, he needed to find a wife. Someone who would be a good mother to his children. Abby's face popped into his mind. As much as he hated to do it, he had to erase that image.

"Over here. I think I found something." Sheriff Long's voice broke through Harrison's thoughts.

Pine needles crunched under Harrison's feet as he made his way to the sheriff, standing at the rocky edge of the Colorado River. There, near the riverbank, lay one of his son's carved horses. Harrison thought he might be sick. He swallowed several times, fighting the sickening image that threatened to overtake him.

White caps peaked as the rushing water barreled into the boulders poking out from the deep riverbed. Harrison closed his eyes, imagining the worst. The sound of rushing water filled the eerie silence.

A large hand cupped his shoulder, and his gaze slid that way.

"Don't go imagining the worst, Harrison. I don't see any sign to indicate they went into the water."

Harrison hoped, and even almost prayed, that the man was right.

Sheriff Long looked around and then pointed toward a large boulder. "There's something over there." He and Harrison hurried toward the giant rock, the moisture from the tall grasses saturating the bottoms of their pant legs as they did.

His sons' socks and shoes lay on the rocky ground

in a heap. Faster than the river water rolling over the rocks below the surface, dread tumbled over and over Harrison until he felt he would drown under the weight of his great loss. He dropped to his knees, clutched the items to his chest and laid his head back. Not caring that he wasn't alone, he cried out, "Why, God, why? Do You hate me that much? What about Abby? She prayed that my sons would be safe. Apparently, You don't answer her prayers, either. What kind of a God are You, anyway?"

"A loving One," Sheriff Long answered.

Harrison's eyes bolted open, and he glared at the tall middle-aged man with the black burly mustache. "How can you say that? My boys are gone."

"You don't know that."

Harrison shot him a look that said the man must be nuts. All he had to do was look at the evidence. His sons' shoes and socks were found near the edge of the riverbank, and his children were nowhere in sight. It didn't take much to figure out what had happened.

A gunshot sliced through the air.

Harrison bolted to his feet, waiting, listening for another.

A second shot sounded.

He held his breath, waiting for a third.

When it came, no joy accompanied it as he didn't know if his boys had been found safely or not.

"It sounded like it came from that direction." Sheriff Long pointed across and downriver, toward the direction of Abby's place. "There's a bridge down that way. We can cross over there."

Harrison rushed forward behind the man, stumbling

and hurrying with barely any direction to his steps. They came to a rough-hewn beam draped across the width of the river, one that didn't look nearly strong enough to hold their weight. "This is a bridge?" Harrison hiked a brow in the sheriff's direction.

"Don't let its looks fool you. This here bridge is a lot stronger than it looks."

It had to be. Judging by its decrepit appearance, that thing couldn't even hold something as light as a hummingbird.

Still, Harrison needed to trust that the sheriff knew what he was doing.

One at a time, they carefully made their way across it.

Three more gunshots pierced the air. Only this time they were louder. They were closer to his boys. Harrison's blood pounded in his ears.

Rocks crunched under their feet as they raced through the uneven ground, shoving branches of various bushes aside.

A large bull snake slid out from under the brush right in front of him, tripping him and crashing his knee against a rock. The snake slithered away.

Ignoring the intense pain, Harrison pushed himself up, brushed the rocks and mud from off his knee and with a strong limp, forced himself to move forward so he could catch up with the sheriff. Pain darted through his leg like a million pins and needles as he stepped over felled logs lying across the narrow pathway. They came upon a small clearing where a group of men were gathered into a circle.

Harrison couldn't see his sons.

One of the young men looked their way and broke through the small group and sprinted over to them. "We found them."

"Are they—?" Harrison couldn't say the word that knifed into his head as he hurried alongside the young teenage boy whose face was covered with freckles.

Harrison was panting now, either from fright or the exertion. He didn't know which or if it was from both.

"They're all right except for a few bumps and bruises and complaining that they want their daddy and Miss Abby."

Abby?

Relief poured through him. Thank goodness for Abby and her prayers. God had answered them. Harrison owed God an apology, but first, he had to see for himself.

The crowd parted to let him through.

"Daddy!" Graham and Josiah both shouted. They pushed off the felled log they were sitting on and barreled into him, throwing their arms around his legs, and holding on to him so tightly, he couldn't get them loose to pick them up. His knee throbbed as Josiah pressed his body against it, but he didn't care. His sons were safe. That was all that mattered.

After moments of frantic joy, Harrison was finally able to convince them to let go of his leg so he could pick them up and hold them. They buried their faces in his shoulder, leaving Harrison no way to wipe away the tears that streamed down his cheeks. Never before had he been so frightened or so relieved as he was now.

Minutes passed before the boys finally raised their heads. Harrison looked at each one. "Why did you boys run away? You nearly scared me to death. You know how much I love you, don't you?"

Graham ran his tiny hands over Harrison's wet cheeks, wiping away the tears. "Don't cry, Daddy. We know you love us. We didn't run 'way. We only wanted to see Miss Abby."

"Well, next time you want to see her, you come and ask Daddy first, all right? Promise me you'll never do this again."

"We promise." Josiah spoke for the both of them.

His attention shifted from his sons to the men around them and ended with Fletcher. "How can I ever thank you all enough for finding my boys?"

"We didn't find them. Fletcher did," the same boy who'd met him when he arrived said.

Harrison looked right at Fletcher, remorse for his earlier thoughts about the man tumbling through him. "Thank you, Fletcher. I owe you."

A deep, rumbling sadness went through the man's dark eyes even as he looked at the three of them huddled together. "No need to thank me. And you don't owe me a thing. I'm just glad we found them." He nodded again, sniffed and let out a long breath.

In that moment, Harrison remembered hearing about Fletcher's sons and how they had drowned. That poor man. This had to be hard on him, had to be resurrecting old memories. Harrison's heart went out to Fletcher. He couldn't imagine how he would feel if his outcome had been equally as bad as Fletcher's had been.

A fresh wave of gratitude flowed over Harrison. He wanted to shake hands with Fletcher, with all of them, but he wasn't ready to let go of his sons just yet. "Where did you find them, anyway?"

"They were sleeping way back inside that bush." Fletcher pointed to a large shrub nestled against a boulder.

"In the bush?" Harrison couldn't quite imagine that.

"We did what Mrs. Wainee did, Daddy."

His gaze swung to his son. "Mrs. Wainee?" Who and what was Josiah talking about?

"Uh-huh. You wouldn't let us stay at Abby's, so we sneaked out and followed the river to her house like Mrs. Wainee did. Only we got lost and sleepy. Miss Abby told us when Mrs. Wainee got lost, she followed the river, and that when it got dark, she found a bush near a rock to hide in."

It finally dawned on him what Josiah was talking about. Abby's sister-in-law Rainee. She'd told that story to him days before. His sons had been busy playing with their toys on the floor across the room. He didn't even know they'd been listening. How could someone so young remember those things?

"Well, Mrs. Rainee is an adult. Not a child. Children do not leave their homes or anywhere else without an adult. Do you understand that?"

His twins nodded their heads, their eyes wide with solemn understanding.

With a breath of relief, Harrison turned his attention onto the men. "Gentlemen, it's been a long morning. Why don't we head back down to Miss Bowen's? She had her cook fix up something for everyone to eat."

"Sounds good. I'm starving," Sheriff Long said.

"Me, too," Josiah added, and of course, Graham mimicked him.

As soon as they arrived at the mansion, Abby rode up in Harrison's buggy. The buggy rolled to a stop, and Abby hopped out, gathered her skirt and ran toward them.

Abby's heart leaped with joy at the sight of the twins, and she barely managed to keep herself from hugging all three of them. "Josiah! Graham! I'm so glad you're okay."

Harrison lowered them to the ground, and she dropped to her knees and gathered them into her arms, hugging them and smothering their cheeks with kisses while tears trickled down her face.

Graham looked at her with sad eyes. "Why you crying, Miss Abby?" His little fingers softly and tenderly brushed the moisture from her cheeks. That sweet gesture sent even more tears cascading from her eyes.

"Because I was so worried about you two. Where were you boys? Why did you run away?"

Josiah stepped from her embrace, planted his tiny hands on his waist and huffed. "We didn't run 'way. We wanted to see *you*."

His sweet words melted her aching heart even through the guilt over the fact that they'd been put in jeopardy trying to get to her. She pulled them back into her arms, closed her eyes and relished the feel of their tiny bodies as she held them close to her. This was, without a doubt, what love felt like.

Seconds later, her gaze slid upward to Harrison.

He smiled down at her warmly. Affectionately, even.

"I'm sorry," she mouthed.

But he just shook his head as his smile widened and he let out a long sigh, which almost brought tears to her eyes.

What was she going to do?

In that instant, she realized that she had not only completely lost her heart to Harrison's sons, but to him, as well.

She tore her gaze away from Harrison, for fear the love she had for him would show in her eyes. And she couldn't have that. His words about wanting more children scribbled through her mind as they had so many times since he'd said them. Each time they had the same effect on her, creating an aching, longing hole in her heart that could never be satisfied.

Later that evening, after things had settled down at the mansion, and everyone, including Fletcher and his men had gone home, Harrison asked Abby to take a walk with him. Although she didn't trust herself to spend time alone with him for fear her heart would expose her true feelings, she could see that whatever it was he wanted to talk to her about was important, so she reluctantly agreed.

At twilight, they walked in silence through the now weed-free garden. Roses of various colors and sizes flooded the light breeze with their luscious scents. A strand of her blond hair drifted across her cheek, and she curled it behind her ear.

Harrison led her to the bench he'd repaired. They sat down and she laid her hands in her lap, waiting for him to say what was on his mind.

"Abby."

She looked up at him, careful to not let her eyes find his. "Yes."

"I couldn't wait to tell you thank you."

This time her eyes did find his. "For what?"

"For praying for my boys this morning."

She blinked back her shock. From what she'd learned, the man didn't believe in prayer. Perhaps this was a start. She sure hoped so, anyway. "You're welcome."

"I must admit when you wanted to pray, I wanted to scream at you. To ask why bother. When I saw their socks and shoes by the river, I wanted to shake my fist at God, and I did, too. I couldn't understand why He hated me so much that He would let my sons drown." His hand found hers, and its gentle warmth made its way into her heart, caressing it tenderly.

She wanted to yank her hand away, but just for this moment, and this moment only, she wouldn't. She would allow herself to enjoy the connection to love that she longed for in that secret place of her soul. The one she kept carefully barred. "God doesn't hate you, Harrison. He loves you." *And so do I,* she wanted to say, but those words remained holed up inside her.

"No. He loves *you*. It was *your* prayers He answered. He's never answered any of my prayers. That's why I quit praying years ago. But I don't want to talk about that. I just wanted to tell you how much I appreciate you being there for me this morning. And to thank you for the strength you covered me with when I felt as weak and as helpless as a newborn."

Abby could see just how hard that was for him to admit. "I'm glad I was here for you." She gave his hand a squeeze before she reluctantly released it. She had no choice but to let it go; the connection to him was too strong for her, and right now she was the weak one, for a much different reason, though.

Letting his gaze go, she stared out into the garden. Her mind wanted to take a turn and dream about him holding her and kissing her and telling her he loved her. That having more children didn't matter to him. That his boys were enough. That *she* was enough.

She closed her eyes to blot out that silly dream, but the dream didn't leave. It took a turn of its own. If only her dreams could come true. Oh, how she hated those if-onlys.

Masculine fingers, strong yet gentle, cupped her chin, tugging it upward.

Soft warm lips covered hers, touching her with a sweetness she'd never known before.

Oh, if only this were real and not just a dream.

Something stronger than the light breeze brushed against her lips.

Words, soft, and barely audible reached her ears. "Oh, Abby. Sweet, adorable Abby."

Abby froze.

Afraid to open her eyes.

This wasn't a dream.

Harrison had kissed her. And she had returned his kiss.

Great stars, what had she done?

Powerless to fight against the strong feelings she had for him, she allowed him to pull her into his arms, and to continue kissing her. When the moment ended, neither spoke. Instead, she sat with her head nestled against his chest, listening to his heart beating a soothing rhythm, knowing this could never happen again.

Time drifted lazily by, and she let it, until finally she asked in a voice quiet and soft so as not to shatter the moment. "Where did you find Josiah and Graham?"

Harrison shifted, and Abby forced herself to leave the comfort of his embrace. "Fletcher found them sleeping between a boulder and a bush." He chuckled softly. "Josiah said he got that idea from you."

"From me?"

"Yes. Who would have thought the boys were even listening the other night when you were talking about what your sister-in-law Rainee did?"

"What Rainee did?" She frowned.

"Yes. You know when she ran away and hid between a bush and a rock."

Blood drained from Abby's face as her eyes went wide.

The boys taking off in the middle of the night was all her fault. They could have died because of her. No wonder she couldn't bear children. God knew she'd make a terrible mother.

Tears stung the back of her eyes.

She shot off the bench and ran as fast as her legs would carry her toward the river.

"Abby! Wait! Where are you going?"

She pushed herself harder, willed herself to run faster. How could she ever face Harrison again?

A band of steel encased her arm, forcing her to stop, and her strength was no match for his. "Let me go." She tried to yank free, but Harrison held her firmly, yet without hurting her.

"What's wrong?" Panic edged his voice, but she couldn't comfort him right now. She had to get away. To flee the demons chasing her.

"Abby, stop. Look at me." With one arm holding her in place, his other cupped her chin and tugged on it until she had no choice but to look at him. "Abby, please talk to me. Tell me what's wrong? Was it the kiss?"

She shook her head vehemently. "No. No. It wasn't that. Although that can never happen again."

He looked shocked at the intensity with which she said it, but instead of voicing that, he simply asked, "What is it, then?"

Her shoulders shook with the pain spinning in her spirit, and no longer able to hold back the flood of tears, she let them loose.

"Abby." Harrison took her and buried her head into his chest and kissed the top of her head. "What is wrong? Please, tell me."

"It's all my fault," she said through hiccupping sobs.

"What's all your fault?"

"That Josiah and Graham went missing. They could have died because of me."

"No. Abby, this wasn't your fault. You couldn't have known."

Oh, if only that were true, but it wasn't. "Yes, it is. I'm always planting ideas in their heads. Like the fishing and the mud."

"How would you know they were listening?"

"I didn't. But still…"

Harrison dipped back and pulled her chin up until she was looking at him. "Abby, listen to me. This isn't your fault. If I were a better father, none of this would have happened."

"No! Don't even say that. You're a wonderful father." How dare he blame himself for something that was entirely her own fault?

"No. I'm not. I'm so lost on this whole father issue. I shouldn't have left them alone. I should have slept in their room with them. I'm obviously doing something wrong because my sons keep running off every nanny I hire."

"That's not true. Zoé and I love them."

His eyes pleaded with her to be honest. "You do?"

"Yes. Who wouldn't? They're adorable, and you're blessed to have them. Not everybody gets to be a parent." With those words, she removed herself from his arms and headed back toward the house, grateful Harrison didn't ask her what she meant. She never wanted him to know about her barrenness. Never wanted to see the look of disgust on his handsome face. With a heavy sigh to bury her sorrow, she realized she would never be a suitable mother—even if she could actually have children. That hurt more than anything else she'd ever endured. At that moment, the dream she'd quietly allowed to grow in her heart since Harrison's arrival finally died. And the pain of that was more than she felt she could ever handle or endure. But endure it she must.

Chapter Thirteen

Harrison lay on the floor in his sons' bedroom, and in his mind he relived his kiss with Abby. Something he now realized should have never taken place. Most of the night, he tossed and turned, trying to figure out a way to make things work between them, but no rational solution came to him. He even made a mental list of why it wouldn't work.

She lived here, he lived in Boston.

Her dream was to own her own dinner theater, something she was extremely passionate about.

His was to right the wrongs his father had done, something he couldn't do from here.

Further, his only goals before arriving here were to restore his family's good name and to claim his sons' inheritance. He couldn't give those up, could he?

No matter how many angles he examined the problem from, he saw no way to make their worlds mesh. Besides, he couldn't subject someone as sweet and innocent as Abby to the people of his society. While she may be able to carry her own here, those people were ruthless. Especially the Bostonian women. So taking her back there was not an option, either.

After hours of agonizing, the verdict was clear—it was best to put an end to any notions Abby may have gotten from his carelessness the last evening.

That decided, he finally got up cleaned and got dressed. Just before sunrise, he got the boys ready and headed down to Abby's, dreading the conversation that he knew must take place.

When he pulled the buggy in front of Abby's mansion, Josiah hollered, "Miss Abby, Miss Abby!" His son leaped up and started to step out of the buggy while it was still moving.

Harrison barely managed to grab the back of Josiah's collar and settle him back onto the buggy's seat. A quick glance over at Abby sitting in her usual early morning spot at the small table on her front porch, sipping her tea and watching them, and he turned his attention back to Josiah. "What did I tell you about leaving your seat before the buggy is stopped, Josiah?"

"To wait till the horsey stopped and till you come and help us down."

"That's right. And why do we do that?"

"'Cause we could get hurt if we don't."

"That's right. Very good, son." He kissed the top of Josiah's head, and then Graham's so as not to leave him out. Thankfulness that he could still do something so simple with them breezed through him. He got out to help them down.

The second their feet hit the ground, the twins darted up the walkway.

Abby met them halfway, dropped to a squat and gathered them into her arms, a place he wished he himself could be. He gave himself a quick reprimand about tormenting himself with such thoughts.

"Good morning, boys. Morning, Harrison," she said, never once looking up at him.

That wasn't good. He needed to have that talk with her as soon as possible.

"Did you boys sleep well?"

Both bobbed their heads.

"I'm so glad. Now, how about some cookies and milk? I know it's not your typical breakfast food, but if it's all right with your father, maybe he'll let you have them just this once." Her uncertain gaze slid up to his as did his sons' eagerly expectant ones.

As soon as he nodded his assent, she quickly looked away, stood and brushed herself off. Hand in hand the three of them made their way up the steps and to the table. They looked so right together, like they were family, and yet Harrison knew he had no right even thinking that way.

She seated his sons at the table and placed a glass of milk and a plate with three cookies on each one in front of them. "Let's pray and then you can eat."

"Why do you pway, Miss Abby?" Graham asked.

She sent a quick glance Harrison's way, searching for his approval to answer Graham's question. Normally he wouldn't allow someone to disillusion his children with such nonsense as prayer, but Abby strongly believed in it. And even though prayer had never done a thing for him, hers had, so he found he wanted to hear her answer to that himself. With a quick close of the eyes and a nod, he once again gave her his consent.

She offered him a half smile before turning her attention back to his sons. "Well, I pray because it makes God happy when I talk to Him. When I thank Him for the things He does for me. And, whenever I need help, I ask God for it, and He helps me. Just like your daddy helps you boys. Do you tell your daddy thank you when he helps you and takes care of you and gives you things?"

They smiled up at him and bobbed their heads. Love for his sons turned his insides to mush.

"Do you think that makes him happy when you do?"

Their eyes brightened and they nodded yes again.

"Well, it's the same way with God. God is the One who provided this food for us to enjoy, so we need to thank Him for it."

Josiah tilted his head, and his tiny brows gathered together. "But Who is God? And where is He?" He raised his hands, palm sides up, and looked all around. "I don't see Him anywhere."

"God is invisible. We can't see Him with our eyes. We can only see Him with our hearts, but He is always here with us. He's the One who made me and you."

"Did he make Daddy, too?" Graham asked.

"Yes. He made everyone and everything. He made the sky, the trees, the flowers, the animals and everything else you see."

"Even the cookies?" Josiah asked with wide-eyed wonder.

Abby smiled. "No. Not the cookies. Veronique made those. But…" She held up a finger. "God provided the ingredients she needed to make them."

"Well, we better pray and thank Him, then, huh?" Josiah rushed out.

Harrison's chuckle blended with Abby's.

Those smiling eyes of hers matched the curve of her lips and lifted his heart. "Yes, we should."

They bowed their heads, and Abby prayed a short prayer.

Breakfast was quickly devoured, and Harrison wiped the crumbs and milk mustache off his sons' mouths. "It's time to find Miss Zoé and go with her."

"Aww. We wanna stay with Miss Abby."

"I know you do. But, Miss Abby and I have things to discuss. So come with me." He stood and gazed down at Abby. "I'll be right back."

She responded with only a nod.

Unable to stand the strain of tension between them, he couldn't wait to drop his sons off with Zoé and get back here so he could clear the tense air between them.

Oh, good-night. Why did he ever kiss her?

Abby watched Harrison head into the house. Normally she and Harrison took the boys to Zoé together, but she needed these few minutes to pray and to gather her thoughts on what she would say when he returned.

For the first time in her life, she didn't know how to act around someone. Their shared kiss had changed everything, and not for the good, either. Harrison was right. They needed to talk. Otherwise, she didn't see how they could possibly continue to work together under this umbrella of tension.

She offered up a silent prayer, confident that God would take care of the situation between her and Harrison. A man she admired and loved enough to realize she had to let him go.

The object of her last thought stepped out of her front door, his face fraught with uncertainty. She understood exactly how he felt. She refilled his coffee cup while he sat down in the chair across from her.

Seconds ticked by until finally Harrison rested his clasped hands on the table. "Abby, about last night." Their gazes touched. "I owe you an apology for kissing you. We were both distraught over Graham and Josiah's disappearance and equally relieved when we found them. However, it was wrong of me to kiss you. There's no excuse for my action, and I do not intend to try and make one. Please accept my sincere apology."

Abby shrugged it off as if her heart wasn't breaking inside her. "It's like you said, I think we were both so relieved that we found the boys safe and unharmed that we just got caught up in the moment. So, there's nothing to forgive. We'll just forget the whole thing ever happened and go on from here." Even the amount of conviction she managed to put into her voice hurt. The whole situation was vastly unfair to all of them.

Still, she had to tamp her inward snort down. As if she could ever forget his kisses. Kisses that had her dreaming about them and the person behind them until the wee hours of the morning.

But that was simply one more thing she needed to give over to God—her need to stop dreaming about Harrison Kingsley.

Another quick prayer went upward before she turned her full attention onto Harrison. "Before I forget, I want to let you know that I promise to be more careful about the things I say in front of Josiah and Graham. None of this would have happened if it hadn't been for me and my big mouth."

"Abby, I told you it wasn't your fault."

Yes, he had, but she knew better than that. Not wanting to discuss the subject any further because it hurt too much knowing she had indeed been the one responsible for the boys' actions, she changed the subject. "I have news."

"Oh?"

"I got a letter yesterday from the acting company I had scheduled to come from Philadelphia. They won't be able to make it in time for the grand opening."

"What?"

She felt bad about the concern that fell across his face. "They double-booked with another festival for the same two weeks, but they assured me they would be here the month after."

Harrison frowned. "So what do we do until then? Delay the grand opening?"

"No."

"What, then?"

"I don't know."

"I'm confused. We have a grand opening coming up, and no actors. Why are you not worried?"

"Because I know that God will work it all out. Last night when I was praying, God impressed it on my heart to write my stepfather and ask him if he could send his understudies until my crew arrives."

He still looked utterly confused. "Do you think he will?"

The peace she felt probably didn't make sense to

anyone else, but she knew this feeling. God would no doubt handle the situation with amazing insights and perfection. "I'm sure he will. He has more than enough actors and actresses in his employ. In fact, I should have listened to him in the first place. He offered to send part of his company with me, but I assured him that the traveling crew I had gotten to know very well from back East would work out just fine."

Harrison nodded and splayed his fingers across his clean-shaved chin. "You really believe in prayer, don't you?"

"Yes. I do." And she didn't quite understand why he didn't. Why anyone didn't, for that matter. But it wasn't her place to judge him or anyone else. Her place was to pray and leave all of the other in God's hands.

"Did you ever have your prayers go unanswered?"

Childbearing, or rather the lack thereof, popped into her mind. So yes, she'd had her prayers go unanswered. But her faith in God and His wisdom was stronger than her feelings and her hurts. Therefore, her faith in Him remained in tact. "Yes. I have. But that doesn't stop me from trusting God. Or from praying."

"Why?"

"Why? Because I love Him, and I know He loves me, and that He has my best interest at heart." God's best interest in her not being able to bear children—she struggled with that one. "I will admit sometimes it's hard. And I don't always understand why things are the way they are or why He answers the way He does. His word says that His ways are higher than my ways and His thoughts are higher than my thoughts.

I've learned to accept that. Well, most of the time, anyway." She chuckled.

"Even so, if God never answered another one of my prayers, I would continue to pray, and continue to trust Him because my faith isn't based on answered prayers. It's based on a God who loved me so much He sent His Son to die on a cross for me so that I could communicate and have a relationship with Him. That's what prayer is really all about—communicating and having a relationship with a loving God."

"How can you call Him loving when He allows so many bad things to happen in this world? And most of the time it's to good people."

Abby noted the anger in Harrison's voice and wondered what had happened to make him so bitter against God. "I don't pretend to have all the answers, Harrison. I only know what I feel in my heart. In here." She pressed her hand to the center of her chest.

"How can you be so sure that God even exists? You can't see Him."

"Oh, but I do." At his frown, she continued. "I see Him everywhere. I see Him every time I look at the sun or the stars or the moon, and I am amazed at how they know just when to show up every day. Look around you. How do you explain the various species of birds and animals and plants and flowers that you see? And how every human being is unique and different?"

"That doesn't prove there is a God. I can see these things, but I can't see Him."

"Okay, let me ask you something. Do you see the air?"

"No."

"Then how do you know it exists?"

"Because I can feel it and breathe it."

"Exactly. It's the same way with God. I can't see Him, but I feel Him." The peace settled over and in her once again. She didn't work for it, it just was.

"That's different."

"Is it? Let me ask you something else. Do you *see* the love you have for your children?"

"No."

"But you *feel* it, right?"

"Yes."

"How do *you* know that love is real? After all, you can't see it with your eyes."

"I just do."

Abby pursed her lips and hiked a shoulder, letting her words sink in.

Harrison remained silent. She could tell he was thinking about what she'd said. Wanting to give him time to do just that, she closed her eyes and listened to the hummingbirds flitting by as she inhaled the pleasant menagerie of sweet scents. But mostly she prayed quietly that God would take her bumbling ways of explaining things and open Harrison's eyes to the truth of His existence and of His amazing love.

Harrison contemplated Abby's words. She really believed all the things she said to him. And she had a point. He couldn't see love, and yet he knew it existed. He felt it every time he held his sons in his arms or thought of them or looked at them. He felt it when he'd met his wife, and now with Abby. Perhaps there was something to what she said, after all. He'd ponder all of that later. Today, he had something he wanted to talk to her about. "Abby, I was wondering if you could help me with something."

"Sure. What's that?"

"Well, next month is Graham and Josiah's birthday. I'd like to do something special for them. I've never planned a party before, so I was wondering if you would be willing to help me. I hate to ask because I know you're busy, but I don't know anyone else that I would trust to help me with this."

She smiled and the whole sun-saturated area paled in comparison. "I'd love to help you. Did you have anything specific in mind?"

He shook his head. "No. Like I said, I've never done this before. The nannies always took care of these things."

"Well, let's see." She tugged her upper lip under her teeth, concentrating long and hard. Nothing came to mind, but she wouldn't give up. She'd think of something. She always did. "Let me think about it, and I'll get back to you, okay? Oh, and while we're on the subject of parties, the Fourth of July is coming up. I'm planning on having a small get-together here at my place around noon."

"Where do you find time to plan and to do all of this?"

"I make the time, and my mind is always coming up with some scheme or another. Gets me into trouble sometimes."

"Only sometimes?" he teased.

"Hey." She whacked him on the arm. "Yes. Only sometimes. Sometimes I come up with some pretty good ideas even if I say so myself. This place was one of them. Anyway, back to my plans for the Fourth. Closer to evening, I'm going to head to the town square. From what I've been told, they have a lot of festivities going on then. In fact, you might want to take Josiah and Graham. I've been told they have games and prizes and lots of things for the children to do. Then when the sky gets dark enough, they're supposed to have a fireworks display. Should be a lot of fun."

"It sounds like it. Would you mind if the boys and I tag along with you?"

"No. No. Not at all. I'd love to spend time with the boys and be able to watch them having fun." *What about me?* Harrison wanted to ask, but he knew he didn't have that right or that privilege.

The more time he spent with Abby, the harder it was becoming to keep his personal feelings in check. What a mess he'd gotten himself into…falling in love with a woman with whom he could never marry.

Chapter Fourteen

Despite the fact the sun bore down on them without mercy, Harrison was enjoying himself. Watching his boys dig for coins in the sawdust pile roped off at the town square and seeing their faces light up when they found them made his heart feel lighter than it had in years.

"They're sure having fun, aren't they?" Abby said from beside him. Having her next to his side felt right. More right than it had a right to.

The other day, when he and Abby had talked about the kiss they'd shared and how it should have never happened, he had thought he would easily be able to forget it and go on. But he hadn't been able to get the kiss out of his mind. After much contemplation, he decided that the kiss hadn't been a mistake, and he had lain awake most of the next few evenings trying to figure out a way to make things work between them. No solution came to him, so he finally decided to simply enjoy every minute with her and to make the best of the time he had left with her. He'd deal with his heartbreak later.

"They sure are. I love watching them. They give me so much joy and pleasure and happiness. And love. Everybody should have children of their own. Don't you think?"

When Abby didn't answer, Harrison gazed down at her. Gone was the smile that had been there just mere seconds ago. "Abby? What's wrong?"

She glanced up at him, and if he wasn't mistaken, he thought her eyes had a sheen to them. He wasn't quite sure, though, because the look of sadness had been so brief.

"Daddy, Daddy! Looky what we got." Graham and Josiah ran up to him, holding their palms upward.

Four shiny copper pennies rested in each hand. He was glad that he'd made a large contribution to the children's games. Fletcher had been in charge of the donations, and when he'd asked Harrison, he'd been only too glad to help out. Thinking of Fletcher, the man strode their way with Julie in tow.

"Miss Abby, look at what I got." Julie held her dainty hand open and three copper pennies glistened in the sunlight.

Abby peered down at the girl. "That's wonderful, Julie," was all she said. No sparkle, no usual joyful response, nothing.

Something was wrong, and he wanted to know what it was.

"We got pennies, too, Miss Abby." Josiah's not-to-be-left-out voice came through.

For one so young, his son was already a very competitive child. He wanted to win at everything he did. Harrison dreaded the day Josiah lost at something. But losing was part of life. Harrison should know. He'd lost plenty. And he would lose even more when he left. Then again, how can a person lose something they never had? Abby didn't belong to him. She didn't belong to anyone.

Not yet, anyway.

He cut a glance toward Fletcher. While the man had made no advances toward her, Harrison could see the admiration in Fletcher's eyes when he looked her way. And he had a feeling that Fletcher wished Abby belonged to him and Julie, too. The thought of Fletcher and Abby together drove a dagger of pain deep into Harrison's heart.

"You sure did."

"Miss Abby? Are you sad?" Graham, always the perceptive and caring one, asked.

She blinked, then as if it dawned on her, she gazed down at his son tenderly. "Who could be sad with you around? And you." She looked at Josiah. "And you." She glanced at Julie, who smiled shyly at Abby.

Josiah lunged toward Abby, threw his arms around her and hugged her. "I love you, Miss Abby."

"I do, too." Graham imitated his brother's actions.

Hearing his sons declare their love for Abby, Harrison knew he had to figure out a way to make things work between them. He had to. Not only for his sons' sake, but for his own, as well. Not once had he started out to do something that he didn't accomplish. Now was no different.

Abby's chest constricted with not only love, but with heartbreak. These sweet boys loved her. And she loved them, too. Oh, if only she could have children. Then perhaps she could win Harrison's heart and not only would these precious boys be hers, but Harrison would be, as well.

But it was all just wishful thinking. She sighed.

No man wanted a woman who couldn't bear children. David was right. Harrison's earlier words were proof of that fact. Just moments ago, he'd mentioned how everyone should have children of their own and how much joy and love and happiness they brought.

At one time she actually thought adoption might be the answer, but even that was out. She was not mother material. The boys' disappearance because of what she'd said had proven that.

Despite all of those things, she made up her mind she would enjoy Josiah and Graham while she could.

"Well, we need to go." Fletcher's attention slid between Harrison and his sons, then ended on Abby. "Hope you didn't mind, but Julie wanted to show you the coins she got."

"Of course I don't mind. I'm thrilled that she did. What are you going to spend your coins on, Julie?"

"A new dolly."

"Have you already picked one out?"

"Yes, ma'am." She nodded. "Over there at that booth." She pointed to a stand yards away from them that had three shelves of porcelain, cloth and crocheted dolls, each wearing bright clothes and hats. "Papa's taking me there now. Aren't you, Papa?"

"I sure am, precious." Fletcher looked at Abby. His gaze lingered for a moment, and Abby thought it strange. "Now, if you all will excuse us, we have a doll to purchase." Fletcher reached for his daughter's hand and they walked away.

Abby turned her attention onto Josiah and Graham. "What are you boys going to buy with your pennies?"

"Toys!" Graham blurted.

"Candy!" Josiah blurted louder.

"Would you like to get them now?" Harrison asked, standing across from Abby

"Uh-huh. Then we wanna race." Josiah bobbed his head.

Abby smiled as the boys led her and Harrison over to the candy and toy booths. Harrison was on one end, she on the other, and the boys were in between them. Like a real family. For today only, just this one last time, she would pretend they were.

After the boys bought a bag of jelly beans, which Harrison insisted they give to him to dole out, they each purchased a wooden sword. Abby cringed, wondering if they would hurt themselves with the toys that looked a bit too real for her peace of mind.

"Time for the sack races, folks." Mayor Prinker's voice rose above the crowd. With that loud, boisterous voice of his, he didn't need the speaking trumpet he held. "If you will make your way to the roped-off area, we can get started."

"Miss Abby, you wanna watch me and Siah race in one of those sacks?" Graham pointed to the pile of gunny sacks near the area where the races would take place.

"I would love to. Lead the way, boys."

Harrison fell into step alongside them. Near the starting line, Zoé came up to them and asked if she could take the boys and sign them up.

Harrison agreed, and off they went. He leaned close to Abby's ear and whispered, "How about you and I run this race together?" Abby ignored the tickling sensation his breath caused in her ear, and she had a feeling his words had a double meaning.

Her mind took a turn back to the past and to another sack race. One in which her sister, Leah, and Jake had run together and the two of them had ended up married.

Nothing like that would happen to her and Harrison. A gal could always dream, though, couldn't she? Wait, wasn't it her dreams that had gotten her heart into trouble in the first place? Even now the thing was yanking her back and forth. Only a short time ago she'd decided to stop the dead-end dreams. Was she that fickle minded that she was so willing to pick them up again?

She sighed. Yes, she was, at least where Harrison was concerned. For now, she was going to have some fun. She'd deal with the consequences of her choice later. "I can't think of anything else I'd rather do." She flashed him her brightest smile, and in return he offered her one, too, only his was escorted by a wink. A wink! One that turned her legs into the texture of warm molasses.

"Miss Abigail. Mr. Kingsley." Mayor Prinker disrupted Abby and Harrison's sweet moment. He and Harrison shook hands.

Abby wanted him to go away, to ignore him, but she wouldn't be rude no matter how much she disliked the man. She plastered on a smile. "Mayor Prinker." She refused to lie by saying how nice it was to see him again, so instead she went with the only other comment that entered her mind. "How are you enjoying this fine, sunshiny day?"

"Quite well. And you?"

"Very well. Thank you."

"Good, good. How is the Royal Grand Theater coming along?"

Did he really want to know or was he just making conversation? "Extremely well, sir. You must come and see it someday soon." Now why had she gone and invited him to do that? She wanted to snatch the words back and then slap herself silly for even voicing such an invitation.

"I already planned on it." He rubbed his meaty fingers over his bulbous red nose and chin. "In fact, the committee and I planned on paying you a visit Tuesday next. We will be there promptly at nine o'clock."

Abby's teeth ached from bearing down so hard on them. What nerve the man had. He hadn't even asked if they could come barging in on her; instead, he told her they were. Sure, she had invited him, but they had planned on coming before she even offered the invitation.

Harrison's hand nudged lightly against her skirt, and she gazed up at him. That same look of understanding passed between them. It meant hold your tongue and let me handle it. "We would love for you to come."

That's how he handled it? Speak for yourself, Abby thought.

"And now if you will excuse us, Mayor Prinker, Miss Abby and I are going to enter the sack race."

The mayor's bushy eyebrows pulled together. "You

and Miss Abby are going to race? Together? As in the same sack?"

Was the man deaf?

"Highly improper, Mr. Kingsley. You need to reconsider that. How would it look to the people of this town?"

Oh. Oh. Just let me at him, she pleaded silently with Harrison. She didn't care what the people of this town thought. Who were they to tell her who she could and couldn't run in a sack race with? Harrison's approval or not, she refused to remain quiet. "Excuse me, Mayor Prinker, but I see nothing wrong with it. Back home it is done all the time and no one thinks anything of it."

"That may be deemed acceptable back where you are from, but it isn't here. I must say, if you think that is acceptable, then I have to wonder if your theater will be as acceptable as you have tried to assure me it will be."

The veins in Abby's neck expanded. Her anger rose to the surface and she was about to spew out a piece of her mind in the mayor's direction, when again, Harrison's hand nudged her skirt. He just better be glad she respected him enough to refrain from letting the mayor have it because right now she didn't care what the pompous windbag thought of her. But she didn't want him to think ill of Harrison, so she mentally pulled all the willpower she could muster to collect herself together.

"Mr. Prinker, if you feel this is not acceptable, then we will respect that and forgo running the sack race."

What! Abby yanked her gaze toward Harrison. Whose side was he on, anyway?

Harrison again sent her that silent, knowing look to let him handle things. She was growing to resent that look. It meant she would once again refrain from lashing out, and she really wanted to let the pudgy little crook have it.

"Miss Abby and I are certain that once you see the Royal Grand Theater your mind will be at ease. We know how important it is to you and the committee to maintain this fine town's reputation and image, and we respect that."

We do? What was Harrison doing? By now she was starting to doubt his ability to settle this matter at all. His handling of it was scratching down her last nerve.

"When you arrive next Tuesday, if there is anything you see that you do not agree with, we will be more than happy to deal with it."

What! What was Harrison saying? Had he gone daft or something? She wasn't going to change anything for those stuffy, old grouches.

Mr. Prinker's brows settled back into place. He grabbed the lapels of his dark gray suit jacket and puffed out his already inflated chest. "Very well, Mr. Kingsley." He smiled.

The man had actually smiled. Abby couldn't believe it, couldn't believe this whole nightmarish scene, actually.

"We will see you on Tuesday next, then." Mr. Prinker shook Harrison's hand and tipped his hat at her.

She wanted to yank his *chapeau* from his meaty hand and whack him with it. Harrison might be calm about this whole thing, but she wasn't. Her insides were stewing. And not just at the mayor but at Harrison, too.

When Mayor Prinker was out of hearing distance, Abby faced Harrison and shot him her worst and fiercest glare. "What were you thinking?" she ground out, trying hard to keep her voice down, but not her anger and frustration. "How dare you! I'm not changing anything for that man."

Harrison glanced over her head to where the boys were standing in line with Zoé. He grabbed her hand and led her several yards away from the crowd. "Calm down, Abby. I've dealt with his kind before. You have to flatter them or they can make your life miserable. Don't you see the man can shut you down? Then all the money and hard work you have put into the place will be for nothing. I don't want that to happen. I want to see your business succeed, and I'm going to do everything in my power to see that it does, even if it means doing something as humbling as sweet-talking the mayor."

Talk about humbling. The man was doing this for her. And as usual, he was being rational while she was operating out of her emotions. Right then, her anger went from blazing logs to a pile of smoldering ashes. She drew in a long breath and was about to partake of a huge slice of humble pie. "You're right. Thank you, Harrison. And thank you for caring about my business. However—" she held up a finger "—I'm still not changing anything for that man."

"You won't have to. We'll just let him think we're willing to. That's all the man wants. He wants to be in control. And if he thinks he is, he'll act as if it was his idea to approve things."

"But what if he doesn't?"

"He'll love it. Trust me."

The following Tuesday, July eleventh, Harrison waited in Abby's parlor with her. Over the past week, they had worked night and day preparing the place for the town committee's arrival.

Despite how tired they were, Abby managed to look refreshed. Instead of the casual attire the little beauty normally wore around the mansion, today she had on an off-white bustle gown sprinkled with forest-green, long-stemmed roses with a ring of forest-green garden flowers six inches from the bottom of her skirt. Dainty red roses and lace lined the modest neckline, the short puffy sleeves and the gathered material at her side. Even her hat matched.

Harrison understood why she had dressed so elegantly. Mayor Prinker and the committee members would be arriving any minute. Harrison couldn't wait to see their faces when they saw just how elegant the theater, dining area and really the whole house actually was. The extra men Fletcher had hired were making great progress. In fact, things were progressing more quickly than Harrison had imagined. To be honest, there were still some kinks that needed to be worked out, but if things kept going the way they were, the grand opening would be much sooner than scheduled.

"The fireworks display was beautiful, don't you think? There's nothing more lovely than seeing those glittering waterfalls and sparkling colored lights exploding against the pitch darkness."

Oh, but there was something more beautiful. And she was sitting next to him.

Abby turned toward him until her knees were almost touching his. "They probably weren't that great to you considering you come from the big city. The fireworks are probably much grander there, I imagine."

"They are. But I enjoyed the Hot Mineral Springs display much better. And it had nothing to do with the fireworks."

"Oh?" Her dainty brows met in the middle of her pretty face. "What do you mean?"

"*Mademoiselle,* I am sorry to interrupt you." Colette breezed into the room. "Mayor Prinker and the town committee members are here to see you. I saw them into the formal parlor as you instructed me to."

"Wonderful. Thank you, Colette." She stood and quickly ran her hands down the front of her dress, tucked a blond curl that had escaped from her chignon back into place and straightened her hat.

"You look fine, Abby. No, make that beautiful."

Abby's gaze shot to his. "Beau-beautiful? Th-thank you," she stuttered while blinking those smiling eyes of hers. Quick as a flash, she squared her shoulders and scurried toward the door.

Harrison caught up with her, wishing they wouldn't have been disrupted. He wanted to tell her how much he'd been enjoying his time with her and how special it had been. He really wanted to tell her how he felt about her, but until he knew how she felt about him, he wouldn't. Besides, now wasn't the right time for that discussion. There would be time later to tell her. Right now, they needed to make a good impression on the mayor.

"Would you please welcome them, Harrison? My mother taught me to welcome people into my home, but I would feel so phony welcoming those people who have made my life miserable."

"Don't you worry your pretty little head about it.

I'll take care of it. You just relax and smile. Can you do that?"

"Like this?" She smiled cheekily at him.

"No, Abby. A genuine smile."

"I know. I know. I was just being silly."

They stepped into the expansive parlor. The men stood.

"Good morning, gentlemen. So glad you could come. Would you care for something to drink before we show you around?"

"No, thank you, Mr. Kingsley. We have a meeting to attend in twenty minutes, so we would just like you to take us on a tour. That is, if you wouldn't mind."

Harrison was surprised the mayor had added the last part. His sweet-talking had softened the man.

"Good morning, Miss Bowen. I hope you are well." Mayor Prinker's smile appeared to be genuine, which is more than he could say for Abby's.

Harrison nudged her, hoping she would get the message to be nice.

"Good morning, Mayor. I am very well, thank you." She gave a nod to each of the committee members. "Gentlemen, good morning."

Harrison was proud of her. She was doing very well considering how much she loathed these men.

"Shall we go, gentlemen?" She turned her attention to Harrison. "Would you please lead the way, Mr. Kingsley?"

Harrison led them out into the massive hall.

"This doesn't even look like the same place," one of the committee members said.

"Sure doesn't," another added.

Harrison wondered if Abby heard them. He cut a sideways glance at her and met her fleeting look with a quick wink. They continued on with the tour.

"Those dark blue-and-gold carpet runners up the stairs look very nice, Miss Bowen." Mayor Prinker shocked Harrison with his compliment, and obviously Abby, too, because her eyebrows spiked before turning into a skeptical frown.

"Thank you, Mayor." She hadn't said it like she meant it.

Harrison nudged her again, and she nudged him back, narrowing her eyes at him in the process.

He and Abby led them up the stairs where the shield-back-style Chippendale chairs with gold, padded seats and matching Chippendale tables were situated. Kerosene lamps with white globes with dainty blue flowers on them and gold filigreed stands centered each white tablecloth with a blue, lace tablecloth over it.

Harrison studied the men's faces. Each appeared very pleased, nodding and smiling.

"Very nice." Mayor Prinker's jowls wiggled as he nodded. "So far what we've seen, you've done a spectacular job, Miss Bowen, of making this an elegant establishment."

"Thank you."

Harrison knew how hard it was for her to say that a second time. "Shall we go to the theater now, gentlemen?" Harrison motioned them toward the stairs.

He and Abby followed the small group of eight men.

Walking along her left side, Abby placed her fingers along the right side of her mouth and for his ears only said, "I can't believe the mayor actually paid me a compliment. Not just one, but two. I didn't know the man had it in him."

Harrison chuckled.

The mayor stopped and gazed up at them. "What's so funny, Mr. Kingsley."

"Nothing you would find interesting."

The mayor seemed satisfied with his answer. Everyone made their way to the theater. When they stepped inside, gasps emitted from the committee members and the mayor.

Rows upon rows of royal-blue chairs filled the audience section. Carpet runners patterned with several shades of blues and grays lined the two aisles. Filigreed gold lamps, like the ones in the dining room, lined the stark-white walls. Various pictures hung on the walls, and heavy light blue drapes with navy swags graced all twelve of the floor-to-ceiling windows.

The completed, polished wood stage sparkled. A dark blue curtain hung off to the side, ready to be pulled shut during curtain calls or change of scenes, and the front of the stage had a light blue swag curtain draped across the front. Abby had done an amazing job. Even in Boston there wasn't anything this grand.

When they said nothing for several moments, Abby gazed up at him. Her mouth cringed, and she raised a shoulder.

"Don't worry, Abby. They love it. Just look at their faces."

Her attention swiveled from him to them. They were talking, waving their hands animatedly, and smiling.

The wrinkles around Abby's eyes disappeared.

"Miss Bowen, Mr. Kingsley, you have done quite a fabulous job here."

"Miss Bowen is responsible for all of this, gentlemen. She had all of this designed before I ever showed up."

"Yes, well, I'm sure you had a hand in it, so stop being so modest."

"I'm not being modest, sir. I speak the truth."

"Yes, well." The mayor loosened his tie. "Just make sure your plays are in as fine a taste as the decorum is."

Even though the mayor had paid her a roundabout compliment, Abby's eyes narrowed. Harrison knew she was about to blast him, so he quickly intervened. "They will be. Of that, I can assure you."

"Well, they'd better be." The mayor pulled out his watch, clicked it open, and snapped it shut. "Gentlemen, we need to be leaving now if we're going to make that meeting on time."

He strode from the room and the men followed after him like a bunch of baby ducks waddling after their mother.

They bid their good-days, and Abby closed the door and leaned against it with her eyes closed. "Am I ever glad that's over." She opened her eyes and pushed herself away from the door. "I need a drink." The way she said it, Harrison laughed.

"I meant tea, Harrison. Nothing else."

"I know, but it sounded funny. When one of the nannies who raised me used to have a stressful day, they would say it in the same tone you did, only they meant they needed a strong drink of spirits."

"Eww. I don't know how anyone could drink that nasty-tasting stuff."

"And just how would you know if it tastes nasty or not, Miss Abigail Bowen?" He waggled his eyebrows.

Her cheeks and ears turned a dark shade of red.

"Ah-ha. So you have tasted it, then. I knew it."

"Only once. When I was little. My brothers brought all of us a drink of water one time. Only mine and my sister's wasn't water. They snuck some of my mother's medicinal alcohol and put it into my and Leah's cups. Unfortunately, I was so thirsty that I drank a huge gulp of it and swallowed it before I realized it. My throat burned so bad, and I was sick the rest of the day. My only consolation was that my brothers had to clean up the messes me and Leah made and they had to do our chores for two full weeks."

"Did you get along with your siblings? I mean, other than that incident."

"Yes. We've always been very close. We still are. And even though they loved us, they pulled pranks on us like that all the time. But we got even with them enough times."

"I'm sure you did. You were fortunate to have brothers and sisters. I wish I did. And very soon, if things go as planned, I just may." Brothers and sisters by marriage that is. His heart smiled at the thought.

Chapter Fifteen

The rest of the morning, Harrison's comment drenched Abby's mind like the raging thunderstorm dumping bucketfuls of rain outside. He was an only child, so his comment about having brothers and sisters soon if things went as planned didn't make any sense unless...

Was Harrison getting married?

If so, to whom?

She hadn't really seen him with a woman, and she knew he didn't mean her. Did he have someone in mind back in Boston?

She slammed her hands over her ears, trying to squeeze out the disturbing thoughts as the whole thing was driving her crazy.

For the umpteenth time, she tried to concentrate on what else needed to be finished before their grand opening, which was going to happen much sooner than expected. Unable to stop from thinking about Harrison's comment, she gave up and chose to go into the theater instead and act out lines from one of the Jane Austen novels that had been converted into a play she'd starred in back home in Paradise Haven. Acting had a way of easing the tension in her.

Setting her pen and paper on her office desk, she made her way to the theater, marveling at how much Fletcher and his men had accomplished. Because of the fifteen extra men he'd brought in from all over the county they were nearly finished. All that remained were a few repairs, a few odds-and-ends jobs and the stage props that needed to be built and painted.

All the food had been ordered, and the dishes and flatware were arriving this afternoon. Brochures and tickets were ready, the plays were printed, as were the newspaper advertisements announcing their first play, which was an adaptation of *Emma* by Jane Austen.

Her stepfather had sent a telegraph that his crew was happy to help her out and that they would arrive within a week by train, costumes and all.

Abby figured she could have her grand opening within the next three weeks. A month ahead of schedule. She should have been ecstatic about the whole thing, but she wasn't because shortly after opening night, Harrison and his precious sons would vanish from her life. Forever. She knew beforehand that she would get attached to them and that it would hurt when they left, but she didn't realize just how much it would until this moment.

Making sure she was alone, she sat on a chair in the theater as tears pooled in her eyes. "Oh, Lord, why did I have to go and fall in love with them? I know You have Your reasons, but I still don't understand why You brought such an amazing, wonderful man into my life. One with two darling children, something You know I can never have." Abby placed her face into her hands and let the dam burst.

Her heart wept tears of grief for the children she would never bear, and for the boys she would soon lose along with a certain wonderful man.

How desperately she wished she could bear children. If she could, she would be so bold as to tell Harrison how she felt, even if he rejected her. But to have him reject her because she wasn't woman enough, because she was a failure as a woman, that she couldn't bear.

When her tears finally subsided, she snuck out of the theater and made her way to her room. A quick glance in the mirror and she sighed. Her eyes were red and her face was blotchy. She poured water into her wash basin and splashed it on her face. She flopped her body across her bed and closed her eyes. For ten minutes, she told herself. Ten minutes only.

"Abby? Are you in there?"

Abby blinked and scanned her bedroom.

Three loud knocks on her door yanked her attention in that direction. "Abby? It's me, Harrison. Are you in there?"

Harrison? What was he doing here? He said he wouldn't be back this afternoon. That he had business issues that needed his attention. His lawyer in Boston had sent papers for him to go over or something like that.

Her eyes felt as if someone had scraped sandpaper across them, so she rubbed them lightly.

What time was it, anyway?

One glance at the clock and her eyes bounced open. 3:45 in the afternoon. Oh, no, she groaned. She'd only meant to close her eyes for a moment. Instead, she'd fallen asleep for almost two hours. "Yes. I'm here." Her voice sounded groggy.

"I'm sorry to disturb you, but we have a problem."

"A problem?"

"Yes."

"What kind of problem?"

"Abby, can you come to the door? I need to talk to you."

"Give me a minute, okay? I'll be right there."

Abby leaped off the bed and did a quick glance in the mirror. Even though her face was no longer blotchy and her eyes weren't red, her blond hair stuck out like a scarecrow's. "Oh, dear me. That won't do." She quickly put her hair to rights, ran her hand over the wrinkles in her dress, strode to the door and swung it open. "What are you doing here? I thought you had work to do." Abby stepped into the hallway.

"I do, but Fletcher came to see me."

Abby frowned. "Why would he come to see you?"

"Well, he wanted me to be the one to break the bad news to you."

"What bad news? And why wouldn't he tell me himself?"

"He didn't know how to tell you, and he thought you would need my support when you heard it."

"I'm not fragile or made of glass. I won't break if I hear some bad news. I can handle it." Most of the time, anyway. The only time she had completely broken down was the day she had received the devastating news that she couldn't... *No! I refuse to think about that now.*

"That's what I told him, but he insisted I be the one to tell you."

Harrison's comment blessed the corset right off her. He obviously saw her as a strong woman. Something she prided herself in.

"The wind last night tore some of the shingles off the roof, causing it to leak in a few places."

"Oh, is that all?" Abby waved her hand at the minuscule problem. "Well, we'll just have him repair the roof when it dries."

"That's not what he's concerned about." Wrinkles formed around Harrison's eyes, alerting her that something else was terribly wrong.

The muscle in her neck tensed. "Oh. What's that?"

"The leak soiled some of the theater chairs."

"How many is some?" And why hadn't she noticed them or the leak? They must have been on the opposite side of where she'd been sitting earlier. And her mind *was* on other things.

"Ten or so as far as we can tell."

"Oh." Her neck relaxed. "That's not too bad. I'll just wipe them down and air them out. I'm sure we can get the water mark out if there is one. And if that doesn't work, perhaps Fletcher can recover them."

"That's not the worst of it."

"What?"

When he hesitated, Abby said it again, only with less patience. "What? Just tell me, Harrison." She wished he'd just say whatever it was and stop prolonging it.

"When Fletcher went to check the attic for leaks, he had an encounter with a raccoon. He got the animal out, but the raccoon made a mess of things up there.

It's obviously been living up there for quite some time and has soiled the floor. He fears the smell will eventually make its way to the theater. Therefore, the floor will have to be torn out and replaced sooner rather than later. Plus, we're going to have to figure out a way to keep that raccoon from coming back. Fletcher says once they've made their home somewhere, it's hard to get rid of them."

Abby seated herself on the beautifully carved oak lion's-head French bench seat situated in the hallway outside her bedroom door. She absentmindedly ran her fingers over the white material with the elegant needlework flowers.

Harrison joined her.

"Did he say how the raccoon was getting in?"

"Yes, through the window."

"I see. Well… God saw this coming." However, she did let one sigh escape. So many, many problems and obstacles. She hoped that wouldn't always be the case. "It's not a surprise to Him. He'll take care of it. He'll show us what to do." She tapped her lips and silently prayed for God's direction and wisdom. "Did Fletcher say if there was anything he could do about this?"

"Yes, he has an idea to keep the raccoon away, but he's more concerned about replacing the floor and the delay that it will take along with the added expense."

"How much of a delay are we talking about?"

"Two. Possibly three weeks."

"Is that over and above the time it will take to complete the other projects?"

"No, that's everything."

"Oh, okay." She pulled her lip under her teeth. "I just

remembered that the tickets have dates on them. So that means that the show will have to go on one way or another. Well, with God's help, I'll figure something out. In the meantime, we need to find Fletcher and tell him to do whatever it takes and to buy whatever material he needs to complete the job." Abby's mind began going through her dwindling funds. With all of the things she had not planned on, the accounts were getting much lower than she had anticipated. She rose, hoping to keep her concerns from being obvious, but before she could take a step, Harrison clutched her hand.

"Abby." He stood and let go of her hand. "I know we had an agreement, but I'd like to help you."

She tilted her head. "Help me. I don't understand. In what way?"

"With the extra funds it's going to take."

If only her father hadn't set it up to where a certain amount of money would be dispersed each year, then she'd be fine. Right now, she had enough funds to take care of the added expenses and to live on until her business took off, but she just didn't have enough to handle too many more problems. All that aside, she had confidence that God would take care of it. He'd never let her down yet. Well, maybe once.

Harrison studied Abby's face. While his finances were stretched tight at the moment, he hated the fact that the cost of the repairs and the items that were stored in the attic would be substantial. He hadn't even told her yet about the two trunks of costumes the animal had destroyed. He didn't have the heart. Yet, he knew he needed to. Now was as good a time as any to tell her.

"Abby, I know you believe God will take care of this, but there's something else you don't know."

"What's that?"

"The raccoon also destroyed two of the seven trunks of costumes you had up there."

Her mouth fell open, then it quickly closed. She dragged in a breath and let it out. "God will take care of that, too." She smiled.

The woman smiled. How could she when so much expense was before her. And how could she have such confidence that God would take care of it? Since starting this business, one thing after another had gone wrong, and yet with each problem, Abby had confidently said that God would take care of it. As much as it pained him to say it, the truth was, God had.

As he stood there, for the first time in Harrison's life, he wanted to know God. The God she knew, that she trusted so implicitly. Harrison wanted to really know Him. The same way Abby did.

It was time to re-read the note his mother had left for him, the one explaining how to have a personal relationship with God. Harrison wasn't quite sure how it went. It had been a very long time since he had read it, but he was going to find out. Abby had convinced him that God did indeed care about their lives. She was living proof of that by the peace she exhibited and the confidence she had in God even in the midst of complete disasters. Therefore, when he got home this evening, he would take his mother's letter out and follow its instructions.

That evening, after his sons had gone to sleep, Harrison took out his mother's Bible. Though he'd never read it, he kept it with him always. It was one of the few things he had of his mother's. Harrison had been told that before she'd drawn her last breath, against the doctor's wishes and even his father's, she used what little strength she had left to write a note to Harrison.

He opened the Bible and removed his mother's note. Many times before he had read through the parts about how much she loved him and how sorry she was that she had to leave this earth and leave him behind. Knowing she soon would, she wanted to leave him with the best gift anyone could ever give to another. The way to salvation. For years, Harrison believed his mother to be delusional, but now, as he re-read them, he cherished those words, words he was ready to read with a hungry heart and an open mind.

At first, he had a hard time finding the scriptures she mentioned until he noticed she had underlined them in her Bible. That made them easier to spot. The first one he read was in the book of John chapter three, verse sixteen. Next he followed her note to Romans chapter ten, verses nine and ten. After that, he read even more scriptures, devouring them like a thirst-deprived man who had just found a river flowing with fresh water.

Three hours later, touched by the love and the truth he found in those pages, he fell to his knees. He asked God to forgive Him and to be the Lord of his life. Immediately, a peaceful sensation, better than anything he'd ever experienced before poured over him and through him. The only way to describe what he was feeling was liquid love. A love so powerful, Harrison bowed his head in reverential awe. The next thing he knew, he was talking to God, pouring out his love to Him and thanking Him for cleansing every inch of him. Harrison now had the loving Father he'd always dreamed of having. It came not in the form of his own father, but someone even better. Someone who loved him unconditionally.

Drained, yet happier than he'd ever been before, he crawled under his sheets and closed his eyes. Tonight he would sleep better than he ever had before because he'd just made the greatest, most important decision of his life.

The next one would be when he asked Abby to become his wife.

The next morning, Abby hurried about, trying to get herself ready for church. For the first time ever, she was running late, so she'd told the Denis sisters to go on ahead without her. Twenty minutes later, she arrived at the white clapboard building with the stained-glass windows, large church bell and white cross.

As she neared the door, she heard the members singing. She stepped inside, slipped into the back pew, grabbed a hymnal, and soon her voice mingled with the rest of the congregation. When the singing ended, she sat down and slid her gaze forward toward the pastor, but it never made it that far. Instead, it froze on a familiar head of light brown hair seven pews ahead of her. Harrison?

During the sermon, Abby barely heard a word Pastor Wells said. She couldn't take her eyes off the back of Harrison's head. Question after question swarmed through her brain, making her dizzy. Why after all this time, had Harrison finally decided to come to church?

Where were Josiah and Graham? Were they with Staimes? If not, then whom?

She wondered about the woman he'd planned to marry. Who was she? Where did she live? What was she like? Would she love Josiah and Graham and Harrison as much as Abby did? The very idea of Harrison getting married and the boys having someone else for a mother other than herself gnawed a hole in Abby's heart. This was not the place to be thinking about those things, and yet she was powerless to control her turbulent thoughts.

When the congregation stood to sing the last song, Abby slipped out of the church and took her time as she made her way back to her property. Broken branches crunched under her feet. Moist leaves and the scent of forest floor, along with sweet flower aromas and pine, filtered through her nostrils.

By the riverbank, she sat on the same log she and Harrison had occupied the other day, and closed her eyes.

Water rushed right on by to only who knew where. Birds chirped in the trees surrounding her, and the chipmunks' tweeting, clucking noise all filled the silence. Normally those sounds soothed whatever troubled her, but not today. Nothing could ever soothe or take away the unease tearing at her heart over the thought of Harrison getting married. Not even God.

"There you are."

Abby's eyes bolted open. A shadow towered over her, blocking the bright morning sun from her view. "Harrison? What are you doing here?" She peered around him, looking for what, she didn't know exactly.

"When I didn't see you in church, I went to your

house. Veronique said she didn't know where you were. I thought perhaps you might have come down here."

"Why would you think that?" She wanted to ask him what he was doing in church as he'd never gone before since his arrival, but she didn't want to embarrass him. She'd already done that before when she'd made the mistake of asking him to pray in front of everyone the day of her get-together picnic. She refused to make that mistake again.

He shrugged. "I don't know. It just seemed like something you would do."

How would he know what she would do? *Only because he's spent the past several weeks with you, you silly goose.*

"Mind if I join you?"

"No, of course not. Please, sit down." She scooted over. It was then she noticed he was carrying a basket. "What do you have there?" She pointed to it.

Harrison lowered his broad-shouldered frame beside her and faced her. "Well, I didn't know if you'd eaten yet, so I asked Veronique if she could throw something together. Hope you don't mind me asking her to do that." His eyes searched hers.

"No, not at all. Actually, I'm glad you did. I didn't have time to eat breakfast this morning and I'm famished."

"Shall we go sit in the shade? On my way out the door, I snatched one of the blankets that you used on the Fourth. Hope that's okay, too."

"Of course it is. That was so sweet of you to think of it."

He stood and offered her a hand up. She placed her hand in his and allowed him to do just that. Except when she was on her feet, he didn't let go. Instead, he looped her arm through his and led her to the same spot where she and her small group had picnicked before.

Abby reached for the blanket so she could spread it out, but he shifted it out of her way.

"Allow me. You just stand there a moment while I spread it out."

"I can help."

"I know you can. But please, allow me."

She spiked a shoulder. "If you insist."

"I do." He snapped the blanket and let it fall to the ground, straightening it afterward. "Have a seat, Miss Abby."

"Miss Abby, huh?" She sat down with her legs off to one side.

Harrison sat next to her and opened the lid of the basket. He reached in and pulled out two roast beef sandwiches. He handed her one and set the other on a napkin in front of himself. Next, he pulled out a bowl filled with thin-sliced, deep-fried crispy potatoes, two red apples, several slices of hard cheese and a plate holding two large pieces of pecan pie and set them on the blanket in front of them.

"That's everything. Shall we eat?"

As was her custom, Abby bowed her head. "Father, thank You for this food. May it nourish our bodies the way You intended it to. Bless Harrison for this thoughtful act. Amen."

"Amen."

Abby cut a peek over at Harrison. She had never heard him say amen until now. His head was bowed and his eyes were closed. That wasn't something she'd seen him do before, either. She quickly yanked her gaze away before he caught her watching him, and picked up her sandwich. "Where's Josiah and Graham? Is Staimes watching them?" She took a bite of her roast beef.

"No. Miss Wright is."

Miss Wright? Abby didn't know a Miss Wright. Was she the woman Harrison planned on marrying? If so, what was he doing picnicking with Abby?

She set her sandwich down and gazed out at the river.

"Is something wrong, Abby?"

Her mind scrambled for an answer. One that wouldn't reveal anything about how she was feeling.

"Is something wrong with your sandwich?"

Now that, she could answer. "No." To keep him from inquiring about things any further, she snatched up her sandwich and forced herself to take a bite. Unable to handle the suspense, she nonchalantly said, "Is Miss Wright from around here?" She picked up a chip and popped it into her mouth. The crunch echoed in her ears.

"No. She's from Boston."

The roast beef turned to stone in Abby's stomach. She didn't want to know any more. She couldn't bear to hear if Miss Wright was the woman he'd referred to when he said if things worked out the way he wanted them to, that he would have brothers and sisters, too. Did she come from a large family? Could she give him the children he wanted? It was back to that again.

If only things were different.

If only she could make her dream become a reality. Her once beautiful dreams were fading quickly before her eyes, being replaced at a rapid pace with her worst nightmares. And at the top of that list was saying goodbye to Harrison and his precious sons forever.

Chapter Sixteen

For the past two weeks since their picnic together, Harrison had made several more attempts to spend time alone with Abby. But each time, either something or someone had interrupted them. If it wasn't one of the actresses or actors who had arrived two weeks ago, it was someone else on Abby's staff, or she was instructing the new hired help on how to wait on the tables and how to address their guests. Times when it appeared there might be a moment to talk with her, he'd been pulled away to attend to his own business matters. Business matters that were definitely looking up.

Now, in less than an hour, the Royal Grand Theater would start their grand opening, a completely sold-out affair.

Harrison had been impressed with Fletcher and his men. As he walked through the mansion just before the guests arrived, he had to admit they had done a phenomenal job of getting everything ready, and much faster than Fletcher originally figured it would take.

Delicious aromas drifted from the kitchen. Veronique's French cuisine was sure to be a huge hit. He was amazed by how proud he was of all of it. Sure it was Abby's, but everywhere he looked, he could see his handiwork, as well. They definitely made a good pair.

The theater was buzzing with last-minute preparations. Maids, waitresses and waiters, dressed in white and black, neatly pressed uniforms ran around making sure the place settings were arranged on each table. The others had a tray of finger foods in hand, ready for the guests to enjoy. Footmen and ushers, dressed in black tails with white, starched shirts, donned their pristine white gloves. Two ticket ladies stood by the door, ready to receive tickets for the night's performance and to hand out the playbills. Musicians tuned their violins, cellos and violas to the sound of the flute.

Such an amazing group of talents they all represented.

Miss Elsa, the mayor's former receptionist, had done a fine job of finding the suitable help Abby needed. Abby had seen to it that the elderly lady's tasks were tailored so she didn't have to walk much on her bad leg. Miss Elsa had turned out to be a valuable asset to their little team. The mayor had been sorry to see her go, but his ruffled feathers had been soothed by the fact that Miss Elsa had a niece who was an experienced secretary and that she could start right away. Otherwise, the mayor may have made things even more difficult for Abby.

Abby didn't deserve what the mayor and his cronies had doled out to her. Long before Harrison had arrived, the woman had every minuscule detail planned out. She had deserved the men's respect and assistance rather than the derision she got.

Thinking of Abby, Harrison glanced in the direction of her chambers. A little over an hour before, after she made sure everyone was lined up and knew what they were supposed to do, she'd left him in charge so that she could ready herself for the grand opening. He couldn't wait to see her, to share this moment that meant so much to her with her. And when the festivities were over to have his long-past-due talk with her.

Abby took one last look in the mirror. The light pink, soft silk bustle gown with burgundy stripes and butterfly lace hung tastefully over her shoulders. Her blond hair hung down her back in one long twisted curl, except for the sides. They were gathered on top of her head and pinned with pink and burgundy dangling beaded combs.

Pleased with her appearance, she picked up her lacy burgundy-and-pink-striped fan and headed down the stairs. Her insides and her knees were shaking so she held onto the handrail for support. Her burgundy silk shoes peeked out from under her dress with each step. Halfway down the stairs she noticed Harrison across the room, talking to one of the hired men.

What a striking figure Harrison made standing there in his finely tailored, gray suit. His light blue shirt was pressed to perfection. A silk, striped tie, in three different shades of blue, along with a matching pocket-square handkerchief sticking out of his suit jacket pocket, and shiny black polished shoes finished his ensemble quite handsomely. Even his beautiful hair was combed to perfection. Hair she'd dreamed of running her fingers through.

Abby! Shame on you. Stop it! No more daydreams where Harrison is concerned. He's taken, remember? Boy, did she remember. With excruciating pain in her chest, she remembered.

She had no right admiring another woman's man. Before he caught her staring at him, she yanked her gaze away from him.

During the past two weeks, she had been extremely grateful that she had been so busy that she hadn't even had time to think about Harrison with another woman. Okay, that wasn't entirely true. She had thought about it often, and every time she had, she had to force her mind to take a turn in another direction. One that didn't include Harrison.

Each step she took down the stairs, her legs got weaker and her insides shook even harder. This was it. Tonight was her grand opening. The day she had dreamed of for so long.

By the time she reached the third step from the bottom, Harrison was there, offering his hand to assist her down the last few steps. She thought nothing of his offer. After all, many a time he had assisted Miss Elsa, Veronique, Zoé and Colette. He was just being who he was, a perfect gentleman. At least that's what she told herself when she laid her gloved hand in his.

At the bottom of the steps he leaned close to her and whispered, "You look very lovely this evening, Abby."

"Thank you, Harrison. You look very nice yourself."

His aftershave, a combination of orange mint, lemon, rosewater, lavender and some other scent she thought to be rosemary, floated around him, swirling her senses. She wanted to draw in a deep breath, to enjoy how masculine Harrison smelled, but she didn't. Instead, she mentally shook her brain to clear it of any romantic notions.

"Are you ready for this?" He looped her arm through his.

She wondered what he was doing until she reminded herself he was only doing what gentlemen did. "To be perfectly honest, I'm extremely nervous. I just hope everything goes well. People have bought tickets from as far as twenty miles away."

"The mayor's happy about that. The hotels are full and people are lavishly spending money at his spa, at the stores, the restaurants and the hotels. Even Fletcher said he's sold a lot more furniture and has enough orders to keep him busy all winter and then some."

"I'm so glad. Not only am I getting to fulfill my dream, but it's blessing others in this town, as well. And you." She gazed up at him. "I have your bank draft ready. Remind me to give it to you later, okay?"

"Bank draft?" Harrison looked genuinely confused. Had he so quickly forgotten that after the grand opening, their business arrangement would come to an end?

"Yes, silly. Remember? The money I promised you when you became my partner? Your original investment, plus the profit I promised you when this arrangement was over?"

"Oh, but you are mistaken, Abby. It isn't over. It's only just begun."

Abby didn't know what to make of Harrison's words or the penetrating look in his eyes. She never got the chance to ask him or to ponder it any further as their first patrons of the evening had arrived. "I see Mayor Prinker and the town committee members have arrived. We'd better go greet them." Holding her head up high, she strolled toward them.

Harrison tugged her back to him before she got too far away. "After everyone leaves this evening, I need to talk to you."

Abby gave a quick nod, wondering what he needed to talk to her about and then strode forward, a perfect lady heading into a perfect evening. "Gentlemen, it's so nice you could come."

Later on, Abby and Harrison stood at the entrance door, saying goodbye to her patrons. Everything had gone off without a hitch. The exquisite French cuisine had been a sheer delight, the play had been perfectly performed with only one minor glitch, but nothing that anyone other than Abby and the performers ever knew happened, and the guests had left smiling with the promise to return with their friends. Some of the ladies had even asked Abby when her women's spa would open. How they'd gotten wind that she was considering opening one, she didn't know. The one thing she did know was, she was definitely going to build one since the interest in it was already so great.

The last patrons to leave were the mayor and his wife, along with the committee members and their spouses.

Abby held her breath as they headed toward her and Harrison.

"Miss Bowen. Mr. Kingsley. I want to congratulate you both on a job well done."

"Abby is the one who deserves all the credit, Mr. Mayor. She had all this planned long before I arrived." Harrison smiled down at her.

Abby beamed under Harrison's praise. "That's not entirely accurate, Mr. Kingsley. You were a huge help."

"You're being too modest, Miss Bowen. I am a man who believes that credit should go where the credit is due. And that credit belongs solely to you." He stepped back. Facing her, he clapped his hands. Within seconds, everyone else joined him.

Heat flooded up Abby's neck and cheeks, flaming all the way into her ears.

As soon as their applause ended, Mayor Prinker's gaze honed in on Abby. "I owe you an apology, Miss Bowen. You have done an amazing job here. All of us—" he spanned his hand to include every one of the committee members "—are all very impressed with what you have done and what you have accomplished. The food was excellent. The play was exquisite and done in extremely fine taste. There is nothing here that would shame our town or damage its reputation in the least. Quite the contrary, actually.

"You have brought culture to our town, Miss Bowen. And I know I speak for everyone here when I say how grateful we are to you and how proud we are of you. You have proven yourself to be a fine, upstanding businesswoman and a fine asset to our community. Therefore, as long as you continue on as you have this evening, there will be no revoking of your business license. You may continue to run your establishment with or without a male business partner."

Joy lit through her, but it was doused almost instantly with fear. Now there was nothing to keep Harrison here.

The mayor and his men along with their wives filed outside to their awaiting carriages.

Abby turned to Harrison with a fake smile in her heart and on her lips, prepared to tell him thank you for all he had done. "Harrison..."

"*Mademoiselle!*" Veronique called from the back of the main room near the kitchen and came running.

Abby spun toward her. "Veronique, what's wrong?"

"*Mademoiselle,* the raccoon, he is back, and he is making a huge mess in the kitchen. Come quickly. I don't know what to do!"

Abby sighed. What else could go wrong?

The next morning, Harrison woke early. He couldn't wait to see Abby today. Before she got too busy preparing for this evening's performance, he needed to talk to her. There would be no more delaying this conversation, especially after hearing the mayor's words that she no longer needed a business partner. He'd intended to talk to Abby after everyone had finally left the theater, but then everything turned to chaos, trying to catch the raccoon and then cleaning up the mess the critter had made. It was late, and everyone was exhausted, so he and Abby had agreed to meet at seven a.m.

Harrison rushed through getting dressed, kissed his boys goodbye with the promise of seeing them later, then hurried to Abby's place.

His stomach leaped into his throat the instant he saw her sitting in her usual morning spot at the table on the mansion's front porch. He hopped out and jogged up the stairs. "Morning," he said with a chipper voice.

"Morning." Her greeting lacked its usual luster and sounded rather formal.

His joy evaporated like the morning fog from the river. He stood and took a seat next to her. "You tired?"

"A little." She poured him a cup of coffee and handed it and a plate of leftover French pastries to him.

"Thank you."

She nodded and said nothing more, wouldn't even look at him.

He picked up the finger-size pastry and popped it into his mouth, then followed it with a drink of hot coffee.

Awkward didn't begin to describe the silence stretching between them. This wasn't quite the atmosphere he had in mind when he decided to propose to her. Even so, he wouldn't let that deter him, but he would start out with something else less life-altering and ease his way into it.

"Abby, I want to share something with you that I found out a few weeks ago."

She looked over at him. The light in her smiling eyes was nonexistent today. "What's that?" she asked with very little interest.

"My butler overheard a conversation between my father's lawyer and a colleague. He was apparently bragging about how much money he had made off my father to enforce the stipulations in his will—stipulations it appears that no court or judge would ever enforce." That caught her attention. "When I found out, I fired my father's lawyer and hired a new one. Mr. Wilkins informed me that the judge reviewed the stipulations in my father's will and declared them unenforceable. Therefore, they will be releasing all my father's assets and money, my full inheritance, next week. I'm telling you this because I want you to know that I could have walked away from this business arrangement of ours a few weeks ago, but I chose not to."

She frowned. "I don't understand. Why did you stay if you didn't have to?"

"For several reasons." He held her gaze tenderly, praying she wouldn't throw him off the porch and out of her life. "One, I wanted to finish what I started. Two. I wanted to make sure your dreams came true, and I wanted to help make that happen. And Three. Because I needed time to figure out a way to make this work between us. To make us work."

"What do you mean 'make us work'? I don't understand." She frowned again.

He raked his hand through his hair. He wasn't going about this very well. "Let me try to explain it this way. I've had the pleasure of being your business partner these several weeks, but that isn't enough for me anymore. I want to be your lifelong partner. I love you, Abby."

Her eyes widened in shock.

He hurried forward before she could say anything. "I even figured out a way for us to be together and still get what we both want. You would be able to stay here and keep your theater, and I would be able to right the wrongs my father has done.

"I've already worked out the details with Mr. Wilkins. When my father's assets are released, I am having a full accounting done for all of my father's affairs, and for those businesses where it appears he took unfair advantage, we plan to make restitution to the extent it's possible." His words swam across Abby's face, but he continued, knowing he could re-explain it later if necessary. "The men that are currently running my other businesses now will continue to do so. They will each check in with me until which time I can sell them off. During that time, Mr. Wilkins will make sure the books are accurate along with keeping an eye on the businesses for me. That way, not only will I fulfill my lifelong dream, but I will also restore my family's name.

"Only I'll do it from here. Truth is, Abby, I've grown to love this town and its people. I love the mountains and would love for my boys to grow up here instead of in Boston. So…" Harrison slipped from his chair and down onto one knee. He reached inside his pocket and pulled out the diamond ring he'd had his butler, Forsyth, send from Boston. His mother's diamond ring. "Abby, I love you. And judging from what I've seen in your eyes when you look at me, I believe you love me, too." Shock danced in her blue eyes at that one. "Will you marry me?"

"Will I what?" She leaped to her feet. "What about Miss Wright?"

"Miss Wright? My nanny?" He stood and stared at Abby, wondering what she was talking about.

"Yes. I thought you were getting married. And since I hadn't seen you with another woman, I assumed that you were talking about Miss Wright."

Now where had she gotten that ludicrous notion

from? "Why would you think I'd be marrying Miss Wright? She's old enough to be my grandmother."

"She is? But—but she's from Boston."

"You're not making any sense, Abby. What does her being from Boston have to do with anything?"

"The other day you said if things went your way you'd soon have brothers and sisters. I figured you already had someone in mind to marry when you said that. Then shortly after that you talked about Miss Wright from Boston. I just assumed..." She let her sentence hang, and he picked it up.

"That that was who I was talking about."

"Yes."

"Well, it wasn't. I was thinking about you." He reached for her hands but she yanked them behind her back the same way she had the day they met. Only there wasn't any reason for her to yank them from out of his reach this time. Or was there?

Abby couldn't believe her ears. Harrison loved her and asked her to marry him. Her heart sighed knowing he had figured out a way for them to be together, and knowing he could have gone home a long time ago but he hadn't.

That he had chosen to stay here for her.

To help her see her dream come to pass.

All of those things endeared her to him even more so, and yet she had to deny her heart of his love and her dreams. She couldn't marry him. She had to refuse him, but how could she do that without telling him why? That was going to take a lot more courage than she had, so she sent up a silent prayer asking God for a huge dose of courage.

It never came.

She had to handle this one on her own, and handle it she would. Not because she wanted to but because she had to. For his and his sons' sakes. "Harrison, I'm sorry for any misunderstandings between us. But before this goes on any further, I want you to know that it hurts me to pain you, but marriage was not part of our original agreement. I have no plans of ever marrying. I'm sorry." With those words she fled past him and bolted into the house. Taking the stairs three at a time, she rushed up them and into her room.

She closed her door and locked it, then darted to her bed and flopped herself on top of her blue comforter. Hands crisscrossed above her head, she buried her face and wept.

How she had wanted to throw herself into Harrison's arms and to smother his face with yeses and kisses, but reality had finally crashed down on her. She wasn't a whole woman, wasn't mother material. Therefore, she refused to saddle someone as wonderful as Harrison with someone like herself. She loved him and his two boys far too much to do that to them.

Harrison stood there, staring at the door Abby had disappeared through, unbelieving of what he'd just heard. Her rejection stung him to the core, deeper than anyone else's who had rejected him or had used him during his life. He shook his head, running his fingers through his hair and settling his hand on the back of his head.

With all his being, he truly believed Abby was different, that she cared about him, loved him, even. But she didn't. It was perfectly clear that she didn't have any use for him anymore, and that he had once again stupidly trusted someone with his heart. Well, he wasn't ever going to make that mistake again. He whirled and stomped down her porch. There was nothing keeping him here now, so the first train heading East out of this town, he would be on it.

That evening, Abby made it through another Royal Grand Theater production, but this time it didn't feel royal or grand. Without Harrison at her side, her heart felt as if it had been yanked out of her chest, and the pain of loss was more than she could handle. He hadn't even come, hadn't even shown up for their second biggest night of all. All she wanted to do was to go to bed and forget the whole day. When the last person left and the staff had gone to bed, she made her way to her room and cried herself to sleep. What good was a dream if when you got there, it hurt this badly? When she awoke the next morning, she had a splitting headache from crying so long and so hard.

She wanted to stay in bed and pull the covers over her head, but she had to get up and get busy. Her mind swam with all the preparations there were to handle. For two more weeks, her company would perform the play *Emma* by Jane Austen. After that, they would be perform *Pride & Prejudice*. There were costumes to make and playbills to script and tickets to fashion. So much to do, and she didn't want to do even one whit of any of it.

Before Harrison had come into her life, she would

have been happy that things were going so well and that she had sold out performances clear on up until December. Without him, she no longer cared. And yet somehow she had to go on. She had to forget him. The best thing to do was to bury herself in her work so she could at least try to. She looked at the clock. Even though it was only five in the morning and no one else would be up and about, she forced herself to get out of bed and to get dressed so she could busy her mind with other thoughts than those of Harrison.

In her quiet office, she started checking her list for things that needed to be done—get the playbill material to Miss Elsa, wash and iron the draperies, order the food, repair the costumes, build new set pieces. About an hour later, she caught a strange whiff of something and stopped. She drew in a longer breath through her nostrils. Was that smoke she smelled? She sniffed again. It was.

Her eyes went wide as she darted through the house, checking for the source of what she now knew to be smoke. When she reached the back door, she spotted flames in the distance. The grass fire just down the hill was popping and smoking and heading directly toward her shed, the very shed that held most of her stage props!

Grabbing her skirt with both hands, Abby raced through the servant section of the house, banging on doors and hollering, "Help! Help! Fire!" Without waiting to see if anyone heard her or would follow her, she ran outside, gathered buckets and gunny sacks. She filled the buckets with water from the pump and soaked the sacks as fast as she could.

Loud clanging from the town's fire bell rang in her ears.

Voices rose above it as men gathered near the place where the flames were eating up the grasses around her shed. Without a thought for her own safety, she raced between the two and began to bat at the flames. They were small but persistent and growing.

Others arrived and helped fill buckets from the well and the pump. They handed them to the men who had formed several lines where they handed off the buckets and sacks to each other. Abby worked side by side with the men. She could not let another assault shatter her dream. She was soaked and sweating and panicked as the flames continued to advance until the orange and yellow overtook their best efforts.

"Miss Abby!" One of the men grabbed her and yanked her free of the firestorm just as the flames licked up the outside of her shed, engulfing the walls within seconds. But she would not give up. She grabbed two buckets of water, ran as close as she could get to the structure and poured the water on the ground, trying to make a perimeter so the grass fire wouldn't reach her house. The shed was gone, a total loss. Now she only prayed that somehow they could save the house. "God, help me. Please don't let it burn my theater down, too."

Chapter Seventeen

Harrison stood at the stagecoach stop, waiting for the vehicle that would take him, his sons, Staimes and Miss Wright to the nearest train station that would take them back to Boston. When he'd asked Abby to marry him and she had refused him, he'd felt like an idiot for thinking she was different from all the other women he'd known, that she was like his sweet Allison. Well, she turned out to be nothing like Allison, and she was just like every other woman he'd known. Women who only wanted him for what he could offer them. Money and opportunity.

He and Abby may have had a business agreement from the very start, but when he had kissed her and she had responded, that had nothing to do with business. When they shared time talking and picnicking, that, too, had nothing to do with business. At least not to him, anyway. And what about all those dreamy looks he'd seen in her eyes? Looks he must have misinterpreted.

He slammed his eyelids shut. What an idiot he'd been. To think that she cared about him. Loved him, even.

He still couldn't believe how much trouble he'd gone through, how many sleepless nights he'd endured to come up with a plan that would work for both of them. Plans that he now needed to get back to Boston to undo.

Loud clanging pierced the air. Harrison jumped and his turbulent thoughts disintegrated into new chaotic ones. What was going on?

Voices of men shouting rose above the thundering hooves of the stagecoach horses.

A man carrying buckets filled with gunny sacks flew past him.

Harrison called after him, "What's going on?"

Without stopping the man hollered over his shoulder, "There's a fire at the Royal Grand Theater."

The Royal Grand? Had Harrison heard him correctly?

A fire? At Abby's?

His whole spirit cried out. *Abby! Lord, no!*

Harrison spun to his valet. "Staimes, don't board that stagecoach." He yanked his coat off and tossed it to him. "Stay here. Miss Wright, watch the boys. I'll be back." He whirled and ran as fast as he could toward Abby's place, rolling up his sleeves as he went.

When his racing feet carried him close enough, he saw the flames devouring her shed and now heading toward the theater. The fire was still a fair distance away from the mansion, but it was closing in fast. "God, don't let it reach Abby's house!"

Just as he arrived, he spotted Abby amid the chaos, running with a bucket in each hand. He rushed over to her, and she stumbled right as he got there. He shot out his hand and caught her, water sloshed all over the legs of his suit pants, soaking them.

Abby turned her soot-covered face up to his. "Harrison?" She coughed. "What are you doing here?"

"I came to help. Give me those." He reached for her buckets, but she yanked them to her.

"No! I need to put the fire out before it takes out my home." She took off running toward the opposite end of the line where the buckets were being passed off. She poured what little water that was left in them onto the ground. What a smart woman she was, trying to place a water barrier between her house and the flames.

Harrison rushed toward the water pump and got to work forming the barrier and dousing the flames.

Sweat soaked his body, the heat from the fire became unbearable, but he pressed onward.

All up and down the line surrounding the house, men passed buckets back and forth. Each bucket dumped doused more and more of the destructive flames. Finally, with the effort of what seemed like every townsperson in the surrounding area, Abby's employees, along with himself and Abby, the flames were finally put out. Thankfully, the gardens and the back side of the theater had sustained no damage at all. The rest was mostly smoke damage, except for the grass and the shed.

Harrison breathed a prayer of thanksgiving as he thanked each and every person who had come to help. He gave Veronique, Colette and Zoé extra hugs as they looked the most shaken. He made sure to search out and shake the hand of every one of Fletcher's men as well as Fletcher himself.

When he had finished thanking everyone, the one he most wanted to speak with was nowhere to be found.

"I think she went down by the river, sir," Veronique said when she found him standing among the diminishing crowd looking around.

His gaze found hers and he nodded. "Thank you, Veronique."

"No. Thank you, sir."

He gave a quick nod. Leaving the others, Harrison hurried to the river. He found Abby there, on her knees splashing water on her arms and her face.

He knelt down beside her and splashed his own face with the cool mountain water, not knowing how he'd be received after not showing up the night before. Harrison waited, hoping she would say something. Anything. All she did, however, was to continue to splash water on her already soot-free face.

Abby glanced over at Harrison, hoping the water would disguise the tears she wanted so desperately to hide from him, but couldn't. Because of his efforts, the town's, and the efforts of her employees and friends, her theater had been spared. She owed him a thank-you at least. Without looking at him, she stared out across the river, seeing nothing but her own pain reflecting there. "Thank you, Harrison," she finally said. "For helping me." She swallowed back the overflow of tears, but was powerless to stop them from completely flowing through her voice. She only hoped Harrison didn't hear them. "I was so afraid. I thought I was going to..." Unable to hold back the sobs rising in her throat, they pushed out, drowning out the rest of her words in the process. She covered her head with her hands and broke down completely.

Within seconds, she felt herself being lifted up and pulled into Harrison's arms. She knew she should push away, but just this one last time, she'd allow herself to be held by him. Right now, she needed the comfort and strength his arms provided.

As she wept, the rhythmic sound of his heartbeat against her ear comforted her. "I don't know what I would have done if that fire had burned my theater," she whispered against his chest a moment later.

"You would have rebuilt it. That's what you would have done." His words vibrated in his chest and her ear, and his breath brushed against her hair.

Abby stepped out of his embrace and shook her head. "No, I don't think I could handle it if I had to rebuild it. Not alone."

"You wouldn't have had to do it alone. I would have helped you." He pulled back enough to be able to see her. His intense stare held her captive. "Abby." He swallowed hard. "I know you said you wouldn't marry me. Is there anything I could do or say to change your mind? I love you so much. I can't bear the thought of living without you."

Abby couldn't bear to see the pain in his eyes. "Oh, Harrison. I love you, too. As much as it pains me to say this, I have to. I—I can't marry you."

"Why, Abby? Why?" An even more intense pain filled his voice.

"Two reasons. One of them I'm too ashamed to tell you about, and the other is, we don't share the same faith."

"Oh, but we do."

Abby's gaze shot up to his. "What do you mean?"

"Ever since I arrived, every time a problem arose, you would say that God would take care of it. At first, I pitied you, knowing you would wake up one day to find that God had let you down, like He had me and so many others I know. But, your faith in Him never wavered. You stayed true to your convictions, and in doing so, you allowed me to see a different God. A loving God. A God that could be trusted.

"The other night, I re-read the note in my mother's Bible and now I've accepted God as my Heavenly Father, and I belong to Christ now."

"Really? Oh, Harrison! That's wonderful!" She threw her arms around him, rejoicing that God had once again heard her prayers. "I'm so happy for you. It's the best decision you'll ever make. God is sooo good." She continued to prattle on until she realized where she was and that her arms were still around him. She clamped her mouth shut, dropped her arms from around him and stepped back.

"That means," he said, tilting his head to look at her. "One of the reasons for you not to marry me no longer exists, so what is the other reason why you can't?"

Abby took another step away from him and placed her back to him. He deserved to know the truth, but she couldn't bear to see the look of repulsion on his face when she told him. She yanked all the courage she could to herself before speaking. "I can't have children." She spoke so low the words were a mere mumble, but loud enough that they rang out with a painful jolt in her spirit.

"What did you say? I didn't hear what you said."

"I said, I can't have children," she said an octave higher.

His presence closed in behind her, but he made no response.

Furious with herself and the whole situation, she whirled on him. "I said I can't have children!" she yelled, watching his face for his reaction and dreading it at the same time.

But he only looked at her with worry and incomprehension. "What do you mean you can't have children?"

As hard as it was for her to explain, she might as well finish what she started and tell him all of it. "A few years ago, I found out I have a dead womb. It means there is absolutely no chance of my ever conceiving a child." She kept her eyes on his face, challenging him to throw her on the trash heap of life, but no repulsion materialized. "I know how much it means to you to have a houseful of your own offspring, so that's why I can't marry you."

For a long minute he said nothing and then the scowl on his face deepened. "Is that it? Are there any other reasons why you can't marry me?"

What was wrong with him? "Didn't you hear me? I said I can't give you the children you want."

"Yes, I heard that." The scowl slid away, replaced by something very close to mirth and amusement. "I have children already. And we could adopt if we want more."

Exasperated, she huffed. "I don't think you get it, Harrison. My fiancé, ex-fiancé, David, made it very clear to me that no man would want me because I can't give him children. That every man wants a woman who can bear him a child. You yourself said you wanted more children of your own. And I can't give them to you. Don't you see that? I'm defective! I'm worthless as a woman!" she shouted at him, letting all the anger she'd had pent up inside her over this issue explode out of her.

The mirth on his face grew until Harrison laughed out loud.

Abby couldn't believe it. He actually was laughing.

She didn't see one funny thing about what she'd just said. Of all the nerve. Here she'd poured her heart out to him, and he was laughing. She narrowed her eyes and pursed her lips. A half second more and she would have let him have it with both barrels and the cannon; however, he didn't give her that chance.

Instead, he stepped up to her, took her hands in his and pulled her into a hug.

"Harr-i-son. Let me go." She tried to yank free, but couldn't. "What—what are you doing?"

"Abby, do you love me?"

She whooshed out a long breath of frustration. "What does my loving you have to do with anything?"

"So you admit, you do love me, right?"

"Yes, I love you. You know that. I've said it. I love you. I'm in love with you. I'm miserable without you, and I'd give anything for you to stay. There. Are you happy?"

He backed up from her, letting her go and retaking her hands in his. "No."

"What do you mean 'no'?"

"No, as in not yet." His twinkling eyes forced hers to stay fixed on his. Unfazed by the mud and dirt he was sure to get on his pants, he knelt and gazed up at her. "Abby, I'm asking you again. Will you marry me?"

Abby stared down at him. The man wasn't running away? He wasn't repulsed? And most of all he still wanted to marry her? Could this even be happening? "Do you mean it, Harrison? Even knowing I can't give you children?"

"Abby, listen to me. When you heard me say I wanted a houseful of my own, that was true. I already have two beautiful sons of my own. But even if I didn't, it wouldn't matter. My life would be nothing without you in it, Abby. I love you so very much. Please say you'll marry me."

"Oh, Harrison." She threw herself at him so quickly, he almost didn't have time to get to his feet before she was in his arms. "Of course I'll marry you. I love you so much!"

Their lips met in the sweetest, dreamiest kiss of her life. Even dreamier than the ones she'd constantly dreamed about. One thing was for certain—reality was so much, much better than her dreams ever had been.

Chapter Eighteen

"Come on, you guys. Please, for me?" Abby pleaded with her brothers. She was the last of the Bowen siblings to marry and she wanted it to be befitting of who she was. "It won't hurt you to wear a costume just this one time. After all, your baby sister only gets married once." She batted her eyes at them with all the flare she had accumulated and then some.

Being the baby of the family had its advantages. She could see all three of them weakening. Just as she had when she had begged them to let her name all the ranch animals. She had named a pig Kitty, a cat Miss Piggy, a bull Taxt, a cute little mule deer Fawns, a horse Lambie and on and on. To this day her brothers still took a razzing over the names from anyone who stepped foot on the ranch. Hey, what did people expect from a little girl?

She eyed each of her brothers and gave them that same pathetic puppy-dog look she'd given them all the other times she'd gotten her way. It was only a matter of time before they would crack and give her everything she wanted.

Haydon, the oldest of Abby's brothers looked over to her other brothers, Michael and Jesse, who looked back at him for his decision before they dared voice their own. Haydon raked his hand through his blond hair and let out a long breath. "What do you say, guys? Surely we could do it just this once."

"Costumes?" Michael spiked a brow.

Jess shook his head. "I suppose we could. But only because it's you, Abby."

"Oh, thank you!" Abby threw herself at her brothers and gave them each a great big hug and a kiss on the cheek. "I love you guys. Thanks!" With that, she whirled and bolted toward the main ranch house. She couldn't wait to tell her mother. She was thrilled that Harrison didn't mind them getting married on her family's ranch. In fact, he thought it was a great idea.

So, she and Harrison, Josiah and Graham had boarded a train shortly after the fire that had destroyed her shed with all her props for the upcoming production of *Pride & Prejudice*. They wouldn't have gotten to come here if it hadn't been for all the townspeople, including the mayor and the town committee members getting together to help rebuild all the props. Once they were finished, Abby and Harrison felt free to go. Especially since everyone knew their routines to keep the theater running while they were gone. She and Harrison felt confident leaving Staimes and Veronique in charge until they returned from the home she grew up in—Paradise Haven in the Idaho Territory.

Abby rushed through the door of the main house. "Mother! Rainee! Selina! Leah! Hannah!" Abby hollered as she strode inside. She would have hollered for the children, too, but the older cousins had taken them on a scavenger hunt to keep them occupied so that she and the ladies could head into town to take care of more wedding details.

Before Abby found where they were, all five of them came barreling in from the direction of the living room, concern and fear marching across their faces.

"What's wrong?" Mother asked, her voice covered in panic.

"Wrong? Nothing's wrong, Mother. Why?"

"What do you mean, why? You came running in here hollering like the house was on fire. Merciful heavens, child. You gave me such a fright." Her mother pressed her hand to her chest and took several deep breaths.

"Sorry, Mother. I didn't mean to. I'm just so excited is all. I finally talked the boys into wearing the costumes for my wedding. Bless their hearts." Abby smiled with pure delight that they were willing to do that for her. She couldn't wait to go pick the costumes out. So with a dramatic swing of her arm outward toward the direction of the front door, in her strong, mock British accent, she said, "Come now, my dears. Make haste, make haste. Let us away to town to Father's theater where there we may obtain said costumes with which to clothe everyone."

Leah, Abby's only sister, darted a glance toward the ceiling before settling her gaze on the other women. "Abbynormal hasn't changed one little bit, has she?"

"Now why would she wanna up and go do that for?" Selina, Michael's wife, asked. "Ain't nothin' wrong with her the way she is. God done a right fine job with her."

"I know that, Selina." Leah smiled. "I was just teasing her, and she knows it." Her gaze softened toward her sister. "I wouldn't want her to change who she is for anything in the world. I love her just the way she is. Drama and all."

"I love you, too, Lee-Lee." Abby hugged Leah but not too close. Abby didn't want to hurt her sister's protruding belly. For the first time since Abby had discovered she couldn't bear a child, seeing one of the women in her family with child didn't bother her. She was certain it had to do with the fact that in three days' time, she would become the mother of two of the sweetest, most precious boys in the world.

"Well, are we going, or are you just going to stand there all day with that silly grin on your face?" Hannah's voice broke through Abby's happy thoughts.

"What? What did you say?" Abby asked Hannah, her brother Jesse's wife.

"Don't mind her, Hannah. She's a woman in love." Leah wrinkled her nose at Abby, and Abby returned the gesture.

Mother shook her head at them. "We're wasting time, ladies." She looked at Abby. "Lead the way, daughter." Mother gestured toward the front door. Abby led the procession out into the hot August sun.

"How ever did you get them to consent to this?" Rainee, Haydon's wife, asked from behind Abby.

"The same way I got them to let me name all the animals." Abby peered over her shoulder at Rainee and smiled with a wink.

"How come that never worked for me?" Leah looped Abby's arm through hers. The two of them strolled arm in arm toward her mother's landau.

"You just don't have my knack and my flare for getting your way, that's how come."

They laughed.

Everyone climbed into the carriage, and all the way to town the five of them chattered about the wedding, about children, about husbands and everything else women talked about, and Abby was loving and enjoying every moment of it. She didn't think something like this would ever happen to her. But it had. God had taken care of it. Because of that, in just three days, she would become Mrs. Harrison Kingsley. Oh, how she liked the sound of that.

This was the day Harrison had dreamed of. Today, he would marry the woman of his dreams. One who loved not only him, but his boys, as well. She was going to make a great mother for Graham and Josiah, of that he was certain.

Harrison tugged downward on the red, silk stripe running down the outside of his pant legs. The costume pants were a tad too short, but he wasn't about to complain. It was either them or leotards, and he wanted no part of those. Harrison shuddered just thinking about wearing those stretchy, leggy things. He still couldn't believe that he almost had to wear them. Even more unbelievable, however, was that he would have, just to see the joy on her face. After all, how could he refuse Abby? How could anyone, for that matter? His fiancée had a knack for getting people to do things they didn't want to do. Like wearing theater costumes to a wedding.

Not just any wedding, either, but his own wedding. Harrison had no idea how Abby talked everyone into the things she did, but he figured he'd better find out soon or he had a feeling that during their marriage he would be doing a lot of things he didn't want to.

He glanced down at his prince costume. He felt like an idiot in the red jacket with shoulder pads and gold cords looped under his arms and over them. The royal-blue pants with the red stripe down the side wouldn't be so bad if they weren't a tad short. His wasn't the only costume that didn't fit just right, he thought, trying to make himself feel not so self-conscious about it. One thing that helped him not to was the fact that at least he wouldn't be the only one wearing one. Besides, who knows? It might even be fun. It would certainly be an adventure, and life with Abby was always that, if nothing else.

Haydon, Jess and Michael, Abby's brothers, along with her brother-in-law, Jake Lure, all of whom he had liked immediately upon meeting them, strode up to Harrison. Wearing those knee-length baggy pants, knee-high boots and puffy-sleeved-shirted peasant costumes and peasant vests took guts. What took even more guts to wear were the white wigs they all had on. Now there Harrison had drawn the line.

Haydon placed his hand on Harrison's shoulder. "Are you sure you're ready for this?"

Harrison's eyes scanned the length of each one of them. "Are you?"

The men laughed, then headed over to take their places in the ranch yard.

Rows of neighbors dressed in costumes ranging anywhere from Roman guards to sheriffs to outlaws to soldiers to nurses to maidens to princesses and everything else in between graced the yard. Some of the women even had masks on. Abby's mother included. Her royal-blue velvet queen costume, complete with a jeweled crown, suited her. Not that Abby's mother acted like a queen or anything, but she was a very lovely, caring lady who had all the style and grace of a queen.

The whole thing was quite a sight to behold. Unlike anything he'd ever seen before. Then again, it fit his Abby perfectly.

Harrison's gaze traveled to the front where the pastor stood wearing a white wig and a knee-length medieval white robe that looked more like a dress to Harrison, with a huge red cross down the center of his chest, and a white cape that hung midway down the calves of his legs. A man in a skirt? Now *that* costume took real guts to wear. Again, Harrison shuddered, thankful *he* didn't have to wear a skirt, too. What he had on was bad enough. Well, he refused to dwell on it. He was doing this for Abby because he loved her.

His line of vision slid down to Graham and Josiah who stood directly in front of the pastor wearing royal blue caps with a single white feather fanned out from each one, white shirts with puffy sleeves, royal blue knickers and white stockings. Each of the twins held a small, white-satin pillow with a tied blue ribbon that held his wedding ring on one and Abby's on the other.

Behind his sons and off to the minister's right, stood Abby's sister, Leah. Beside Leah was Rainee, Hannah and Selina. To the minister's left stood Jake, Haydon, Jesse and Michael. All costumed to perfection. Well, almost. Harrison smiled.

The sound of a bell clanging rang out across the yard,

and a loud voice came from the direction of the barn drawing Harrison's attention to it.

Abby's stepfather, Charles, dressed in a town-crier costume, rang the hand bell and cried with a boisterous voice, "Hear ye, hear ye. All rise. Here comes the bride."

With that, Abby came into view sitting sidesaddle atop a white horse wearing a white satin dress and white slippers. On top of her head sat his mother's diamond-and-sapphire tiara. The matching necklace graced Abby's sleek neck.

Harrison smiled. He'd never seen a more beautiful bride. His bride. His heartbeat kicked up, and a passel of butterflies fluttered about in his stomach.

Today, the lovely Miss Abigail Bowen would become his wife.

Abby's eyes sought out Harrison's and locked onto them. Her soon-to-be husband stood at the beginning of the aisle looking like a real-life prince. Her very own prince. And this wasn't one of her dreams, either. Well, it was, but it was about to become a reality. Her heart skipped.

She reined the horse to a stop in front of Harrison. His strong arms reached up to help her down while Charles held the horse for them.

Harrison held her securely while he helped her off the horse. As soon as her feet were settled on the ground, the pastor's voice boomed, "Who here gives this woman to this man?"

Charles spoke up in a strong, commanding voice. "Her mother, her brothers, her sisters and I do."

"Very well, then you may come forward."

Abby was so proud of everyone and so grateful. It was exactly as she had envisioned it for so many years.

Harrison looped Abby's hand through his arm, and they strolled up the aisle between their wedding guests whose smiles lit the pathway to the preacher.

When they reached the front, Abby leaned down and gave Josiah and Graham a quick hug, careful not to tip the ring pillows they held in the process.

Strands of Pastor James's red hair peeked out from under his white wig. He opened his Bible and started to read about how a man should leave his father and mother, and two people should become one flesh, and how no one should enter into the marriage union lightly. Abby breathed it all in and exhaled as joy filled her heart. The vows were coming when they would commit to love one another all the days of their lives. She had to force herself not to tell the pastor to hurry up.

Finally, he closed the Bible and looked first at her.

"Abigail Bowen…"

Abby wanted to correct Pastor James and tell him it's Abby, not Abigail and that Abigail sounded too stuffy, but she held her tongue. Now was not the time nor the place.

"Do you take this man, Harrison Kingsley to be your lawfully wedded husband?"

"Yes, she does!" Josiah burst out.

Everyone laughed, including Harrison and Abby.

Abby looked at the preacher. "Yes, she does." Then she looked right at Harrison. "Yes. I do." She had never meant three words more.

They finished repeating the vows and exchanged the rings, without any further interruptions. Finally, Pastor

James smiled at them and said, "You are now husband and wife. Harrison, you may kiss your bride."

"Gladly." He cupped Abby's face and kissed her. Not just a little short kiss either, but a long knee-locking one. When he finished, his loving gaze settled on hers. "I love you, Abby," he whispered.

"I love you, too, Harrison," she whispered back.

"I now present to you, Mr. and Mrs. Harrison Kingsley." Pastor James's voice broke through their tender moment. But she didn't care. She knew there would be many, many more.

"Don't forget us," Josiah said.

"Yeah. Don't forget us," Graham mimicked.

Everyone laughed again.

Abby squatted down to their eye level. "Now you know we could never forget you boys. We love you both so very much."

"We love you, too," Josiah and Graham said at the same time.

Abby's heart sang with their declaration.

"Can we call you mommy now?" Graham asked shyly.

"You sure can."

Both boys' lips curled so far upward that Abby thought they would split. Joy and happiness rushed into her as she gathered them into her arms. She now had her very own children. Not by birth, but love bound them together and that was just as wonderful. She gave each one of them a hug and a kiss on the cheek, then she stood and turned her gaze to Harrison. The love in his eyes left no doubt whatsoever in Abby's heart that he saw her as a whole woman—complete and wonderful in every way.

He smiled at her and then scooped her up into his arms and carried her down the aisle, whispering words of love as he did. She'd never intended to marry her business partner, her unintended groom. But oh, was she ever so glad she had.

> *And we know that all things work together for good to them that love God, to them who are the called according to His purpose.*
> —*Romans 8:28 KJV*

* * * * *

Janet Dean grew up in a family with a strong creative streak. Her father and grandfather recounted fascinating stories, instilling in Janet an appreciation of history and the desire to write. Today she enjoys traveling into our nation's past as she spins stories for Love Inspired Historical. Janet and her husband are proud parents and grandparents who love to spend time with their family.

Books by Janet Dean

Love Inspired Historical

Courting Miss Adelaide
Courting the Doctor's Daughter
The Substitute Bride
Wanted: A Family
An Inconvenient Match
The Bride Wore Spurs
The Bounty Hunter's Redemption

Visit the Author Profile page
at Harlequin.com for more titles.

THE BRIDE WORE SPURS

Janet Dean

My grace is sufficient for thee:
for my strength is made perfect in weakness.
—*2 Corinthians* 12:9

To my friends and family
who believed I'd achieve my dream. Your support
means everything, then and now. Thank you.

Acknowledgments

A huge, heartfelt thank-you to Mary Connealy
and Becke Turner for their invaluable help with
researching this story. Their expertise enabled
this greenhorn to ride into the Old West largely
unscathed. Any errors are my own.

Chapter One

Bliss, Texas
Spring, 1888

The wrong man showed up to collect Hannah Parrish at the train station. And he was late.

Matt Walker.

Hannah bit back a groan. Of all the people in Bliss, why him? Matt never saw her as grown-up and capable. Instead he still treated her like a child, like the young girl he'd teased.

The man was too sure of himself. Tall, broad-shouldered, long legs encased in denim, his suntanned face hidden by the wide brim of a black Stetson, Matt's every inch oozed cowboy. And every one of those inches oozed irksome.

He came to a halt in front of her, boots planted in a wide stance as if buffeted by the winds that blew across the open range. With a smile, Matt doffed his hat, the late afternoon sun gleaming in his dark wavy hair. The man was good-looking, she'd give him that, but the only man she ached to see was Papa.

"Welcome back," he said. His Texas drawl was polite, yet the pucker between his brows was far from friendly.

"Good to be back." She scanned the crowd milling about the depot platform, retrieving baggage and greeting family. "Have you seen my father?"

Matt plopped his hat in place, throwing his chocolate-brown eyes in shadow. "Martin asked me to pick you up."

Surely after being apart for a year, Papa wouldn't miss meeting her train unless...

Was something wrong? She swallowed against the sudden knot in her throat. "Why didn't he come himself?"

"Didn't say. Better not keep him waiting."

Before she could question him further, Matt took her by the elbow and guided her across the wooden platform, dodging two rambunctious youngsters running through the throng.

Was it only four years ago she'd tagged after Zack, Matt's youngest brother? At the time, Matt had been married to Amy, his high school sweetheart, and had reveled in teasing Hannah at every opportunity. That had been before Amy's horse threw her and she died from a broken neck, when Matt's laugh came easy.

Now, he looked tense. Did he resent picking her up? Well, she wasn't any happier about the switch.

Still, to be fair, she should ease her attitude toward the man, give him the benefit of the doubt. From what

Papa had told her, he'd closed himself off after his wife's death.

They stopped before the baggage cart's perspiring attendant. Hannah pointed out her bags and large camel back trunk.

The porter surveyed her luggage, mumbling an oath under his breath.

Heat flushed her cheeks. If she'd had a choice, she would've left every dress behind in Charleston. But, Papa had tired of seeing her in denim and had insisted she return with a new wardrobe. Aunt Mary Esther had made his wishes her mission.

Matt slipped the attendant a tip. "I'll take it from here."

With a snaggletooth smile, the porter doffed his hat, then turned to the next traveler.

Matt hefted the trunk onto his shoulder, letting out a grunt. "A man could bust a gut toting this load. Must've brought the entire state of South Carolina back with you."

"That's not my fault, I—"

"If you packed them, I'd say that makes them yours," he said before she could explain the large number of cases weren't her idea.

He balanced the trunk then grabbed a valise's leather handle, straining muscles that pulled his shirt tight over powerful shoulders and arms, producing an odd flutter in the pit of her stomach.

"Stay put," he said. "I'll only be a minute."

"I'm perfectly capable of carrying..." Her voice faded as he swaggered off. How dare he treat her like a hothouse flower.

She grabbed the three remaining cases and marched after him, the sun glaring on her back, her lungs heaving against her cast-iron corset. The ostrich plume on her gray felt hat drooped into view, tickling her nose. Her aunt would say the hat made fashion sense. More like fashion insanity.

Papa had sent her away to gain grace and style and all those put-on manners the finishing school had drummed into her. Now she supposed she was indeed finished.

But not as Papa intended.

Her aunt's aimless life had made Hannah all the more determined to remain a rancher. What she did on the Lazy P had significance, and gave her satisfaction.

Without a free hand to swat at the tormenting feather, she blew a puff of air. The feather fluttered, then came to rest against her nose.

Matt stopped, turned back. His gaze settled on the feather. He gave a smirk. "I'd prefer you'd wait until I can return for the rest."

"I prefer doing my part."

Surly eyes gave her a cursory glance. "In that?"

Hannah's gaze swept her traveling dress, all flounce and ruffle, as uncomfortable as armor thanks to the torturous corset. "Don't judge me on my attire."

He harrumphed. "Like Charleston hasn't changed you."

She jerked up her chin. "It hasn't. At all." Another breath lifted up the feather. This time it stayed put.

"Whatever you say, Miss Parrish."

He headed down the boardwalk. She followed, perspiration beading on her forehead. At the wagon, she dropped the load with a clatter at Matt's feet—feet clad in cowboy boots, high quality, Texas made. And he accused her of being a clotheshorse.

Matt leaned against the wagon, apparently untouched by the heat. "Didn't that fancy finishing school teach you to allow a man to give you a hand?" he drawled.

"It taught me to take care of myself."

Not exactly the truth. The headmistress's main message was a proper lady relies on a man for everything, not merely heavy lifting. Well, Hannah tried to never rely on anyone for anything.

His amused expression disputed her claim. "Course you can."

She slapped her arms across her chest, arms that ached from carrying that load, but she'd never admit as much by rubbing them. "Are you questioning that?"

"All right, then. Go ahead. Take care of yourself." He gestured toward the trunk.

On the ground. Six feet below the bed of the wagon.

"You mean put that…in there?"

"You said you could take care of yourself."

To admit she needed help would mean admitting defeat. She bent, the feather quivering in front of her eyes, then gripped the leather handles and heaved with all her might, releasing a decidedly unladylike grunt. And managed to budge the trunk three whole inches before she let it drop. A year in Charleston had made her soft.

"Give up?" Matt asked.

"Never." Heat flooding her cheeks, she gritted her teeth and tried again.

"We'll be here all day while you try to prove your point." He bent down, grabbed the trunk as if it weighed less than the obnoxious feather on her hat and shoved it into the wagon, then stowed the rest of her bags.

"I could have done that." She met his amused gaze. "Eventually."

"Next time the trunk is all yours." With a chuckle, he rounded the wagon and gave her a hand up.

His touch trapped the air in her lungs. Since when did Matt Walker affect her this way? Exhaustion had muddled her mind into mush.

He climbed up beside her. His fluid movements revealed how comfortable he was, how completely at ease. Whereas she felt thrown off balance, as if she'd stepped into somebody else's skin with a whole set of reactions she didn't understand. Or appreciate.

She wanted to go home, to see her father, to soak in the tub until not one speck of travel dust remained.

Home. To the cattle, to the land she loved, the limitless expanse under the Texas sky. Home. Where she'd shuck her frills and finery and don her usual garb and favorite Stetson, clothes she could move and breathe in. Home. To Papa.

With large, capable hands, Matt took the reins, then clicked to the horses. The wagon jerked forward as the horses pulled away.

Beyond the depot lay the bustling town with wagons, buggies and horses jamming the streets. After a year in Charleston, returning home was like easing into comfy boots.

Hannah removed her hat, her gaze caressing each edifice they passed. The courthouse dominated Main Street, teeming with storefronts, saloons, Bliss State Bank, Bailey's Dry Goods, The James Hotel, the post office, the office of *The Banner Weekly* newspaper and two groceries. They passed the blacksmith shop, O'Hara's livery stable, the sheriff's office and the Calico Café, owned by the widow Shields with two rooms to let upstairs if boarders met her strict standards.

At the outskirts of town, they headed toward the ranch. No longer distracted by the racket and dust of Bliss, she turned to Matt. "Is my father well?"

Matt glanced at her, then away, staring at the horses' rumps. Just as she decided he wouldn't speak, he cleared his throat. "Martin's had a rough few months. When I stopped in last night to check on him, he asked me to meet your train."

"Check on him? Why? Isn't Rosa there?"

"Yes, of course." Matt shifted on the seat. "Wait to talk to him."

"I need to know what's wrong before I arrive."

"He's facing…some challenges." He met her gaze. "Having you home will lift his spirits."

And lift a load from Papa's shoulders. If he was sick, she could run the ranch. Oversee the foreman while Papa recovered. If only she'd known he needed help.

"Why didn't he send for me?" A rut in the road sent Hannah's hat tumbling to the floorboards. She retrieved it, then whacked the crown against her knee, raising a puff of dust. "I didn't want to go to Charleston in the first place."

He shot an amused glance at the mound of baggage in the wagon bed. Proof he didn't believe a word. What did she care?

She'd take the focus off her. "How's Zack? Is he out of school?"

"My little brother graduated and joined a law firm in Dallas." He arched an eyebrow. "He's still single."

"I'm surprised he hasn't met someone."

"Figured he was waiting on you. Or you on him."

"You figured wrong. I'm in no hurry to get married."

Dark eyes bored into hers with the force of an auger. "From what I've seen, most women are downright desperate to get hitched."

Desperate to get hitched, my eye.

The claim didn't deserve a retort. From what Hannah had seen, a wife was either a household drudge or an ornamental knickknack. Determined to ignore him, Hannah kept her gaze on the road, away from the vexing man at her side.

At last they drove onto Parrish land, passing a field of bluebonnets carpeting the earth to the horizon. A sense of serenity absent in Charleston seeped into her spirit. But then her mind niggled, filling her with troubling disquiet.

Matt had danced around her questions about Papa. What wasn't he telling her?

Matt eased back on the reins, slowing the horses to pass through the Lazy P gate. At his side, Hannah soaked up the terrain. Barely nineteen, yet certain she had her future mapped out. The set of her shoulders, her ramrod back, the tilt of her jaw, all pointed to one determined woman.

He swallowed hard. One determined, beautiful woman.

The skinny tomboy in baggy clothes, who sometimes could outride, outshoot and outrope Zack, had grown up. He forced his eyes away from the pretty woman at his side and onto the Parrish house up ahead.

The past year, he'd fallen into the habit of spending evenings here with Martin, discussing politics or cattle business over a game of checkers. With Hannah away, this ranch had become his refuge, his second home. Here he could unwind, away from haunting memories of Amy in his parents' house, away from the watchful eyes of his loved ones, away from his father's tight control.

As he'd gotten close to Martin, he hadn't seen the signs of his friend's waning health, but when he grew weak, pale, Matt could no longer deny Martin was sick—too sick to run the ranch. Without shirking his responsibilities at the Circle W, Matt had overseen operations of the Lazy P. The additional work pushed him to his limits, but nothing compared to the agony of watching a friend's body deteriorate.

Like a crouching lion, a sense of helplessness, sorrow and anger had sprung up inside him, awakening feelings he'd had when he lost Amy. Feelings he'd tried to bury with endless work, collapsing into bed at night, too drained to feel anything.

He'd seen the flash of fear in Hannah's eyes as he'd spoken of Martin's health. Unless God wrought a miracle for Martin, she'd have her heart broken.

This spitfire in a skirt, about as competent as a man with his hands tied behind his back, could no more handle this ranch than a cowpoke could handle city life. No matter what she said, she'd need to sell the land. Go back to Charleston where she fit, where she could find herself a husband.

The thought of the anguish awaiting her stung the

backs of his eyes. He blinked, clearing the mist, and strengthened his resolve to stay clear of entanglements. He'd do all he could for Martin. But, the debutante's future wasn't his problem. He'd hold himself apart, keep that armor in place. The only way he could be of use to anyone.

He halted the horses in front of the Parrish house, a low-slung solid structure with an inviting shady porch sheltering a cluster of twig furniture. A quiet spot where a man could catch a sunset. Catch his breath. Catch a moment with God.

He climbed down and headed toward Hannah. Before he reached her, she'd grabbed a fistful of skirts, jumped down and dashed up the steps. No doubt impatient to see her father.

The door swung open. Rosa, the Parrish housekeeper, stepped out, plump arms thrown as wide as the welcoming smile on her face. "Hannah!"

Rosa had to be around Matt's parents' age, yet her dark hair held only an occasional strand of silver and not a single wrinkle creased her round face. With one eye on the happy reunion, Matt unloaded and lugged the baggage to the porch.

Before he toted them to Hannah's room, he'd check on Martin, see that he was prepared to greet his daughter. The man couldn't stomach appearing weak, looking like an invalid.

Across the way, Rosa cradled Hannah's face in work-worn hands and kissed her on both cheeks. "You left a girl and came back a woman. You favor your mama more and more."

Tears running down her cheeks, Hannah hugged the older woman. "I've missed you, Rosa."

Why women cried at happy occasions baffled Matt. At least they weren't weeping in his arms.

Rosa smiled at him. "Hello, Señor Matt."

"How's the finest cook in the county?"

Rosy-cheeked and beaming, the housekeeper giggled. "You try for cookie. They cool in kitchen." She tucked an arm around Hannah. "Come. I help you unpack."

"I want to see Papa first."

"Hannah, I'd like a minute with Martin. Why don't you take a second to…" He glanced at Rosa for help.

"*Si,* wash face, hands." The housekeeper led the way inside.

"I'll only be a few minutes," Hannah said, pleasant enough, but her pointed stare warned him not overstay his welcome.

With a nod, Matt rounded the corner and strode down the hall to Martin's room. He rapped on his door then poked his head in. As he suspected, Martin was stretched out on the bed fully dressed, but from his bleary eyes, he'd been dozing.

A smile lit his face as he struggled to rise. "She's home."

"Yes, freshening up." Matt helped Martin stand. Once he was steady on his feet, they walked the short distance to the office. Martin dropped into his chair behind his desk, his back to the window.

Matt sat in a chair across from him. "You sure you're up to dinner guests tonight?"

"I'm fine."

Those words belied Martin's appearance. Yet Matt understood the need to save face, to ignore what was plain to see.

"My illness is going to flip Hannah's world upside down. She can't keep the ranch," Martin said, his tone weary. "I've got to make her understand that her future is in Charleston."

Martin spoke the truth. Yet that truth hurt Martin and would hurt his daughter.

"I let that girl run wild." A smile lifted the grim line of Martin's lips. "Can't wait to see the change in her."

Tomboy turned debutante would please Martin. "If you have everything you need, I'll be on my way."

"Thanks for picking Hannah up at the depot." Martin's gaze dropped to his hands. "Appreciate it if you and your folks kept silent about my troubles. I aim to give my daughter a happy homecoming."

"Of course. You can count on us to—"

The sound of shoes clicking on the floorboards cut off Matt's words, then halted outside the open door.

"Papa!" With a smile riding her face, Hannah rushed to where Martin sat, the late afternoon sunlight putting him in silhouette. As she reached him, her smile vanished. Wide-eyed, she gaped at Martin. Shock was on her face at seeing her once robust father a shell of his former self, a frail man, his face etched with lines, his skin an unhealthy gray.

"Hannah, dear, I've been waiting all afternoon for my daughter's kiss."

She leaned down, kissed his cheek then stepped back, plopping hands on hips. "You're too thin. Are you ill? Are you eating properly?"

"Been ill. Feeling much better now that you're home. You need to change for dinner. The Walkers will be joining us."

Stormy blue eyes flashed Matt's way then turned back to Martin. "Of course. I'll wear one of my new dresses and relay all the news from Charleston."

"That's my girl."

"I'll see you later, Papa. Rest, okay?"

She pressed a kiss to Martin's forehead then strode to the door, grabbing Matt's arm and hauling him with her.

"See you tonight," Matt said over his shoulder.

As the door clicked shut, Hannah whirled on him. "What's going on with my father?" she said in a harsh, hoarse whisper.

"He told you. He's been ill."

"That doesn't tell me anything! Ill with what?"

With a shrug and sealed lips, he met her gaze. He wouldn't betray Martin's confidence.

Her eyes narrowed, latching on to him like a terrier to a bone. "Who's running this ranch?"

"I am."

"The Lazy P belongs to us. You have your own ranch."

"I'm only helping out."

"That was nice of you, but he has me now."

Matt fought to keep a straight face. "You?"

"You think I'm nothing more than a debutante." She poked him in the chest, her dainty forefinger carrying a surprising wallop. "I'm what I've always been, Matt Walker. A rancher."

"That's absurd. The sooner you realize you have no business running the ranch, the better."

"The sooner you realize what I do is none of your business, the better," she said, then stormed off.

A young, inexperienced female boss was about as welcome to cowpokes as a rattler in the bunkhouse. How long before Hannah learned that truth the hard way?

Chapter Two

A nuisance stood on the Parrish threshold. Or so Hannah tried to tell herself. Taller than her by several inches, Matt's dark mesmerizing eyes locked with hers.

"Evening," he said as he stepped inside.

He looked far too appealing, even chivalrous as he swept off his black beaver Stetson, giving access to his features. Pressed flat on the sides from the pressure of the headband, his hair curled around his nape. His full lips and long lashes would make most women envious.

The deep tan of Matt's face and arms were in sharp contrast to the white cotton shirt beneath his leather vest. Open at the neck and rolled up at the sleeves, the snowy fabric revealed dark curly hair on his forearms.

Before she could gather her wits and take his hat, he'd hung his Stetson on the hall tree, obviously very much at home. He'd admitted running the ranch. Give the man his head and he'd encroach on every facet of their lives.

She pasted on a smile, as if she didn't have a care in the world, and glided across the foyer with a ramrod carriage even the persnickety headmistress in Charleston would approve of.

Inside the dining room, candlelight flickered, shimmering in the high gloss of the tabletop. The silver serving pieces, possessions her mother had brought west, looked out of place in the rustic room's whitewashed walls and dark beamed ceiling.

At the table, Matt's parents sat talking to her father. Papa looked even more frail beside the Walkers.

Robert Walker's hair might be streaked with silver, but he possessed the same broad shoulders and dark brown eyes as his son, no doubt the picture of how Matt would look when he aged.

Were father and son preparing to acquire the Lazy P?

Ashamed of her suspicion, Hannah cringed. Just because Matt helped on the ranch, like any good neighbor would, didn't make him underhanded.

Victoria Walker, tall, big-boned and pretty with soft blue eyes and silvery hair, wrapped Hannah in a hug. A strong woman with a contagious laugh and good heart, Victoria could have a sharp tongue. Or so Hannah had heard. A trait that had surely come in handy raising three ornery sons, one son in particular.

Wrapped in a clean apron, Rosa waited, ready to serve from a table laden with steaming platters and bowls emitting enticing aromas. "The food looks and smells wonderful, Rosa. Thank you."

"I cook your favorites, Hannah."

Once they'd taken seats, Papa said grace. Everyone sampled the food—steak, corn pone, mashed potatoes and gravy—and declared every bite delicious. Smiling, Rosa returned to the kitchen.

"A father couldn't be more proud of a daughter than I am of you, Hannah."

"You're a wonderful father."

Papa cleared his throat. "A picture of your mother, you possess not only her beauty but her spirit."

Fleeting flashes of gentle hands, a loving smile, a nine-year-old girl's memories of her mother. The portrait hanging over the fireplace mantel a reminder that Melanie Parrish had been a lovely woman. "Thank you, Papa."

"Martin's right," Victoria declared as she buttered a bite of cornbread. "For an instant earlier, I thought I was seeing Melanie. Gave me quite a start, too."

"Hannah wasn't eager to go to Charleston, but I wanted her to visit the city where her mother and I fell in love." Papa smiled. "High time she got acquainted with her mama's kin, too."

Finishing school wouldn't help her work a ranch, but Papa had been insistent, as unbending as steel.

"Growing up surrounded by cowhands and cattle wasn't fair to you, Daughter. I wanted to give you the social graces your mother would've taught you had she lived."

Etiquette might mend fences, but not the sort made of barbed wire. Still, Papa had good intentions, always thought of her first. Hannah squeezed his hand.

"So, Daughter, tell the Walkers about Charleston."

"The city's beautiful. The grand piazzas and private gardens tucked behind ornate wrought-iron gates are charming."

Victoria put her hand to her chest, feigning horror.

"Surely the gardens aren't prettier than our fields of bluebonnets and Indian paintbrush?"

"Nothing is prettier than Texas wildflowers."

"Spoken like a true Texan," Victoria said.

Robert ladled gravy on his potatoes. "South Carolina could never overshadow the great state of Texas."

"True, but with my eight cousins and their friends coming and going, I loved Aunt Mary Esther's garden, the one place I could find solitude."

Matt cut into his steak. "Any damage remaining from the earthquake of '86?"

"The brick buildings that survived have been stabilized with iron bolts. Otherwise I saw few signs of the quake."

Victoria's brow puckered. "Was your aunt's house damaged?"

"Yes, they had to rebuild, as did most people. The city's done an amazing job of restoration."

"After the hectic pace of Charleston, Bliss must seem dull." Matt's tone issued a challenge.

"Hardly." Dull was hours spent practicing stitching, drawing and elocution, but she wouldn't disappoint Papa by saying as much. "I botched needlework and painting. My poor aunt struggled for something charitable to say about my pitiful efforts."

"Your cousins would find working on the Lazy P equally difficult," Victoria said.

Hannah chuckled. "I can't imagine Anna Lee and Betty Jo riding astride, cutting calves or mending barbed wire."

"Do you plan to teach those fancy manners to the

young ladies in town?" Robert said. "Maybe start a school?"

"No, I'll work on the ranch as I always have."

Matt turned dark censorious eyes on her. "The work is hard, even dangerous. Not the place for a lady."

Hannah clamped her jaw to keep from sharing a piece of her mind with Matt, a piece that would not fit his image of a lady.

"Matt's right, you're a lady now." Papa patted Hannah's hand. "Nothing would make me happier than to see you marry and settle down with a doctor or lawyer, someone to take care of you, to give you a life of ease."

"Zack's a successful lawyer and single," Matt reminded them, eyes twinkling.

A well-placed heel on his instep would wipe that smirk off his face.

"Zack would make you a fine husband, Daughter."

"I've got two sons needing a wife," Robert said, shooting Matt a pointed look.

Heat flooded Hannah's cheeks. "I'm not looking for a husband." She glared at Matt. "I've never been hurt working on the ranch."

Papa patted her hand. "Wear those dresses you brought back from Charleston. Practice your stitching and painting. Leave the ranch to the men."

The food in Hannah's stomach churned. What had gotten into Papa? Before she'd left, he'd given her free rein. Now he insisted she conform to his image of a lady. Wear clothing that would impede her freedom and make ranch work difficult. She wanted to please him. But the thought of spending hours confined in the garments designed for the "weaker gender"—though any honest woman would admit the clothes took great fortitude to wear—chafed against every nerve.

"I'd like to know what all they taught you at that school."

"I'd be glad to show you, Papa. I brought back paintings, needlework…"

"I heard from Mary Esther that you're a master at elocution." Papa's gaze traveled the table. "Who'd like my daughter to recite a poem?"

Victoria smiled. "That would be delightful."

"Oh, ah, maybe another night. I'm…tired from the trip."

"I'd love to hear a poem." Matt's grin spread across his face. "Nice and loud."

Hannah arched a brow. "Why don't you sing for us, Matt? You're certainly loud enough in church."

"The evening is in your honor, Hannah, not mine. Besides, I'd enjoy listening to a master at elocution."

"I would, too," Robert said.

Papa slapped his hands together. "That settles it. Before Rosa serves dessert, rise and recite a poem, Hannah."

All eyes turned on her. One pair filled with amusement. She wanted to run, but Papa wore a proud smile she couldn't destroy.

She scrambled for a poem, a short poem. The only verse that came to mind was by Elizabeth Barrett Browning, in Hannah's mind the perfect map of love. How could she recite a love sonnet with Matt nearby, no doubt laughing at her?

With Papa's pat of encouragement, she struggled to

her feet, hands cold, cheeks as red-hot as a horseshoe in a blacksmith's forge.

Matt sprang up and pulled out her chair, then returned to his seat, watching her.

She glanced at each guest as she uttered, "How do I love thee?" First Robert, Victoria, then Papa. "Let me count the ways." Her gaze landed on Matt. She jerked it away, focusing on the gilt-framed landscape over the fireplace. "I love thee to the depth and breadth and height my soul can reach…" The words flowed from her. "I love thee freely…I love thee purely…" If she ever fell in love—that *if* towered in her mind—she'd want this sweet, deep, true love. "I love thee with the breadth, smiles, tears, of all my life; and if God choose, I shall love thee better after death."

Robert clapped heartily. "Bravo!"

For a second she'd forgotten the audience. Her legs turned to jelly and she plopped into her chair. If only the floor would open up and drop her clear to China.

"Lovely." Papa's pale face glowed. "Just lovely."

Matt leaned in. "The way you were caught up in that poem, I have to wonder if you're pining for some gangly boy back in Charleston."

"Of course not!"

Rosa's arrival cut off conversation. She carried a tray of delicate, amber flan, the dessert of her homeland and normally Hannah's favorite. But her appetite had vanished.

The others dug in with abandon, discussing the drought and Cattlemen Association business while Hannah picked at the flan.

"This dessert makes me think, Matthew. Jenny Sample brought a cake by this afternoon. Said she had extra eggs and knew angel food was your favorite. That's the second cake this month."

A wide grin spread across Robert's face. "Appears she'd like the job of feeding you permanently. Why, Jenny dangles her baked goods in front of your nose like bait on the end of a line. Fishing for a husband, I reckon." He raised a brow. "You could do worse."

A flush crawled up Matt's neck. Amused at his discomfort, Hannah giggled. "One of those women you spoke of, desperate to marry," she said, her tone as loaded with sugar as the dessert.

Something akin to a growl slid from his lips.

Victoria glanced at Papa, took in his hunched shoulders, then laid her napkin beside her plate. "It's gotten late. We should be going. We've had a lovely evening, Martin. Please express our thanks for the delicious meal to Rosa."

With both hands, her father pushed against the table, half rising to his feet.

Hannah's heart lurched. Why, the evening had tired him. "I'll see our guests out," she said.

Papa flashed a grateful smile. "I'll say good-night, then."

While Matt stayed behind, speaking to her father, Hannah accompanied Robert and Victoria to their carriage and waved as they pulled away.

In the cooler night air, Hannah lingered for a moment, listening to the plaintive sound of a harmonica drifting on the breeze from the bunkhouse. In the moonlight, long pale shadows of outbuildings instilled the ordinary structures with a sense of mystery. She tilted her head back and studied the star-studded sky, bright as diamonds.

God had created this land long before the Parrish family lived upon it. The land would remain long after they were gone. The permanence of the land and of its Creator slid through her, wrapping her in tranquility. In gratitude.

Until Matt loped to her, leading his horse by the reins. From the smirk on his face, he'd come to taunt her. At the end of her rope, she hoped he had the good sense to keep his smart-alecky mouth nailed shut. Nothing would give her more pleasure than showing that naysayer she could run the ranch and run it well.

Matt chucked Hannah under the chin. He'd do what he could to encourage Martin's wish to see his daughter settled in Charleston. "You gave quite a performance earlier. Proof you're well suited for Charleston's social life."

She swatted his hand away. "Stop trying to stuff me into a box labeled debutante. That's not who I am."

"Kind of testy, aren't you?"

"I was enjoying the peace of this beautiful night before you came along."

The glint in those blue eyes gazing up at him had nothing to do with reflected moonlight and everything to do with an urge to wallop him. He had no idea why he'd been hard on her, especially with her concern for Martin. "Look, I'm sorry."

Her eyes widened, as if she couldn't believe her ears, then she gave a brisk nod.

Surely on a night like this they could find a way to

get along. He tilted his head, studying the starry expanse. "When I look up at that sky, at the number of stars and planets, I feel part of something big. Part of God's creation."

"I know. I only caught snippets of the sky in Charleston, but here…" Her voice caught, then trailed off. "I love this land."

It was one thing they had in common. "Who wouldn't?"

Her gaze landed on him, intense, eager. He couldn't tear his eyes away.

"Then you understand how much the ranch means to me. Why I have to take charge until my father's on his feet."

"You'd be wise to set your heart on something else before you get it trampled."

At his words, the accord between them evaporated faster than dew on a hot Texas morning.

Hannah planted her hands on her hips. "You'd be wise to keep your opinions to yourself, Matt Walker."

"I know these cowpokes—"

"I've known most of our cowhands all my life. Why, except for Papa, I'm better suited than anyone to handle the job."

"You can mend a fence, move cattle, muck a barn, I'll give you that, but operating a ranch is more than that."

She harrumphed. "You're exactly like the men in Charleston. They treat women as if we are delicate porcelain or, worse, dim-witted. I can run the ranch as well as anyone."

How could he make her see reason? He doffed his hat and ran his fingers along the brim, gathering his thoughts. "You're not fragile or dim-witted. I don't doubt that you could learn to manage the financial end. But, truth is, cowpokes don't cotton to taking orders from a female, especially one as young as you."

"They will if they want to be paid."

Matt stifled a sigh. How could he make her understand what was at stake? Cowhands saw her as the boss's daughter, more capable than many perhaps, but still young and inexperienced, hardly prepared to run a spread like the Lazy P.

"It's not about money, Hannah. It's about respect. Something that's earned, not bought."

Alarm traveled her face. She sighed, clasping trembling hands in front of her. "You make a point. I'll need to earn their respect and earn it fast."

Respect wasn't earned overnight. Nor were these men eager to give it. But to say more would get her dander up. "Let me handle things for now."

"You're no longer needed here." She pinned him with a fierce, chilling gaze. "I don't want your interference."

If looks could kill, Matt would be a dead man.

How would Martin have managed if Matt hadn't—as she called it—interfered? He'd call it lending a hand, being neighborly. How in tarnation did the dainty debutante think she'd manage roundup?

Not his concern. She'd made that abundantly clear.

He jammed his Stetson on his head and swung into the saddle. Without a backward glance, he nudged Thunder in the flanks and rode in the direction of the Circle W, the peace of the starry night shattered.

Hannah Parrish had no concept of the trouble looming on the horizon. Trouble she'd bring on herself, as if she needed more.

She saw him as an enemy instead of an ally. Any action he took, she'd misconstrue. He'd warned her, it was all he could do. Except for checking on Martin and looking after his needs, Matt would stay clear of the little spitfire.

How long before her plan to run the Lazy P single-handedly blew up in her face?

A rooster's call pierced the muggy morning air drifting through the open window. Hannah stirred then opened her eyes, stretching languidly, relishing the pleasure of waking in her own bed.

A smile curved her lips. In the dream she'd had, a handsome cowboy, tall, dark, held her in his arms.

She reared upright. All the events of yesterday slid into her sleep-fogged brain, rousing her faster than a cold dip in a horse tank. Her stomach knotted, as she recalled Matt's attitude toward women, and Papa's poor health and sudden determination to make her a lady.

Lady or not, she had work to do. Last night she'd looked the part of debutante. Today she'd show Matt Walker, her father and the Lazy P cowhands she could run this ranch, if need be, wearing skirts. That ought to earn their respect. And wipe that smug smile off Matt's face.

Hannah donned a pair of denims and a shirt, her hands trembling. What if she failed to earn the crew's respect? What if they wouldn't listen to her? What would she do then?

One glance around her room's familiar belongings

slowed her breathing. The quilt her mother had stitched, the rocker beside the open window, curtains rustling in the morning breeze. Peaceful, normal.

Her stomach clenched. With Papa ill, normal had fled faster than a calf freed after branding.

At the washstand, she splashed water on her face and brushed her teeth, then ran a fingertip over the chip on the blue-and-white ironstone bowl, the result of a carelessly tossed hairbrush years before.

Her possessions might not be perfect but this room was an oasis in a world flipped upside down. "Oh, please, God, don't let Papa…" Her voice trailed off, the possibility too horrible to speak aloud.

Surely things weren't as dire as they appeared. She took a calming breath. She'd see that Papa ate well and got plenty of rest. Whether Matt believed in her ability or not, she'd run the ranch, gladly taking the burden from her father and returning the operation of the Lazy P to its rightful owners.

She braided her hair, shoved her feet into scuffed boots, grabbed her leather gloves and Stetson, then strode out the door.

In the kitchen, Rosa removed a pan of biscuits from the oven.

"How's Papa this morning?"

"Sleeping. You up with rooster."

"I'm heading out to help with the chores."

"I fix big breakfast when you finish."

"Thanks."

Hannah downed a hot biscuit and coffee, then strode to the stable. A few feet away, the pungent odor of manure and horseflesh teased her nostrils, softened by the sweet smell of hay, a welcome relief from the overpowering scents of potpourri and eau de cologne permeating her aunt's house.

She stepped into the dim interior and a ray of sunlight dancing with dust motes lit a path to Star's stall. As she approached, she spoke the mare's name.

With a nickered greeting, Star poked her bronze head over the stall door, bobbing it in recognition.

Hannah pulled the mare's nose against her shoulder, rubbing the white irregular shape that earned her name. "Oh, I've missed you," Hannah murmured. "Later today I'll take you out."

Hannah grappled with the feed sack, watching the oats tumble end over end into the feedbox. A sense of peace filled her. Here in the stable, among crusty cowpokes, unpredictable livestock and her steadfast steed, she fit. This life filled her as she'd filled Star's feedbox, to the brim, to overflowing.

Across the way, Jake Hardy lugged two buckets of water into the stable. Stooped and wiry, he'd worked on the Lazy P for as long as Hannah could remember. "Hi, Jake."

"Well, welcome home, Miz Hannah!" Jake entered Star's stall and tipped water into the trough. "Star missed you something fierce. Reckon lots of folks like me are glad you're back, specially your pa."

"Thanks, Jake. How's that back?"

He grinned, revealing the gap between his front teeth. "'Bout what you'd expect for an old coot throwed too many times from breaking broncos."

"Any news from your niece?"

The light in Jake's gray eyes dimmed. "No idea

where Lorna's gone off to. I don't mind telling ya, she's got me worried. What kind of a woman leaves her child?"

What else had Papa kept from her? "I'm sorry to hear that."

"My sis is taking care of Lorna's girl, Allie."

Lord, help Lorna do what's right. "I'll pray for her."

A smile crinkled his leathery face. "'Preciate it."

If anything happened to Jake's sister Gertie, Jake would have to take care of Allie. He wouldn't know what to do with a seven-year-old girl any more than Hannah would.

Finished with the morning chores, Hannah glanced outside. "Do you know where I can find Tom?"

"I'll fetch him." Jake hobbled toward the bunkhouse, pitched forward from the waist, his legs curved as if permanently astride. Thanks to multiple injuries, Jake looked older than his years, but he was sinewy, his disabilities didn't slow him down.

While she waited, Hannah checked the tack room. Oiled leather hung on the wall. The horses looked well cared for. Even with Papa's poor health, the ranch appeared to be operating efficiently. How much credit was Matt's? How much was Tom's?

She wandered outside and spied the foreman rounding the corner of the corral, ambling toward her, his frame reed thin, a bandana around his neck, spurs jangling. She raised a hand in greeting.

He touched his hat. "You looking for me, Miss Hannah?"

"I want to thank you for keeping the ranch running smoothly."

"Just doing my job."

"Before I left for Charleston, my father and I discussed the need for a well on the south range. When I arrived yesterday, I noticed nothing had been done. I'd like you to get the digging underway first thing tomorrow. I'll arrange for a windmill."

Tom removed his hat and scratched the back of his head. "The boss didn't mention nothing about another well."

"With his illness, the plan must've slipped his mind." She knew ranching. Soon Tom, the entire crew, would see that too, and give her respect. "Progressive ranchers don't rely on nature to supply water to their herds."

Tom shuffled his feet. "I'll check with the boss."

That was the last thing Papa needed. Hannah bristled. "That won't be necessary."

"Ain't no trouble." The foreman tipped his hat, polite enough, but the sullen look in his eyes said otherwise.

As she watched Tom clomp to the house, an unsettling sense of foreboding gripped her, squeezing against her lungs. What would she do if Tom refused to work for her? How could she run the ranch? From the conversation at the table last night, the cows were dropping calves. That meant roundup was only a few weeks away, which was the reason she'd wanted to get the well dug now. Perhaps she'd been hasty in pushing the issue with the foreman.

Across the way, Matt emerged from the house, swung into the saddle and rode toward the Circle W. No one paid a social call at this hour. She sighed. More likely, he'd helped her father dress and shave. Thoughtful of him and easier on Papa's pride than turning to her or Rosa for assistance.

Had Matt heard Tom question her authority with Papa? Perhaps, if she asked him to intervene, he'd set Tom straight. But she wouldn't ask. She couldn't build respect with the men if she didn't handle things herself.

She strode to the house and met Tom coming out. The smug expression he wore steeled her spine.

"Ain't going to be no well dug," he said.

Was her father too ill to stick to his plan, to stand up to his foreman? "Do you think you're running this ranch?"

"Nope." He guffawed. "Appears you ain't either."

Hannah stepped around him. Inside she found Papa at his desk, dressed and freshly shaven.

"Morning, daughter. Have a seat." He looked at his hands, instead of meeting her gaze. "We need to talk."

With an arrowed spine, she sat across from him, her hands knotted in her lap.

"A company back east is buying up land in the area. No reason they won't buy our spread. Without the responsibility of the Lazy P, you'll be free to return to Charleston."

Never. But she wouldn't upset him with a refusal.

"Papa, can we discuss this later? I just talked to Tom. He claims you don't want a well dug on the south range."

Martin motioned to the books spread in front of him. "That was the plan but we've had a tough year. Last year's low beef prices and high costs have put the ranch in jeopardy."

Why hadn't Papa told her all this? Did he see her as some fragile female unable to face realities?

"I've curtailed expenses. Had to let two hands go."

"If I'd known about our financial trouble, I wouldn't have made a fool of myself in front of Tom."

"What Tom thinks doesn't matter." The steely determination in his eyes, something she rarely saw, stabbed into her. "What I think does. Denims aren't fitting for a lady. Change into one of your dresses. If you want to help, help Rosa in the kitchen."

With roundup a few weeks away, how could Papa relegate her to the kitchen? If this drought didn't end soon, they risked overgrazing the land and would need to thin the herd. That meant punching cattle to Fort Worth right after roundup. With only two drovers and Tom, she'd need to lend a hand.

Besides, what if Rosa resented the interference? Years of managing the house had proved she didn't need help.

Roundup wasn't the huge undertaking it had been when cattle freely roamed the range. Still, how did Papa expect to handle branding the calves without her? Or if rain didn't come, driving cattle to Fort Worth to sell without her?

Her breath caught. Was Papa too ill to grasp the work that loomed? "Papa, with few drovers, what's your plan for handling roundup?"

"Matt and I were talking about that this morning. He'll bring a couple of the Circle W hands. We'll get by."

"Why isn't the Walker ranch struggling, too?"

"Things are tight, sure, but they're a bigger operation. Better set financially."

Were the Walkers hoping to pick up the Lazy P for a song?

She wouldn't sit back and twiddle her thumbs. If dresses pleased her father, she'd work in dresses. She'd ride astride in dresses. She'd run this ranch in dresses. But she wouldn't turn over their ranch to anyone.

In her room, she changed into one of the simple dresses she'd owned before Charleston, then joined her father in the kitchen for breakfast. Rosa had prepared hotcakes, eggs, steak, biscuits and gravy—food to keep a working man and woman going.

Throughout the long day, she tested the corral, the gates, then rode fence, assisting with repairing barbed wire, as she had before she left for Charleston. The cowpokes tipped their hats and spoke politely, treated her like a lady.

But, when she gave instructions, they played deaf or openly rebelled. By the day's end, she'd seen and heard enough to know their hands and foreman were used to taking orders from Matt, but refused to listen to her.

Matt had used the pretense of helping her sick father to worm his way into running the Lazy P. Why would he do that? Did he expect to benefit financially?

She saddled Star and rode for the Circle W, determined to have it out with the man.

Chapter Three

Trouble in a skirt was heading Matt's way. Trouble he'd tried to avoid by doing exactly as Hannah asked. Except for helping Martin dress and shave, he'd kept his distance from the Lazy P. So why the long face?

Unless—

His heart skidded. Had Martin taken a bad turn?

No, by the looks of that ramrod posture, the no-nonsense set of her shoulders and those flashing eyes, the filly was out for blood.

His.

As if she were a bounty hunter and his face topped a Wanted poster, Hannah had tracked him to the far border of the Circle W. Not that she looked like any bounty hunter he'd ever seen. Her feminine dress was hiked to reveal dusty-toed boots in the stirrups. Her black Stetson slung low completed an enticing mix of female and rancher that would've held an appeal, if not for that bloodthirsty look in her eyes.

He removed his hat, swiped the sweat off his brow and then arched his back, stretching achy muscles. With his pa slowing down, Zack a big-city lawyer and Cal overseeing his in-laws' spread, Matt barely kept up with the work. He slapped his hat in place. Now he had to take time to deal with an irate female.

She dismounted, standing there waiting.

He turned to the cowpoke working beside him. "If I'm lucky, I'll only be a minute." He released a gust of air. "More likely you'll have time for a siesta."

"Sounds good. Looks mighty good, too." He winked. "If you need help, holler."

"I'll manage." Though when it came to women, his past had taught him to curb expectations.

Matt strode to where the feisty female stood. Chin sky high, arms folded across her chest, she started yammering at him before he reached her.

He held up a palm. "Now slow down, little filly."

Hannah stiffened. "Don't call me that."

"What's wrong with filly?"

"I remind you of an awkward young horse?"

"Way back when, you reminded me of a newborn foal, all legs, yet I knew you'd be a beauty."

Who could help noticing the red highlights in her auburn hair shooting sparks in the sunlight. Without thinking he lifted a hand to a tendril coiled along her jaw.

As if his touch branded her, she jerked back, but then gathered her wits and anger and leaned toward him.

You're in for it now, Walker.

"Thanks to your meddling, our drovers are accustomed to taking orders from you and won't listen to me."

"Martin's not up to running the ranch. A foreman needs someone looking over his shoulder, making sure the ranch operates efficiently. I stepped in because I had to."

Those sky-blue eyes of hers narrowed in a vise of disapproval. "Isn't it more that you want to take over the Lazy P?"

He snorted. "Why would I want to do that? I've got more work than I can handle here."

"Good question. The only answer I can come to— you're in it for the financial gain."

Those were fighting words. If she'd been a man, her implications would've raised his fists. "If you knew anything about ranching, you'd know that profits are at a record low. I'm not earning a dime from the Lazy P."

She harrumphed, as if she didn't believe a word.

"Examine the books," he ground out. "You won't see any mysterious loss of funds. Your father is overseeing the accounts. Talk to him."

"I will." She whirled to go.

Why had he said that? "Wait, don't. Leave him be."

"My father has a right to know what's going on."

"Nothing's going on." Matt let out a breath. "He doesn't need the worry. Not now."

Alarm sprang to her eyes. "What aren't you telling me?"

"That you're going to ruin that land you love with your confounded stubbornness," he said, edging away from the truth.

Martin was dying. Nothing she did, nothing Matt did could turn that tide.

The alarm faded, replaced with a stony stare. "I want you to talk to our hands. Tell them I'm in charge of our ranch."

"I told you that cowpokes resent taking orders from a woman, especially one as young as you. That's got nothing to do with me."

"So you say, still I want you to make clear that I'll be giving the orders until my father's health improves."

"Hannah, you need every ranch hand to keep things running. Cowboys are an independent bunch. If you get them riled, they'll quit."

A flash of doubt traveled her face, but then she squared her shoulders. "I'll hire more." She planted gloved hands on her hips. "Set them straight today. If you don't, I'll suspect you of malicious intent."

"Get this straight, Miss Parrish. I'm not your lackey. I've got a ranch to run."

"Then stop trying to run mine!"

He crossed his arms, stepping toward her until the toes of his boots touched her hem. "You're one stubborn woman. I'll enjoy watching you run your ranch into the ground."

She looked stunned, as if he'd slapped her. His stomach gnarled with regret. Before he could apologize, she stomped to where Star grazed. With a swish of skirts, she mounted, then glared his way. "I can't understand how good people like your folks got saddled with a son like you," she said, then rode off.

He couldn't remember the last time he'd been told off by a woman. He wasn't partial to it, especially when he'd spent months slaving for her ranch.

Still, he'd let his temper get away from him.

Hannah might not believe it, but Tom would have no difficulty getting another position if he rebelled against a female boss. He couldn't let her run the Lazy P into the ground. He owed Martin that much.

He'd talk to her. Apologize.

If the words didn't stick in his throat.

Hannah rode hard for the Lazy P, every muscle tighter than a well-strung fence. She could've slapped Matt's face for suggesting she'd run the ranch into the ground. That he'd enjoy seeing her fail. What cruel arrogance.

She'd accused him of swindling.

A sigh slid from her lips. *Forgive me, Lord.*

She didn't really consider Matt a crook. Yet every word out of his mouth raised her hackles. Why, he'd even forbidden her to talk to her father. *He doesn't need the worry. Not now.*

A shiver slid through her. What was Matt keeping from her?

On Parrish land, Hannah hauled on the reins and reversed direction. She'd ride to town. Visit Doc Atkins. Ask him what ailed her father.

The decision made, Hannah's limbs and neck relaxed as she and Star soared over the familiar terrain. Horse and rider blending as one, the miles melted away. The freedom and exhilaration of the ride filled her with hope. Surely, nothing was terribly wrong with Papa.

On Main Street, Hannah tied Star to the hitching post and strode onto the walk, passing the weathered sign, Earl Atkins, M.D.

Inside, she rapped on the open door of the examining room.

"Miss Parrish. Heard you were back. Been expecting you." The doctor motioned to a pressed-back chair across from the examining table. "Have a seat."

Doc's no-nonsense tone carried such authority Hannah dropped into the chair he'd indicated. A short man with white thinning hair and shaggy brows, his faded blue eyes often held a fierce expression, perhaps from handling the harsh realities of life and death. Today his eyes had softened with kindness.

"I'm worried about my father. He avoids talking about his health, but he can't do much. He's lost weight. His skin tone isn't good." The words escaped in a rush. She bit her lip, waiting for Doc to allay her fears.

With a sigh, Doc Atkins leaned against the examining table. "I'm sorry I don't have better news. Martin's got a cancerous tumor in his abdomen."

Pain exploded in her chest. Tumor? Cancer? Papa? Her trembling fingers found her lips. "Oh, no."

"I'm sorry."

"Isn't there an operation? A medicine?"

He shook his head. "I've done all I can. The specialist in Dallas agreed."

"Papa saw a doctor in Dallas?"

"He treats nothing but cancer. He tried what he knew, but…"

The "but" said it all. She released a shuddering breath. Nothing could be done. "How…how long?"

"Only God knows, but he's…failing fast. All I can do is ease his pain."

Doc turned to an oak cabinet and withdrew a bottle. "I'll send out more pain medication with you." He scribbled the dosage, then handed her the paper and bottle. "Wish I could do more. If we'd found it sooner, he could've gone to St. Mary's, an excellent hospital in Minnesota, but...I'm sorry."

With herculean effort, she rose and walked to the door, her limbs slogging through an invisible thick haze, the shocking verdict vibrating with each step she took.

"See that he takes the medicine." Doc laid a gentle hand on her arm. "I'll be out to see him in a few days."

"Are you sure this isn't some horrible mistake?"

Doc shook his head, his eyes glistening. "I never get used to the losses, especially of someone like Martin."

As if she were a sleepwalker, Hannah found herself outside, dazed and disoriented, her hope shattered. She leaned against the building, shivering in the glaring sunlight, head and heart pounding.

Papa is dying.

A sob tore up her throat. She stuffed a fist to her mouth, biting down on gloved knuckles. What would she do without him? Papa and the ranch were her life. A squeezing fist of fear encircled her neck, closing her throat. She lifted her gaze to heaven. *Lord, help Papa. Help me handle this.*

She breathed slowly. In. Out. In. Out.

As she did, her heart regained its rhythm. She straightened, tamping down the paralyzing panic. Papa needed her. Needed her to be strong. She wouldn't waste precious time she could spend with her father wallowing in despair.

She pushed away from the clapboards, untied Star and rode for home, happy memories with Papa parading through her mind.

In the stable, she met up with Jake. Eyes averted, he toed the ground.

"What's wrong?"

"Tom picked up his back pay, said he don't see a future here."

"He what?"

"Said he wouldn't work for a woman today or tomorrow." Jake sighed. "Our top hand went with him." He huffed. "Was a time when a man took pride in riding for the brand."

The news slammed into her like a stampeding herd. She fought for footing. Matt had been right. What would she do?

"You have a problem working for me, Jake?"

"Nope. Way I see it, money is money no matter who's paying." He met her gaze with moist eyes. "I reckon this here's my home."

"Thank you." She laid a hand on his arm. "The Lazy P is your home and always will be." If the ranch survived. But she wouldn't say that.

"Want me to round up some new hands?"

"I'll take care of it." How, she didn't know. But Jake would have more than enough to do.

Once the last heifer dropped her calf, they needed to drive the cattle into pens, brand and cut the calves. Without a foreman and only two hands, how could she handle roundup? Especially now that she'd told Matt to stay away?

She believed in God's power. With every breath she took, she prayed for a miracle for her father. Without one, Papa wasn't getting better. Tears stung her eyes. Her father had spent his life running the Lazy P. If Papa didn't make it, she wouldn't let the ranch die with him.

Lord, please give me wisdom. Show me how to keep the ranch.

Only yesterday her world seemed secure. Only yesterday her future brimmed with rosy hopes and dreams. Only yesterday she welcomed the challenge of running the ranch.

Today Papa was dying. The foreman had quit. Most of the hands had either been let go or quit. Only two drovers remained.

She took a calming breath, steadying her wobbly emotions, and headed inside the house. Outside her father's room, she pinched color into her cheeks and forced a smile.

Papa was lying down but not asleep. The bed dwarfed him. The pale color of his skin matched the pillowcase beneath his head. Were the lines edged into his face lines of suffering?

"Hi, Papa," she said, then set the pain medicine on his nightstand.

His gaze settled on the bottle. "You know."

"Yes." She dropped onto the bed and clasped one of his hands in both of hers. Tears burned the back of her eyes. She blinked them away.

"I'm sorry, Daughter. I'd hoped to keep it from you a little longer." He raised his other hand, cupped her jaw. "I'd do anything to change things. To be here for you."

"I know." She sucked in a breath. "Tom and our top hand quit."

As if warding off the bad news, Papa closed his eyes, then met her gaze. "You've got decisions to make. I'm sure Matt will step up and run things until you can sell the spread."

"I won't sell."

"Hannah, you've got no choice. It'll take a while, but we'll manage. I'll hang on as long as I can. When my time comes, I want you to return to Charleston, live with Mary Esther. They'll treat you well, be the family you'll need."

She wouldn't leave the ranch. She couldn't. Never.

With the strength of her will, she squared her shoulders. She and Papa couldn't give up. She moved his blue-veined hand to her lips and kissed it. "You have plenty of time. Let's talk about something else."

"I have to know you'll be taken care of after I'm gone. Please, hear me out on this. You can't stay. This ranch is too much for a lone woman."

Weary lines carving his face, Papa closed his eyes.

She tucked the blanket under his chin. "You're right, Papa. Rest."

"That's my girl." A smile curved his lips, yet his eyes remained closed. The smile eased, his breathing slowed. He slept.

Hannah slipped out of the room and headed for the stable. She had to give her father peace. But how?

Her mind churned with Doc's diagnosis, the approaching roundup and Papa's determination to sell the ranch. She needed the wisdom of God but with everything churning inside of her mind, she couldn't hear His quiet voice.

A ride would clear her head. She threw a blanket and saddle on Papa's horse. Lightning probably hadn't been ridden much and needed the exercise.

She found Jake in the tack room. "I'm going to ride out to the north range."

"Always do my best cogitatin' on horseback."

"Me, too." She gave him a weak smile then led Lightning from the stable, mounted and headed north.

In her entire life she'd never carried the weight of responsibility she shouldered now. What if she couldn't find the hands she needed? Most honest, hardworking cowpokes were employed. She didn't trust those loafing around town.

She bit her lip. Matt had been right. She couldn't handle things by herself. Not a camel back trunk, not a cattle ranch. Not her father's death.

God, please, help me. Show me what to do.

Near the copse of cottonwoods alongside the creek winding through the Lazy P, Hannah slowed Lightning then stood in the stirrups. Her gaze scanned the herd dotting the landscape, a mix of breeding Hereford and longhorn, evidence of one of the many changes in ranching, along with fenced pastures, wells, windmills, earthen tanks and short drives to railroad heads. By fencing their cattle, they'd protected the land from overgrazing. Or so she hoped. Without rain they still faced that risk. They'd raised hay and saved half of their herd during the harsh winter of '86 and '87. Exactly why she couldn't deplete their supply in spring.

She dismounted and the leather creaked, loud in the stillness. A fly buzzed near Hannah's head then lighted on the horse's flank. Lightning flicked his tail but the fly persisted.

Hannah shooed the pest, then walked the horse to a patch of shade, struggling to gather her thoughts and come up with acceptable options. Each alternative that paraded through her mind was worse than the last.

Her gaze roamed the pastureland she loved, settling on the prairie dogs playing tag across the way. The cattle lowing in the background was a sound she'd heard all her life. A few calves bunting each other brought a smile to her face.

How could she leave the ranch? She'd shrivel up and lose herself in Charleston. To remain on this land and give her father peace, she'd do whatever she had to do.

In the distance she spotted a lone rider. Even from here she could identify him and his horse. Matt. A man who cared about Papa and would understand her grief.

Papa trusted him. Matt had only been helping Papa, not trying for financial gain. He'd been right about the cowhands, but instead of listening to his advice, she'd suspected his motives. She'd misjudged the man. She had nothing to fear from Matt, a man she could lean on.

He loved the land. He'd help her find a way.

Matt had come to apologize. The fire he'd seen in Hannah's eyes earlier had vanished, replaced with a gut-wrenching sorrow that slammed into him.

God help her, she knows.

Huddled on the ground in the shade of a cottonwood, she exhaled a shaky breath, turning her gaze to the pastureland beyond. Her shoulders sagged, as if the starch had left her spine.

"Papa's dying," she said, tugging on a weed that wouldn't budge.

To hear the words from her lips, each word laden with anguish, knotted his throat. He sat back on his heels beside her. "I'm sorry."

She stopped fiddling with the weed and folded her hands on her knees. "Mc, too."

"Your father doesn't deserve this." But then, who did?

"How long have you known he has…he was sick?"

"About a month, since I took him to the specialist in Dallas." He took her hand. "What are you going to do?"

"I don't know." She raised determined eyes to his. "But I'll tell you what I'm not going to do. I'm not going to leave this land."

He'd seen Hannah as a nuisance, incapable of facing realities. Yet look at her now. Strong. Not falling apart as most women would've done. He bit back a sigh. Strong or not, she couldn't run this ranch alone.

"Martin needs the peace of knowing you're with family, back in Charleston. Best thing you can do for him is sell the ranch."

"I'd do anything to please him." Her voice broke. "Anything but that." She rose and turned her back to him, swiping at her eyes. Yet that ramrod spine spoke of spirit and strength. Silhouetted against the horizon, small and alone, she had no one to turn to for comfort.

Except him.

Matt crossed the distance in two strides and gathered her into his arms. Something he'd do for anyone struggling with sorrow, for any one of his brother's friends.

She laid her face against his chest, her tears dampening his shirt. He cradled her close, his heart pounding like the hooves of a herd of wild mustangs. What was happening to him?

"I can't run the ranch alone," she said, lurching away. "I can't handle the roundup without a crew. I can't make

Papa well." She lifted glistening eyes rimmed with spiky lashes, eyes filled with desperation.

"I'll help any way I can." He wanted to ease her burden. Ease her heartache, but he didn't have the power. *God, help her.*

As if deep in thought, she stepped away, eyes fixed on the horizon, filled with a faraway look. What was she thinking?

She turned to him, resolve on her face. "You'd help me even after the way I treated you earlier?"

"Yes, of course. I care about Martin. About what will happen to you. I'll do whatever I can to help."

She gave a nod, resolute blue eyes nailing him with the force of a blacksmith's hammer shoeing a horse.

Something in her gaze made him take a step back, unsure he wanted to hear what was coming.

"If you mean that, marry me."

Chapter Four

Matt held up his palms and took another step back, tripping over a tree root, but managed to stay on his feet. Barely. What the tarnation had just happened?

Assistance with the coming roundup he'd expected. A helping hand on the Lazy P, sure.

But marriage?

Nothing could've been further from his mind. Hannah Parrish, that gangly girl from the neighboring ranch, his kid brother Zack's tagalong, had proposed?

To him?

"Did you just say…marriage?"

"I did," she said.

His gaze swept over her slender yet curvy frame, wide blue eyes, wind tossed red-brown hair. That gangly girl had grown into a fine-looking woman. Still, the idea of marriage was crazy. Why, Hannah could barely tolerate him.

Not that he hadn't been at fault for raising her hackles. Since he'd laid eyes on her at the depot, he'd teased her about her finery, her debutante days in Charleston, her elocution. He'd done it to keep her attention on him and off her father.

He bit back a sigh. Why not be honest? He'd become an expert at holding women at arm's length. He had no intention of falling for a woman, especially a female with an iron will.

A scowl on her face, Hannah folded her arms across her chest. "You look like a man sentenced to hang."

An apt description considering his throat had constricted with the pressure of a squeezing noose. He took a step closer. Lifted a hand toward her. "I'm sorry, I... ah, you surprised me."

She whirled out of his reach. "Forget it!"

"Wait." He shot after her, taking her by the arm. "You can't blame a man for being taken aback. A request for help doesn't usually include a marriage proposal."

"These aren't usual circumstances."

He released a gust of air. "No, they're not."

"I don't want marriage any more than you do." Her eyes flared. Then drifted in the direction of her house where disease and worry dwelled. "I don't see another option."

"Reckon marriage to me means you get help with your pa, an experienced cowhand and a husband all rolled into one."

"Husband?"

"That is what you call the groom once you tie the knot."

"I..." Her cheeks bloomed. "I hadn't thought about a husband."

"A husband does come with the wedding band," he ground out.

That chin of hers shot up. He hadn't meant to sound testy, but matrimony was sacred, not to be entered lightly. If they wed, they'd be hitched for life. With that stubborn streak of hers, marriage would feel like a life sentence, too.

Her gaze dropped away. She fiddled with the sleeve of her dress. "We're not in love so we'd, ah…well…"

"Have no proper marital…union, is that what you're trying to say?"

"Yes."

Why didn't he feel relieved by her answer? If he married, a marriage without love was what he'd want. Even four years later, Amy's death haunted him. He clamped his jaw. He'd never again risk that kind of anguish.

Tears brimmed in Hannah's eyes. Eyes filled with desperation. Disquiet. A host of emotions he couldn't handle. A damsel in distress. How could a man look into those eyes without wanting to save her?

But, at what cost? "What do I get out of this marriage?"

Her eyes widened. Like the question surprised her. "You?"

"Yes, me. I'd be half of the man and wife." He didn't mention her opposition to a proper man and wife relationship, but the arrangement hung over them just the same.

"Well, you'd, ah, get a home. Good food. Rosa's an excellent cook. And—" she wrinkled her nose that cute way she had "—you wouldn't have to ride to the Lazy P twice a day to help Papa and…" Her words trailed off. "That's not much."

Without a doubt, Hannah wouldn't have turned to

him if she'd had another candidate for the position of husband. "What I'd get is another ranch to run." He removed his Stetson and slapped it against his thigh, raising dust and his ire with each whack. "You've resented what you called my interference. Now you're asking for it?"

She straightened her shoulders, but didn't look him in the eye. "I'd prefer you not interfere. I'd make the decisions on how to run the Lazy P. I will work on my ranch. None of that nonsense about leaving the job to the men."

Mercy, if he married her, he'd have to put up regularly with this spitfire. One thing he'd give Hannah, she had bravado, more like audacity, considering her lack of alternatives.

"All I need a husband for is…" Her brow furrowed, groping for the word.

"Respect," he finished for her.

She nodded. "I'm seen as an upstart, not a boss. With a husband—" She shot him a defiant stare. "In name only, well…if you showed your support, the hands would listen to me, figure the instructions came from you."

That much was true.

"Well, will you marry me or not?" She crossed her arms over her bosom, trying to look in control, but her lips trembled like a terrified toddler.

As long as he'd peered into those pretty, haunted eyes, how could he expect to make an intelligent decision? Could any decision be called intelligent that involved marrying a woman he didn't love? And who didn't love him?

Lord, I need the wisdom You gave Solomon.

"I'll think about it. Pray about it. This isn't an agreement a man enters into lightly."

With that assertion, he plopped his Stetson on his head, strode to his horse and rode for the Circle W, leaving Hannah behind, from what he'd heard, sputtering. Had she expected his answer on the spot?

He needed time to wrap his mind around her proposal. He supposed marriage to Hannah would mean no risk of entangling his heart and no more of Jenny Sample's cakes. And, marrying Hannah would allow him to care for a dying man he saw as a second father.

Amy's death had killed his capacity to risk his heart. A marriage of convenience would work for him, but didn't seem fair to Hannah. She deserved love. Even if he could love again, he didn't deserve her, any woman.

If only—

He refused to let his mind travel to the day of Amy's death. As much as he lived with regrets, nothing could change the past.

A bright, sunny morning didn't fit Hannah's mood. As she and Jake finished the last of the chores, she'd prayed for an answer to her dilemma. Never thinking God would put words in her mouth, she'd never have spoken if she hadn't been desperate to give Papa peace. *Marry me, Matt,* she'd blurted out. Yet marriage was the last thing she wanted. If Matt agreed, would the solution bring even bigger problems? If he refused, she'd have no recourse but to sell.

She felt out of control, swept along like the cattle she'd often witnessed in Fort Worth, driven through narrow chutes and onto waiting railroad boxcars that would deliver them to their final destination.

Annihilation.

She shivered. Surely marriage wouldn't be that bad. She knew little about wedded life, had no more than an outsider's view. Would a husband want to herd her into the narrow shoot of his will and destroy the freedom she held dear, freedom to work, freedom to run the ranch? To have purpose and meaning, be part of something bigger than her?

Across the way, Matt emerged from the back door, no doubt finished helping Papa shave and dress, the actions of a thoughtful, caring man. Why had she thought he had ulterior motives for his kindness?

With a strong, hardworking, no-nonsense air about him, Matt's long legs gobbled up the distance as he strode to his horse. Where was he headed?

She caught up with him just as he took Thunder's reins. "Heading back to the Circle W?" she said, trying to sound casual, when every muscle tensed with wondering if he'd come to a decision about marrying her.

He turned to her, a smile on his lips. The sight of that dimple winking at her and his dark eyes, soft, kind, whooshed the breath out of her lungs. Why couldn't she stop reacting to the man? He saw her as a gangly kid to be teased, barely tolerated.

"Several of your cows will be dropping calves. Thought I'd ride out to check on them."

Here was an opportunity to take back the reins of her life. "If you can wait while I change out of this dress and saddle Star, I'll ride along. See for myself how the herd looks."

And along the way ask a few questions about the ranch. Make sure he saw her as being in charge. Prove she wasn't the debutante he believed her to be.

"I'll saddle Star for you," he said, then disappeared into the stable.

Within minutes, she'd told Papa her whereabouts, changed into denims and returned just as Matt emerged leading Star.

"That was quick," he said, his gaze sliding over her.

"Papa's determined to see me in a dress. I'll change back before he sees me."

With an impish grin on his face, Matt gave her a hand up. "I don't understand Martin's position. You look mighty good in pants."

Her cheeks heated and the smile wobbled on her lips. At least Matt wouldn't insist on her wearing dresses if they married, but would she lose the freedom she cherished?

Lose her identity like Belle, her married friend? Once she and Belle had shared the thrill of riding, of lassoing calves, of shooting tin cans off fence posts. Now Belle had turned into a lady, answering to her full name Marybelle, spending her days cooking and cleaning, washing and ironing, mending and gardening. Not that Hannah shunned hard work, but she'd find such confinement suffocating.

With maids and a cook to do the work, Aunt Mary Esther spent her days socializing and didn't appear to have an independent thought from Uncle Clyde. That existence would be even more unbearable.

In comparison with the alternatives, marriage to Matt looked tolerable.

They rode out toward the north range, the view from horseback exhilarating. But then the realities of life invaded her mind, dashing her pleasure like a deluge doused in hot coals.

"How does Papa seem to you?" Hannah asked.

"Having you home has lifted his spirits."

If Matt agreed, Hannah knew their marriage would give Papa peace. And her the certainty of staying on the land she loved. He hadn't broached the topic, probably still praying about his answer. She wouldn't press for his decision, for fear that pushing him would raise his ire and he'd give a hasty no.

Instead she'd focus the conversation on the ranch and look for ways to resolve the problems. "Did we lose many cattle last winter?"

"Nope. Mild winter. Another year or two like that and the herd will come close to its size before the winter of '86–'87."

That was a terrible winter and spring. Cattle that survived the blizzard were swept away in floods. They'd lost half the herd, more fortunate than some, but still they'd taken a serious punch in the pocketbook.

Ahead of her, the cattle dotted the fenced pasture, their large frames of every imaginable color. Their horned white faces bent toward the grass. "Crossbreeding longhorns with Herefords makes an interesting herd."

"Yep, the offspring are the best of both breeds, eventempered, early maturing and mighty fine eating. They fatten up fast and handle drought. The cows make excellent mothers."

At the entrance to the north pasture, Matt guided

Thunder alongside the fence, opening the gate from horseback, letting her ride through before closing it behind them.

Up ahead two calves bunted each other, then stopped to stare as they rode slowly through the herd, counting calves. A few of the babies were overcome with fear and rushed to their mamas to nurse and be comforted.

Hannah grinned at Matt. "Aren't they cute?"

"Yep, better yet, they're profit on legs. I—"

He rose in the saddle, then with a nudge of his knees, urged his horse forward. Hannah followed. Up ahead, away from the herd, a cow lay on the ground. At their approach, she staggered to her feet, took a few steps then lay down again.

Matt frowned. "She's calving and in distress."

When they were a few yards from the animal, the cow rose, scrambling away from them, revealing the emerging calf's snout.

The first time Hannah witnessed the birth of a calf she'd been a tyke riding in front of her father. She knew the front legs should appear before the head. Head first meant trouble.

Matt grabbed the lasso draped on his saddle horn, twirled it overhead, then released the line. The loop settled around the cow's neck. He tightened the hoop, then hauled the cow toward a fence post. She trotted a few steps, then lurched to the side, attempting to get away, but rider and horse cut off her escape.

At the post, Matt dismounted, heaved the lariat around the wood and, using the leverage, pulled the animal closer, then knotted it, holding her in place.

Breath coming fast and shallow, the cow bellowed as

a contraction slithered through her. Matt strode to her hindquarters. "Front legs are folded back."

Hannah tethered the horses, then moved to Matt's side. "Poor thing."

"I've got to fish for the front legs." He didn't look up, merely unbuttoned his cuff, then jerked his head toward the horses. "Stand by Star. Turn your back. Can't have you fainting on me."

"I've seen calves born countless times." She jerked up her chin. "Besides, I'm not the fainting type."

One arched brow said he doubted her claim. "Suit yourself, but don't say I didn't warn you."

Hannah may have seen calves born, but had no idea what to do in this situation. She bit her lip, grateful Matt didn't hold back, and took fast action. He tried to slide his hand past the calf's head. Once. Twice. A third time. "My hand's too big."

"I'll try. What should I do?"

Matt's eyes lit with something akin to admiration. "See if you can find a small flat surface right below the jaw. That's the calf's knee."

Lord, help me. She slipped her hand in. "Found it."

"Follow it back till you find the hoof. Bring it forward."

"Oh, no, the calf pulled his leg away." Perspiration beaded her brow. "Wait, the legs are straight now. Got 'em. Slippery."

The sweet scent of amniotic fluid filling her nostrils, she hung on, guiding first one leg, then the other, producing the calf's fully extended front legs and head. With the next contraction the body followed in a whoosh

of fluid and slid out onto the grass, a slick dark speck-
led lump.

A motionless lump.

Holding her breath, Hannah slid away the sack, waiting for the calf's chest to rise, fall. Nothing. She ran
to Star, jerked her bedroll from behind her saddle and
wrapped the blanket around the glistening calf, rubbing
the fibers over its hide.

"Come on, baby. Breathe," she said, warming the
calf.

The calf jerked and sucked in air. Its eyes opened and
stared up at her. Hannah peered into those dark eyes.
"Well, hello there, little guy."

The cow lunged against the rope, determined to
reach her calf. Matt grabbed Hannah's hand, pulled
her out of harm's way, then untied the rope and removed
the lariat. The cow paid them no mind, merely circled to
the now bawling calf and proceeded to lick every inch
of him. Within minutes the calf staggered to his feet,
swaying against the pressure of his mother's tongue,
keeping his balance, barely. A quick maneuver by the
mother and he found nourishment.

His grin as wide as the outdoors, Matt met her gaze.
"Looks like they'll both make it, thanks to you."

"And you. You told me what to do. If you hadn't decided to ride out here and check on the cows dropping
calves…"

"Most likely they'd have both died. We'll head to
the south range." He winked. "Maybe next time, you'll
help birth twins."

"I've had enough excitement for one day."

With a chuckle, he swept a hand toward her. "No debutante would be caught looking like that."

Hannah glanced at the damp smears streaking her shirt and denims. "I'm no debutante, remember?"

"I'm starting to believe it. You and I make a good team." The mischief left his gaze. A gaze that suddenly turned tender. "You love this land, the ranch, the cattle. Everything."

"I do."

"I do, too." He touched her hand. "Reckon with all those I dos, we'd better get hitched and keep you here."

Her gaze locked with his. She lost herself in his eyes, dark, mysterious, full of life and offering marriage.

"See something you like?" he said, dimple twinkling.

Heat surged to her cheeks. Nothing about the man met her disapproval. "No, nothing much."

When had she uttered a bigger lie?

Matt's self-assured, relaxed posture said he was sure of himself—and of her, most likely. Why wouldn't he be? She'd done the proposing. First.

"With the six-year difference in our ages and your year away, we don't know each other all that well. But, we're alike in our bond with this land." Expression earnest, Matt leaned toward her. "I can think of far worse reasons to marry."

Just like that, with few words, the bargain was sealed.

"We need to do this right," he said, taking her hand and sending a shiver along her spine. He moved as if to get down on one knee.

With a gasp of protest, she snatched her hand away. "This marriage is business only. No need for a proper proposal."

"Is it really? Just business for you?"

Her gaze settled on those eyes searching hers, as if peering into her soul. She wouldn't get swept up by a handsome face and fall for a man. Not even a man with a dazzling smile and a dimple begging for her touch.

At her silence, he took a step back, erect, formal. "Hannah Parrish, will you marry me?"

A lump rose in her throat. Once she agreed, there'd be no turning back. Yet what choice did she have? "Yes, I'll marry you."

"We'll need to marry soon."

Hannah stiffened. "How soon?"

"Today's Monday. Can we get it done by Thursday?"

Get it done. As if marriage was on his list of chores. Her stomach clenched. How could she be ready in three days?

"Martin's a very sick man," he reminded her. "He'd want to see you wed."

For Papa she could do anything. "Yes," she said in a voice that wobbled.

"I'll do my best to be a good husband." His soft tone matched the kindness in his eyes.

She had no idea what constituted a good husband... or for that matter, a good wife. Could she fit into a husband's expectations? Especially a mature man like Matt?

One thing Hannah knew, she could never abide a bossy spouse. Papa seldom gave her orders. Until now. She'd grown up making her own decisions and had felt stifled under Aunt Mary Esther's thumb. She couldn't imagine a lifetime of being dictated to by a man. Would Matt allow her the freedom she needed?

Her gaze swept the land. To remain on the ranch, to keep her way of life and to give her father peace, she'd marry.

If only they had more time.

If only Papa wasn't dying.

If only they were in love.

She thought of the tenderness that had fleetingly appeared in Matt's eyes. Perhaps love was possible... eventually.

No, that expectation was a foolish peg to hang her heart on. A fairy-tale ending wasn't what she wanted. She would deal with the real world. Papa was dying. To run the ranch and remain on the land she loved, she'd marry a man she didn't.

Chapter Five

Wound tighter than a coiled spring, Matt rode into the Circle W stable, stripped leather, then brushed Thunder's coat. As Matt led the stallion to his stall, fed and watered him, large, wide-set eyes alert with intelligence gazed back at him. Quick, smart and high-spirited, much like his future wife.

But Hannah was a woman, not trained to bridle and bit. Truth was, she held the reins, using him to keep her ranch. Not that he didn't want the same.

At the pump, he scrubbed his hands and doused his face and neck. Had his admiration for Hannah's cool-headed competence during a calf's difficult birth triggered his proposal?

No, he had prayed for wisdom. Felt a deep certainty he'd been led by God and had done the right thing. He wanted to give Martin peace. He wanted to help Hannah. He didn't want love. The lack of expectations in this marriage fit him perfectly.

Cal and his family were joining them for supper. Normally a good time, but with the task of telling his family the news, his steps lagged. No doubt they'd question his sanity.

He found his mother and Cal's wife, Susannah, in the kitchen preparing the evening meal. "Smells good, Ma," he said, letting the screen door slap behind him. "Hi, Susannah."

Blond silky hair swept into a sleek bun, Susannah looked up from laying plates on the table and smiled. Fair and blue-eyed, Cal's petite wife had an innocent, delicate quality about her, yet had a mind of her own if the occasion warranted.

Victoria turned from the stove. "Hoped you'd get here in time for supper."

He hung his Stetson on a peg beside the door, then walked to his ma. "Let me help with that." He took the potato masher from her hand and battled lumps in the potatoes. An easy skirmish compared to what lay ahead.

As if led by their noses, Cal with his son, Robbie, tucked in his arms, and Pa trooped into the kitchen. Matt greeted them, then turned the pot over to his mother, who scooped the creamy potatoes into a large crock.

"Hey," Cal said, clapping Matt on the shoulder, "you look down in the mouth."

"Hush," Victoria scolded. "Your brother's been over to the Parrish ranch. You know Martin's poorly."

Cal's gaze clouded. "Sorry. Martin's a good guy."

At the moment, Matt's disquiet involved the task at hand, not merely Martin's health. He'd like his family's blessing, and would get it…in time.

They gathered at the table, Robbie tucked in his high chair between Susannah and Cal. Pa offered grace, thanking God for the food and asking His mercy on Martin. After a hearty amen, Robert nabbed a piece of fried chicken, then passed the platter on.

Susannah tied a bib around Robbie's neck. "Hannah has no family in these parts. What will happen to her?"

"She should sell the ranch and go back to Charleston," Robert said. "Running a ranch isn't a woman's place."

"The Parrish family has endured a lot. First losing both Melanie and the baby in childbirth, now Martin." Ma's voice caught. "Poor Hannah. Makes me want to weep."

Susannah handed Robbie a spoon. The boy promptly dug into the potatoes and managed to get a spoonful into his mouth. "Hannah loves the ranch. I can't believe she'd leave willingly."

Appetite gone, Matt moved his potatoes around his plate with a fork. Might as well get it said. "I asked her to marry me."

Stunned silence followed his declaration. All eyes turned on him, while the startling news sank in.

"So when is the wedding taking place?" Susannah asked.

Martin was dying. They had no time to cement their relationship. "If Pastor Cummings agrees, Thursday at the Lazy P."

Ma gasped. "Mercy, that's fast. Are you sure about this?" she said, searching his face.

Matt had seen that look before. Knew Ma was trying to read his thoughts, zipping him back to when he was ten and had played hooky from school. Ma had been judge and jury, meting out justice. As he recalled, he'd had to muck out the barn every night for a week.

He glanced away from those perceptive eyes. "I'm sure."

Ma didn't smile, merely nodded instead. "I'll drive over to see how we can help."

"You can't possibly love the girl," Cal said. "Why, you barely know her." He plopped his elbows on the table, his expression aghast, as if Matt had grown two heads. "Hannah's a great kid. One thing to feel sorry for her, and I do, but quite another to marry her."

"Obviously, Cal, you haven't seen Hannah since her return," Pa declared. "She's all grown-up."

Cal plopped tiny bites of chicken on Robbie's tray. "There's always been pretty women around. Why the sudden decision to marry this one, big brother?"

Matt would never reveal that Hannah had proposed first. He couldn't explain their decision to marry without revealing the personal details of the agreement, something he'd never do.

"May be overstepping," Cal went on, "but I trust grief over Amy isn't making you settle for a loveless marriage."

Hands balled into rock-hard fists alongside his plate, Matt glared at Cal. "Keep Amy out of this."

As if held at gunpoint, Cal raised his arms, palms out. "Whoa, brother. I want you to have what Susannah and I share. I'm just saying—"

"Saying what? That I don't have the sense to know my own mind?"

"Matthew! Calvin! You're behaving like bullheaded toddlers," Robert said. Then he nodded his head, a smile forming on his lips. "A merger with the Lazy P makes sense. By pooling our resources, both ranches might survive dropping cattle prices and the bad economy."

Leave it to his father to see marriage as a business opportunity. "Hannah hasn't agreed to a merger," Matt said.

"See that she does." Robert glanced around the table, at the untouched food. "Enough of this talk. Eat."

"Eat!" the food-smeared toddler ordered with pride, then stuck a gooey spoon in his hair and grinned.

Everyone laughed, easing the tension at the table.

Matt settled back in his chair, taking a deep breath, trying to slow his breathing. His father tried to run every facet of his sons' lives. It was the reason Zack had turned to the law. And Cal spent most of his time at Susannah's folks' spread.

Still, the ongoing strain between Matt and his father didn't explain Matt's reaction to Cal's concern. He'd thought he had peace about the decision to marry Hannah, but in truth, he was entering uncharted territory.

One grim possibility after another marched through Matt's mind. Without the benefit of a loving relationship, he and Hannah would deal with Martin's illness and without a miracle, his death. This marriage could backfire in a myriad of ways.

Matt had grown comfortable with the emptiness of the past four years. Each day had held a blessed sameness, with neither highs nor lows, just a flat, hollow monotony. He had filled those days with work. The highlight of his week were evenings spent with Martin, another lonely man fighting his own demons. Martin's waning health triggered painful memories of Amy's death.

Still, none of this excused his treatment of Cal. "I'm sorry for overreacting, Cal."

His brother met his gaze, an apology in his eyes. "Me, too."

"To see Hannah wed will give Martin peace," Ma said. "Hannah's a lovely young woman, a rancher at heart. A good match for you."

Robert gave a nod. "Marriage to Hannah is a solution for everyone."

Cal looked pained, as if he'd taken a bite of cactus.

At her husband's silence, Susannah frowned at Cal. "Hope you and Hannah will be very happy," she said, then reported Robbie's latest humorous antic and conversation resumed as usual.

Matt's mind wandered back to how all this started. During his visits to the Lazy P, Martin spoke often of Hannah, the daughter he obviously adored. The day Martin was diagnosed with cancer, he'd shared his heavy burden for his only child's welfare. Matt shared that concern. Hannah was in a tough spot.

Yet, to wed a nineteen-year-old without love scared him silly. Marriage might be a solution for her, but marriage would also create new problems.

Unlike Cal, Matt knew why he'd proposed. He couldn't risk love, but at twenty-five, he wanted a new beginning. He'd settle for companionship, settle for a woman to share his dreams and goals, settle for a woman who'd share his way of life.

The honest truth was that he was tired. Tired of dodging unsuitable women with matrimony on their minds. Tired of feeling alone in a houseful of people. Tired of fighting his father's control.

By marrying her, Matt would see that Hannah could remain on the land she loved. He hoped that would make her happy. If not happy, at least content. Something he'd come to appreciate.

Matt had come, hoping for his family's support of the marriage. For the most part he'd gotten it. Cal would come around. But Pa.... Would Pa's expectation of a merger between the two ranches wind up causing trouble?

Two days till Hannah lassoed and tied herself to Matt Walker. Married. The word twisted in her stomach. Wedding vows meant until death do us part, faithfulness, respect.

She stiffened. Obedience. She hoped Matt could tolerate giving up one of those promises. If he tried to keep her on a short tether—

She swallowed against the sudden lump in her throat, shoving down all the misgivings trying to spew out of her mouth and into Papa's ear.

Instead she helped her father to his desk. Last evening Matt had asked for Papa's permission to wed. Papa had clapped Matt on the back, declared he already thought of Matt as a son and nothing could make him happier than seeing Hannah in good hands.

As if she wasn't capable of taking care of herself.

Still the news had eased the tension around Papa's eyes and put a big smile on his face. That was reason enough to bite her tongue.

Hannah glanced out the window. The Walker buggy

was coming up the lane. She kissed her father's cheek. "Matt's here."

"While you're in town, spread the word about the wedding. A chat with the town's bench sitters and Pastor Cummings should do the trick."

Hannah dreaded the townsfolk's reaction, but forced a bright smile.

Martin motioned to the package in Hannah's hands, "Is that your mama's dress?"

"It is. I'm taking it to Miss Carmichael's for alterations. Are you sure you'll be all right while I'm gone?"

"You're in more peril in Biddy Carmichael's shop than I could ever be here."

"Papa!" Hannah laughed. No matter how much he suffered, her father made the effort to bring laughter to others. "You know her name is Belinda, not Biddy."

"How could I make such a mistake?" He winked. "Now skedaddle. Don't keep your groom waiting."

She kissed him once more, her heart swelling with love, and then walked as fast as her dress would allow, more tortoise than her usual hare. Who could abide such restriction?

Outside, she popped up her frilly parasol, an accessory Aunt Mary Esther had insisted upon. On such a sweltering day riding in an open buggy, Hannah welcomed the shade.

Matt rounded the conveyance, his gaze traveling from the hat perched atop her head to the silk toe of her pump. He doffed his Stetson. "The debutante is back."

"You looking for a fight, Walker?"

"No, ma'am, I'm not." He grinned wickedly. "One

thing's sure. Whatever garb she's wearing, the filly's a Thoroughbred."

Hannah thrust up her chin. "I'm becoming your wife, not joining your stable."

Obviously not the least bit repentant, his impish smile held. "Kind of fun having two of you, debutante and cowgirl, all wrapped up in one very nice parcel."

At his perusal, butterflies fluttered in her stomach. She corralled her skirts, then allowed him to assist her into the buggy. Whether she would be in good hands as Papa had said, was to be seen, but his grasp was strong, secure.

"You have an admirer in Rosa. She's very excited about our wedding," Hannah told him.

"It pays to be on good terms with the cook. Since I've been made to understand that won't likely be you, I plan on buttering her up."

"So the way to a man's heart is indeed through his stomach."

He cocked a brow. "Are you sure you want to know the way to a man's heart, Hannah?"

A shiver slid along her spine. She quickly looked away from the amusement in those dark, smoldering eyes.

"The filly's a tad skittish," he said. Then with a flick of the reins, they got underway. "Know what kind of a wedding you want?"

"A simple ceremony at the Lazy P, outside if weather permits."

"Sounds good."

She sighed. "Papa insists on inviting half the town and hosting a barbecue afterward."

"He doesn't want his illness to cheat you out of a pretty wedding. Most women want that."

Hannah had been thirteen when she and Papa attended Matt and Amy's wedding, a grand affair. Hannah recalled the glow on their faces as they'd recited their vows. After such a love match, Hannah found Matt's acceptance of a marriage of convenience baffling. Perhaps he'd understood that no one could take Amy's place in his affection and wanted companionship.

She plucked at her skirts. "What he doesn't realize, and I can't tell him, is I can't abide the thought of putting on a charade. We aren't an ordinary couple."

"True, but a private wedding might set tongues a-waggin'."

"I suppose you're right, but a party seems...deceptive."

"People marry for many reasons, Hannah." His gaze locked with hers. "If we're committed to one another, then our wedding won't be a charade. I believe we'll be as happy as we choose to be. That's what I want. Do you?"

As she looked into those dark orbs that penetrated her soul, she vowed to do everything in her power to make the marriage work. "Yes," she said softly.

A smile curved the corners of his mouth. "God will bless us, help us find our way."

He took her hand in his. At that moment, the sense of connection between them felt as meaningful as the vows they'd speak on Thursday.

Matt released her hand. "I told my family our decision to wed."

"What did they say?" Hannah asked, her heart in her throat.

"They were…surprised, at first." He shot her an impish grin. "But then, no more than I was."

"Did you tell them I did the proposing?"

"Nope, that's our little secret."

"What did they say?"

"They think you're a lovely young woman and wish us happiness."

Had Matt omitted much of his family's reaction? What had they really said? Perhaps she was better off not knowing. She'd have to get accustomed to the startled reactions of others, those who'd question their sudden nuptials.

On Main Street, Matt pulled up in front of Miss Carmichael's shop, rounded the buggy, then placed his hands around her waist. As she rested her palms on his shoulders and he lifted her down, she stared into warm cocoa eyes, gentle, kind, appealing. Too appealing. She gathered her package, keeping her eyes anywhere except on him.

"I'll stop at the church and ask Pastor Cummings to perform the ceremony. After that I've got business at the bank. What do you say we meet at the Calico Café at noon?"

"That should give me time to visit Leah."

"We won't leave town until you're ready," he said, then loped up the street to set the wedding plans in motion.

An urge to call him back, to renege on the proposal lurched through her. Foolishness. If she'd had another choice, she'd have taken it.

She threw back her shoulders and stepped inside the shop, in actuality, Miss Carmichael's parlor. Overhead a tiny bell jingled. Cases and tables held gloves, hats, bolts of fabric, and baskets of feathers, silk flowers and papier-mâché fruit, the tools of her trade.

Belinda Carmichael bustled through a curtain separating the shop from her private quarters. Behind wire-rim glasses, the spinster's hazel eyes missed nothing. Nor, for that matter, did her ears. Tall, thin, as prim and proper as a starched collar, Belinda gloried in her role as town gossip. No doubt she would gossip about the suddenness of her and Matt's marriage. Still, Hannah wouldn't trust Mama's dress to anyone else.

"Good morning, Miss Parrish. I heard you were back from Charleston." She glanced at the package in Hannah's hands. "What can I do for you?"

Hannah untied the string and wrapping, revealing her mother's wedding dress, an off-white silk confection with a row of pleats edged with lace at the hem, at the flared sleeves and on the draped overskirt.

"I'd like you to alter this dress to fit me."

Miss Carmichael's fingers skimmed over the bodice that tapered to a point below the waist. "The stitching is impeccable. Let's see what needs to be done."

She guided Hannah behind a screen and helped her change, then turned Hannah around, studying the fit. "I'll need to add length. If I trim the sleeves and hem with the matching lace on this overskirt, no one would suspect the additions aren't part of the original dress."

Hannah agreed the solution would be perfect. She skimmed her palms over the overskirt, proud to wear this lovely dress. If only she were marrying a man she loved. She tamped down the thought. Love didn't matter. The Lazy P did.

The bell over the door danced a cheery tune. A second customer entered the shop. "Be right with you," Miss Carmichael called.

"No hurry." The newcomer removed her hatpins, then her hat, obviously eager to try on one of Miss Carmichael's creations.

Miss Carmichael leaned in. "I'm curious, Miss Parrish. Why are you having this dress altered? Surely your relations in Charleston didn't give you their hand-me-downs." Miss Carmichael's tone oozed sympathy. "You might want to consider having something new made. I have several beautiful fabrics that would compliment your coloring."

"Thank you, but I came back with a trunk full of dresses, more than I'll ever wear."

The seamstress's expression soured. "Then why alter this one?" Her eyes widened. "Unless you intend to wear it for sentimental reasons, like at your wedding." She smirked. "How silly of me. You have no beau." She raised a brow. "Unless you met someone in Charleston."

No point in avoiding the truth. Papa said to spread the word about the wedding, no better way than to tell the seamstress. Hannah steeled herself for Miss Carmichael's reaction. "This is my mother's wedding dress," she said. "I want to wear it at my wedding Thursday. You won't have any difficulty getting the alterations finished by then, will you?"

Hazel eyes gleaming, Miss Carmichael clapped her hands. "For a wedding, it'll be my priority! Who are you marrying?"

"Matt Walker."

"Matt Walker! From what I hear, he's a most elusive catch." Her shrewd beady eyes resembled a predator moving in for the kill. "You've only been home a few days," she said. "Isn't this wedding rather sudden?"

Sudden hardly described it.

"To marry that quickly, why, you must've fallen in love at first sight." She tittered. "Not really first sight, of course, but first sight since your return." Her hands fluttered like tiny birds in flight. "How romantic!"

Heat flooded Hannah's cheeks. Love at first sight had not been the reason for the marriage. More like, at first sight of her ailing father. At first sight of her foreman's refusal to follow orders. At first sight of Papa's worry about her future.

Harsh realities had led her to propose, not romance, not affection for the man. Still, she'd play the role of blissful bride. She owed Matt that much. "Isn't it exciting? Matt's a very persuasive man."

Miss Carmichael's gaze sharpened. Perhaps the waver of Hannah's smile or the wobble in her voice had raised the seamstress's suspicions. Thankfully, the older woman didn't pursue the topic, no doubt unwilling to risk a paying customer's ire. After all, the seamstress had to make her own way.

A wave of sympathy for the woman swept through Hannah. Belinda Carmichael carried a load of responsibility and had no one to help share the burden. At least with Matt she'd have a partner.

All business, Miss Carmichael grabbed a tape measure and whipped it from the edge of Hannah's hem to the toe of her shoe, then wrote her findings in a tiny notebook. She did the same for her sleeves. "I have all I need. Let me help you change."

Behind the screen, the seamstress eased the garment over Hannah's head. "I'll have the dress finished by tomorrow afternoon and drive out to the ranch and deliver it personally."

"That's too much trouble."

"Not at all, if you'll show me the fashions you brought back from Charleston," Miss Carmichael said with a smile, then rushed toward the waiting customer.

On the way out of the shop, Hannah passed Miss Carmichael and the shopper, their heads together, their smiles couldn't cover the speculative look in their eyes.

As she escaped into the sunshine, Hannah heaved a sigh. She'd survived Miss Carmichael's reaction, so surely she could survive anyone's.

Up ahead, Bertram Bailey swept the entrance of Bailey's Dry Goods. Thin as the broom in his hand, and not much taller, Mr. Bailey propped the handle against the building. "Good to have you home, Miss Parrish," he said, then followed her inside.

She handed the proprietor the list. "Rosa needs a great many things to prepare for a barbecue at the Lazy P Thursday."

"Ah, a celebration for your homecoming," he said, scanning the order.

"Actually a celebration of my wedding."

Mr. Bailey blinked. "You don't say. Who are you marrying?"

"Matt Walker."

"Well, if that don't beat all. I waited on Mrs. Victoria Walker a couple days ago. Never said a word about her son marrying. Reckon she's better keeping secrets than most folks."

No need to tell Mr. Bailey that Matt's mother didn't know about their wedding a couple days ago. For that matter neither did she nor Matt. "Since the order is sizable, I'll pick it up this afternoon before we leave town."

"I'd appreciate it. I'll add this to your bill."

Bills got paid when cattle got sold. That's the way things were done in Bliss. "Thank you."

A glance at the clock on the wall revealed she had an hour before she'd meet Matt. Enough time to visit Leah.

Down the street the town's bench sitters watched the comings and goings in town. At her approach, all three doffed their hats, grins wide on their faces, evidence of their bright outlook despite the infirmities of age. The realization that Papa would not be as fortunate slugged her in the belly like a fist.

"Good to have you home, Miss Hannah. How's your pa?" As the oldest at eighty-four, Mr. Cooper acted as spokesman.

"About the same, thank you. How are y'all?"

"Fair to middlin'" Reed thin, his bushy, untamed eyebrows all but hiding his pale blue eyes, Mr. Cooper's knobby hands wrapped around the handle of his cane. "Ben here is a tad riled. The Fowler twins chucked rocks our way and hit him smack-dab on the nose. They high-tailed it for home before we could catch 'em!"

The image of these men swinging their canes in hot pursuit of the notorious eight-year-old boys had Hannah stifling a giggle. Until she took a look at the poor man's swollen nose. "Should you have Doc check it, Mr. Seller?"

Two gnarled fingers skimmed his bulbous nose, ruddier than usual. "Had worse. Don't know what the world's coming to when a man ain't safe minding his own business. Little imps hadn't ought to be out amongst decent folks."

Hands looped around his suspenders, Mr. Brand laughed, his belly bobbing with each cackle. "Seller, you oughta see Doc and give Fowler the bill. Why, that'd make him sit up and take notice. Fowler's so tight he'd walk a rotten rail over the Rio Grande to save hisself a nickel."

Mr. Cooper sputtered with laughter that dwindled into a wheeze. "If Fowler kept as tight a rein on them young-uns as he does on his wallet, this town would be a whole lot safer."

Three grizzled heads dipped in agreement.

"I want you gentlemen to be among the first to know that Matt Walker and I are getting married. The wedding is Thursday afternoon at the Lazy P, outside, weather permitting."

"Well, ain't that the best news!" Mr. Brand said. "The Circle W and Lazy P are joining forces."

Was a merger the first thing everyone would think of when they heard of their wedding?

Mr. Cooper smiled. "Don't worry none about the weather, Miz Hannah. If rain was coming, my knees would be hollering."

"That's good to hear. I hope you gentlemen will come. We're having a barbecue afterward."

"Jake Hardy making his famous sauce?" Mr. Seller asked.

"We wouldn't serve anything else."

Mr. Fowler grinned, revealing two missing teeth. "Count on me. Ain't missing the chance to see you two hitched. And have a visit with your pa."

"Pass the word along, will you?"

"You can count on us," Mr. Cooper promised, already surveying the block for someone to tell.

Hannah had accomplished what she'd set out to do —pass the word about their wedding. Thus far, she'd dodged a bullet. No one had openly questioned the match.

So why did she feel like she'd taken a slug in the heart?

Chapter Six

Hannah darted across Main Street, then hustled along Oak Avenue, lined with live oaks and large imposing houses. Only an occasional barking dog disturbed the quiet.

Friends since childhood, she and Leah had shared their girlhood dreams of romance and marriage. How naive they'd been. She batted away tears welling in her eyes. She wouldn't confide in Leah that her marriage was one of convenience and crush her friend's fantasy.

At the Montgomery house, Hannah climbed the steps, then lifted the brass door knocker. She studied the fanciful stork standing on one leg amongst cattails etched in the oval glass of the door. The stork seemed appropriate here.

Her gaze swept the planked porch littered with toys left behind by Leah's four younger brothers and sisters, Abe, Anna, Peter and Susie. In the gap between Leah and her twelve-year-old brother Abe, two precious Montgomery children had died. Perhaps that was the reason the parents didn't fret about disorder. The large, rambunctious family thrived in a house where bedlam reigned. Far different from Hannah's quiet, tidy home with only a caring housekeeper and doting father to keep her company.

Hannah's throat knotted. How could she abide losing Papa?

Leah flung open the door. Blond, blue-eyed and prettier than ever. "Hannah! When did you get back?"

They wrapped their arms around one another, then leaned back to inspect the changes a year had brought. Leah had inherited the best qualities of both parents, her mother's fair beauty and openness, balanced with a good measure of her father's steadfastness.

Mrs. Montgomery, blond hair twisted into a chignon, blue eyes harried, dashed out the door, almost colliding with them. She scooped Hannah into an embrace. "Hannah, you've grown up! I'm amazed how much you resemble your sweet mother."

Hannah might look like Mama but she was her father's daughter.

"Keep Leah company while she looks after the rest of my brood. Better yet, stay overnight. I'll drive you home tomorrow."

"Thank you, but I'm expected back."

"Well, another time then. You're always welcome, dear. Please give our best to your father." Mrs. Montgomery gave Hannah's cheek a pat, peering into her eyes. "If you need anything, anything at all, come to me." Hannah nodded, then the older woman spun off with a moan. "I'm late!"

Leah tugged Hannah into the house and up the stairs. "Everybody's in school and I'm not scheduled today to clerk at Bailey's. We can spend the entire afternoon together."

"I can't stay."

In Leah's room, an oasis of tidiness in the disheveled house, they sat on the brass bed facing each other. Leah's eyes welled with tears. "We know how sick your father is. I'm sorry."

As if a dam had broken, words poured out of Hannah—Doc Atkins's dire diagnosis and the foreman and top hands quitting.

Leah listened, never once interrupting, then took Hannah's hands in hers. "I wish your father wasn't sick. But, wishing doesn't make it so. I've been worried about what would happen to you. What are you going to do?"

"I've got…news. Matt Walker and I are getting married."

Leah shrieked and threw her arms around Hannah. "You're getting married! Oh, how exciting!" Her brows puckered. "How did this happen? You've been in Charleston for a year."

"I've never forgotten Matt. We've seen each other at church, at community events, even at the Lazy P when he'd stop by on occasion." Heat bloomed in her cheeks. "When I came back to town, he picked me up at the depot and…sparks flew."

That much was true, though those sparks stemmed from a clash of personalities, not from attraction.

Hannah's breath caught. Why not be honest? Any woman would notice that cowboy physique, that attractive face.

That arrogance.

"You're blushing." Leah's eyes lit. "How romantic.

Matt's perfect, a rancher like you, and no one in the county's more handsome. Unless you count his brother, Cal, but you can't because he's married to my cousin Susannah."

Leah raved about the handsome Matt Walker, as if appearance could cement a relationship.

Countless times she and Leah had shared dreams of marrying a prince, a knight in shining armor, depending on the last book they'd read. The one constant in those stories was the couple's unshakable love, the happily-ever-after ending. Not a marriage based on life's harsh realities.

"Marrying Matt must give your father peace of mind."

"Yes." It was the reason Hannah had proposed. She'd swapped that fairy-tale groom she and Leah daydreamed about for survival. Now sitting here with Leah, away from the ranch, away from Papa, that decision seemed hasty.

"Every unmarried woman in town has been after Matt, and he chose you." Leah pulled Hannah to feet and turned her toward her dressing-table mirror. "Any man would be proud to have you for his wife."

The reflection in the mirror might look all grown-up, but Hannah didn't feel ready to marry. Anyone.

With a dreamy look on her face, Leah swayed to some soundless melody. "Matt Walker's not like boys our age, who all but drool when they steal a kiss." She leaned closer. "I'll tell you a secret. I've flirted with Matt's brother Zack." She sighed. "I'm sure he'd make a woman feel things right down to her toes."

"What are you talking about? Do you think you're ready to get married?"

"Oh, yes! I want to have my own home and a man to care for and love." Brow puckered, lips turned down, Leah paced her room. "I'm sick of taking care of my brothers and sisters. I feel more like their mother than Mama."

Not that Leah handled everything. Able to indulge his wife, Mr. Montgomery employed a cook and a laundress to ensure timely meals and starched shirts.

If she married, Leah might not have that luxury. "If you marry, you'll most likely end up with kids. And have to do all those tedious chores that involve looking after children and a home. I much prefer roping cattle and riding herd."

"I love the little kids and don't mind caring for them, not really. I'm just ready to live *my* life, to have a man to love, to share our home, our thoughts, our children. With Zack's and my blond hair, our children would be towheads." She plopped her arms across her middle. "Why do you prefer hard, dirty jobs on the ranch? Instead of the genteel pastimes of your mother?"

Hannah shrugged. "I'm more like Papa. Strong."

"Well, you look exactly like your mother. You'll be a beautiful bride." Leah's voice dropped to a whisper. "If Matt's kisses are anything like Howard Honeywell's—"

"Who is Howard Honeywell?"

"A college friend my cousin Mark brought home for the Christmas holiday. I met Howard at a party. He asked me to walk outside to get some air. He kissed me, really kissed me."

Speechless, Hannah gaped at her friend. In Charleston, when a boy acted like he wanted to kiss her, she'd had an urge to giggle.

"I'm sorry I didn't write to tell you about Howard, but I only saw him a couple of times." Leah shrugged. "Before Mark left, he admitted Howard has a special girl at school."

Hannah touched Leah's sleeve. "I'm sorry, that must hurt."

"I didn't really know him. Maybe I wouldn't have liked him if I did." She sighed. "But, I'll always remember him."

A knot lodged in Hannah's throat. In three days, she'd marry a man she barely knew. A man she'd never kissed.

"If not for your papa's health, I'd say you're the luckiest girl alive!"

Hannah tried to work up a bright smile but failed.

Leah gaped. "You don't look…happy. Is something wrong?"

"I'm just upset about Papa." Leah gave a sympathetic nod as the grandfather clock in the hall downstairs struck noon. "I've got to go. I'm meeting Matt at the café."

"Wait, when is the ceremony?"

"Oh, I forgot. Will you stand up with me?"

"Of course. We've always promised to be in each other's weddings. This is so exciting. What time is the wedding?"

"Thursday at three o'clock. At the Lazy P."

"Those must've been some sparks!" Leah said, chuckling.

"We want Papa to see us wed."

Leah absorbed the significance of her words, her eyes softening with compassion.

To avoid that sympathetic gaze, Hannah strode to Leah's wardrobe. "Let's look at your dresses. See what you might wear."

"Miss Carmichael made this for Mark's graduation party," Leah said as she pulled out a frothy dress. "It'll be perfect for an outdoor wedding."

"It's lovely." An image of Leah wearing the pale peach confection as she stood beside Hannah made the wedding all too real.

Leah's eyes widened. "What are you going to wear?"

"Miss Carmichael is altering Mama's wedding dress to fit me."

"Oh, the gown in the portrait. You'll look beautiful."

"Thank you. I've got to go. I'm late."

Arm in arm, they walked to the door, then faced each other.

"Matt's perfect, Hannah. Not a knight, not a prince, but a cowboy groom is the perfect match for a tomboy."

Hannah nodded, then marched to the Calico Café, her clamped jaw shooting pain up her face. Easy for Leah to rhapsodize over Matt Walker. To babble on about stolen kisses. Courting was one thing, marriage quite another.

The grim reality was that Papa was dying, and she'd proposed to Matt. She had no one to blame for this marriage but herself.

Matt fingered the slim gold band in his pocket. To ensure the fit, Rosa had cut a string the size of the ring Martin had given Hannah for her sixteenth birthday.

The door opened, and Hannah crossed the café. Tendrils of her shiny auburn hair had pulled loose, swaying in rhythm with her steps. Any man would be proud to call this lovely woman his.

Yet, one look at the disquiet on her face knotted Matt's gut. Leah must have reacted badly to their upcoming nuptials. During the meal, he'd do what he could to smooth the rough waters he suspected Leah had churned up.

He rose to help Hannah into her chair, then took his seat. Might as well get to what was troubling her. "How did Leah react to news of our marriage?"

Hannah's gaze dropped to her hands clenched in her lap. "She's thrilled."

Unlike the bride.

"She's excited to stand up with me. Has the perfect dress."

"Good. As soon as I got to town, I wired Zack. Already got his acceptance. He'll arrive Thursday morning."

"I told Miss Carmichael, Mr. Bailey and the bench sitters about our wedding."

Matt grinned. "In that case, everyone in town will know by nightfall. I talked to Pastor Cummings. He agreed to marry us."

Finally. No need to tell Hannah that the preacher had cautioned them not to rush into marriage. As if they had the luxury of taking things slow.

"Plans are coming along at home. Rosa's cousin will help clean and cook. Jake will dig the pit, make the sauce and handle the barbecue."

"We're making progress." Matt took her hand. "I'm sorry we'll have no honeymoon."

A flush rose to her cheeks. "No reason to go anywhere," she said, then snatched her hand from his.

If he hadn't understood the boundaries of their marriage, that said it all. Not that he disagreed. Far better to rely on common sense than on emotion, an unreliable foundation for happiness.

Carolyn Shields, her salt-and-pepper hair swept back in a bun, a crisp white apron over her middle, arrived at the table. "Know what you want?"

They settled on the special, beef and noodles. The widow left to dish up the food.

"You seem upset." Matt glanced around him, then kept his voice low. "Are you having second thoughts about our marriage?"

The eyes she lifted to his might not look like an excited bride, but they were steely with determination. "Marriage is what I want. Are you changing your mind?"

"No, ma'am." He grinned. "I'm corralled and ready for branding. Thing is, which brand will I wear?"

"The Lazy P, what else?"

"And you're just the woman to get the job done."

She grinned back at him. "Never doubt that, cowboy."

Good to see her feisty side back. A man didn't hanker to be led around by his nose, but if pretending Hannah was boss would put a smile on her face, that's what he'd do.

But he couldn't help wondering at what point a marriage based on pretense would blow up in his face?

Chapter Seven

The rooster's crow jolted Hannah awake. For a moment, she lay between sleep and wakefulness, listening to the swelling pitch of the rooster's call. Then the significance of the day slammed into her. She sucked in a breath and shot upright in bed. Today she'd become Mrs. Matthew Walker.

Was she ready? Her stomach tumbled. She'd better be. She had no way to undo this. Not now.

She crawled out of bed, padded barefoot to the window and pulled the curtain aside, revealing the glow of the rising sun in a pink and blue sky dotted with fleecy clouds Papa called featherbeds for weary angels. From the looks of the morning sky, the Lord had blessed their plan for an outdoor ceremony.

Hannah had laid awake most of the night. Too edgy to return to bed, she braided her hair, then pulled on a simple dress to please her father, rather than her usual denims.

She glanced in the mirror, staring into the anxious eyes of a nineteen-year-old on the verge of taking the biggest step of her life. A lump rose in her throat. If only she could turn back the clock. To the time when Papa was healthy and strong and she rode the land with joy in her heart, free and full of confidence. Her life had been simple then.

Since her return from Charleston, she'd felt caught in a maze, bumping into one obstacle after another. She'd chosen a way out. Where would that path lead?

She refused to question an answer God had given her. Her stomach tumbled. Hadn't He?

As she passed the dining room, stacks of dishes, boxes of silverware and glasses they'd borrowed from the Walkers, Montgomerys and Rosa's cousin to supplement their supply, covered the table.

Mingling aromas of breakfast led Hannah to the kitchen where Rosa bustled about, keeping an eye on iron skillets of potatoes and sausage gravy as she popped a pan of biscuits into the oven.

"Morning, Rosa," Hannah said. "Breakfast smells delicious."

"Good morning, Hannah. Beautiful day for a wedding."

"Yes." As Hannah carried three white ironstone plates to the stove, she kept an eye out for Matt. Some claimed if the groom saw the bride before the wedding, they'd have bad luck.

Not that she believed in luck, bad or otherwise. Her hesitancy was cowardice, the fear that Matt would see the jumble of emotions churning inside her. Or worse, that she'd see he was having second thoughts.

She didn't have to wait long. Matt rode up the lane to help Papa start his day.

"I'm going out to do chores. Jake's got his hands full watching over the fire," Hannah said, fleeing the house by the back door.

By the time she'd finished, Matt's horse was gone. She heaved a sigh. He'd returned to the Circle W. At the pump, she washed her hands, then headed for the house.

Papa sat at the kitchen table, pale, thin, but with a twinkle in his eye. "How's the bride feeling on her wedding day?"

"I'm fine, Papa."

"Your groom looked mighty chipper."

Rosa joined them at the table, setting a large vase of roses in the center. The flower's sweet, spicy scent mingled with the aroma of fresh brewed coffee. "Señor Matt cut flowers for the wedding."

"He did?"

"Your mother cherished her roses," Papa said, "and tended them daily."

Exactly as her father had done all these years. No matter how busy life got on the ranch, he'd check the roses for bugs, disease, drought. The roses, a symbol of Mama, of her life in Charleston that Papa would not let die.

"Tell me about Mama," Hannah said, then nibbled on a biscuit.

"She loved you. Beamed with pride as you grew from baby to toddler to little girl."

"Was she disappointed I was a tomboy?"

"She would've never been disappointed in anything about you, sugar. But, it wasn't until after your mama died that you traded dolls for lassos and spurs." He smiled. "I wish she could see you married. See grand-children."

If only Mama and Papa were both strong and healthy, how different life would be. But grandchildren…

Hannah shifted in her chair, picking at her food. Papa expected her and Matt's marriage to produce children. Not possible with their arrangement. Still, Hannah could barely imagine motherhood.

She scrambled for another topic. "Tell me again how you and Mama met."

"I was in Charleston to buy a stallion. This beautiful young woman and I had our eye on the same horse. Melanie knew horseflesh and prevailed in the bidding. I pestered the stable owner until he introduced us. We fell in love at first sight. A month later, I brought my bride and her stallion home to Texas." He chuckled. "Melanie always claimed I married her to get that horse."

Her parents' marriage was a far cry from her and Matt's marriage of convenience.

"Your mother loved the slower pace of Charleston. Yet, she gave all that up for me."

Life on a Texas ranch must've been as foreign to Mama as Charleston's frantic social scene had been for Hannah. She couldn't imagine giving up the vastness, the wildness, the challenge of this land. "She loved you, Papa."

"Yes, and I her." He toyed with his fork, turning it around and around in his hands, then lifted moist eyes to Hannah. "I've wondered if bringing Melanie here killed her."

"Why? Women die in childbirth in Charleston, too."

"Yes, but this life is hard, especially for a delicate

woman like your mama." He took Hannah's hand. "I sent you to finishing school for the social graces, the skills to marry, to run a home. So you wouldn't spend your life battling bad weather, cattle diseases, trying to make a success of the ranch."

"I'm not like Mama."

"I'll admit you're sturdier, stronger than your mother. In many ways you're more like me."

"I love this land, Papa. I'm as connected to it as deep-rooted cottonwoods, as enduring as perennial bluebonnets."

Brow creased, his eyes searched hers. "Enough that you will marry to keep it."

Papa understood that romance had nothing to do with the decision to marry Matt. Not having to pretend with Papa somehow eased the tightness in Hannah's chest.

"Hannah, if you're marrying Matt for my sake, if this isn't what you want, don't go through with it."

How could she not? Without her parents, without this land, she had nothing. Nothing of the life she knew, the life she loved. By marrying Matt, she'd keep that way of life. She'd keep this land and give her father peace. "I've made my decision, Papa."

"You sure?"

"I'm sure."

He smiled, relief plain on his face. "I can rest easy knowing you'll be looked after when I'm gone. Matt's a good man. You have much in common. He'll make you a good husband."

The prospect of being yoked to a man she didn't love and who didn't love her flopped in her stomach. Yet, she believed Matt was a good man. She could do worse.

"Promise me you'll give Matt a chance. In time, I'm sure love will come."

"I promise."

Papa sucked in air, the sudden grimace on his face a reminder of the pain he endured. "Reckon I'd better take a dose of my medicine."

With a lump in her throat, Hannah helped Papa to his feet. By the time she had settled him in his room, had given him a dose of his pain medication, then helped Rosa with last-minute food preparation, she needed to start getting ready.

As she filled the tub with water, she thought about her conversation with Papa. Deep within her soul, she wanted that true love her parents had, wanted it with a desperation that took her breath away. To have a love so strong that nothing else mattered—not location, not traditions, not a way of life—was implausible. But she'd have all the rest, the things that gave her security, that filled her life with meaning, that gave her purpose. That and God would be enough. Enough for a lifetime.

She bathed and washed her hair, then rinsed it with vinegar for shine. On the porch, she lifted and finger-combed the strands, letting them dry in the gentle breeze.

Strange how the day felt ordinary when she'd soon take the biggest step of her life. Somehow she managed to eat a few bites at noon, then went to her room to dress and finish her hair.

Rosa had laid out Hannah's wedding finery in a fan of silk on the bed. True to her word, Miss Carmichael had brought the dress out yesterday. The alterations done perfectly, the dress was pressed and ready to wear.

"I hope I'm as prepared," Hannah whispered, as she swept her hair onto the top of her head, anchoring it with hairpins and pulling shorter ringlets free around her face.

There was a tap at the door. Forehead beaded with perspiration, the strings of her apron flapping behind her, Rosa barreled into the room, a bouquet of roses in one hand. "Oh, your hair so pretty," she said a she set the flowers aside. "I come help you dress."

Rosa cinched Hannah into her corset, the hated contraption she rarely wore on the ranch, then carefully lifted the dress and slipped the skirt over Hannah's head. With the help of several hairpins, Rosa secured the halo of waxed orange blossoms to Hannah's hair, then smoothed the attached filmy veil that fell almost to the floor.

The mirror reflected an uncanny likeness to her mother's wedding portrait hanging over the mantel in the parlor. Hannah had viewed the painting her entire life, but today she felt as if she had stepped into the portrait…had become Melanie Parrish.

With shaky fingers, Hannah smoothed the gown over her petticoats. The toe of a white satin slipper peeked from beneath the hem. She felt like a princess in the fairy tales she and Leah had read as youngsters.

"The bride is most beautiful in all Texas!" Rosa gushed, then retrieved the roses tied with a silky ribbon and handed the sprig to Hannah.

Hannah blinked back tears and buried her nose in the petals, inhaling the heady scent, the fragrance of Mama.

"You are sad?"

"I miss Mama."

Tears flooded Rosa's eyes. "*Si,* a bride needs her mama on her wedding day." With both hands, Rosa cupped Hannah's face and kissed her on both cheeks, then tapped her heart. "She here. She here for you."

"Thank you, Rosa."

"I go change clothes." She smiled. "Señor Matt helped your papa shave and dress."

A gentle warmth slipped through Hannah. Without fanfare, Matt recognized and quietly met the needs of others. Papa was right when he'd said she was marrying a good man.

As Rosa hurried out the door, Hannah bent over her jewelry case and removed the dainty pearl earrings Mama had worn at her wedding. As she fastened the pearls in front of the mirror, troubled blue eyes looked back at her. Nothing like the smiling eyes in Mama's portrait. This dress, the dress in the wedding portrait, had been worn by a bride deeply in love with her groom. A bride willing to leave everything behind and move across the country to share his life.

If only Hannah felt that deep love that mattered more than anything on this earth. If her mother could see from heaven, would she be disappointed in her daughter? Disapprove of giving up girlhood dreams for grown-up realities?

Determined not to surrender to the sudden tightness in her throat, Hannah took one last look in the mirror. Would Matt think her pretty as he had Amy on their wedding day? Ashamed of such foolishness, Hannah tamped down the thought, eyes misting. The image before her blurred.

The jingle of harnesses, the squeak of a wheel took

Hannah to the open window. Buggies were pulling in the lane, parking in the barnyard.

Settled in an armchair in the shade of the pecan tree, Martin greeted their arriving guests.

Please, Lord, help Papa handle the long, tiring day.

Hannah heard a shriek and reeled to the doorway.

"Oh, you're a beautiful bride!" Leah said, charging into the room. "Are you excited?"

"Of course!" Hannah despised the lie but what else could she say? "You look lovely, Leah."

"Thank you." Leah spun in a circle, a wide grin on her face. "I adore this dress."

Leah looked fetching indeed in her delicate peach frock with a modestly scooped neckline and deeper peach sash at the waist. A wide-brimmed straw hat, trimmed with flowers and matching ribbon and white gloves completed her outfit.

"You better hurry. The yard is full of people and the preacher is here," Leah said. "Matt is pacing out front, looking more handsome and nervous than I've ever seen him."

What had happened to the confident cowboy? Was Matt having second thoughts? She tamped down the temptation to look out the window to see for herself, afraid she'd see regret on his face.

"Zack looks gorgeous in his Sunday best," Leah went on. "If you don't need me for anything, Rosa gave me strict orders to bring you down. It's almost time to begin."

"All I have to do is slip on these gloves."

Leah again clutched Hannah's hands. "I know you'll be happy. Matt's the best catch in the county. He's going to fall even more madly in love with you the minute he sees his beautiful bride."

Nonsense. Leah's head was filled with romance, not reality. Some sentimental part of Hannah wished he would, but love would complicate everything.

"Where will you stay tonight?" Leah said, her blue eyes gleaming.

"What do you mean?"

"You know, where will you...ah, sleep?" Leah's gaze traveled to the full bed.

Tonight. Her wedding night. Perception dawned, trapping the breath in Hannah's lungs. Leah had skirted a subject too personal to broach, even with a best friend. Hannah's stomach knotted. The expectation would be for her and Matt to share a room. The knot cinched tighter. She'd do what she could to hide the truth that Matt would stay in the guest room down the hall.

"We'll stay here," Hannah said. "We don't have to travel far for the honeymoon."

Leah giggled. "That's a surprisingly sensible thought for such an impulsive wedding."

Hannah worked a smile to her face. "I'm almost ready. Go on ahead. I'll be right along."

After Leah left, Hannah battled back tears. Everyone was here, the time had come. A part of her wanted to run. To take off the gown, release her hair, dash to the stable. Let Star take her away from all this.

She walked to the window. Papa sat on the front row of chairs beside Rosa, too weak to walk her down the grassy aisle, but looking happy. Her gaze swept the land, Parrish land all the way to the horizon as far as the eye could see.

For her father and for this ranch, she could marry Matt. She turned to the mirror, pasted on a smile and a brave face that didn't reveal the uncertainty underneath, then before she had second thoughts, grabbed the bouquet of roses and hurried from the room.

In the entry hall, Robert Walker waited, a wide, teasing grin on his face. "Your guests are roasting and need a bride before they're as barbecued as that beef. You look most fetching, Hannah, a stunning bride. My son is a lucky man."

"Thank you. No more than I, to be joining your family."

Wearing a pleased expression, Robert offered his arm. Together they walked out into the sunlight, the scent of roses overridden by the tantalizing aroma of barbecue.

Up ahead Leah sashayed toward the front, serene and in her element, carrying a bouquet of Mama's pink roses.

Under the rose trellis, Matt waited with Zack and Pastor Cummings, looking expectant, nervous and so handsome he took her breath away. Boots planted wide, freshly shaven, his curly dark hair combed into obedience, he wore a dark suit, as befit a proper groom.

His dark eyes focused only on her, filled with unmistakable approval. Her heart leaped, then pounded in her chest. She offered a tentative smile.

He smiled back, the expression on his face content.

With newfound confidence, she proceeded up the aisle, passing their guests. Hannah met Mrs. Montgomery's tear-filled eyes and unwavering smile. Jake gave her a wink and a nod. Matt's mother, Victoria, blew her a kiss. Papa sat beside Rosa, his pale face glowing with pride, with joy.

Robert took a seat beside Victoria. Hannah leaned down and pressed a kiss to her father's cheek. "I love you, Papa."

"I love you, Daughter."

She stepped to Matt's side and accepted the solid warmth of his grasp. Together they faced the preacher as butterflies tap-danced in her belly.

With a smile, Pastor Cummings glanced at those seated before him. "We are here today to witness Hannah Lorraine Parrish and Matthew Aaron Walker united as one in holy matrimony."

Holy matrimony. A permanent union, sanctioned by the church, by God. *Lord, I promise to commit to our vows.*

The ceremony passed in a blur, with Hannah barely aware of the words the preacher uttered. Yet moments of utter clarity branded her brain. The sincerity in Matt's eyes and the strength of his voice when he recited his vows. The warmth of the gold band he slipped on her finger. The scent of roses rising from her bouquet and the trellis.

And then finally, the words she had both dreaded and anticipated. "You may kiss the bride," Pastor Cummings said.

Hannah's heart skipped a beat, fluttering in her chest. A moment passed, then Matt lowered his lips to hers, his gentle, feathery touch tingled through her, trapping the air in her lungs until she had to remind herself to breathe.

He drew back, but her brain lingered on that kiss

and on the riot of emotions and reactions churning in her belly. What had just happened? A part of her had been swept away, caught up in some fantasy of happily ever after.

She steeled her spine. He didn't love her. She wouldn't let herself care for him. She wouldn't.

Matt's heart thudded in his chest, as he gazed down at his bride, her lips slightly parted, cheeks rosy—from the heat or from his kiss? Had she been as stunned by the reaction to his lips on hers as he had?

Long dark lashes fluttered as she opened her eyes and stared up at him, looking dazed, vulnerable and oh, so beautiful.

His throat clogged. The responsibility for her that once weighed on Martin's shoulders shifted to his. This time, he would protect his wife from harm.

Within minutes of the ceremony, Pastor Cummings ushered Matt and Hannah into Martin's office to sign the license. Behind them, dapper in a three-piece suit, Zack walked beside a radiant Leah, obviously smitten with Matt's brother. Hannah's signature never wavered, the strokes precise and straightforward much like the woman. Matt added his own signature, then thanked everyone.

"Let's give the newlyweds a moment alone," Zack said, after the preacher took his leave.

"Very considerate of you, little brother." Matt grinned. "Though I suspect your plan is for a moment alone with Leah."

Leah giggled, blushing like a want-to-be bride, then

removed Hannah's headpiece and floor-length veil. "Can't have you tripping when you dance."

Once the others left the house, Hannah stopped at the open front door, scanning the yard where their guests milled about, chatting.

Matt took her hands, engulfing them in his own. The delicate bones of her fingers proof that women were fragile and needed protection. "I'll take good care of you, Hannah," he promised.

A flash of disquiet traveled her face. She tugged her hands away. "I'm a big girl. I don't need coddling."

"Is that right? Or is it cuddling you don't need?"

"That, too. Don't let the flowers and my finery fool you." She nailed him with her gaze. "We married for convenience, remember?"

A chuckle rumbled inside of him. "Married only a few minutes and you're already putting me in my place."

Exactly where he wanted to be, a distance from Hannah, in a place of contentment. Not of infatuation or a rush of emotion, as unreliable and perilous as a tattered saddle cinch.

"I'm sorry. I didn't mean to sound harsh."

She laid a gentle hand on his jaw, peering up at him. At her tender touch, his heart tripped. An urge stormed through him to cradle her hand, kiss the palm and each fingertip.

A bright smile on her lips, she removed her hand. "That should pacify our guests," she said.

Tarnation. She'd played the role of blissful bride so perfectly, even he'd fallen for the charade.

With every ounce of his will he tamped down his reaction and turned away. To keep that distance they both wanted would require fortitude and willpower. If all else failed, a reel of barbed wire should blockade his heart. No matter what, he'd not fall again into the trap of impulsiveness and risk another unhappy wife.

"Shall we join our guests?" Hannah said. "I promise they'll never suspect this marriage is a business deal, at least not from watching me."

She had no idea how much she'd affected him. "Of course," he croaked, then cleared his throat. "Everyone is waiting for us to get our food first."

At dinner, he and Hannah smiled into each other's eyes. She touched his arm, a hand, snuggled near. Perhaps that fancy finishing school taught acting classes. Hannah was putting on quite a performance. With each touch, he steeled himself, determined to remain aloof, as they played the game. Yet the dishonesty of feigning love and happiness roiled the food in his stomach.

When their families and guests had eaten their fill, Zack stood, fulfilling his role as best man. "Hannah, you'll need a load of patience to put up with Matt's bossy nature."

"I'm only bossy with those who require direction, Zack." Matt grinned. "Like you, not my wife."

Their guests chuckled at the banter.

"But underneath that, ah, slightly rough surface, Matt's solid, a godly man." Zack raised his glass. "I wish you both every happiness."

Not to be outdone, Cal stood. "Matt and Hannah, may you have a long and happy life together with the blessing of many children. Susannah and I intend to give you a goal to strive for in that department." With a wide grin, he glanced at his wife and small son.

The clink of glasses filled the spring air. Matt pulled his collar from his neck. Children. He adored children.

But he and Hannah wouldn't have any. He'd be a good uncle, spend time with Robbie and other babies that arrived. Fill the empty place inside him with Susannah and Cal's offspring.

Eyes aglow, Martin struggled to his feet. "God bless you, my children. I wish you a long and happy life filled with the joy you've given me today."

To see Martin happy, at peace, confirmed he and Hannah had done the right thing.

Tears in her eyes, Hannah rose from his side and embraced her father. Matt and Martin shook hands then clapped their arms around each other.

As Martin took his seat beside Robert, Matt's father stood. "Hannah, welcome to the family. To Hannah and Matt!" he said, lifting his glass.

The wedding guests cheered his toast—no doubt believing he and Hannah were in love.

Matt rose, and cleared his throat. "I'm blessed to have this special woman as my wife." He stared into Hannah's eyes. "Hannah, I will love you as long as I live," he said, not tripping over the word love, but perspiration beaded his brow.

He leaned down and brushed his lips over hers. Her smile never wavered, even as tears welled in her eyes. He knew full well these were not tears of happiness.

He felt like he'd stepped onstage. He and Hannah were the main actors. He didn't know who'd put on the better performance but the joy on everyone's faces was their applause.

Donned in her best finery, Belinda Carmichael sashayed up and tapped Matt on the arm with her fan. "I'll admit I was suspicious you two had married for reasons other than love. But seeing you together, the looks, the touches." She sighed. "I've never seen a more lovesick couple. I wish you much happiness."

"Thank you, Miss Carmichael. And thank you for altering my wife's wedding dress. I've never seen her look more beautiful."

The rest of the afternoon passed with all the traditions of a wedding. Rosa led them to the tiered cake festooned with white swags and sugary roses and placed a beribboned knife in Hannah's hands.

Then Hannah tossed her bouquet. Leah scrambled to retrieve it and winked at Hannah as she lifted the sprig of roses in victory.

All afternoon Zack had hovered at Leah's side. Both were flirting openly. There was no pretense on Leah's part, but Zack...who knew?

Hannah nudged Matt. "They'd be perfect together."

No doubt their guests thought the same about him and Hannah. "You'd better warn Leah. Zack has broken more than his share of hearts."

"Don't underestimate her. Leah might be the woman to tame him."

"Like you've tamed me?" he said, chuckling.

Head thrown back, eyes twinkling, she laughed. "You're about as tame as a wild mustang, Matt Walker."

"Hardly." He leaned in to her, catching the lingering sweet scent of roses. "But, I must admit, I'm glad you think so, Mrs. Walker."

As much as he wanted a marriage of convenience, a powerful temptation to take his bride into his arms, to hold her close gripped him. This newlywed game they played had undermined his judgment and opened a crevice in the steel casing around his heart.

Where would all this lead?

Chapter Eight

Drained from playing the part of happy husband, Matt saw off their departing guests. Each one expressed appreciation for the delightful evening of barbecue, guitar music and dancing.

Determined not to get close to his wife, who was in the kitchen thanking Rosa and her cousin for all they'd done for the wedding, Matt stowed the bag of toiletries and satchel of his clothes in the foyer. Then he returned to the porch where Martin waited, cane in hand.

He helped Martin down the hall to his room, got him settled for the night, then gave him a dose of pain medicine.

"Thanks, Matt. For everything."

Matt met Martin's eyes, and understood what he'd left unsaid. Martin was thanking him for marrying Hannah. "Thanks for trusting me with your daughter."

"No one I'd trust with Hannah more," Martin said, voice soft and reedy. "No one I'd trust with this ranch more. With only Jake to help, you'll carry a heavy workload."

"I'll see that things get done."

"I won't let you kill yourself handling two spreads."

"Pa is handling the Circle W. Besides, I'm tougher than an overcooked steer."

"I used to be." Face lined with fatigue, Martin chuckled. "Weddings make a man tired."

"That they do."

Behind him, he heard a rap on the doorframe. Hannah entered, still wearing her wedding gown. "Thank you for the lovely wedding and party, Papa. Our friends and neighbors enjoyed themselves."

"Nothing like a wedding to bring folks together for a good time."

She leaned down and kissed Martin's cheek. "I love you. Sleep well."

"I love you, sweet daughter."

Matt laid a hand on Martin's shoulder. "If you need anything, call."

"Hannah, my bit of fatherly advice—look to your husband for leadership."

"I'll…try, Papa."

Martin gave a wan smile. "Reckon that's where you'll need patience, Matt."

"We'll find our way."

Eyes weary, Martin nodded. "Know you will."

He and Hannah left the room, leaving Martin's door ajar and walked to the entry. Matt opened the front door. They stood side by side studying the night sky yet not touching. The awkward silence between them spoke volumes of uncertainty about their new status.

To fill the void, Matt scrambled for a topic. "Looks like we'll have another nice day tomorrow."

As if his words had the power of gale winds, she wobbled and brushed against him, then jerked away, obviously as jumpy as he was. "Yes. Though we could use the rain."

"The water's evaporating from the earthen tanks. The windmill pumps water into the tank in the north pasture. We'll have to move the herd there."

Hannah sighed. "And risk overgrazing."

When had a bride and groom had a more absurd conversation on their wedding night?

He closed the door, then gathered his belongings. They retraced their steps. Hannah's room was directly across from Martin's. Where would he sleep?

She walked past her door, hugging the wall as if she feared they'd touch. At an open door just down from hers, she stopped and faced him. "This is your room."

He met her skittish gaze. "Thanks."

"Well, if you don't need anything…" her voice trailed off "…I'll say good-night."

"Sleep well."

"You, too."

Head held high, back erect, as if she had a broom handle wedged along her spine, Hannah rushed to her room. At her door, she paused and glanced back at him, then ducked inside. The door clicked shut behind her, the sound as clear-cut as a no trespassing sign.

Matt lugged his possessions inside his room, lit the kerosene lamp on the nightstand and surveyed the large space. The windows opened to the back of the house, to the paddock and pasture beyond.

As he put his toiletries on the shelf below the washstand, his thoughts turned to the wedding ceremony. To the moment Pastor Cummings declared him and Hannah husband and wife.

Married. *Again*.

Unlike the first and despite its speedy execution, this marriage was not an impulsive act, far from it. He'd prayed repeatedly about the decision, felt guided by God's wisdom and had been filled with peace when he'd accepted Hannah's proposal. A levelheaded decision motivated by his concern for Martin, his concern for Martin's daughter and his desire to get on with his life in a way that honored God.

Yet right now, that decision felt anything but sensible. He hadn't expected his response to Hannah's touch. He was a red-blooded male. Could he kiss Hannah, hold her hand, touch her soft skin without opening his heart to his wife?

Somehow he would.

He'd treat his wife as he would a good friend. He'd be considerate. Supportive. Share the work. If he kept his distance, kept his focus on the ranch, on Martin, not on the woman down the way, he could carry out their agreement.

As Hannah made preparations for bed, what was going through her mind? Did she regret her insistence on a marriage of convenience? Or did she thank God for a solution to her problem?

He shoved the drawer closed on the last of his belongings, then hung his shirts in the wardrobe and put his Bible on the nightstand by the double bed. A chair across the way would be a likely spot to shove into his boots. The room resembled what he had at the Circle W. Except this room was next door to Hannah.

His wife.

Of its own volition, his mind traveled back to Amy, to the hole her death had left in his life. A hole he'd filled with regret and self-recrimination.

He dropped into the chair and lowered his head to his hands. He'd loved Amy, but their marriage had been far from tranquil. If he hadn't been blinded by attraction, he'd have seen that she cherished activities in town, daily encounters with friends and wouldn't be happy with the life he'd chosen. The life he couldn't give up.

During their courtship, he'd found ways to leave the work and get to town to see her. But once they'd married, he'd expected Amy to enjoy ranch life as much as he did. To find her own purpose, while he concentrated on proving himself to his father. Yet, she'd resented the hours he spent working on the ranch, claiming the Circle W took him away from her as surely as a mistress.

With time on her hands and little interest in housekeeping, she made frequent trips into Bliss or spent her days moping. During their evenings and Sundays together, her unhappiness with the life he loved chipped away at their relationship until the tension between them was a wall they couldn't penetrate.

He swallowed hard against the lump in his throat. He could've made concessions, could've found a way to spend more time with Amy, but hadn't. Then one horrible day, Amy was thrown from her horse and died.

Too late to make amends. Too late to compromise. Too late to make her happy.

He shed his dress boots, wiped dust from the toes with his handkerchief, restoring the shine. If only he could clean up his past as easily, clean up the mistakes he'd made.

Each day he lived with the knowledge he'd failed his wife. That heartache had taught him a lesson—to never make decisions with anything other than clear logic. To never just fall into a pattern as they had. Months of courting had led to expectations of marriage, as if they traveled a river flowing to a preconceived destination. Instead of scrambling up the bank for a clear view of their prospects for happiness, they'd paddled along with the current, never discussing anything of importance. Making assumptions. How wrong they'd been. How little they knew each other. How little of importance they'd shared. That negligence had cost them a terrible price.

He rose and laid on the bed, staring out at the night sky. He didn't understand the mysteries of the heavens, but he was grateful God was there. God was here. God was inside him. That gave him hope that with Hannah's love of the ranch, her knowledge and appreciation of the life he held dear, they'd have what he and Amy hadn't. Contentment.

Yet this strong attraction to Hannah caught him off guard, put his gut in a twist. If they got close, fell in love, what would happen then? Would her expectations change? Would she want something from him, some level of closeness and awareness he couldn't comprehend, much less give?

And would he fail her, too, as he had Amy?

He rose from the bed and paced the room. He'd share with Hannah a love for Martin, a love for the ranch, a love for their way of life.

That was enough. More than enough.

Tomorrow he'd ride the range, check on the last of the cows dropping calves. Then do the same at the Circle W. Each day he'd work tirelessly until he fell into bed exhausted. Too exhausted to think about his new wife one door down.

As tired as Hannah had been when she'd gone to bed, she'd tossed and turned all night. Finally, toward morning, she'd given up on sleep and sat at the window, soaking up the peace of the sky, of the resting land with only the hoot of a barn owl to disturb the quiet.

Her thumb traced the slender gold band on her finger, for most brides, a symbol of love. Her marriage was a sham. If she wanted proof, she need only acknowledge she'd spent her wedding night alone. Worse, she'd had to go to Rosa's room off the kitchen and ask for help getting out of her wedding gown. And reveal that Mr. and Mrs. Matt Walker were married in name only. Rosa would keep their secret. Still, she'd no doubt grieve that Hannah didn't have the love of her life as Rosa had believed.

The marriage was exactly what she'd wanted, yet beneath the levelheaded reasons for their business deal lay a heavy heart. She'd thought she'd tossed aside her girlhood dreams, but they clung to her still.

Lord, help me handle this loveless marriage. Help me appreciate the answer Matt has provided. Let that be enough.

Matt had agreed to her stipulations and had no idea that she struggled with the cold reality of the life she'd chosen. No matter what, she'd never let him know her misgivings. She'd keep a smile on her face. Work the ranch, learn all she could. The ranch would give her purpose and satisfaction.

She'd learn about the accounting side of ranching. See when to order and pay for supplies at local merchants, learn how to negotiate cattle prices. Last year's books should reveal how things were done.

As the sun rose in the east, she slipped into a skirt and blouse, brushed her hair, then hurried to the kitchen, determined to make this first day of married life productive and peaceful.

Rosa was nowhere in sight. No doubt exhausted from handling the food and cleanup for the barbecue, she'd slept late.

Hannah lit the cookstove, then made a pot of coffee. She was about to pour a cup when Matt appeared in the doorway.

She jumped, slopping coffee. "I didn't hear you coming."

With his boots dangling from one hand, he motioned to his bare feet. "Not trying to sneak up on you."

"Good thing." She grinned. "Men have been shot for less."

His dimple winked. "Guess I should be relieved you're not wearing a gun."

"Sure should." She lifted the pot. "Care for coffee?"

"Please."

With shaky hands, she poured, proud of not spilling a drop, then handed him the cup.

He thanked her, then leaned against the counter and took a sip. "Mmm, good."

Odd to share an early morning cup of coffee with a

denim clad, barefoot husband with his shirttail out, hair mussed, the stubble of his beard shadowing his jaw.

A crazy urge to run her fingers through the hair curling at his nape slid through her. Fingers tight on her mug, Hannah took a swig of the steamy brew, then hissed. She grabbed a ladle of water and cooled her burning mouth. It was a painful reminder that focusing on Matt presented a greater risk to her than gulping hot coffee.

"You okay?" Matt stepped closer, invading her space, trapping the air in her lungs.

"Coffee's…ah, hot," she muttered.

"Yep, supposed to be."

"I forgot." Could she sound more stupid?

Truth was, she'd forgotten pretty much everything, where she was, what she was doing. But she wouldn't admit how much his early morning presence unnerved her.

Bloodshot eyes met hers. "Hope you slept well last night."

"Fine. And you?"

"Like a log."

Apparently they were both good at concealing the truth. But what could she say? *I didn't sleep a wink knowing you were next door?*

"I thought you'd sleep in—after the hectic day," Matt said.

"I like rising early. Besides, with morning chores to do, I never had the privilege."

"I figured that fancy finishing school didn't start the day till noon."

She shot him a glare. "I'll have you know that classes started at nine."

"Never thought you were a shirker, Hannah, but for all your lessons on deportment, you're mighty easy to rile."

"You might want to blame yourself for that."

He smirked. "You're fun to tease. Thanks for the coffee." Matt set his cup on the counter. "What time is breakfast?"

"Knowing Rosa, she'll have a hearty breakfast on the table at eight."

"Wouldn't miss it." He stomped into his boots, then grabbed a cold biscuit off the table. "See you then."

This first morning of their marriage she'd make it clear that she wouldn't be confined to the kitchen. "I'm coming."

She grabbed her Stetson and dashed after him. A stiff breeze whipped the brim of her hat and her skirts. She held onto both until she stepped inside the stable, out of the wind.

As they fed and watered the horses and mucked the stalls, Matt whistled a soft tune, as if he were happy, at peace. If only Hannah could capture that tranquility, instead of feeling skittish, like a colt being trained to the bit.

She and Matt tramped from the feed bin and pump to the stalls, hauling feed and water to the horses. Each time they passed, she averted her eyes. As they worked, their movements were awkward, a dance of stops and starts, first sidestepping, then motioning the other to move on ahead. All done clearly to avoid brushing against one another, as if contact were a crime.

The stable had never felt so confining. Or its occupants so tantalizing. Muscles bulging, Matt insisted on carrying the water, a pail in each hand. As quickly as she scooped up feed, he'd be there to tote the bucket. He was trying to be thoughtful, but she felt restricted, confined, edgy enough to crawl right out of her skin.

How long before she got used to having him around all the time? Until they figured out who did what, without this awkwardness?

Jake entered the stable, a welcome disruption.

"Morning, missus," Jake said.

At the label, heat climbed Hannah's neck. "Morning."

"Not sure she's used to the missus part, Jake," Matt said, then shot Hannah a teasing grin.

Hannah tried to return the smile, but it wobbled on her lips. One glance at the ring on her finger, shiny like a new penny, reminded her of the vows binding her to Matt. This simple gold band was as much a brand of ownership as the Lazy P brand. If only she could leave it in her jewelry box, claiming wearing it was hazardous. But to keep up the charade, she must.

Determined to keep her mind off Matt, Hannah turned to Jake. "Any word from your niece?"

The furrow between the old cowpoke's eyes deepened. "Got a letter from Gertie yesterday. I could throttle Lorna for going off with a no-account man and leaving my sis to clean up the mess."

"Taking care of a child must be hard on Gertie."

Jake bobbed his head. "Gertie loves Allie like any grandma would, but sis ain't no spring chicken. Running after a seven-year-old day in and day out has her plum tuckered out."

"Lorna hasn't contacted Gertie?"

"Nope, too selfish, I reckon. Ain't easy to explain such behavior to a child."

No doubt Jake felt as helpless as Hannah did watching Papa grow weaker every day. At least by marrying Matt she'd given her father peace. Yet, she could barely comprehend life without him.

With a wave, Jake hobbled out the door, heading toward the barn.

Matt shoved his hat back on his head. "Jake looks like he's carrying the weight of the world on his shoulders."

"His niece Lorna's been a worry for years."

"You're the opposite of Lorna. Responsible, considerate of your pa, a daughter he's proud of."

Hannah's throat knotted. What would Matt think if he knew doing the right thing for Papa had cost her peace of mind?

He sent a clod flying from the toe of his boot. "I'm sorry you're going through this. Martin, too. Sometimes life's a kick in the teeth." He cupped her jaw with his hand, and peered down at her. "Just know that I care. I'm here to help."

"Thanks," she said, leaning into the comfort of his palm, if only for a moment before she pulled away.

With the chores in the stable finished, she and Matt washed their hands at the pump, eyes averted as if this ritual was somehow too personal to share. As she scrubbed her nails with a bar of lye soap under the cold blast of water, Hannah shivered. Inches away, water splattered Matt's boots. He was standing so close, she could feel the heat from his body.

She took a step back, wiped her hands on her skirt. "The water's cold this morning," she said. Ridiculous thing to say on a warm Texas morning in May.

He took her hands and rubbed them between his.

She jerked them away. "While you're warming my hands, our breakfast's getting cold," she said then strode for the house.

In a few steps he caught up with her. "Happy to warm you up, anytime you say," he said, then gave her a wink.

Heat climbed her neck, flooded her checks. Though she wouldn't admit he already had, the blush she wore surely did.

They entered the cozy kitchen. As always, wonderful aromas of Rosa's home cooking filled her nostrils.

While Hannah and Rosa dished up the food, Matt helped Papa to the table. He slumped forward, resting his elbows on the wood as they all took seats. Lines of pain etched Papa's eyes and mouth. The backs of Hannah's eyes stung. She blinked, warding off tears. Yesterday had been one of his good days, but the wedding and party had worn him out.

As Martin murmured a blessing for the food, Hannah silently formed a prayer of her own.

Lord, please heal Papa, let him live. I need him, God. I promise I'll work hard. Even listen to Matt, if you'll save Papa. I'll do anything You ask. Anything.

No matter how often she'd prayed for healing, her father grew weaker. God could heal with a spoken word. Yet Scripture didn't promise healing or a trouble-free life. Only that God would walk with them through those troubles.

As her husband, Matt would also share those troubles, a thought she found oddly comforting. Losing Papa would hurt Matt, too. Just watching the two of them revealed the respect and trust they had for each other. And for God.

If only she could trust like that. But every time she thought about life without her father, her veins flamed, her throat went dry, her heart rattled in her chest.

Fear. Fear had her by the nape. She wouldn't let fear win.

"You planning on bringing Tom back," Papa asked, his gaze on Matt.

"No, your foreman didn't exactly endear himself to Hannah. Your two drovers along with me, Pa and Cal can manage both roundups."

"Good to hear." Papa laid down his fork, having eaten only a couple of bites. "Want to let you all know where I stand on a few things."

Face grave, Matt nodded. Hannah took her father's hand.

"Jake's an old codger like me. He's worked here since I brought Melanie here as a new bride." He smiled at Rosa across the way. "He and Rosa are family and will always have a home here. Take care of them."

"Consider it done. Anything else?" Matt said.

Hannah's hands went cold. Papa was making arrangements. He wanted to ensure Matt understood people mattered more than money. People mattered more than productivity. She'd never loved her father more. "We'll take care of everything."

He gave Hannah's hand a squeeze, then glanced at Matt. "Sorry to ask, but I'd like to lie down."

As Matt helped her father to his room, Hannah glanced at his full plate, then met Rosa's troubled gaze. "The barbecue tired him," she said. "He'll be stronger tomorrow."

"*Si.*" Rosa turned her back, fussing with the stove.

Rosa couldn't admit the truth, anymore than Hannah could. Each day Papa grew weaker. Yet, Hannah wouldn't lose hope. Hope for more time with Papa.

She'd see that he ate better. Got his rest, didn't overdo. She would never stop praying for a miracle.

Chapter Nine

Matt found Hannah in the office hunched over the Parrish account book, her pen hovered over a sheet of paper scribbled with notes. No doubt trying to understand the particulars of the ranch's finances. From that pucker between her brows, she was losing the battle. A ride would do her good.

"Having fun?" he said.

She jumped, then set down her pen with a sigh. "Not at all. All I'm sure of is we owe a pile of money due upon the sale of our cattle."

"That's how things work."

"If we have to cull the herd early, I have no idea who to contact."

"We'll need to wire ahead to make sure a cattle buyer will be in Fort Worth. We drive the cattle, corral them, agree on the tally, then make a deal."

"That's it?"

"Well, in a nutshell." He smiled. "I'm riding out to the north range. Want to ride along?"

"I'll change." She popped to her feet, heading out the door before he'd gotten the invitation out of his mouth.

"Meet you outside."

In the stable, Matt slapped leather on the horses. By the time he'd finished, Hannah appeared clad in denims, hair loose under her Stetson, eyes smiling. His wife loved nothing more than a ride, the outdoors. Already the tension he'd seen in her shoulders had eased, which was the reason he'd suggested she accompany him. Not that this hardworking tomboy would be left behind.

She must've found that year in Charleston stifling. He'd find being cooped up in an office just as suffocating.

"Well, Mrs. Walker," Matt said, glancing at the gold band on her hand. "Ready to deliver a calf or two?"

"Nothing to it," she said, shooting him a saucy grin.

They rode side by side to the north pasture and stopped their horses to survey the cattle cropping grass, quiet and peaceful.

Hannah shifted in the saddle. "The outstanding bills on the books and that loan payment due in September make me uneasy."

"If you studied last year's numbers, you know the herd's growing. The Lazy P should show a profit this year. The price in the spring may be lower, but the sale of your cattle should make more than enough to handle the bills."

"Good to hear."

"Too pretty of a day to talk invoices." On their own volition, his eyes sought her lips. "Too pretty of a woman to talk business," he said, then raised his gaze to hers.

Their gazes locked and heated, the pull between them a powerful living thing.

"Not talk business?" she repeated, a dazed look in her eyes. "Can't think of anything more important."

"Your peace of mind is more important."

"Hard to have peace with Papa so sick. With all those perplexing numbers to wade through."

Much troubled her. How could he bring her comfort? "Try to live one day at a time." He took her hand. "Enjoy the good. Trust God for the rest."

She glanced at his hand, then lifted her eyes to his. "You're kind," she said. "I'm grateful you're helping me run this ranch. Helping me with my father."

His gaze lingered on her lips. One hand gripping the saddle horn, he leaned toward her, cupping her jaw with the other. "I want to make your life easier."

Matt nudged Thunder closer until their knees touched, gazing at her upturned face. The dreamy look in her eyes, those parted lips beckoned. Surely she wanted his kiss. The insight trapped the air in his lungs. He leaned toward her. Lowered his head.

Her eyes went wide, she reared back, then kneed Star. The horse leaped forward. "Race you to the creek!" she hollered. "The loser mucks the barn. Yeehaw!"

Bent forward in the saddle, hat dangling, her hair flying out behind her, horse and rider devoured ground.

With the force of a right hook to the gut, memories assaulted him. As the horror played out in his mind, he broke out in a cold sweat. Amy. Racing her horse toward the creek. Her mare stepping into a prairie dog hole, stumbling, falling, throwing Amy to the ground.

He'd reached her in seconds, cradling her limp body in his arms, willing her to breathe.

Too late.

She was already dead from a broken neck.

With a shake of his head, Matt cleared the image, kneed Thunder into action, racing to intercept Star before Hannah met the same fate. A larger animal with a longer stride, Thunder's pounding hooves pulled him closer. Then Star and Thunder raced neck and neck.

Her eyes dancing, Hannah slapped the reins, urging Star on.

Thunder inched ahead. Matt leaned out, grabbed Star's bridle and tugged back, slowing the mare's pace from a gallop to a canter to a walk. Soon both horses stood muzzle to muzzle, lathered and heaving.

Hannah slapped at his hand. "What are you doing?" she demanded, eyes blasting like a six-shooter.

"Saving your pretty little neck."

"I ride as well as any man."

"That may be, but racing Star with the huge prairie dog colony between here and the creek is insanity," he shot back.

"I'm careful."

"Careful? At that speed you can't see the tunnels."

She slammed her Stetson in place. "When did you become a fraidycat, Matthew Walker?"

Her words cut off his air. Once, he had been a risk taker, even toyed with danger. Life had changed him.

Hannah's expression softened, her eyes filled with regret. "I'm sorry, that was thoughtless of me. I forgot about Amy's accident. But, I know this land. I know every tree, every gully, every blade of grass."

"You've been away for a year. The terrain is constantly changing."

Eyes downcast, she sighed. "You're right. I should be more cautious." She patted her mount's neck. "But, Star and I love the thrill of a race, don't we, girl?" Star bobbed her head up and down, slinging lather, as if taking her mistress' side.

Matt motioned to the trees. "Let's give the horses a breather." And give his stomach time to move from his throat to its rightful location.

Shoulders squared, Hannah rode alongside him to the creek and the canopy of cottonwoods at the water's edge. They swung out of the saddle, then walked the horses under the trees, letting them cool down.

At the creek, Matt filled his hands and offered a gulp to both horses, careful not to give them too much and risk colic.

Once they'd settled the horses in the shade, Matt doffed his Stetson, wiping his forehead on his sleeve, then plopped the hat in place.

One glance at those pursed lips of Hannah's told him plenty. Had he overreacted?

"I understand what happened back there and I'm sorry for scaring you. But a ring on my finger doesn't give you the right to tell me what to do. I'll be careful, but ultimately, I decide what's risky for me and what's not."

He released a gust of air. "I can see keeping you alive will be a full-time job."

"If I listened to you, I'd be sitting in the corner like little Jack Horner, twiddling my thumbs."

"Jack didn't just twiddle those thumbs. He put one

into a Christmas pie, pulled out a plum and said what a good boy am I."

Her jaw dropped. "How did you know that?"

"I have a nephew who's fond of nursery rhythms."

"Don't expect me to say you're a good boy for stopping the race." She snorted. "I suspect you were afraid of losing."

He chuffed. "Didn't you notice you had a head start yet I still caught up with you?"

"Well…yes. The point is, you have no confidence in me or my abilities. I thought you were different than Tom and the others. That you believed I could carry my weight."

"I'm not saying you aren't capable or a hard worker. You're all those things, but I won't let you risk your life. Ranch work is dangerous. Spend every minute you can with your pa. Allow me to shoulder the load."

A flash of pain crossed her face. "Papa sleeps more than he's awake. I need to—" she bit her lip "—keep busy."

"Do some of that painting, stitching that Martin admires. Stay close to the house in case—"

"What? In case I hurt myself? That's no way to live."

"Can't say I have a yen for a strong-willed wife, but that's what I got. And I'd like to keep her safe."

"I know you loved Amy. I can understand that her death makes you cautious, affects you still."

Matt stared at the water flowing serenely between the banks, picking up sticks and leaves, moving the debris along until the creek rounded the bend and disappeared from view. Like that stream, he needed to move on, to hang on to the good and let go of the heartache, the bad times.

He turned back to Hannah. "Amy's gone. I'll always care, but that doesn't mean I don't care about you. As a friend, I can't allow you to risk harming yourself to prove some fool point." He leaned closer. "Like you tried to do at the depot."

"Lifting that trunk risked nothing, except maybe a toe."

Laughter burst out of him. "You're not an easy woman to tame, Little Filly."

"Stop calling me that." She doffed her hat, then shook her head, the mane of her wind-tossed hair settled along her shoulders in waves of umber. "I'm all grown up and no filly."

"I'm not sure I'd want to tame you if I could."

"Good thing," she said, then plopped her hat on her head and strode to the horses. She grabbed the reins then swung into the saddle and nudged Star into a quick getaway. Back ramrod-straight, her chin lifted skyward. He should recognize those feisty gestures. He'd seen them often enough.

He'd nicknamed her Filly, but the pet name in no way described the woman she'd become. Truth was, he hadn't thought of her as a child since she'd helped deliver that calf.

Hannah was a flesh and blood woman, a powerful temptation to let go of the reins of his heart and take a risk.

Not that he would.

He'd once walked the fine line between fearless and wayward. He'd prized challenges, pitted himself against nature, against man and beast, pushing his limits and beyond. He'd lost the yen for that boldness the day Amy died.

Since then, he'd tamped down his penchant for danger, the carefree cowboy part of him. Yet the decision to play it safe warred within, in constant battle with his temperament, leaving him in turmoil. Sometimes the tight grip on his reckless side chafed like too many hours in the saddle, but that's what he'd do. Nothing was worth the penalty of his impetuous nature.

Nothing.

No matter how lovely Hannah was, if they got close and fell in love, he could end up making her miserable.

Icy fear twisted inside his gut. Or worse, he could lose her, too. He'd hold his new wife at arm's length.

It was all he could do.

All during supper, Hannah struggled to keep her eyes on her plate and off Matt. She wouldn't behave like a woman enthralled with her husband. Not when her husband had called her a friend.

A friend watched out for a friend. Gave a helping hand, even a shoulder to lean on. To have a friend was nice. Especially now, with Papa sick, and the Lazy P to run.

A friend did not ogle the other, did not come close to kissing either. Yet wasn't that exactly what Matt had been about to do? Worse, wasn't that exactly what she'd wanted?

Shaken by her reaction and to put distance between them, she'd challenged him to that race. Protective of her safety, he'd stopped the race and started an argument, shriveling the connection between them.

If some vague discontent churned inside her, she'd ignore it and focus on learning more about running the ranch.

Finished with supper, Rosa had insisted on cleaning up the kitchen alone. Hannah, Papa and Matt retired to the porch. Soon Jake ambled over from the bunkhouse.

A breeze had kicked up, stirring the unusually hot night air. Beyond the porch, birds flitted about, darting in and out of bushes and trees. Hannah loved spring, the time of new beginnings, of birth, rebirth.

Even Papa seemed stronger. He sat on the settee, reminiscing of the days of long cattle drives. She sat beside him and held his hand in hers.

"When I was young, Daughter, we'd trail our cattle north to the railhead in Abilene where our longhorns were shipped to stockyards in Chicago," he said. "Nowadays, with windmills pumping water into earthen tanks, and the range divided by barbed wire, we're ranchers, not cowboys."

Jake chuckled. "Cowpokes once raised Cain. Nowadays we're raising hay."

With the loose swagger and lean frame of a cowboy, Matt ambled to the porch railing, leaning against it. He was better looking than a man had a right to be.

Hannah struggled to turn her attention to the conversation. She treasured these times with Papa and wanted to absorb every word, learn everything she could about ranching. Then and now.

"Tell us more about those drives," she said.

"Martin was trail boss," Jake said. "He assigned duties, scouted for water, kept an eye out for trouble. Us drovers punched cattle. Nothing purty about heat and dust and risky river crossings. But a man likes a challenge."

What role would Hannah take? When she knew so little, the men wouldn't see her as trail boss. Was there enough water for the herd between here and Fort Worth?

"Challenges were the norm," Papa said. "On almost every drive a thunderstorm spooked the longhorns into stampeding. Getting the beeves under control made for a rough night. Every drive we'd lose several head. Sometimes a man."

If the herd spooked, Hannah knew how to get a mill going, until the herd formed a tight circle and wore down. But they couldn't afford to lose one animal. The weight of the responsibility rested heavy on her shoulders.

As the men talked, bringing to life the hardships of the two or three months on the trail, heat lightning flashed around them, but giving no promise of much-needed rain.

One of the brief flashes illuminated the porch. Hannah's gaze slid to Matt's. His dark eyes locked with hers, a silent connection she didn't want. Matt was a friend, nothing more. She quickly looked away.

"'Tweren't nothing to move two, three thousand head with only ten men. We took turns night herding." Jake shook his grizzled head. "Seen men rub tobacco juice in their eyes to stay awake."

"Rough life," Matt said. "When I was twelve, I yearned to go. My pa wouldn't hear of it."

"Probably trying to protect you from a rough bunch,

especially once the drive reached Abilene. Most cowpokes spent every dime they earned on gambling and…" He glanced at Hannah and cleared his throat. "Whatever."

Heat climbed Hannah's neck. She scrambled for a change of subject. "How much did you earn?"

"Twenty-five, thirty dollars a month. Forty dollars tops. Not much, but trailing cattle gets into the blood."

"After I married your mother," Papa said, turning his head toward Hannah, "I never went on another drive."

"Why not?"

"Didn't like the idea of leaving her."

Papa loved her mother with every ounce of his being. How hard to lose her in childbirth, along with his son. Hannah would've liked to ask him more about those days, but not in front of the others.

Martin looked at Matt. "I may sound like a sentimental fool, but once you've been married a while, Matt, you'll feel the same."

"You know your daughter better than that, Martin. She's not one to be left behind."

"Reckon I do." Papa chuckled, giving Hannah's hand a squeeze.

Good, at least Matt understood she wouldn't be denied the right to make her own decisions.

"All this reminiscing has made me bone tired. Will you help me into the house, Matt?"

"Reckon I'll turn in, too." Jake bid everyone goodnight and ambled toward the bunkhouse.

Matt helped Martin to his feet and offered his arm. "Are you hurting bad?"

"Won't turn down a dose of that medicine."

"First thing," Matt promised.

Hannah's heart swelled with gratitude for Matt's affection and concern for her father.

"I'll check on you later, Papa."

Hannah laid her head against the back of the chair and closed her eyes. Her father's talk of earlier days connected her to their heritage, to a time when cattle drives tested man and beast. She treasured every minute, a sweet interlude in a day with more ups and downs than a bucking bronco ride.

In the quiet, Hannah drifted off toward sleep. The screen door squeaked. Her head popped up. Matt joined her on the settee, laying his arm across the back.

She gave him a smile. "Thanks for your help with my father."

"Glad to do it. Couldn't be easier now that I'm living here."

A reminder that no matter what Matt had said, he was her husband, not merely a friend. A husband who might get amorous thoughts on such a beautiful night. She rose to her feet, intent on escape. "I'm going for a walk."

He took her arm. "I'll go with you."

Not what she planned, but what could she say? *I'm afraid you've got kisses on your mind, like we came close to sharing on horseback?*

They left the porch, walked to the rose trellis where they'd recited their vows. The air was filled with the heady, sweet fragrance of the roses hidden among the shadows.

"My mother brought these climbing roses with her from Charleston. Other plants, too. Papa favors the red, but I prefer the pink. The scent is more vibrant. The blooms are larger. When they unfurl, they have the prettiest centers." Her voice trailed off. Mercy, she'd been chattering like a magpie, trying to conceal her awareness of the man at her side.

The moon appeared from behind the clouds, lighting his face. A rugged, strong face. Deep-set eyes. Full lips that smiled at her. She swallowed hard.

"When I was a little kid," Matt said, "I picked all the lilacs off the bush, at least the ones I could reach, and presented them to my mother, proud of the gift." He chuckled. "Well, Ma had planned to use those lilacs for some fancy function at church, a week off. That incident taught me not to come between a woman and her flowers."

"Aw, you must've been a sweet little boy."

"Sure was," he said, a grin wide on his face. "Never deserved a single one of her reprimands."

The impish look in his eye said otherwise. "Hmm, from what I've heard you and your brothers were a handful," she said, smiling up at him.

As he stared into her eyes, the smile slipped from his face, as if mesmerized by what he saw. "You got me pegged," he said softly.

Lost in those dark depths, Hannah couldn't turn away. Could barely think. What had he said?

Strong hands slid around her waist, pulling her to him. The solid strength of his chest beneath her palms and the thundering beat of his heart beneath his shirt trapped the air in her lungs. She lifted her face and looked into his hooded eyes, heavy with longing. Time stood still, wiping everything from her mind but the two of them.

He lowered his head, brought his lips inches from hers, close enough to kiss. With a soft sigh, Hannah closed her eyes, slid her arms around his neck, teasing the hair at his nape with her fingers. Her heart pounded in her chest as he brushed his lips over hers, sending a shiver along her spine.

His hands fell away and he jerked back, rubbing the back of his neck. "I...ah." He cleared his throat. "I'd better get you inside," he said, then stepped away.

Dazed, Hannah groped for her bearings, for footing in a relationship with ever-changing rules. The truth slammed into her. What a fool she'd been. *Friend.* He'd called her *friend.* Yet she'd all but invited his kiss.

She stumbled toward the porch, Matt at her heels. At the door, he reached around her and opened the screen door. "See you in the morning," he said as she walked inside.

"Aren't you coming?"

"In a minute."

He was avoiding that awkward walk down the bedroom hall, then separating, Matt to his room, she to hers.

Why had she asked if he was coming inside? She sounded needy, dependent on him, when that's the last thing she wanted.

Outside Papa's open door, she heard his soft snore, his even breathing. *Thank you, Lord, that Papa is having a good night.*

Inside her room, she changed into nightclothes, brushed her teeth, then took down her hair, reliving those moments in the rose garden. The way she'd reacted to him, his charm. He appeared to care, then stepped away, remote. She wouldn't fall for his antics again.

Finished with the hundred strokes, she laid her brush aside and climbed into bed, stretching out her weary body with a sigh.

Down the hall, a door closed. Matt had come inside.

He appeared in control, strong and caring. He did everything he could for her father. In many ways, he was an admirable man. A man she could care for, if she dared. But his words and actions conveyed contradictory messages. One moment he called her friend. The next he came close to kissing her. Was he toying with her emotions like a cat with his prey?

Tonight's discussion on the porch had proven she needed Matt's help on the cattle drive. If only she didn't have to rely on a taciturn cowboy claiming to be a friend, then behaving like a husband. Matt couldn't have it both ways.

Why not be honest? She had conflicting emotions, too. For both their sakes, she'd keep her distance. No point ruining a practical agreement. She needed Matt to help her manage the ranch. But she wouldn't let him manage her heart.

Chapter Ten

Matt, as fireman in charge of the fire and the irons, swiped the sweat out of his eyes, stinging from hours spent hovering over a red-hot fire. The iron in his hand had the Lazy P mark, a P laying on its back. The brand had been approved by the Cattlemen's Association and registered in the courthouse. Brands were meant to impede cattle rustling, not much of an issue these days with the demise of the open range, but even so, the brand proved ownership.

Finished with roundup at the Circle W, his father and Cal had joined him and the remnant of the Parrish crew, to round up and sort the Lazy P cattle, then brand and cut two hundred and fifty spring calves.

Across the way, Hannah rode Star, singling out a calf, her long braid under her Stetson swinging with the peg pony's movements. A bandanna over her nose and mouth kept out dust. Denim pants and a long-sleeved shirt protected her skin in the blistering sun.

At first, whenever his wife chased down calves, Matt's heart spent more time in his throat than in his chest, ready at a moment's notice to protect her. She soon impressed him with her ability with the lasso, the ease with which she rode her horse.

Even the drovers respected Hannah's skill with a lariat, but still looked to him for instructions. He didn't need to be a mind reader to see that stuck in Hannah's craw like a chicken bone. Something he understood, having lived with a father who usurped Matt's authority at every turn. Matt had harped at the men, reminding them Hannah was boss and insisted they look to her for orders. He'd even walked away when asked for direction.

Yet, the men refused to change. Change had turned cowboys into farmhands. They'd lost the open range, the long cattle drives, their way of life. He suspected Hannah paid the penalty for pent-up resentment.

She deserved their respect, having handled the long hours in the saddle and the hard work as well as any man. With each passing hour, admiration for his cowgirl wife grew.

Hannah and the cow pony knew exactly what to do. As he watched, Star changed course with the elusive calf, giving Hannah access to her target. She swung the lasso, the rope snaked through the air, the noose settling over the calf's neck.

With the press of her knees, Hannah directed Star to back off, taking up the slack in the rope tied to the saddle horn, bringing the calf to the ground.

Two cowpokes wrestled the animal on its side, wielding a knife, while Matt pressed the Lazy P brand into the hide, barely aware of the stench of singed hair and the raucous bawling. As the men stepped away, the calf scrambled to his feet. Familiar with his mother's voice, he trotted straight to her.

Hannah appeared at his side. "That's the last."

"Thanks to your skill with a lasso, we got it done in record time."

"Thanks, but Star deserves the praise."

"You and Star make a good team." He chucked Hannah under the chin. "So do we," he said, his gaze capturing hers.

"Spoken like a true friend."

She'd thrown his words back at him. Not that he blamed her. He didn't understand his behavior any more than she did.

Hannah motioned to the spring calves. "A year with their mamas and they'll be chubby as butterballs."

"Yep, two years from now, half the spring babies will be full-grown heifers, ready to breed. The other half, full-grown steers, ready to sell."

"I'd like to see the heifers bred to the best of the Walker bulls. I want to strengthen the herd."

Matt nodded. "That's understood."

Without a drop of rain, both ranches had made the decision to drive the cattle to Fort Worth. He directed Hannah's attention to the penned steers and aging cows. "You've got three hundred head set aside to sell." He grabbed his bandanna and swiped the grime from his face. "We'll join your cattle with Pa's four hundred. Unless we encounter trouble we should reach Fort Worth in two days. Without cattle, one day back here."

Martin's words came back to him. *One day, Matt, you'll feel the same and not want to leave your wife.*

Matt looked forward to having three days away from

Hannah. With every passing day, he found it more and more difficult to think of her as a friend, no matter what he'd claimed. A few days of separation should ease the pull.

"Well, if I'm not needed here," Hannah said. "I'm going to groom Star." She looked down at her smudged, sweaty shirt, the dusty toes of her boots. "Then clean up myself."

He watched her go, her steps slow, no doubt painful after days in the saddle. Grubby as a cowpoke or fresh as a debutante, either way, Hannah looked fine.

With effort, he tore his gaze away and swung into the saddle, moving the cows and their calves toward pasture. The sun eased to the horizon as the calves frolicked at their mothers' sides, none the worse for wear after their ordeal.

Once the herd had gotten underway, the drovers took over and Matt returned to the stable. He found Jake grooming Star in her stall. "Where's Hannah?"

"She's gone in to clean up and spend time with her pa. Told her I'd see to Star."

Matt released a weary sigh and peeled off his gloves, then rubbed his forearm across his face. "The men will be back soon, hungry and tired."

"Vittles are ready soon as they are."

"Knew I could count on you," Matt said, slapping Jake on the back.

Matt saw to his horse, then joined Cal and his father at the pump. Wearing tired but satisfied grins, they scrubbed off grime and sweat, dousing their heads under the cold stream, rising up and slinging water like drenched dogs.

Pa pulled a clean bandanna from his hip pocket and wiped his face, yet his eyes stayed on Matt. Matt recognized the look. His pa had something on his mind.

"I'll handle the sale in Fort Worth while you young pups see to separating the herds. While I'm at it, might as well handle the transaction for Martin."

"Martin asked me to handle the sale of his cattle. I intend to carry out his wishes."

His father flapped a hand, as if Martin's request was of no consequence. "No point splitting hairs. See you at sunup."

He and Cal sauntered to their waiting horses, mounted up and rode toward the Circle W, the horses' hooves kicking up dust.

Matt slapped his hat against his thigh. He was a grown man, yet Pa didn't trust him to close a simple deal. He'd foolishly believed that moving out of the Walker homestead would give him breathing room. But no, his father oversaw everything down to the smallest detail.

Scripture demanded children honor their parents, something Matt had tried to do, to the point that he'd let Robert take over his life. The time had come to stand his ground. The cattle drive to Fort Worth presented the perfect opportunity. He intended to take it.

Hannah walked outside, letting the screen door slap closed behind her. Exhausted from days in the saddle, she looked forward to a quiet evening, then planned to get to bed early. They'd leave for Fort Worth at first light.

Overhead the sky glittered with stars, barely diminished by the light from a full moon. As she ambled toward Matt, she glanced at the moon. *See the man in the moon?* Mama used to say. *He's always got a smile.*

Unlike the man standing across from her.

"You look troubled," she said. "Something the matter?"

"I...." His voice trailed off, then he cleared his throat. "Just planning the particulars for tomorrow. On a short drive like this, all we'll need is a canteen of water and a couple days rations in our saddlebags. I'll pack a gun, makings for coffee, a tin of matches, medical kit."

"Doesn't sound like much to worry about."

"Nope, just the usual. Most likely the hands won't be coming back with us."

"Why not?"

"They'll spend a month's pay in Fort Worth carousing."

"Apparently cowboys haven't changed much since those long trail drives Jake talked about. Oh, that reminds me, Rosa will serve breakfast at five-thirty so we can get an early start."

He frowned. "We?"

"Well, yes, I'm going." She drew herself up and met his gaze. "Of course."

Before she'd gotten the words out, Matt was shaking his head. "No need for that. We have ample drovers. You can stay here, spend those three days with Martin."

"Part of that herd is Parrish cattle. That makes the drive and sale my responsibility."

"You have enough to handle." He chuffed. "Martin asked me to handle the sale. My pa is claiming the responsibility, but I intend to follow Martin's directive and negotiate the price." He took a step closer. "Or don't you trust me?"

Her breath caught. Did she trust him? The question alluded to far more than handling the sale, at least for her. "You'd never cheat us, but you're trying to cheat me out of an opportunity to learn. If I'm to run this ranch, you said I need to earn respect. The best way to earn the respect of the hands, the buyers, even the men running the Cattlemen's Association is to prove myself by moving the cattle, negotiating the deal, handling the paperwork. That's what I intend to do."

"Hannah, I'm your husband. I'm supposed to ease your burden. Not to ask you to take on another one."

"We had a deal, Matt. A deal that enables me to run my ranch, to make decisions." Her chin shot up. "I'll be riding with you."

"Do you realize we'll sleep under the stars? With only enough food to get by?" He let out a gust. "This is no picnic or society ball."

She bristled at the implications. Did he still see her as the debutante? Not as a woman who could handle a horse, a ranch, a cattle drive? "I've gathered a bedroll, canteens of water, jerky, dried apples and hardtack, everything I'll need, my gun." She ticked the items off on her fingers. "When I was young, Papa used to take me out on overnight jaunts to mend fence. We slept under the stars. I've had experience camping out."

Matt ran a hand over his chin, shadowed with the day's growth of his beard. He met her gaze. "Are you prepared to handle acting like newlyweds?"

"What?"

"How will it look if we don't..." His voice trailed off.

He took a step closer, until the toes of his boots touched her hem. "Sleep close?"

Heat flushed her face then slid through her limbs. With his father, brother and the Lazy P hands looking on, they'd have to play the part of a recently married couple. "Well, I don't have a problem with it if you don't."

The expression on his face said he did. Did he find the idea repulsive? Or did the idea make him edgy?

"I agree we'll have to…stay close. But no more than a friend keeping an eye on a friend."

The grating sound she heard—was that Matt gnashing his teeth?

He stepped even closer. Within kissing distance. "Are you challenging me, *wife?*"

The way he said the word sent a shiver down her spine. Wife implied everything they had agreed they would never have, such as tender kisses. "I'm just saying I can sleep near you. Well, unless you snore."

"Maybe you're the one who snores." He gave a smug grin.

She raised her chin. "Never."

He trailed a finger down her cheek and over her lips. Her heart thudded in her chest. Lost in his eyes that held not one morsel of humor. Lost in his eyes that looked tormented, revealed a man at the end of his rope.

"We'll have plenty of time to find out the truth, won't we?" he said, his dimple winking with his lopsided grin.

She gulped. Nodded.

"I will be a perfect gentleman. So you have no worries I might…take advantage of the situation." He took a step back, breaking the connection, severing the magnetic pull between them. "Be ready at first light, prepared to ride," he said, then without a backward glance, he clomped off the porch, heading toward the stable.

With Hannah's heart banging inside her chest like a barn door with a broken hinge, she sucked in a breath. Then another, until she'd shoved all these reactions deep down inside of her.

Those moments on the porch with Matt were fantasy, here today, gone tomorrow. She had no patience with such silliness. She had a job to do.

In the next two days, she would once again play the biggest make-believe role of her life, that of the blissful bride. This time, in front of a handful of drovers and Matt's father and brother.

With a husband who appeared to want to change the rules.

Or perhaps he was trying to scare her off from going on the drive to Fort Worth. If so, he'd soon learn she didn't scare easily.

With the sun below the horizon, Hannah led Star out of the stable, spurs jangling, her saddlebags loaded with provisions for the trip, determined to use this opportunity to prove herself. To prove herself, she'd ride drag at the rear of the herd. To prove herself, she'd not lose a single straggler. To prove herself, she'd handle the sale of Lazy P cattle in Fort Worth.

Robert and Cal Walker sat on horseback, talking to Matt.

"Morning, Hannah," Robert said. "Going for a morning ride?"

Matt looked up from checking Thunder's saddlebags. "Hannah will be riding with us."

"No reason for her to do that." Robert frowned, his eyes black as coal. "We're not shorthanded. A woman will add complications."

"Believe I said she's going."

Hannah's breath caught. Matt was actually standing up for her right to go, when she knew he'd prefer she stayed behind.

The pucker between Robert's brow smoothed. "Reckon that's newlyweds for you. Can't stomach being apart."

"Not for a second," Matt said, then strode to Hannah's side, lowered his head and swept his lips across her cheek.

At the husband-like act, heat flooded her face and sent a shiver snaking along her spine. She forced a smile, then allowed him to give her a hand up.

He patted her knee, searching her eyes. "You all set?"

"Yes." With Cal and Robert's scrutiny, the sooner they got underway the better.

"Looking forward to sharing the day with my pretty wife." He plopped his Stetson in place, then leaned closer. "And the night," he whispered.

Heart pounding, Hannah turned away, then searched the horizon. "Where are the Circle W beeves?"

Cal shifted in the saddle to the sound of creaking leather and pointed west. "Our drovers are holding them about a mile from here with a good stand of grass. We'll join up with them there."

"Cal and I will work as pointers near the head of the line. You and Hannah work the flank," Robert said.

"Can't have this young lady eating dust." He motioned to the two Lazy P drovers on horseback inside the corral. "Your cow punchers will bring up the rear, make sure cattle don't wander off."

Hannah understood Robert's desire to lead. But, to act as if she couldn't handle the cattle rankled. "I'd prefer to take the drag position. Star and I enjoy rounding up stragglers."

"Then it's settled. We'll take the rear," Matt said.

As if he'd argue the point, Robert's lips flattened, then he chuckled. "Sounds more like you and your wife want privacy."

Hannah looked away from Robert's amused eyes.

"Ready to move?" Jake hollered, hand at the gate.

Matt said a prayer for safety and a successful drive, then glanced at Hannah. At her nod, he raised an arm. "Let 'em loose."

As Jake opened the gate, two drovers on horseback rode behind the milling cattle, punching them out of the pen. They came slowly, plodding along in the dim light. Soon, a few steers took the lead, the aging cows falling back. Robert and Cal rode off to take positions on opposite sides of the herd that now strung out in a long irregular line.

Matt guided Thunder to Hannah's side. Close enough their horses rubbed noses. Mercy, even Star and Thunder feigned romance.

Last night, when Hannah had agreed to behave like newlyweds, to give the little gazes and touches that spoke of love, she hadn't understood the cost.

She'd never felt more devious.

Nor more attracted to the man.

Surely, her reaction stemmed from Matt's support of her right to join the drive. Once again she was beholden to him. How long before he'd insist on changing the rules of this game they played—and expect a real relationship?

Her thoughts were muddled from Matt's kiss last night and his peck on the cheek earlier, Hannah hoisted the bandanna over her mouth and nose. She hoped this scrap of cloth would protect her from dust, and from Matt's teasing mouth.

She wouldn't get near enough to give him an opportunity. She'd see that there would be no dawdlers—not cattle, not she and Matt. Her heart thudded in her chest. The trek had only begun but couldn't be over soon enough to suit her.

Matt kept an eye on Hannah as they punched cattle along the trail. Drag riders had the most difficult position on the drive. No doubt Hannah had chosen the position for that very reason, trying to prove herself. Drag riders dealt with the herd's most uncooperative varmints that often hung back and tried to make a run for it.

All morning, Hannah and Star, an agile cutting horse, one of the best, had done an admirable job. Still, cattle were dangerous. Only one of many hazards on the trail that included flooded river crossings, stampedes and rustlers. The list was long. Not likely to happen on this trip, still Matt didn't ride easy.

A man never knew when a mean steer would swing its big, long horns at a horse with the aim of killing. Or when a cow would turn on a drover unexpectedly and charge, spooking the horse into rearing and throwing the rider. He'd seen a drover trampled by milling cattle.

He'd keep a sharp eye on his wife. An easy task. He couldn't keep his eyes off her. Even with her Stetson tugged low, a bandanna across her face and her long tresses worn in a braid down her back, he could picture her vibrant blue eyes, those full lips, the red in her brown hair sparkling in the sunlight.

Keep your mind off your wife and concentrate on the job.

Distraction got people hurt. He wouldn't focus on his wife, no matter how much he found her appealing, no matter how much he felt connected to her, no matter how much he cared about her safety.

Toward noon, Matt unearthed a string of jerky from his saddlebags and gnawed on it, then washed it down with a long swig from his canteen. On such a short drive, they managed without a chuck wagon, but he'd worked up an appetite. Already he looked forward to Rosa's cooking.

He'd ride over to make sure Hannah took a drink, got a bite to eat. He grinned, then tugged on the reins. Who was he kidding? All he could think about was getting near his wife.

Across the way, Hannah and Star cut right, chasing down a cow. Within minutes they'd returned the straggler. A few feet from the herd, they passed an outcropping of rocks. Suddenly Star reared without warning.

Matt kicked Thunder and they raced toward Hannah as she fought to keep her seat. He closed the gap— twenty feet, ten feet, five feet. And then he saw the trouble.

Rattlesnake. The lethal creature had coiled into a tight spiral, tail rattling, forked tongue darting, head still, waiting to strike. Star snorted, prepared to rear again. Hannah held tight to the reins, speaking softly to her horse, but her face had paled and he saw fear in the tight set of her shoulders. He pulled his .45 Colt from his holster, cocked the gun, ready to fire.

Star reared again. Hannah lost her grip, falling to the ground not far from the snake.

"Don't move! I'll shoot it," Matt shouted.

In a flash, she rolled to her hip, metal flashed in the sunlight as she yanked out her pistol, took aim and fired. The snake writhed, then lay motionless. Star shied, but held her position.

As Matt swung from the saddle, his gaze scanned the herd. A few cattle bellowed but they kept moving forward in a wide column. He helped Hannah to her feet. They inspected the snake to make sure it was dead. "That was an amazing shot."

"That one even surprised me," she said, giving a weak grin.

A cowpoke galloped their way, no doubt checking on the gunfire he'd heard. Matt waved his hat, signaling all was well.

He put his hands on her shoulders, felt the tremor running through her. For all her bravado, in her eyes he saw fear. "You okay?"

She reached a trembling hand toward him. It was all the invitation he needed to tug her into his arms. She flattened against him, her hand on his chest. Surely she could feel his heart beating beneath his shirt, racing with an erratic rhythm.

"I think so," she said, taking a step back, staring up at him.

He dipped his head and kissed her full on the lips, slow and easy as sensations of longing flooded him from head to toe.

Hannah pulled away. "We've got cattle to tend."

"This promises to be a very long day, Mrs. Walker," Matt whispered near her ear.

They swung into the saddle and rode toward the herd, separating on either side of the moving column.

She'd scared him silly, but she'd handled things fine. Hannah Parrish Walker was no debutante. No filly. No tomboy.

His wife was all woman.

Chapter Eleven

$\mathbf{M}$att's awareness of Hannah had him tighter than a water-soaked peg. That moment of closeness after the scare with the snake had him longing for more. To make matters worse, the entire day they'd played the role of newlyweds. The attraction between them palpable.

Why had he suggested such a foolish thing?

To appease his family's expectations?

He heaved a sigh. Be honest. Underneath he wanted that closeness to his wife. When he'd accepted Hannah's terms for their marriage, he hadn't realized the difficulty of keeping her at arm's length. With each passing day, his feelings for her grew. Not part of the plan. The plan was sensible, far safer than giving in to feelings. Feelings changed.

Dusk had fallen, they'd bedded the cattle down for the night and had eaten cold rations and had drank hot coffee by the light of the campfire.

Under the cottonwoods alongside the creek, Matt ducked beneath the ropes corralling the horses, carrying feed and water. With a night to rest, the cow ponies would be champing at the bit to get underway tomorrow.

Not that he'd sleep a wink with Hannah curled up nearby. Still, a man never knew what wild animals, snakes, even bad hombres might roam these parts. He wouldn't let his wife out of his sight. To protect her. To keep her safe. Nothing more.

One glance at their camp across the way, at Hannah's perky profile as she sat by the fire confirmed what he knew—looking out for this woman was a privilege, not a chore. He admired her spunk, her appreciation of the life he prized, her devotion to her dying father, a man more father to him than his own. She could've whined about life's unfairness. Instead she faced each day with faith, with courage, with determination to learn everything about ranching.

So she wouldn't need him?

The thought cooled his mood faster than a tumble into an ice-crusted trough. No matter how much he was drawn to his wife, he wouldn't act on those emotions.

Not that she'd allow it if he tried.

If upon occasion her breath caught at his touch, that didn't mean she welcomed the contact or the reaction. More likely, she'd been caught off guard.

A shape moved out of the shadows. Pa. "We need to talk."

With Pa, talk inevitably led to a lecture. Matt squared his shoulders. "What about?"

"You need to get your wife under control."

From this distance Hannah wouldn't overhear, still Pa's censure fisted Matt's hands at his sides. "Hannah's not out of control. Today and during both roundups, she did the work of a man and then some."

"I'll give you that." Pa folded beefy arms across his chest. "But when a woman tells a man what to do, she needs a firm hand."

"Hannah wasn't telling you what to do. She merely stated she'd prefer the drag rider spot, which is her right. Half this herd is hers. Isn't it more that you resent anyone but you making decisions?"

"Nonsense. Victoria runs the house as she sees fit. But she doesn't give me orders on how I'm to run the ranch or handle a drive." He shook his head. "Can't imagine what's gotten hold of Hannah. She was the sweetest gal."

"Hannah's an owner, same as you. She has a right to make decisions."

Robert harrumphed. "I'm not against considering another way, but she's giving orders, telling *me* what *she'll* do. And telling you, too. A husband shouldn't stand for that."

"Be honest." Matt plowed his fingers through his hair. "No one can take the lead, have an independent thought without raising your ire. No matter what you believe, your way isn't the only way."

"My way has made the Circle W a success. But do you thank me for that? No!"

"I am grateful and respect what you've accomplished. But—"

Robert raised a hand. "Quit your yapping. See that your woman doesn't wear the pants in Fort Worth and disgrace us all."

Pa strode off. No doubt confident of Matt's compliance.

And why not?

For years, Matt had taken the backseat to his father, a decent God-fearing man, but a man unable to give up one smidgeon of control. Pa never sought his and Cal's opinions. Even overrode Matt's instructions, humiliating him in front of the hands.

Hannah carried his name. If she wanted to negotiate the sale of her cattle, he'd support her right. She had plenty to learn, but he'd be there to help if she needed him. He wouldn't rule his wife like Pa tried to rule him.

A glance at the horses satisfied him that all was well. He ambled along the creek in the direction of their camp, giving himself a few moments to rein in his temper. As Hannah's husband, he would put her welfare first, ahead of his father.

In the clearing, he found his wife alone staring into the fire, her face relaxed, at peace. If only he felt the same.

On the other side of the campfire, Pa had stretched out on his bedroll, his back to the fire, already snoring. Cal had ridden out to stand first watch with two of the Walker drovers. The two Parrish hands slept nearer the herd. Around two o'clock, Cal would return and shake Matt awake for his shift. He was tired, but with the encounter with his father churning inside him, not ready to sleep, not yet.

He sat beside his wife. "Star's dozing on her feet," he said. "You should get some sleep, too."

Hannah leaned back on her palms, surveying the sky, the twinkling stars overhead, the sliver of the new moon, looking happy, content, beautiful. "I'm soaking up the serenity of just…being," she said softly. "Out here, with only God and His creation."

And him.

In the light from the fire, the dancing flames flickered on her features, the contented smile on her face. That smile towed him to her like a well-thrown lasso. On such a night as this, a man could get accustomed to huddling close to his wife, could visualize many such nights. With everything in him, he resisted the pretty picture he painted, the happily ever after. Nothing was that simple.

Even if wedded bliss were possible, he didn't deserve happiness, a second chance.

In the distance, a coyote howled. The notes of a plaintive melody drifted to them on the breeze. One of the hands soothing the cattle, or perhaps himself, with a song.

"Except for that rattler, we didn't have a single problem today," Hannah said, her tone filled with elation. "The cattle behaved themselves, as if they've taken this trek before."

"They haven't, but we have. More times than I can count. We know the watering holes, the available stands of grass along the way."

"Like I know the Lazy P."

"You said Martin took you camping. Tell me about it."

"After Mama died, Papa would take me along to ride fence, looking for breaks in the barbed wire. At dusk, we'd make a fire, eat beans, boiled eggs and cornbread." She grinned. "And those sugar cookies of Rosa's you're fond of. As we ate, we'd talk and take swigs out of the same canteen. I'd swipe the dribbles of water running down my chin in the crook of my arm, just like Papa." She chuckled. "No wonder he sent me to finishing school."

"What did you and Martin talk about?"

"Oh, lots of things. The stars, school, Mama." Her voice caught. "Heaven. The gold streets, the jewels, the light of God."

Matt couldn't remember sharing anything personal with his father. Robert lectured better than he listened.

She met his gaze. "As the fire would die down, I'd fall asleep cuddled against Papa. Come morning, I'd awaken tucked into a bedroll. Never figured out how I got there without waking. He said us ranchers sleep best under the stars." Tears glistened in her eyes. "Those memories are precious, especially now."

With an urge to comfort her, to give her what Martin always had, Matt tugged her close. "Martin's a wise man. He understood the importance of giving you his time. Time to remember your mother. Time to heal from her loss. Time for the two of you to grow closer."

In the circle of his arms, Hannah swiped at her eyes. "Did you and your pa camp?"

"If the work kept us away from the house, we'd bunk in a line shack, not under the stars."

"What's your favorite memory from your childhood?"

"That's easy." He smiled at the memory that popped into his head. "The day I turned six and got my first pony. Having a horse of my own changed my life, gave me the freedom to come and go. On horseback I was king of everything I surveyed. The land, the cattle, God's creatures—the jackrabbits, lizards, prairie dogs, buzzards circling overhead. I felt as much a part of the land as those cottonwoods growing along the creek." He motioned toward the trees. "As any living thing that grew here."

"If you were king, then I was queen." Hannah chuckled. "Your childhood must've been fun."

"I had chores, but lots of free time, too. By the age of nine, I was a pint-size ranch hand. I found work satisfying and my efforts pleased my father."

"Any special memories after that?"

"Oh, yes. On my tenth birthday, Pa gave me my first handgun and taught me to shoot. I practiced every chance I got, determined to make Pa proud."

And Matt had. Pa had once been generous with his praise, but something had changed. Now, a man in his own right, competent and skilled, he rarely got his father's approval. Instead Pa hammered him, an attempt to keep him under his thumb.

"Horse and gun, a Texan's path to manhood." Hannah smiled. "Things weren't so different in Charleston."

He cocked a brow. "Are you comparing me to those dandies?"

Eyes locked with his, she sobered. "I'd never make that mistake."

Her answer warmed him more than the heat from the fire.

"You want your father's approval as much as I want Papa's." She sighed. "Papa once approved of my tomboy ways. No longer."

Matt knew better. "No father could approve of his child more."

Hannah lifted troubled eyes to his. "You two are close. Do you understand why he wants me to wear dresses? To behave like a debutante when he knows that's not who I am?"

"I suspect he thought your only option was to return to Charleston so he probably wanted you to embrace that life."

"But we're married so why does he encourage me to take the role of a homemaker instead of running the ranch?"

"I'm not sure. Maybe he believes if your mother had lived, you'd desire a more traditional role."

She sighed. "Running a house could never give me the satisfaction of running a ranch."

He cupped her jaw. "You're fine, Hannah, just the way you are."

Tears filled her eyes. "Thank you." She laid her hand over his. "That means a lot."

Those tears would be his undoing. He cradled her hand in his own, then raised her hand to his lips and kissed her palm and each fingertip.

The sharp intake of her breath said his touch affected her all right. As much as hers did him. Where would this connection lead?

Cal would be rousting him out soon enough. "We'd better get some sleep."

He helped Hannah to her feet. She strode to the spot where they'd stowed their saddles and saddlebags and unfurled her bedroll. He did the same.

"Don't hesitate to wake me if you need anything," he said.

"I'll be fine." In a flash of moving arms and legs, she shucked her boots and burrowed into her nest, putting her back to him.

He doused the flames, kicked dirt onto the ashes, then yanked off his boots, stretching out on his blanket beside hers, close enough to touch. An urge to pull her to him, to hold her in the crook of his arm and cuddle her close roared to life inside him like a raging bull. He wouldn't give in to the impulse. He wouldn't let emotion override common sense. He wouldn't love her.

To keep from reaching for her, he clasped his hands over his chest, lacing his fingers so tightly his bones hurt.

"Comfy?" she asked.

With Hannah within reach, yet off-limits, he was about as comfy as a man clinging to a prickly cactus. "Uh-huh. You?"

Another howl of a coyote.

Hannah jerked upright. "That sounds close," she whispered.

Though tempted to offer his protection, Matt knew the coyote presented no threat. "Naw." Her only threat was her husband, a man yearning to hold her.

But he wouldn't. Not when he knew that opening his heart could destroy the one thing he had. Contentment.

When had he told himself a bigger lie? Contentment didn't describe his state of mind. At all. Not when the prospect of a lifetime of celibacy twisted inside him, rising up like a coiled rattler, fangs bared, ready to destroy all his well-laid plans.

He wouldn't give in to these impulses. And risk another discontented wife. Not when it appeared he and Hannah had forged a kind of truce. To keep that peace, he'd see that she got to handle the sale of her herd. Even if supporting her meant earning more of his father's disapproval.

At the rear of the herd, Hannah rode on the right, Matt on the left, as they punched the cattle into the untamed town of Fort Worth. Corrals teemed with milling, bawling cattle. Hollering cowpunchers prodded steers through shoots, their hooves stomping up ramps into railroad cars ready to haul them to slaughterhouses and meatpackers in Chicago. Dust and noise everywhere. Obviously with the drought, most of the area cattlemen had decided to sell.

Alert for any sign of stampede, Hannah sat tall in the saddle, scanning the herd, moving Star with quiet commands. A steer dodged right, attempting a getaway. A tug on a rein, her right knee pressed into Star's side, the cow pony wheeled, outdistanced and cut off the animal's escape, then returned the renegade to the herd.

Robert had ridden ahead with documentation of the Circle W and Lazy P brands and the number of cattle in each herd. With a wave of his hat, he directed them to empty corrals. As the lead animals entered the pen, men were perched on the fence, counting each brand. Hopefully their number would agree with Hannah's tally.

The chaos before her was a huge contrast to the peace of the previous night and the quiet interlude between her and Matt. In that one evening, they'd shared more about themselves than in all the years of their acquaintance.

Yet the peace and quiet didn't mean Hannah had been serene. With Matt lying so close, she'd had difficulty falling asleep. When Cal had shaken Matt awake, she'd also awakened. To avoid more connection to her husband, she'd feigned sleep.

And knew the moment Matt had pressed his lips to her cheek.

No matter how much she tried not to think about that husbandly act, the gentle sweetness of that kiss lingered. With a sigh, she laid a palm on her cheek. Had he kissed her in case Cal was watching? Or was a taciturn cowboy transforming into a tender companion?

If so, dare she trust the change in him? Or was this side of him temporary? Part of the pretense of wedded bliss? A romantic night under the stars?

With the last of the cattle corralled, Hannah and Matt leaned against the pen, inspecting the herd, waiting for the tally. On the trek home, without cattle to punch, they'd make good time. Wouldn't need to set up camp. That meant the closeness of the trail, the closeness to Matt would end. Inside her a battle waged. Part of her ached with disappointment, the other part heaved a sigh of relief. She didn't know how to handle all these contradictory feelings.

At last, she and Matt stood inside the sales office while Robert confirmed the number of head of Circle W cattle and negotiated his price.

Hannah was next in line. She strode toward the counter.

Robert stepped in front of her, blocking her way. "I'll take care of this. No need to worry your pretty head with all these figures."

"This is Lazy P business," she said, holding her ground.

His mouth set in a grim line, Robert bent toward her. "I'll get you as good a price as I got for my herd," he said, voice low. "Leave this to the men."

In two long strides, Matt stepped between his wife and his disgruntled father. "You can handle the sale, Hannah. Do you know what your cattle are worth?"

Papa had told her what she should expect to get for the steers and older cows. Besides talking to Papa, she'd studied past sales figures, had soaked up every bit of information.

Ignoring Robert, she leaned toward Matt and recited the number she'd worked out in her head during the drive.

With a nod and a smile, Matt motioned toward the waiting buyer. "Go on and get your price, Mrs. Walker," he said, then took his sputtering father by the arm and led him outside.

Hannah emerged from the office with a smile on her face and joined Matt. "I did it!" she said, her tone light with satisfaction.

"Knew you could." Matt's dark brown eyes softened. "I'm proud of you, Hannah. Proud of how you've handled the deal and the herd. You're becoming a capable rancher."

His approval slid through her, as warm and soothing as hot milk and honey to a sore throat. "Your confidence in me means more than I can say."

She'd negotiated her first deal, had trailed her first drive. Inside, she bubbled with confidence. She could handle anything. Anything, that is, except her marriage.

Her marriage wasn't real, a proper relationship. All that talk about how proud he was of her—why wouldn't he be? As business partners, he wanted her to be capable. He saw her as a rancher, nothing more. Perhaps he'd used her desire for independence more as an excuse to stand up to his father more than to confirm his confidence in her.

In an instant, her elation fizzled like thunder without the promised rain. Truth was, she and Matt might be attracted to each other, but something held them apart.

The more she got what she wanted, the more she realized having this deal they called a marriage wasn't all that wonderful.

Chapter Twelve

At dusk, Hannah rode into the Lazy P with Matt at her side. She hoped Papa was still awake so she could celebrate handling her first cattle sale with him.

A glimpse of the horse and buggy hitched at the rail trapped the air in Hannah's lungs. Pastor Cummings. He wouldn't pay a call this late, unless…

Heart in her throat, she dismounted, telling herself that at least, Doc Atkins's buggy wasn't waiting outside.

One look at her face and Matt took the reins from her hands. "Go on in. I'll see to the horses."

Weak-kneed and wobbly on her feet, Hannah lurched to the house. She met Pastor Cummings coming out the door. Brown hair threaded with gray, his eyes soft and serene, Pastor Cummings tugged his waistcoat over the bulge of his belly.

"Is Papa…all right?"

"He's weaker, but awake and eager to hear how things went in Fort Worth."

A sigh heaved out of her. "Thanks for coming. I know he appreciates your visits."

"Martin's ready, Hannah. Let that be a comfort to you." He laid a hand on her shoulder. "Give him permission to go."

In those gentle eyes, Hannah read his message. For her sake, Papa was hanging on. Suffering. Hot tears pricked the back of her eyes. Unable to speak, she clamped her lips together, gave a nod.

Inside, Rosa exited Papa's room, dark eyes filled with sorrow, the plate of food in her hand untouched. "He not take medicine before he see you."

Hannah glanced at her grimy garb. She'd give Papa his debutante daughter. "I'll only be a minute." She raced to her room, changed into a simple dress, grabbed the proof of the sale, then smile firmly in place, sped to Papa's room.

Breathing hard, her father lay propped against the pillows, pale, his skin almost translucent. He lifted his hand. "Hannah, my beautiful daughter, so like her mama."

Her smile quivered, but held. "I'm trail dusty, Papa, but I put on this dress for you."

"I was wrong to keep you in dresses. You wear what's comfortable." He patted the bed. "Now, tell me all about the cattle drive and the sale."

She settled on the bed, facing her father, and handed over the receipt for three hundred head of cattle. The paper quivered in his unsteady hands.

"I remembered everything you said, Papa, and negotiated the sale myself."

"You did good, Daughter. I'm proud of you."

His approval slid through her. She took his hand. "Thank you, Papa."

A sigh slid out of him. "I'm surprised Robert didn't interfere." No need to tell Papa that he had. "He needs to ease his hold on the reins and give Matt his head."

Perhaps the tension between father and son explained Matt's fondness for Martin.

Papa looked exhausted from his effort to talk. "I rest easy knowing with God at the helm and Matt at your side, you'll be fine."

Tears welling in her eyes, she kissed his cheek. "I will be fine, Papa."

A soft moan on his lips, Papa squeezed his eyes shut and sucked in a breath, his face carved with pain. He groped for the medication beside the bed.

"I'll get it." She loved him for attempting to smooth the signs of pain from his face. He only thought of her, always trying to protect her. After giving him a dose, she sat stroking his hand, to touch this loving man who'd always put her welfare before his own.

How could she bear to lose him? Her heart plummeted. How could she want him to suffer more?

Once a vital, active man, Papa would loathe being bedridden, unable to participate in the life of the ranch. Was she holding on to him, keeping him here when he wanted only to go to a better place? To join her mother and brother? The thought of losing him burned inside her, yet how much harder to watch him endure this relentless pain. She had to relinquish him into God's care. To do otherwise would be the worst kind of selfishness. But how?

Lord, I love him. Help me release him to You.

A calmness Hannah couldn't explain enveloped her.

She bent over her father, felt his breath upon her face. "Papa, can you hear me?" He squeezed her hand.

Matt entered the room and stood behind her, his hand on her shoulder.

Her father opened his eyes. "Matt."

"Yes, Martin. I'm here."

Their eyes held in silent communication. "Take care of her."

"I will."

A smile, then Papa looked into her eyes, his gaze soft, tender. "I love you, Hannah."

"I love you, Papa." Her chest squeezed until she felt she couldn't breathe. "Go in peace."

The tension in his face, in his brow eased. "To your mama and brother."

"Rest, Papa," Hannah said, rubbing his hand. Within minutes the fingers under hers relaxed. She laid her head on the bed, listening to him draw each ragged breath.

Throughout the night, Matt sat beside her, held her close, while Hannah spoke words of love to her father, sang his favorite hymns, watched the struggle in the rise and fall of his chest.

Matt's strong arms made her feel safe and secure. Just for tonight she'd pretend she was in love with her husband. Just for tonight she'd pretend he loved her in return.

Toward morning, the time between Papa's breaths lengthened, each one more shallow than the last.

Hannah laid her palms on either side of his face, then leaned close to his ear. "Goodbye, Papa. Godspeed."

As the sun was rising, streaking the heavens with rosy light, Martin Parrish stopped breathing.

Hannah turned and stumbled into Matt's arms.

He gathered her close. "I'm sorry," he whispered.

She choked back a sob, looking into her husband's kind eyes, grateful that she had Matt to lean on. "Our marriage gave him peace," she said, her lips trembling.

"Hannah, you don't always have to be strong. It's all right to cry."

Pulling her close, Matt nudged her head against his broad chest. Wrapped in his strong arms, she wept.

Matt knew where he'd find Hannah. At the family burial plot, making her daily visit to Martin's grave. Where he'd found her every day since her father's death. His gut tightened. He'd never felt more helpless.

Martin Parrish had been a man respected and mourned by all who knew him. Upon his death, neighbors, parishioners and friends rallied around his daughter, bringing food, attending the wake and funeral, offering sympathy and support.

As they'd uttered condolences, many spoke of the blessing of Hannah and Matt's love, that they had each other in this time of grief. The comments were meant to comfort, but Matt suspected the assumption made Hannah feel all the more alone.

Yet, that outpouring of love had gotten Hannah through those first days. But now, three weeks after the funeral, she merely went through the motions of living, barely eating, steps lagging, devoid of energy and unable to make the simplest decisions. He missed his feisty wife.

Inside the fenced enclosure, Hannah stood beside her father's grave, head bowed, hair swept up, a few tendrils curling along her slender neck, full skirt billowing in the breeze. She placed three red roses at the base of the headstone. The third rose for her baby brother buried with her mother. Each day Hannah exchanged the withered blooms with fresh cut flowers. The ritual seemed to bring her comfort.

Yet, Matt knew the futility of this daily pilgrimage. Undergirded with guilt, he'd wallowed in his grief for Amy. Only to learn that his only hope for survival was to get back to living. At first that meant merely going through the motions, but over time, he'd found his salvation in work, in his friends, in the Psalms.

For three weeks now, each evening on the porch Matt had held Hannah, listened to her memories of Martin, offered comfort, but the time had come for her to move forward.

He squatted beside her, his boots mashing the tall grass alongside the mound of earth. She lifted her face to his. The lost expression in her bleak blue eyes snared his heart.

Matt reached for her hand. Her hand fit his perfectly. In many ways they were well suited. They both grieved Martin and shared their sorrow, yet the time had come to be direct. "Your father would want you to get on with living, not come here every day and put flowers on his grave. In fact, knowing Martin, he'd have a stern word for you about now."

"I'm…trying."

That sorrow-laced claim tore at him. He remembered the sorrow of losing Amy. Even with the issues between them, he'd loved his wife. He hadn't known how to fix those problems, any more than he'd known how to ease his sorrow over Amy's death. But he'd had a mother with a will of iron and friends who wouldn't take no for an answer.

She needed a diversion to pull her out of her despondency. "I have an idea. Let's go on a picnic."

"A picnic?"

He swept a hand. "The day's too fine to waste working. What do you say?"

"It's kind of you to offer, but—"

"You think I'm kind for wanting to spend time with my wife? Truth is, I like seeing her have some fun." He slid a finger across her lips. "I've missed that smile."

A weak smile formed on her lips, as if her mouth had forgotten how.

Still, that smile was a start. "Ah, there it is."

He offered his arm and she slipped her hand through the crook. They left the plot, closed the gate behind them, then strolled to the house.

One word to Rosa and she set to work making sandwiches while Hannah poked around in the icebox looking for leftovers.

In a matter of minutes, Matt had hitched Lightning to the buggy and helped Hannah onto the seat, then climbed up beside her, depositing the basket and blanket at his feet.

As they followed the trampled path toward the creek, he glanced at his wife's profile. The broad-brimmed straw hat she wore shaded her face, hiding her expression. Still, with the slump of her shoulders, her gaze focused on the hands in her lap, she looked sad.

"Spring is my favorite time of year," Matt said. When she didn't reply, he went on, "The grass is green. Calves are born. We're not sweltering. Yet."

Apparently caught in her grief, she didn't respond. They passed a field of bluebonnets. Women liked flowers. He pulled the buggy over.

"Why are we stopping?"

"You'll see." He helped her down and then took her hand and practically towed her into the middle of the field.

She stood amidst the flowers, gazing around her. "I love bluebonnets."

He released her hand, then stooped, gathering flowers fast and furious. With a bewildered expression on her face, she stared at him, as if he'd lost his mind.

"Hold out your arms."

She complied and he piled them with bluebonnets. Dozens and dozens and dozens of bluebonnets.

"Stop!" Laughing, she gazed down at her loaded arms. "Any more and I won't be able to carry them all."

He cupped her jaw with both palms and gazed into the prettiest blue eyes he'd ever seen. "They match your eyes."

As if uneasy under his scrutiny, her gaze shifted. Then she shoved the flowers at him. "Race you to the buggy!" She gathered her skirts and sprinted across the field, her laughter trailing behind her.

The blooms tumbling out of his arms, he sped after her, his heart all but bursting with joy. He had his feisty wife back.

With a smug grin on her face, her eyes twinkling like the North Star, Hannah leaned against the buggy.

He skidded to a stop in front of her.

"I won," she said.

"I let you win." He knew full well his claim was ridiculous, but he couldn't resist teasing her.

"Did not."

"Okay, maybe not, but admit it. You had a head start and I had to run with my arms full."

"Not full for long." She pointed to the trail of flowers he'd left behind.

He stared at his empty arms. "I wanted to give you a field of posies," he said, his voice laden with regret.

"Oh, but you did," she murmured, then turned to him, smiling, truly smiling. "Thank you."

The radiance of that smile smacked him in the gut. When he'd said he missed her smile, he hadn't realized how much. To see the numbness and pain replaced, even temporarily, by playfulness, lifted an enormous weight from his shoulders. He knew then that Hannah would be all right. He'd see that she kept smiling, even if it meant losing a race every day of his life.

Tranquility transformed her features as her gaze traveled the horizon, scanning each field, the grove of pecan trees up ahead. "What you said about spring, the green grass, the birth of the calves—made me realize how thankful I am for Papa's new life in heaven."

"He will dwell in the house of the Lord forever."

"The twenty-third Psalm," she said. "One of my favorites."

"As a rancher, I'm not much for sheep, but I find the message of the Good Shepherd protecting His flock reassuring."

He took her hand and helped her into the buggy. As

they drove beneath the canopy of the pecan grove, not far from the creek, he tethered the horse, then wrapped his hands around her waist and lifted her to the ground.

Had she lost weight? If so, he'd see that she ate. The picnic was the perfect place to start. He grabbed the basket and they strolled through the trees toward the creek, the branches swaying in a windy dance.

At the water's edge, he set down the split oak basket and unfurled the blanket that flapped in the breeze, then fluttered to the ground. Then anchored it with the basket.

A gust of wind caught the wide brim of Hannah's straw hat, sailing it through the air toward the water. Matt chased after it and grabbed the brim, then returned it to her. "At least your hat didn't beat me in a race."

She giggled. "My hat had a head start, too. But this time, you didn't whine about that."

"It would've been a whole lot less embarrassing to be beaten by the wind, than by my wife."

Their laughter carried on the breeze, chasing away the shadows of Martin's death. Leaving only the two of them. She met his gaze, her blue eyes wide, filled with uncertainty.

He touched the lock of hair that had fallen from its moorings and tucked it behind her ear. Soft, silky. A temptation to unpin her hair left him gulping. He sucked in a steadying breath. Then her lips parted, sweet, enticing, ripe for kissing. The need to kiss her exploded within him. *Sweet Hannah.*

A pang of uneasiness niggled in his muddled mind. *Careful, Walker. You've walked this road before.*

He turned away. He knew where this intimacy would lead. To a true relationship.

Memories of Amy's dissatisfaction and his resentment, of bickering, then silence as the gaping wound of their marriage scabbed with apathy.

He wouldn't let attraction spur him to an impulsive decision, as he had with Amy. Better to focus on the picnic, on giving Hannah a fun day, and leave well enough alone.

In the cool, dim interior of the stable, Hannah brushed Lightning's coat, her mind replaying the playful moments in the field of bluebonnets, the relaxed picnic by the creek, all the things Matt had done to get her mind on other things, to lift her out from that dark cloud she'd been living under.

All those good things made her feel closer to him, made her think they were turning a corner in their relationship. But then he'd turned away from that almost kiss, making it clear he didn't want anything more.

A sigh escaped her lips as she watched the dust from Lightning's coat drift to the floor. She carried Matt's name. Might even be attracted to him. Might respect and admire much about him. Might share work on the ranch and grief for Papa. But her husband had no intention of cleaving to her.

With Papa gone, she missed the love he gave her, so badly she hurt. Hurt or not, she'd live with her agreement. She couldn't expect more from herself and from Matt than they could give. They both were wounded by deaths of loved ones.

As unfair as the feeling was, when Mama died, she'd

felt abandoned. Lost. She could no more risk that pain again, than she could walk on water. Even reckless Peter had sunk.

"Hannah."

Matt stood in the open doorway, framed by the sun; tall, lean and tanned, every inch the cowboy. He doffed his hat, uncertainty in his eyes, and held out a bunch of bedraggled bluebonnets. "I want you to have these." He strode toward her, stopped inches away, then pressed the bluebonnets into her hand. "They're not much, but they're a part of Texas, a part of this land, something you and I treasure."

The stems in her hands were drooping but not severed. Like herself, bent but not broken. "Thank you."

The gaze he turned on her held tenderness. They might not be in love but they were committed. "I'm glad you're my wife, Hannah."

The statement rocked her. She swayed on her feet. "Why? Now that Papa's gone and you no longer need to be here to help him, why are you glad you married me?"

"We share a commitment to each other, to the land. During the weeks since we married, my respect and admiration for you has grown."

"What do you admire about me?" Hannah wanted— no, *needed*—to know.

"I admire you in that dress, though no more than I do in denims." He let his gaze roam over her. "You're a lovely woman."

The sweet words and the gesture of the flowers captured her heart as surely as if he'd used a lariat.

Not that she'd let him know. Hannah harrumphed. "A sound basis for respect, Mr. Walker."

"I've heard of worse." Matt grinned down at her.

She noticed the lighter lines around his eyes from squinting into the sun. As he pushed a shock of hair off his brow, a band of paler skin on his forehead revealed where his hatband rested and that work ethic she admired.

"What else? What else do you admire?" she asked, gazing into his dark eyes.

"Apparently my wife craves compliments." He smiled. "That being the case, I'll list your many admirable qualities." He touched her hair. "You have beautiful hair that sends off sparks in the sunlight." His fingers slid to her brows. "Eyes that change hue at whim." Then traveled her cheek to her lips. "A smile that would light the darkest night."

Laughing, Hannah covered her ears with her hands, the bluebonnets waving wildly above her head. He was teasing her. "This is a business alliance. You don't have to woo me."

With a nod, he took a step away, giving her room to breathe. There were needs and goals she and Matt could meet for one another. They were friends united in a business cause. In many ways they were well suited, giving her hope they'd find a way to travel the uncharted waters of a marriage based on convenience. That they'd find contentment in companionship.

"Thank you for taking me on the picnic," she said. "It's time to get back to work. Tomorrow I'll go to town, deposit the money from the sale, pay the Parrish bills and order supplies. Then go over the Lazy P accounts until I'm as savvy with running the ranch as any man."

He studied her face, then with a brisk nod, ambled out of the stable.

She glanced at the bluebonnets in her hand. She would put them in a vase. Not that the flowers represented anything more to Matt than his love for all things Texan. For the land. For the way of life. Not that they implied Matt loved her.

That honor belonged to Amy, the young woman buried in the church cemetery.

Chapter Thirteen

Hannah sat at an enormous desk in the president's office of Bliss State Bank, a desk that confirmed his position but failed to hide Mr. Thomas's wide girth, and signed her name.

Across from her, Mr. Thomas shoved his spectacles up his nose and craned his neck toward the form. "Ah, I need to remind you that you're Hannah Parrish *Walker*."

Cheeks aflame, Hannah stared at her signature, barely able to believe she'd signed her maiden name. "Oh, I'm sorry."

Below his neatly trimmed mustache, Mr. Thomas's mouth twitched in an effort to contain a smile. "No problem. Plenty of room to add your married name."

With a nod, Hannah lowered the nib to the paper, then paused. The Walker name affirmed her wedded status. But, what would a real marriage be like? A marriage in more than name only? She bit back the sigh trying to shove up her throat, tightened her grip on the pen and scrawled Walker.

The last of her errands completed, Hannah emerged

into the sunshine and turned toward Leah's. She'd end the hectic afternoon with a visit to her friend.

As she passed the Western Union office, Mr. Katter sped out the door, hatless and huffing for breath. "Miss Parr—Ah, Mrs. Walker, mighty glad I saw you. We just received a telegram for Jake Hardy. If you'd take it to him, that would save our delivery boy a trip out."

"Happy to." Hannah tucked the envelope in her purse.

Mr. Katter's face hadn't revealed anything about the contents, but a telegram rarely brought good news. The visit to Leah would have to wait.

On the drive to the Lazy P, Hannah soaked up the peaceful pastureland, the cattle grazing in the fields. As she neared the stable, she slowed Lightning, then stopped the buggy. A few yards away, Matt and Jake leaned against the corral fence. Matt waved a hand, then ambled over, a welcoming grin on his face.

"Hello," he said, gazing up at her.

The warmth in his dark eyes slid through her, left her unsteady on her feet. With strong hands, he clasped her waist, then lifted her down. Her heart thudded in her chest. This marriage might not be real, but the man most certainly was.

Odd as she'd felt signing Hannah Parrish Walker, for the briefest moment in town, she'd wished for a real marriage. Now gazing into Matt's eyes, hunger for that closeness rose inside her.

"Everything go okay in town?" Matt asked.

Had her expression revealed the turmoil inside her?

"I opened an account in my name at the bank and deposited the profit from the cattle sale. Paid the bills at

Bailey's and the feed store and ordered supplies. Our attorney verified Papa's last will and testament. Shouldn't take long for probate to confirm the will is valid."

"Knew you could handle things."

"Thank you." Matt's confidence in her soothed like butter on a burn. "Some people underestimate me. Papa's lawyer and the bank president both expressed surprise I'd come without you."

"You're smart, capable. You don't need me holding your hand." He arched a brow. "Though I'd be happy to oblige."

Their eyes locked, tugging her closer. "I'll keep that in mind."

Jake ambled over to where they stood. "How are things in Bliss? Any news?"

Mercy, she'd been so caught up in Matt, she'd forgotten the telegram. She reached into her purse and handed Jake the envelope. "I was asked to give this to you."

With trembling hands, Jake tore open the envelope, then read the telegram. He lifted tear-filled eyes to hers.

"What's wrong, Jake?"

"Gertie fell. Broke her back." He sucked in a breath. "No idea how long my sister will be laid up, probably all summer."

"Oh, I'm sorry." Poor Allie. Her mother had deserted her, now her grandmother was bedridden. At Gertie's age, recovery would be slow.

"Not sure how to help, what with my job here." Jake sighed. "Suppose Allie could go from neighbor to neighbor."

To leave the ranch had been hard, but at least Hannah

had the support of family in Charleston. Allie needed that too. "Bring Allie here."

Jake rubbed his forehead. "Is that too much, so soon after losing yer pa? With the ranch to run and all?"

Hannah knew the pain of being motherless. "She'll be happier here than shifted from pillar to post. On the ranch, she'll have room to run, animals galore, fresh air. That should help take her mind off her troubles."

"You sure?" Jake asked.

"I'm sure."

Matt nodded. "I agree. Bring Allie here."

"If it's all right, I can leave tomorrow. A train runs to Amarillo on Fridays."

"Tomorrow is fine," Hannah said.

"I should be back to work by Monday. Allie can stay in the bunkhouse—"

"The bunkhouse is no place for a child. Allie will stay in the main house." Hannah touched Jake's sleeve. "I'll do all I can to help her adjust."

"'Preciate it. She needs a woman's touch."

Hannah gulped. Emotion had overpowered her common sense and she'd invited the girl on impulse. She'd make a mess of mothering a child. What did she know about kids? About this child, a girl she'd never even met?

She tamped down the panic rising inside her and took a calming breath. When she'd lost her mother, Rosa had provided a warm lap, fresh baked cookies and gentle ways. Hannah wasn't a cook, but surely she could read to Allie, hug her, tuck her into bed. But what if Allie wouldn't allow that?

"Losing your folks, Miz Hannah, you'll understand if Allie misses Gertie, misses her mom."

Hannah's heart lurched. Allie's parents had deserted her willingly. Abandonment she couldn't imagine. "I'll do my best."

Tears welled in Jake's eyes. "Can't thank you enough. Reckon I'd better pack." On bowed legs, Jake trudged toward the bunkhouse.

On their way to the house, Hannah turned to Matt. "Jake expects me to comfort Allie, but what if I say or do something to make things worse?"

"It'll work out. I'll do what I can to help." He rubbed his jaw. "Maybe you and Allie can connect over a favorite toy or something."

"That's a great idea. She might like to play with my dolls. They're packed away in a trunk in the attic." Though in truth, Hannah had no idea what this seven-year-old girl might treasure.

"I'll haul down the trunk." Matt's dark brown eyes bored into her. "You probably haven't thought where she'll stay, but the room I'm in faces the paddock. Maybe she'd like seeing the horses."

"Where would you go?"

A thought zipped through her. A crazy hope he'd ask to be a true husband and room with his wife.

"If it's all right with you, I'll take Martin's old room."

"Oh. Yes."

She forced a smile to her face, masking the disappointment tumbling inside of her. She should've known Matt didn't want to change their sleeping arrangements. Well, fine. No matter how good she felt nestled in Matt's arms, no matter how good Matt's lips felt on hers, she didn't need a real husband; the business deal they had suited her perfectly.

Hannah shot up her chin. "Allie *should* have the nicer view."

Matt gave a nod, then glanced around him, as if getting his bearings. "I'll see to the trunk," he said, then veered toward the stairway leading to the attic.

To keep her mind off her husband, she'd focus on Allie's arrival. The move would be hard for the little girl. Along with missing her mother and grandmother, she'd lose her routine, her home, her security.

A huge responsibility. Still…

Something akin to joy bubbled up inside her. Having Allie here would provide a diversion. A diversion from the loss of Papa, from the emotional ups and downs of her and Matt's relationship. With Allie here, Hannah would have another chance to prove herself, more importantly, an opportunity to help a hurting child.

Lord, help me give this child what she needs.

Love, Allie needed love. With Papa gone and a husband in name only, Hannah had pent-up love to give. She'd make a cozy place for the child. Give Allie love like Papa had given her. Smiles of approval. Hugs and kisses. Time alone with her.

Why, with Allie here, Hannah might forge a family. A family she wouldn't get in this business-only relationship with Matt.

Eager to make preparations for Allie's arrival, she entered the guest room. Her gaze leapt from Matt's boots with fancy stitching propped in the corner, to his shaving mug and brush resting on the washstand, to the open door of the wardrobe where his shirts and pants hung. All proof a man occupied this room. That man was her husband. What would it be like to watch him shave? To see him shrug into a shirt? To look across the pillows at his sleeping face?

"Where do you want this?"

Heart in her throat, Hannah whirled toward Matt, then took a steadying breath, reminding herself he couldn't read her mind.

"At the foot of the bed," she said. Her voice sounded hoarse, unsteady even to her own ears.

Mesmerized by the rippling of Matt's muscles as he lowered the trunk to the floor, Hannah's mouth went dry.

He ambled about the room, gathering his clothes, his toiletries, his Bible, each movement masculine.

She'd once feared falling in love with Matt and having a real marriage, believing he would tie her down and treat her like a hothouse plant. But he had stepped aside, letting her make decisions on the ranch, encouraging her to handle the sale of her cattle. Her fear had been unwarranted. He'd been there for her, with the ranch, with her father's passing, yet their relationship hadn't moved beyond friends.

As much as she longed for love, to share every facet of her life, did she want that? Really? She'd lost her mother. She'd lost her father. Those she'd loved most. She couldn't bear to go through that again.

She tamped down such foolish thoughts. How could she lose a man who'd never been hers?

Arms full with his belongings, Matt stepped passed her, keeping his distance as he moved to his new quarters. She gulped. Right across the hall from her.

Determined to get back to the task at hand, Hannah knelt before the trunk, blew dust off the lid. Hand on the latch, she hesitated. More than possessions were stored in this trunk. Memories were stored here, too. Memories of Mama.

Matt strolled into the room. "I'm settled in," he said, then squatted beside her.

Close. Much too close. Yet for some reason she couldn't understand, she welcomed his presence. Welcomed the comfort of having him near when she opened this door to the past.

She lifted the lid, inhaling the sweet scent of roses wafting from a bar of soap nestled in a tatted handkerchief. Folded nearby was the baby quilt Mama had made for her from patterned snippets of pink and green.

"My mother made this quilt for me. It'll be perfect for Allie to wrap up in."

He smiled at her. "Nothing tomboy about that."

She laid the precious keepsake at the foot of the bed, then lifted out the tray. Several boxes filled the bottom of the trunk. Tucked inside the first, Hannah found Ruth wrapped in a cloth. She lifted the doll and inspected her sweet bisque face.

"Mama gave me Ruth on my sixth birthday. Far different than the pony you got."

"You remembered."

She recalled everything he'd said about himself. But she wouldn't tell him that.

"The doll's open-and-close blue eyes and wavy, brown hair were as close to mine as Mama could buy."

"You were a pretty little girl."

"You said I was gangly, remember?"

"That was later, when you were growing like a locoweed."

She plopped hands on hips. "Not sure I appreciate the comparison to a weed that sickens cattle."

"Is growing like a thistle better?"

"No." Giggling, she traced a finger along the kid leather body, jointed arms and legs, smooth and soft as velvet. "Mama and I gave tea parties for my dolls."

"Dolls? There's more?"

She gently laid Ruth aside, opened a pillowcase and pulled out the ragdoll. "I got Baby on my first birthday. Papa said I loved the soft floppy doll at first sight." Hannah's throat clogged. "Mama made Baby, stitched the pert nose, blue eyes, bowed lips. She had a knack with a needle and patience I could never match."

"I remember your mother's lilting accent, her ladylike ways. She was a Southern belle."

Hannah was nothing like her mother, but her heart gave a little flip that Matt remembered Mama. Not that he shouldn't.

"I was fifteen when your mother died." He touched her hand, his eyes filled with compassion. "You were only nine, too little to lose your mother."

Tears brimmed in her eyes as she choked out the words, "After Mama died, I'd cuddle Baby close, wrap her arms around my chest. Pretend they were Mama's arms."

Matt tugged her close. "My arms are available," he said, offering her his handkerchief.

She swiped her eyes. "Hugging that doll brought me comfort, but still, at nine, I knew reality from make-believe."

At nineteen, she was old enough to realize the same. Matt might want to give her comfort, but he wasn't offering love.

Hannah slipped from Matt's arm and rose to her feet with both dolls. She propped them against the bed pillows. Perhaps they would console Allie, as they had Hannah all those years ago. As they still did. These dolls, the baby quilt, all bought or made by her mother, triggered warm memories. The effort Mama had taken to buy or make the perfect gift evidence of her love.

She returned to the trunk. To the stack of books she'd read many times over. *"Grimm's Fairy Tales, Bible Stories for Children, The Adventures of Tom Sawyer, Little Women, Jane Eyre."* She glanced at Matt. "Some of these are too advanced for Allie."

"Tom Sawyer was a favorite of mine."

Hannah stacked the books on the nightstand. "Perhaps come winter, we'll read it again."

Matt rose, leaned against the doorframe, glancing around the room. "Looks like a little girl already lives here. You've thought of everything."

"I'm no mother."

"You were a little girl once," he said with a grin. "Do with Allie what you liked to do as a kid. Maybe have one of those tea parties. You'll figure it out."

Easy for him to say. She cocked her head at him. "So, I suppose that means you'll figure out how to be a father?"

As if jabbed by the horns of a steer, Matt lurched upright. "That job belongs to Jake."

"A man in his seventies can't keep up with a child. Besides, she'll need other people, too. As old as I was when I moved to Charleston, I missed being away from Papa, from everyone and everything familiar. I want to help Allie fit in, to be happy here."

Matt's brow furrowed. "I teased you about finishing school, but never thought how hard it was for you to move clear across the country. Leave the life you knew and loved." He took her hand. "That experience should help you reach out to Allie."

She stared down at their clasped hands, how perfectly her hand fit in his, then looked into his eyes. "We have a marriage of convenience. Allie may not fit our idea of convenience, but you and I are in this together."

As if to protest, he raised a hand.

"You hear?" she said, leaning close. "This isn't my job only."

"Yes, ma'am." He smirked. "Can't imagine Allie will be any harder to handle than her new ma."

She harrumphed.

"Okay, we'll do this together."

He stroked his lip, staring into space. Matt Walker, the problem solver. As if he could handle everything with logic. With action.

"You two can play with the dolls, draw pictures, bake cookies." He snorted. "Oh, I forgot. You'll have to ask Rosa to teach her that."

"You think you've got it all worked out. But what if Allie is more like me? Prefers to roam, ride and rope?"

"In that case, I'd say we're in deep trouble." He winked. "In way over our heads."

"I already feel in over my head, and she hasn't arrived."

He took a step closer. So close Hannah could feel the

heat emanating from his body. "We may be in over our heads, but buck up, wife. I'm a mighty good swimmer."

She took a step back. Matt thought he had all the answers. This marriage had made sense, but with every passing day, the matrimonial waters grew more treacherous, the churning surf more unmanageable. Matt might be a good swimmer, but whether he knew it or not, she was on the verge of drowning.

If they weren't careful, they'd all go under.

In his room directly across the hall from Hannah's, Matt sprawled on the bed, arms behind his head, gazing out the window at the night sky. Moonlight streamed in, lighting the room enough to see. A shooting star streaked through the heavens, vanishing as quickly as it came. Then another. God was putting on quite a show. A show far better appreciated outdoors.

If only he could share the sight with Hannah, but he'd never consider knocking on her door.

He tugged on his boots then opened the door, fiddling with a button on his open shirt and walked into the dark hallway.

Right into soft curves. A gasp. *Hannah.*

"I'm sorry. I didn't see you there." He cleared his throat. "Can't sleep?"

"No, I hoped a glass of milk might help. What about you?"

"I'm on my way outside. To look for more shooting stars. Care to join me?"

She hesitated for a moment. "I would."

In the entry, he opened the wooden door and they stepped into the night. Another star streaked through the sky. Matt watched Hannah's upturned face, aglow in the moonlight. She looked young, at peace, even... happy.

Something akin to joy expanded then exploded in his chest. He might not be the reason for the contentment on his wife's face, but he'd brought her out here, given her this moment. Could he find ways to bring her many more such moments?

They stood there, soaking up the peace of the night. Soaking up the knowledge that God was in His Heavens. No matter what a mess they made of things on earth, God was in control, all the reassurance Matt needed.

"On a night like this, I feel God's presence everywhere, surrounding us, loving us, within us." Hannah sucked in a gulp of air, then turned to him. "Why didn't God save my father? I knew He could. I prayed and prayed He would, but He didn't."

The quiet question, spoken so softly, banged against his heart. The tortured uncertainty he heard in her voice sought an answer he didn't have. "I don't know. All I do know is Martin is at peace."

She turned to him, put a hand on her heart. "I feel that, too. I know my family is safe and happy in God's arms." She gazed up at him. "Thank you for bringing me out here to see the wonder of this night."

Hair flowing down her back, standing there in floor-length nightclothes and bare toes, she looked beautiful. Beautiful and oh, so vulnerable. An urge to protect her swept through him. To make certain she never faced such heartache again. Yet that was not in his power to do.

He encircled her in the cradle of his arms, gazing down at her upturned face. "Your beauty far surpasses this night."

Was that shimmer in her eyes tears?

Before he could ask, she lifted her face to his, closed her eyes, offering her lips.

"Oh, Hannah...dear, Hannah."

He kissed her with tenderness, brushing her sweet lips with his, then deepening the kiss, tightening his hold on her. She rose on tiptoes, pressing against him, kissing him back with a fervor that left him shaken. And had his heart galloping in his chest like a herd of wild mustangs.

Then she pulled away, fingertips pressed to her lips. "I... Good night," she said then fled inside.

As the door closed behind her, he stared up at the night sky, fighting for composure. How long could they go on this way?

Chapter Fourteen

Matt knew his wife. Knew the stiff smile on her face as she greeted Allie covered a passel of qualms. Well, he wasn't any surer of his role of temporary father. Nor could he guess how the child's presence would impact the strain between him and Hannah.

Jake stood beside his great-niece, his hand on Allie's shoulder, a proud smile on his face.

Slender, even wiry, Allie Solaro toed the ground, her dark hair falling around her face like a silk curtain, hiding her eyes. Clothed in cotton stockings and a frothy pink dress, the bow drooping like a saddle-weary drover, Allie would've looked downright citified, if not for the cowboy boots and hat Jake had bought her in Bliss.

Matt heaved a sigh of relief. No worry that this little lady would be a handful, like her temporary tomboy mom. More likely, she'd be scared of anything that moved.

"The Lazy P is your home for the summer, Allie," Hannah said.

Allie glanced at Jake, took in his reassuring nod. How well did the little girl know her great uncle? Yet she appeared to trust him and took the hand he offered.

Hannah rose to her feet. "You'll sleep in the main house."

Allie raised her gaze, her eyes misty, forlorn. "Can't I stay with Uncle Jake?"

"The bunkhouse is no place for a girl. Jake will take his meals with us so you'll see him often."

"That's right nice of you, Miz Hannah."

Matt clapped Jake on the shoulder. "Rosa's cooking will fatten you up."

"Ain't never had an ounce of fat on these bones. Reckon I'll enjoy Rosa's efforts to try."

"Let's see your room, shall we?" Hannah reached a hand to Allie. The little girl released her uncle's grip but didn't take Hannah's hand. "We'll get you settled in."

Eyes on their feet, as if answers for their circumstances could be found in the blades of grass, Allie and Hannah trudged toward the house.

The slender woman and child looked like a family. A lump rose in Matt's throat. A family wasn't what he and Hannah intended. Every day their marriage got more complicated, destroying the contentment he'd prized. In truth, contentment no longer satisfied. Now he yearned for companionship.

Marriage to Hannah was like riding a bronco without a saddle, every buck in their topsy-turvy existence flung him skyward, then landed him hard. He hung on, as if his very life depended on his grip, determined to tame the beast.

Allie glanced back at Jake, uncertainty in her eyes.

Matt's heart went out to the little girl. And to the woman in charge of her. He vowed to do all he could to help, knowing full well that tomboy Hannah felt as lost as he did. Whether they wanted it or not, they were cobbling together a family.

Lord, help all of us give Allie love and security.

Beside Matt, Jake grappled with Allie's trunk, grimacing at the effort. "I'll haul in her things," Matt said, then heaved Allie's trunk to his shoulder and followed.

Inside Allie's room, he deposited the trunk under the window where Hannah indicated. "Girls tote a lot of stuff." He glanced at Hannah. "I'm mighty grateful Allie didn't bring as much as you did from Charleston."

"You still moaning about that measly trunk at the depot?"

"That trunk was twice the size of this one. As I recall you also had five, six pieces of luggage. Not that you wear many of those fancy dresses."

"Are you saying you're partial to dresses?"

"Reckon I'm partial to whatever you're wearing."

A blush bloomed in her cheeks. A chuckle burst from his throat. Hannah tried to stare him down, but failed.

She shot up her chin, then opened the lid of Allie's trunk. A brown bear nestled between stacks of clothes. "What's your bear's name, Allie?"

Lips pressed together, the little girl stepped away. She clearly had no intention of talking to Hannah.

With perseverance Matt admired, Hannah put on a bright smile, then showed Allie where to put her clothes. Once she'd stashed her belongings, he and Hannah gave Allie a tour of the large parlor and the dining room with a table that seated ten.

"Lots of room for you," Hannah said, then led Allie to the cozy kitchen.

Rosa sat at the table beside a plate of sugar cookies and a jug of milk.

Eyes on the snack, Allie moved closer.

"This is Rosa, Allie. She made the cookies." Hannah put her arm around the housekeeper. "She'll give you a snack while Matt and I handle chores."

Allie plopped into a chair. "Okay."

"When you're finished, you can come out to the barn. Rosa will show you where."

Allie sat beside Rosa nibbling on a cookie as Matt and Hannah stepped outside.

"Rosa's cookies should improve her outlook," Hannah said.

Matt grinned, holding up two cookies and offering one to Hannah. "Exactly why I nabbed a couple for us."

"Thanks. Not sure who needs them more," she said with a giggle, then promptly ate hers as they walked to the barn.

Inside the dim interior, Matt hauled a sack of feed, then dumped grain into the manger for the cows while Hannah fed the pigs. Matt joined her, propping a foot on the bottom rail of the pen.

"Allie's not happy about being here," Hannah said.

"Give her time."

"Time doesn't take care of everything. Love does."

"Love?"

She dusted her hands together, then sidestepped him as if he posed a threat. "I'm not saying we love her. We don't even know her, but if we're kind and gentle, she'll respond."

In a couple of steps, he moved in front of her, cutting off her retreat. "If I'm kinder, gentler, will you respond?"

Her uneasy gaze skittered away. "This isn't about us."

"Isn't it?" Matt's heart lurched then thundered in his chest, like a stampeding herd. Surely, she could hear the wild beat. "Really? Aren't we in need of affection, too?"

Those sky-blue eyes filled with disquiet. She flicked out her tongue and moistened her lips. "I'm afraid."

He took a step closer until the toe of his boots touched her skirt. "I would never hurt you. Never." Swallowing hard, he rested a hand on her arm. "My touch is gentle, nothing to fear."

The edgy look in her gaze eased. "I know," she said, then her eyelids drifted closed.

He lowered his head. Was inches away—

"Rosa said kittens are in here."

Matt and Hannah jumped apart like they'd been jolted by a cattle prod as Allie darted inside the barn, then raced past the cows watching her with large serene eyes.

"There they are!" Allie crouched across from the litter of striped kittens nestled beside their mother near the grain bin. Eyes barely open, the kittens mewed softly, jostling for position.

The next thing Matt knew Allie had claimed one of the litter as hers and named the kitten Tiger. "Can I keep it?"

Matt and Hannah's gazes met and they smiled. The kittens would help the little girl connect to a new place.

"The kitten needs to stay with his mama," Hannah said.

Matt squatted beside Allie. "You can visit every day."

Tears flooded Allie's eyes. "If Tiger didn't have a mommy, he'd be sad."

The child looked lost, dejected. A lump lodged in Matt's throat, but he had no idea what to do.

"Yes, he would. Now he'll have his mommy and you," Hannah said then opened her arms.

Allie stepped into the circle of those arms. "I can be Tiger's friend."

Hannah nodded. "And we can be your friends, too."

"Would my little friend like to see the horses?" Matt said.

"Yes!" Allie ran a gentle fingertip along the kitten's spine. "I'll play with you every day, Tiger, I promise."

With Allie tucked between them, Matt and Hannah walked toward the stable. The child flitted along beside them like a little pink bird. Yet inside she carried a heavy load.

They found Jake mucking out a stall. Between the roundup and losing Martin, they'd gotten behind with chores.

Jake leaned on the shovel. "Having fun, Allie?"

"Yes!" Her grin revealed a missing tooth. "I've come to see the horses."

Hannah bent to Allie's level. "I've got paperwork that needs my attention. I'll see you at supper, okay?"

"Okay," Allie said, then strolled along the stalls.

Matt turned to Jake. "How's Gertie getting along?"

"She's in pain, wearing a back brace. A widow from church is staying with her for now."

"Is her doc giving her anything for the pain?"

"Yep, but she says the upset stomach the medicine causes is worse than the pain."

"Sorry to hear that," Matt said, scanning the aisles for Allie. She was nowhere in sight. "Where did Allie go?"

A few frantic minutes later, Matt and Jake found the little girl climbing the gate to the pasture where seven bulls grazed.

His heart in his throat, Matt snatched her off the rail. A few minutes more and she could've been inside. Gotten herself killed. He hoisted the little girl to his shoulder. As he explained the importance of staying clear of the bulls, his cheek twitched. The minute he'd finished explaining the danger, she flapped her arms like a bird taking flight. Had she understood a word he'd said? Or even listened?

"I'm high," she crowed, then leaned down and peered over his head, smiling into his eyes.

As much as she'd scared him, he chuckled, unable to resist the little charmer.

Inside the stable, he swung her to her feet in front of Star's stall. "This is Star, Hannah's cow pony."

Allie gasped. "A cow has a pony?"

"No, that name means Star is skilled at moving cows."

"Where'd they move?"

With a glance at Jake, Matt nudged his hat back. Jake just grinned, was no help at all. "Ah, from one pasture to the next."

"But not to the bull's pasture," Allie said, eyes wide with alarm.

Apparently he'd gotten through to her after all. The tic in his cheek eased. "That's right. Not there."

"Can I get on?"

"Sure." Matt lifted Allie onto Star's back. She leaned over the horse's neck, burying her face in the mane. "I like her. Can I take a ride?"

Jake smiled. "Need some help?"

"If you'll lead Star around the paddock, Jake, I'll hold on to Allie."

From her perch on Star's back, the little sprite scowled down at him. "I won't fall off."

"Well, okay. I'll just walk beside you."

Matt held his breath as the threesome circled the enclosure, but Allie had no difficulty staying astride with her tight grip on Star's mane. "Want to help feed and water the horses?"

A smile lit her face. "Yes!"

Soon she was skipping along, carrying oats, toting buckets, slopping water on her dress and boots.

Goodness, Allie was one active, determined child. Strong, too.

By the time Rosa called them in to supper, Allie's face was smudged, her stockings had holes where the knees had been, her dress was filthy and had a rip in the sleeve.

And Allie's dark eyes carried a new spark.

That was good, wasn't it?

Still, one look at Allie's ruined dress and Hannah might not agree. Most likely would question his supervision.

He and Jake followed Allie as she skipped to the

house. When had he felt more wrung out? Yet accomplished less?

Inside the kitchen, the aroma of chicken and noodles put a rumble in his stomach. The table was set. Dishes piled high. Ready for a hungry man.

Hannah blocked their progress toward the table, eyeing Allie's clothes. "What happened to you?"

Mute, hat in hand, Jake stared at Matt, as if Matt had deliberately destroyed the child's clothing.

Matt doffed his hat, and met Hannah's perplexed gaze. "She's...active," he said. His defense sounded weak, but what other reason could he give? "But she didn't get hurt. Not that she didn't try," he muttered.

Hannah's blue eyes twinkled with amusement. He had no idea why she found that funny, but at least she wasn't mad.

"Your ruined dress is my fault, Allie. I should have had you change clothes," Hannah said. "From now on, we'll remember not to wear your Sunday best when you're going out to play."

Play? Is that what Hannah called that frenzied race from one activity to another?

"Let me see those hands."

Allie held up hers, then frowned at Jake and Matt. "We're supposed to show our hands."

Matt held his up. Jake, too. Tarnation. The three of them looked like outlaws surrendering to the sheriff.

"Back outside. Wash up at the pump."

How had Hannah, in a matter of hours, managed to sound exactly like Matt's ma confronting her dirt-caked sons?

At the pump, they scrubbed up. With a shriek of

laughter, Allie funneled the spray with her hands, shooting water at Matt and Jake, then stomped in the puddle, chortling.

From her behavior when she arrived, Matt had expected Allie to sit around morose and inconsolable. Perhaps time away from her elderly grandmother's quiet home felt like a holiday. He had no idea if the cookies or the kittens had changed Allie's attitude, but whatever had brought that smile to her face, he was mighty grateful.

Back inside, shiny-eyed with faces to match, Allie and Jake sat side by side. Matt joined Hannah across the table. Rosa took Martin's spot.

"Would you bless the food, Matt?" Hannah asked, her voice unsteady, no doubt missing her father saying grace.

Allie folded her hands and bowed her head, as they all did. Matt thanked God for the bounty before them and was about to say amen when something made him take a peek at the little girl.

Eyes dancing, she waggled her fingers at him.

A laugh scrambled up his throat and shot out as a strangled cough and a croaky, "Amen." Then he coughed again.

"You feeling okay, Matt?" Hannah asked.

"Feeling fine." He smiled across at Allie, sharing their secret.

She might be a handful, might exhaust him and risk her neck at every turn, but she added something this house needed badly. Laughter. A diversion from the sorrow of losing Martin, from the tension between him and Hannah.

He wasn't sure how he'd manage to work with that magpie's tendency to get into mischief. A ranch was a dangerous place. Surely, between Hannah, Jake, Rosa and him, they'd manage. Perhaps they needed a schedule. A schedule to make sure Allie was never on her own. Tonight, after Allie slept peacefully, he would suggest that very thing to Hannah.

Matt took a bite of chicken and noodles, his gaze roaming the table, the ragtag family gathered here. Four adults determined to give Allie a good summer. A safe summer.

Tonight Matt would share this first bedtime ritual. After Allie's long day, she'd surely be exhausted, eager for sleep.

Tomorrow, he'd put Allie to work mucking the barn. Garbed in suitable clothes, she'd expend some of her boundless energy.

Why, he might be getting the knack of this parenting thing.

Three hours later, Matt admitted he'd been an idiot. At bedtime, a new version of Allie appeared. A child determined not to sleep. She asked for more water, more stories, a snack for her, a snack for Ginger, as if a toy bear needed food.

At ten o'clock, Hannah declared the kitchen closed. "No more delays, Allie. It's late. You need your sleep."

Allie's face crumbled. She rolled to her stomach and sobbed into her pillow, her slender body shaking. "I... want my...grandma," she wailed between sobs.

He and Hannah exchanged a frantic look.

Tears flooding her eyes, Hannah scooped Allie up,

cuddled her close, rocking back and forth. "Hush, sweet girl, don't cry. We'll take good care of you."

Matt sagged to the mattress, put his arm around Hannah who surely would be crying next. The three of them huddled there. Matt praying and cradling them in his arms with no idea what else to do.

The sobs subsided. Allie's breathing slowed, she slumped against Hannah.

"She's asleep," Hannah whispered, then tucked her into bed.

They walked into the hall, then looked back at the sleeping child. Peaceful and sweet.

Matt turned to Hannah. "That didn't go too badly."

She snorted. "I don't know how it could've gone worse."

"Tomorrow night will be easier." Or so he hoped. "You did a great job." He brushed his lips across her forehead.

As he turned to go to his room, she grabbed his hand. "Thanks for staying with me until she went to sleep."

"You said we were in this together and you were right. Sleep well," he said. "Unless you'd like me to tuck you in."

He shot Hannah a teasing grin. In the dim corridor, their eyes locked and held. The smile died on his lips. Heart racing like a horse nearing the finish line, he dropped his gaze to her mouth. He knew how full and soft her lips would feel beneath his. How sweet they'd taste.

Careful, Walker.

He might want to kiss her, hold her. But where would that lead? To the exact place it had in the past. To two people in the same house, yet worlds apart. He'd failed Amy. No matter how much he prayed, he couldn't seem to put that burden down. He wouldn't risk what he and Hannah had.

"I'll see you in the morning." Without a backward glance, he strode to his room.

Yet with Allie here, he couldn't run from the responsibility of helping care for the child. The cost of this growing longing for a real marriage was steep, a high price to pay. But, pay it he would as long as Hannah wanted him in her life. The day he knew she didn't, he'd set her free.

Hannah curled up in her bed, the pillow clutched in her arms, tears sliding down her face. She and Matt had been married for weeks. In that short span of time, they'd rounded up and sold cattle. They'd lost her father. They'd taken in a child in need of a temporary home.

All the work and grief and distractions didn't conceal the fact that their one-month anniversary had come and gone without fanfare. A sob escaped her throat. Nothing to celebrate about a loveless marriage. About the aching loneliness inside her.

As much as she tried to pretend otherwise, she was attracted to her husband. She admired Matt's strong grip on his faith. She admired his work ethic. She admired his commitment to this ranch. His commitment to her. Even as they tiptoed around each other, she knew he'd never forsake their bargain.

Yet underneath, she sensed Matt hid something. What, she didn't know. Whatever the reason, a barrier stood between them, a wall she wouldn't climb. She sighed. Why not be honest, at least with herself? Half of that barrier belonged to her.

When she'd proposed, she sought the freedom to keep the land and run the ranch. She'd feared Matt would try to take over, but he'd proved his trust in her by backing her up on the cattle sale. She had everything she wanted, or so she thought, but something was missing. Love was missing.

She'd lost her mother. She'd lost her father. No matter how lonely she felt, she didn't want to care about anyone that much again.

The kisses she and Matt had shared brought them closer, tethered them to one another with a stronger and stronger thread of connection. To risk love, knowing from experience she could lose it, would take courage. Courage she might find inside herself, if she believed Matt had gotten over Amy. Hannah couldn't risk loving a man who wouldn't love her back.

In the days ahead, she'd stay close to the house. Look after Allie. Muck the stalls. Finish planting the garden. Keep so busy she wouldn't feel the hole in her heart.

A hole her mother and father left. A hole where love used to live. A hole Matt was unwilling to fill.

Chapter Fifteen

Matt couldn't take his eyes off Hannah as she scooped the last shovelful of manure from Star's stall and dumped it into the wheelbarrow. Even with splattered boots and britches, the smudge on her cheek, her braid swinging along her back, he found his wife captivating.

Determined to keep his mind on his work, not on his wife, he entered the empty stall, dropped a pitchfork of straw in the middle of the floor, then another and another. "Have at it, Allie," he said.

With a grin, Allie dragged a rake, spreading the straw around the floor. Donned in the same garb as Hannah, Allie's small hands swallowed up in too big gloves, the empty fingers sticking out at an angle and flapping as she moved, Allie looked cute as a bug's ear.

More importantly, she looked happy.

With her eyes on Allie, Hannah leaned against the wall, the proud smile on Hannah's face, the softness in her eyes evidence that she'd already taken the child into her heart.

He'd done the same. The last thing he'd expected. Or

wanted. In September, Allie would return to Amarillo and leave a void he and Hannah could not fill. September was months away. No point in borrowing trouble.

Matt gripped the handles of the wheelbarrow and pushed it toward the garden plot south of the house. Weeks ago he'd plowed a small section that Rosa had planted with lettuce, cabbage, radishes and onions. The lettuce was up, the tops of the vegetables waved in the breeze. But Martin's illness had delayed planting the main garden.

A knot closed off Matt's throat. He missed those checker games, Martin's listening ear. But couldn't wish the man back. Not the way he'd suffered at the end.

Matt spread the load of manure onto the plowed red earth. Then he grabbed the spade propped against the gate and chopped the muck into the soil. As soon as he finished cultivating the garden, he'd hoe furrows and help Hannah and Allie plant sweet corn, beans, melon seeds.

Back in the barn, he pitched straw into another stall. As he straightened, he heard a giggle and turned. A clump of straw hit him in the face. Allie and Hannah, hands filled with ammunition, laughter rising from their lips, raced away.

Not to be bested, he scooped up a handful of straw. "You'll be sorry," he said and chased after them.

Eyes wide, they changed direction, darted around a post. He charged after them, grabbed Hannah by her throwing arm and rained down straw on her head. Shrieking, she yanked her arm out of his hands, stumbling as she did. He made a grab for her but off balance, they tumbled into the pile of fresh bedding.

Hannah's laughter echoed through the rafters, music to his soul. "You're not fast enough for me." He looked down at her nestled there in his arm.

"Maybe I wanted to get caught," she said, then her eyes grew wide, her cheeks flamed at the implication in her words.

"Hmm, that makes this all the more interesting." He leaned on one elbow, smiling down at her, his face inches from hers.

"I...I merely meant I could outrace you if I'd wanted to."

Laughter burst out of him. "Yeah, and you can lift a trunk into a wagon bed, too."

Caught in the absurdity of her claim, Hannah grinned. Their gazes met and locked, the smile on her lips faded. He heard a soft sigh. Her indigo eyes, bluer than he'd ever seen them, softened with longing, then lowered to his lips.

With a whoop, Allie sprang toward them, her boots slipping on the straw. Matt freed his arms just as the little girl launched into the air. With both hands, he caught her in flight. She hung there midair, her eyes twinkling with mischief. Thunderation. If he'd been one second slower, she'd have conked her head on the boards.

With a sigh of contentment, oblivious to the risk she'd taken, Allie wiggled between them, then leaned pointed little elbows on Matt's chest. "You were going to kiss," she said, wrinkling her nose as if she found the notion disgusting.

No chance of kissing Hannah with this child around. One day Allie would understand and value the kiss between a man and woman. Assuming she lived that long.

Allie snaked out a hand and tossed straw in Matt's face. "I got you!"

He flicked the pieces away, then scooped the child under one arm and scrambled to his feet, offering Hannah a hand. "Ladies, we have work to do," he said, then put Allie down, giving her a stern look or trying to. "No time for games."

"Allie, remember this. Men don't like to lose."

Matt picked straw from his clothes and headed out the barn door to the sound of laughter. Hannah's laughter—Allie joining in. He'd laughed at Hannah's claim she could outrace him, but apparently the last laugh was on him.

He chuckled. Nothing could make him happier than bringing joy to the two feisty females in his life. Well, perhaps one thing could. But, shared laughter was far safer than shared kisses.

Hannah leaned against the pen where the cows stood chewing cud. Instead of getting the milking done, what she'd come to do, she watched Allie pet the kittens. The contentment on the child's face no doubt mirrored her own.

Allie was filling that hole in Hannah's heart. The wonder of that notion slid through her. She inhaled sharply. How could she bear to lose that child when Gertie's back had healed and Allie returned to her grandmother?

Hannah tamped down the thought. She would enjoy these times, enjoy the fulfillment of nurturing a child.

Not that Hannah had ever considered motherhood. She'd spent most of her life resisting the typical roles of women, viewing household chores and frivolous pursuits as tedious and confining. The lure of the land, the excitement of a cattle drive, the fulfillment of seeing the ranch prosper gave her purpose.

But with Allie here, Hannah had seen that womanhood wasn't just fancy, confining clothes and dull domestic tasks. Womanhood could involve mothering a child, nurturing, protecting, teaching and loving a child, things mothers did every day.

She'd seen with Allie that motherhood was a high calling deserving of respect. Even menial tasks mothers performed were essential to a child's welfare. Those tasks might be tedious, as tedious as keeping financial records or keeping track of supplies or keeping the barns sanitary, but they were important.

The peeved look on Matt's face when Allie had unintentionally interrupted his kiss had made her smile. Then later, when he'd left the barn, a walking scarecrow, he'd triggered a fit of laughter. Laughter bubbled up again inside of her. She buried a smile in her arms, crossed atop her knees.

When had she had more fun? When had she wanted to open her heart more?

She dusted off her britches, grabbed the milk stool, then plopped down beside the cow, leaning her forehead against the cow's side. The first spray hit the pail with a ping.

Allie dashed over. "Why do cows make milk?"

"God made them for that purpose."

As the ranch was hers. Or did God want more for her? Was she afraid to examine the purpose He might have for her life?

The mother cat rubbed against her pant legs. "Will you get her bowl, Allie? Then play with the kittens until I'm finished."

Allie dashed off and returned with the dish, then wandered over to the kittens. Imagine, instant obedience. Perhaps Hannah was getting the knack of parenting.

The spray squirted into the dish, spraying the cat's head as she lapped up the milk with her pink tongue.

As Hannah milked, she hummed "Rock of Ages," Papa's favorite. Oh, how she missed him. His quiet strength. His steadfast love. His endless patience. She'd seen how much energy taking care of Allie required. Dealing with a tomboy daughter had surely taken a lot of effort. Hannah had been nine when Papa had taken over her care. With Rosa's help, but still, the burden fell to him. Never once had he made her feel like a nuisance.

Papa, I wish I could tell you how grateful I am for all you did for me. Your endless patience.

Patience was not Matt's or Hannah's strength, but they were showing improvement.

Finished milking the first cow, Hannah moved to the second.

A bloodcurdling scream froze her hand, raising goose bumps on her arms. She jerked to her feet. The cow stepped sideways as Hannah raced toward the sound. Her gaze darted to the kittens. No Allie. Where was Allie?

Chest heaving, Hannah sprinted toward the stable. "Allie!"

Inside the dim interior, her eyes took a moment to adjust. Then a movement in the straw, a moan.

"Allie!" She dashed to the spot, dropped to her knees beside the little girl, lying face down in the straw. "Allie, can you hear me?" Her shaking hands hovered over the child's head, her body. Dare she move her?

Allie lifted her head, shaking it as if dazed. "Oh, bright lights."

"What hurts?"

"My head."

"Can you turn over?"

She rolled onto her back. Her forehead was scraped, a lump already swelling.

"Can you see me?" Hannah said.

"Yeah."

A gust of air heaved out of Hannah. *Thank God.* She ran gentle fingers over the bump.

"Ouch."

"I'm sorry, Sweetie. Did you fall down?"

Allie pointed to the ladder that led up to the loft. "I fell off there."

Hannah gasped. "Off that ladder?"

"Yeah, I was at the top. I…I don't know what happened."

"It's okay. You're going to be fine." *Please God. Let her be fine.* "Tell me if this hurts." Hannah ran her hand over each arm and leg, over hands and fingers.

Tears spilled down her cheeks. "My whole self hurts."

The clatter of hooves. Matt led Thunder into the stable. "What the—?" He dropped the reins, ran toward them. "What happened? Is she hurt?"

With Matt there, Hannah's heartbeat slowed. He

would know what to do. "She fell. Either off the ladder or from the loft."

Matt crouched on the other side of Allie, staring at the bump on her forehead. "You okay, Pumpkin?"

"I saw lights, like stars. Now I can see you."

"Nothing appears broken." Hannah didn't want to convey her fear to Allie so she tried to control her shaky voice and failed.

"Let's get her inside, get some ice on that bump." Matt slid his hands under Allie's torso and rose with her in his arms.

Hannah led Thunder into his stall, then hurried after them.

Allie's fall from that ladder had surely taken a year off Hannah's life. And had given her insight into Matt's cautious nature. All those times he'd warned Hannah against taking risks, he hadn't been trying to control her life, he'd merely wanted to protect her. Not that accidents wouldn't happen. Not that some risks weren't worth taking, but for the first time she understood her husband's vigilance.

In the kitchen, they gathered around Allie. Matt held cold compresses to the lump on her forehead and checked her pupils. Hannah swabbed her scrapes, thanking God that the child didn't appear seriously hurt.

"Can I have a cookie?" Allie asked.

"A cookie is good medicine," Hannah said.

Allie sat munching the treat, littering the tabletop with crumbs, looking happy, as if nothing had happened.

But something had happened. Something more than Allie's accident. She and Matt had shared their concern and affection for the child. Allie was bringing them closer. Something far riskier than any hazard on the ranch.

Matt met Hannah's gaze. "She'll be fine."

In that moment, Hannah knew she and Matt were on a collision course. The barrier between them was still solid and steep. When they hit that wall, someone was bound to get hurt.

Nothing held Allie's attention for long. To keep her in the house and quiet meant taking on a domestic chore Hannah avoided. Cooking.

At the kitchen table, Allie sat coloring on the back of a blank ledger sheet. The cow she'd drawn was pretty good for a seven-year-old city girl.

"Nice picture." Hannah smiled at Allie's upturned face. "Does our little artist want to make applesauce? I found wrinkly apples in the cellar."

Elbow on the table, chin in one hand, Allie shoved the curtain of hair out of her eyes with the other. "I want to make a pie."

"Ah, that sounds complicated." Especially with Rosa off visiting her cousin and with Hannah having no clue how to make a pie.

"I always make pies. Pies are easy. Pies make me happy."

For a moment, Hannah was tempted to say that pies made her very unhappy. But that sounded childish.

Allie pushed out of her chair and twirled across the floor. "Me and Grandma Gertie bake all the time. Mama likes pie best." Allie stopped her dance. "On Mama's birthday, me and Grandma maked a pie for her." Her face crumpled, tears welled in her eyes. "Mama never came."

Her own eyes stinging, Hannah looked away, unable to bear the pain of a mother's abandonment in Allie's eyes. Hannah had to ease that hurt. Fill that void Allie's mother left in her life. Even if that meant making a pie.

"When your mother comes back, Allie, you'll know exactly how to welcome her home. With a pie you made yourself. You'll make her proud."

The wide smile on Allie's face bloomed in Hannah's heart. She had to get this right. She couldn't let Allie down. "I saw a can of cherries in the cellar."

Somehow she and Allie would make a cherry pie. Within minutes she'd returned from the cellar with the cherries and found a recipe for basic pie crust in a cookbook. Flour, lard, a pinch of salt, water. Fewer ingredients meant fewer mistakes. Or so she hoped.

Once they'd washed their hands, they dumped the flour and salt into a bowl, spilling flour as they did. Lard came next.

"Grandma uses her fingers," Allie said, then dug right in.

No point in both of them getting into that mess.

"It's mixed," Allie said, then held up doughy fingers and wiggled them like attacking claws.

Hannah chuckled, then grabbed a spoon and scraped off what she could, then checked the recipe. "Water comes next. Cold water."

"Grandma Gertie puts ice in the water."

Hannah chipped a chunk of ice off the block in the icebox and dropped it into the small bowl Allie held.

"Says to add three tablespoons of cold water or whatever is needed to make a soft dough."

As if Hannah knew what was meant by a soft dough. She belonged on horseback, not in front of a recipe.

But, Allie appeared fearless. She added the water, tossed the mixture with a fork. The peaceful look on the child's face was worth every knot in Hannah's stomach.

Allie declared the dough ready and divided the glob into two halves, patting them like a cherished pet. "Use the rolling pin to flatten the dough into circles," Allie said, then marched to the sink to wash her hands.

Hannah plopped one glob in the middle of the floury surface and shoved the rolling pin into the dough. The dough stuck to the wood like gummy glue.

"You forgot to flour it," Allie said.

To avoid Allie's shrewd eyes, Hannah kept her gaze on the pin as she scraped off the mess, then washed and dried the rolling pin.

With a fistful of flour, Allie dusted the rolling pin. "Now you can roll it," she said, handing the utensil to Hannah.

This time the dough didn't cling but took the shape of the pie plate.

"You're doing good." Allie shot her a big encouraging grin.

"Thank you," Hannah muttered, feeling more child than adult, then lifted the dough and dropped it into the plate. It landed off-center.

"You gotta pat it. Like you're tucking it into bed, Grandma always said."

"Oh…oh, okay. Well, why don't you do that?"

With a satisfied smile on her face, Allie patted the

dough into the pan, then swiped her floury palms together, dispersing a cloud of white. She giggled. "I'm making it snow."

"Imagine that? In May. Have you ever seen snow, Allie?"

"No, but I've seen snow in storybooks. Snowmen, too," she said. "Grandma Gertie has."

Hannah opened the can of cherries then glanced at the recipe. "Let's see, we need—"

"You gotta do the other one." Allie pointed to a blob of dough. "One for the top. One for the bottom."

"Oh, of course."

The second attempt went more smoothly. With the crust made the worst part was over. The recipe said to mix the ingredients then cook the filling. Hannah added kindling to the embers in the firebox, then more wood. Soon the stovetop radiated heat.

With white palms leaving prints on everything she touched, Allie stood on a stool at the stove and dumped the juice into a saucepan, spattering dots of red on their clothes. "Whoops!"

"It'll wash." Or so Hannah hoped.

Hannah measured and added flour to thicken the juice, inadvertently puffing flour in Allie's face.

Allie coughed. "I can stir," she said, grabbing for the spoon. "How long does this take to cook?"

Hannah had no idea. "You look like a snowman, Allie."

With a mischievous look in her eyes, Allie lifted her hands and patted Hannah's cheeks. "You're a snowman, too," she said, giggling.

Hannah chuckled. "We sure have made a mess of this kitchen and of each other."

One glance around them, at the flour on the table, on the floor, the spatters of red on their clothes, and they both were giggling.

"Any chance I could get a cold glass of lemonade?"

Hannah and Allie turned toward the door. Matt stood on the other side of the screen, taking in their silliness, a somber expression on face. Why, he looked unsettled, like an outsider observing a family he longed to be part of.

Matt doffed his hat and wiped the sweat off his face. He looked weary. Flushed from the heat. So handsome she couldn't move, couldn't tear her eyes away.

"Don't want to put you out," he said, then turned to go. "I'll get a drink at the pump."

His words heated Hannah's face and spurred her to action. "Wait!" She grabbed the pitcher from the icebox, poured him a glass, then strode to the door. "Don't you want to come in?"

"Too dirty to track inside."

With the lack of rain, the walk behind the plow had left him covered with a fine film of dust. But this was no snowman. The eyes he turned on her radiated heat. She swallowed hard, opened the door, handed him the lemonade, then stepped outside.

Matt drained the glass in one long gulp, his Adam's apple bobbing. "Working up the garden is thirsty work," he said, then swiped the back of his hand over his mouth.

One very appealing mouth. Hannah's went dry.

"You saved my life." He handed the empty glass back to her. "Thanks."

"You're welcome." And he was.

Stuck in the kitchen, making that pie, or trying to, she missed working with him. "Besides tilling the garden, have you had a busy day?"

"Fed the stock, the horses, rode out to check the herd. Calves are growing, getting friskier. The windmill's squeaking. First chance I get, I'll grease the gears."

The man worked tirelessly. "I should be helping you."

"No, you're looking after Allie. That's more important." He plopped his hat in place. "She doing okay?"

Allie raced to the door. "The pan's boiling over!"

"See you ladies later," Matt said, then marched off, a man on a mission. No doubt to put himself as far from them as he could get.

At the stove, Hannah slid the pan off to the side and stirred the mixture.

A frown on her face, Allie sighed. "I wanted to surprise Matt. Is it ruined?"

"We're lucky. Nothing stuck to the bottom and the filling's thickened," she said, then grabbed the cherries, ready to add them to the pan.

"I want to do it."

Hannah glanced at the red dotting her shirt. They'd be covered in red if Allie did it by herself. "Let's do it together."

They dumped the fruit into the pan, then Allie stirred it a few more times.

At the table, Hannah held the pan while Allie scrapped the filling into the crust, then lifted the top crust into place. She scrambled onto a chair, got a cup from the cupboard, then added a ladle of water. "Water sticks dough together. Grandma showed me." She plopped floury fingers into the water and moistened the inside edges of the crust. "Grandma said some bakers twist the edges, but she does it like this." Face solemn, Allie pressed the tines of a fork around the rim of the pie plate, careful not to miss a spot or overlap.

"Nice job, Allie." Hannah lifted the pie plate, ready to put it in the oven.

"Wait! We got to poke holes in the top or it'll explode."

"Explode?"

"Yep." The little girl poked the crust with her thumb. "Grandma told me that when Mama was a girl, one time she forgot the holes. Made a big mess in the oven."

With the four holes Allie had dug in the crust promising no explosion, Hannah popped the pie in the hot oven and checked the clock on the wall.

The messy kitchen wasn't quite as funny now. "Time to clean up," Hannah said.

"Ruth's calling me." An impish grin on her face, Allie raced off.

Hannah chuckled. Allie had outsmarted her. She should've helped, but Hannah had to admire her ingenuity. If not for the inconvenience she would cause Rosa, she'd want to get out of the chore, too.

Finally with the kitchen tidied, Hannah swiped a clean damp cloth over the smudges of flour and spatters on her shirtwaist. Why hadn't she thought to wear an apron? She'd change into the blue dress with sleeves to the elbow and a scooped neckline that would be cool in this heat.

Her breath caught. Her entire life all she ever wanted was to wear pants. She treasured the freedom of wearing pants, but was discovering she also liked feeling like a woman. Would she see approval of her appearance in Matt's eyes?

Chapter Sixteen

At noon, Matt slogged into the kitchen, hair wet from a dousing at the pump, the collar of his cotton shirt open at the neck, his sleeves rolled up, revealing tanned, muscled forearms.

The sight of him trapped the air in Hannah's lungs. Brawny, hardworking, all male, Matt dominated the kitchen. Everything else shriveled in importance.

Hannah's cheeks heated, and she felt conspicuous, out of her element. She stood frozen in place, wishing she'd donned pants.

His dark gaze traveled her blue dress from the scooped neck to the floor-length hem, then darted to her face. "You're prettier than a bushel of bluebonnets, Hannah. After working in the hot sun, looking at you in that dress—" he swallowed hard "—is refreshing."

She should've been out working with him, had no business in this kitchen. Had been more of a hindrance to Allie than a help. "Thank you, but I'm no debutante. I'm a rancher."

He tossed his Stetson on the hook. "I haven't forgotten," he said, his tone chilly, as if irked by the reminder.

Hannah pivoted toward the table where the pie sat in the center. "Allie and I made a pie. Well, Allie did most of the work."

Allie bounced into the kitchen, waving the picture of the cow. Matt admired her drawing, then they gathered at the table with a plate of beef sandwiches Rosa had made before she'd left.

As they munched on sandwiches, Hannah couldn't take her eyes off Matt. How could he have this powerful hold on her?

As if avoiding her gaze, he leaned over and took a whiff of the pastry. "Can't think of the last time I had a piece of cherry pie."

Hannah cut Matt a large slice and a smaller one for her and Allie, then slid them on plates. The filling didn't run. The crust didn't fall apart. So far so good.

Not that she wanted to be a woman praised for her cooking. She'd done this to help Allie recapture happy times with her grandmother.

Matt dug his fork into the pie and took a large bite. His face scrunched up, one eyelid drooped low.

"What's wrong?"

He wiped his mouth with his napkin. "Nothing. I like cherry pie on the tart side."

"Tart?" Hannah took a bite, then spit it into her napkin. "Oh no! I must've forgotten the sugar."

Hannah sighed. This proved she wasn't cut out for the kitchen. As if she needed it.

"It's good—really," Matt said.

As if to verify his claim, he took another bite, much

smaller than the first. This time he kept his face composed, though the effort must've cost him dearly. The cherry filling was sour enough to bring a pucker to a man-hating spinster.

She couldn't follow a simple recipe. She should've taken the precaution of tasting the filling before putting it in the pie. "I can't cook."

"You can rope and deliver calves, drive cattle, handle the business end of the ranch. Makes a man wonder if he's needed," he muttered.

Why had his words stabbed at her: Hadn't he said what she'd wanted to hear—praise of her abilities on the ranch? But underneath she wanted a role no cowhand could step in and fill.

"It's easy to fix." Matt dumped a couple spoonfuls of sugar from the bowl on the table onto his slice.

Allie dumped sugar on her pie. "Look at me," she said then took a bite. The face she made had them all chuckling.

Not to be outdone, Hannah added sugar to her sliver, then took a bite. The tartness made her shiver and scrunch up her face.

Allie pointed at her, howling with laughter. "You look funny!"

Matt chucked Allie under the chin. "No funnier than you and I did."

Soon all three of them were trying to surpass one another's silly faces, winking eyes and shivering shoulders.

Hannah giggled, then met Matt's amused gaze. As they studied one another, the smile on his face faded.

The intensity of his gaze bored into her. Something passed between them. Something personal. Meaningful.

"Can I have a cookie?" Allie asked.

Welcoming the interruption, Hannah took a breath, composing herself. She rose, put a plate of cookies on the table. "Rosa's cookies should get rid of that sour taste in your mouth."

Allie grabbed a cookie in each hand. "Cookies are almost as good as pie." Allie looked at Matt. "Hannah and me tried real hard, Matt. We wanted to surprise you."

"I know you did, Pumpkin. Thanks for going to all that trouble for me."

"It was fun." Her lips turned down. "Pie's no good without sugar."

Hannah scooped up all three plates and dumped the contents into the slop jar beneath the sink. Would the hogs reject her first attempt at baking?

To put distance between her and Matt, she cleared the table, swished soap in the dishpan and added boiling water from the teakettle.

Matt met her at the sink and laid a hand over hers. "It's okay, Hannah. Your skills aren't in the kitchen."

"I wanted this to work."

"Why?"

She shrugged then turned away.

"Tell me."

She pushed past him. How could she explain that by messing up that pie, she'd messed up the chance to connect with Allie's grief over her mother's abandonment? When Matt believed they'd made the pie for him?

He stepped closer. "You're avoiding me."

"Hardly."

"Thanks for making that pie for me." He leaned close and brushed his lips over hers. "My way of a thank you."

At his touch, she could barely stand, could barely think, barely breathe. "I don't cook for just anybody."

"That's good to hear."

"Only for tall, dark-eyed ranchers," she said as if the words had been pulled out of her.

"Could be a few of those around."

He stood inches away. Her fingertips slid through the hair at his nape. "With black curly hair?"

Why had she said that? What was wrong with her? This silly flirting wasn't who she was.

"Still might be a couple of those," he said, lowering his head, trapping the air in her lungs.

Losing herself in his eyes, she wobbled, then steadied herself with a hand on his chest. "With shoulders as wide as the great outdoors?"

Matt's eyes lit with something too personal. Too close. "After this," he said, his hand trailing her cheek, "sugarless pie will be a favorite of mine. Still, I have to wonder how you forgot the sugar."

"This fiasco was your fault."

"Mine?"

"When you came to the kitchen door asking for a drink, you and your rugged good looks and charm turned my brain into mush. And I forgot what I was doing."

A smile carved his face, softened every plane. "If it makes you feel any better, the rows in our garden aren't as straight as they ought to be."

He tugged her to him, his mouth claiming hers and reminding her exactly why this man kept her distracted.

The feel of his lips on hers, the warmth of his arms, the strength of his grasp surrounded her, pulled her in.

Hannah circled her arms around his neck, and gave him all the sweetness the pie had been missing.

Then she pulled away. Matt had made her forget more than the sugar. He'd made her forget she wanted only one thing. To be taken seriously as a rancher.

Matt wore a dazed look on his face. "I, ah, almost forgot. I told Pa I'd ride over to the Circle W to lend him a hand," Matt said, then sped out the door.

As the screen door slapped shut behind him, Hannah collapsed into a chair and laid her head in her hands. Why not admit it? Matt Walker had a crazy power over her. She could no more have stopped her reaction to him, than she could stop a stampeding herd singlehandedly.

Matt could not blame his tension on the hard work, the scorching heat, the strong stench of mucking out Pa's stable. Those things were all part of ranch life in Texas.

He'd fled the Lazy P and been driven to the Circle W out of fear. Fear of what he and Hannah might cook up if he stayed with her. He'd come into the kitchen for dessert, and ended up with something far sweeter. Far more tempting, and oh, so bad for him.

Nothing wrong with kissing his wife. In an ordinary world. But their world was far from ordinary. Their marriage was a business arrangement. A solution for Hannah. A solution he'd agreed to, a solution he'd wanted, a solution he'd expected would protect his heart.

No more risk. No more heartache.

Trouble was, a kiss like that tempted a man to open up and let the risk and heartache in. He and Hannah teetered on the edge of a precipice. If they fell for each other, plunged over that sheer drop into a hotbed of emotion, they'd reap the consequences. Pay a terrible price.

He knew that from experience. No one could circle back and change the past. If he could, Matt had far worse regrets than that kiss. One long ago regret in particular.

Matt dumped a shovelful of manure into a wheelbarrow. If only he could discard all the rubbish inside him. The mistakes he'd made. He wouldn't think about all that now. He wouldn't. God had forgiven him. If only he could forgive himself.

The task of making certain he didn't let down another wife was his. And his alone.

To make matters worse, his plan to help his father, perhaps mend the discord between them, had backfired, adding another knot in his stomach. He couldn't blame the sour cherry pie or even his regret at kissing Hannah for this knot.

No, his problem stood across from him, leaning on his shovel, bossing him around. As only his father could do.

Matt lifted another shovelful out of the stall and into the wheelbarrow. "I'm doing the best I can, Pa." His arms ached, his back hurt, but the disquiet from earlier brimmed in his chest. "The best I can here, and at home."

"This family needs you." Robert raked straw over the stall beside him. "And you're over there—"

"With my wife. Helping her run her ranch."

Robert harrumphed. "Exactly. *Her* ranch. A man doesn't let a woman tell him what's his and what isn't. You ask me, your place is here. One day, you'll inherit this ranch."

The knot tightened. If Matt helped Hannah, he'd let Pa down. If he helped Pa, he'd let Hannah down. Why was his father putting him in this position?

Matt shoved his hat back and scrubbed the sweat from his brow with the back of his gloved hand. His gaze wandered out the stable door to the paddock beyond where the horses grazed, the peace of the scene in sharp contrast to the tension in the air.

"You should stay and run this ranch. The Circle W is your legacy, not the Lazy P."

"Pa, I can't live here. I'm married." Matt didn't understand what went on inside Pa's head, but he knew what needed saying. "But even if I could, your idea wouldn't work."

"Why not? Hannah can sell the Lazy P and the two of you could move in here."

"If I did, you wouldn't want me to run the ranch. You'd be trying to run me. I'm twenty-five, yet you're holding me back, keeping me from being the man you are."

"You're always over at that ranch," Pa said, flinging a hand in the direction of the Lazy P, ignoring Matt's point. "Even before you married Hannah, you were there, every day."

"Martin was ill, Pa. He needed my help—"

"I needed your help!" Robert's voice vibrated the timbers of the stalls. He released a blast of breath. "Just go. You want to be there, not here, so go."

The frustration bottled up inside Matt flared. For a second, he considered doing that very thing. Then he looked over at his father. What he saw in Robert's face wasn't anger—

What he saw was hurt.

"Pa, I'm sorry. I never meant to hurt you by helping Martin."

"You didn't hurt me." But the furious way Robert raked at the straw told another story.

"Everything I know I've learned from you." Matt set the shovel aside. "I value your wisdom. I value your experience. I value your work ethic. But you won't accept that I'm capable, can manage on my own."

"Can't say you've done a good job managing everything in your life."

The words slammed into him, a barely veiled accusation he couldn't deny. He'd failed Amy. Pa knew that as well as Matt. Matt turned away, plunged the shovel through the debris, every muscle coiled. Why had he tried to talk to his father?

A hand on Matt's back slowed his frenzied shoveling. "I'm sorry, son. That was cruel." Tears welled in his eyes. "Amy's unhappiness wasn't your fault."

Matt pivoted to his father. "Of course it was!"

He took a steadying breath, determined to avoid talking about his first marriage and get to the trouble between him and his father. "I've made mistakes. But, this is my life you're trying to lead." He sighed. "Pa, you used to allow me to try my own way, and yes, sometimes to fail. That freedom is how men are made. You taught me that."

"This is my ranch. Things *should* run my way."

"Your way isn't working. We need to find a new way. *God's* way."

As if his knees had gone out from under him, Pa sank onto a bale of straw. "Surely God doesn't disapprove of a father expecting his son to claim his birthright."

"Cal and I won't turn our backs on the Circle W. We love this ranch. We grew up here. But we're both married. Married to women with ranches. But if you'd hand over some of the control, you might be surprised how much we'd choose to come to you for advice."

"Like you did Martin." Eyes damp, Pa glanced up at him.

"I'm sorry. I…" How could he explain his relationship with Martin without adding bricks to the wall between them?

"Martin was a good guy." With a sigh, Pa stood, faced Matt, defeat in his eyes and something else, too. An apology. "Truth is, overseeing you and Cal is wearing me out. You're right, I need to let go of the reins. Still, old habits dic hard," he said. "I'll try to stop telling you boys what to do and how to do it."

For years Matt had believed the way to honor his father was by keeping his mouth shut, but his pent-up frustration had made him avoid Pa. That distance had hurt his father, especially when Matt had turned to Martin to fill Pa's shoes.

"What do you say? Want to play a game of checkers one evening?" Matt said.

"If you think you're man enough to beat me, come

ahead." No matter what Pa had said, the wide grin on Pa's face revealed his pleasure.

"I don't mind losing. As long as I get to play the game."

Matt and his father had taken the first step toward reconciliation. Not all that long ago, Matt wouldn't have believed they could spend a pleasant evening together.

Lord, help Pa and me heal our relationship.

He suspected progress between them would be two steps forward and one back. Whatever happened, Matt intended to keep taking steps in the right direction, here and at the Lazy P.

The trouble was, how would he know where those steps would lead him?

Chapter Seventeen

Hannah stepped into Bliss Christian Church, seeking peace for the havoc of her life. Every time she thought she had a handle on her existence, that peace was derailed faster than a train on poorly laid tracks.

With Allie's hand in hers and Matt at her side, Hannah entered the sanctuary, steeling herself for the first Sunday she'd attended services since Papa's funeral. To be here, where Papa's casket had sat, where Pastor Cummings had preached his funeral, took every bit of her willpower.

She and Matt introduced Allie to everyone they met, distracting Hannah from her sad memories. The parishioners greeted them warmly with hugs and smiles. Hannah had missed her church family, this quiet building, the stained glass window splashing a rainbow of color on the white walls.

Here in God's house, she'd find peace and strength. Here with Matt and Allie, she'd worship through prayer and hymns. And avoid the space at the end of their pew where Papa had always sat.

Leah stepped up to them, an expectant smile on her face. "Who is this sweet little girl?"

"Leah, this is Allie Solaro, Jake Hardy's great-niece. She's staying with us for the summer."

"Hi, Allie." Leah motioned to her parents ushering her well-groomed siblings into a pew, a pew they all but filled. "Now that school's out my brothers and sisters would enjoy a new playmate. Ask Hannah to bring you for a visit."

"Can we, Hannah?"

Why hadn't she thought Allie would want to play with children? She'd take the time to bring Allie to town this very week. "We'd love to come."

A visit would give Hannah a good opportunity to ask Leah's advice on handling Allie's ploys to delay bedtime. She and Matt might be too easy on the child, but they didn't want to risk making her homesick for her grandmother.

Hannah, Matt and Allie settled into their pew near the front. Allie craned her neck to gawk at the Montgomery family two rows behind them. Hannah named the children for Allie and gave their ages.

In the pew behind the Montgomerys sat a stranger, unusual in this town. A lovely woman, her dark hair swept up beneath a wide-brimmed hat, she was staring at Hannah. Or was it Matt? Hannah smiled at her. The woman smiled back. Upon closer inspection, she looked vaguely familiar, yet Hannah couldn't place her.

Bertram Bailey shot to his feet, tugged on his waistcoat and rattled off a page number in the hymnal. On Sundays, he led singing with the same energy he ran his store. Soon voices blended with the piano, filling the sanctuary with harmonious tribute to God.

At the conclusion of the last song, Pastor Cummings stood behind the pulpit. He smiled down at her, as if welcoming her back, then opened his Bible. "Today, I'm reading from the Book of James, Chapter Three." The words the pastor read warned believers to tame their tongues. He reminded them that gossip, lies and curses all came out of the same mouths as mercy, truths and blessings. "But the tongue can no man tame; it is an unruly evil, full of deadly poison."

Many chattered about other people's comings and goings in Bliss, but thankfully Hannah hadn't known anyone to try to ruin reputations or to deceive.

After the closing prayer the congregation rose, chatting as they headed toward Pastor Cummings shaking hands at the door.

The dark-haired stranger stepped into the aisle. Parishioners greeted her as they flowed past. She nodded and smiled, but had her eyes fixed on Matt.

As they reached her, the woman beamed. "Matthew, how good to see you."

Hannah glanced at her husband's face. His blank expression slowly transformed into a smile. "Julia? Julia Phillips?"

"You remembered," she said.

The quiet joy in her tone, as if his remembering mattered, sent a shiver down Hannah's spine. Who was this woman?

Matt cocked his head. "I haven't seen you in, goodness, six, seven years."

"Seven."

"What brings you back to town?"

Her expression flooded with sympathy as she rested a gloved hand on Matt's sleeve. "I heard about Amy." Her gaze landed on Hannah, then slid back to Matt. "I'm sorry for your loss."

"Thank you. Ah, Amy's been gone four years."

"Well, I just heard."

Matt glanced at Hannah. "Oh, forgive me. Julia, this is my wife, Hannah. And this is Allie," he said motioning to the child.

"Your wife," Miss Phillips said blankly, as if she couldn't understand the term. "I didn't realize you'd remarried."

"We haven't been married long."

Miss Phillip's gaze landed on Allie. "She isn't your daughter?"

"Allie's the great-niece of a friend. We're enjoying her stay at the ranch."

"Oh, how nice." A smile on her lips, Miss Phillips leaned down, peered into Allie's eyes. "Aren't you the prettiest little girl? Why, you're the age of…" Her voice trailed off, then she straightened. "Matthew, I'm sure I'll see you around town. I'm glad to meet you, Hannah," she said, but her gaze remained on Allie.

"You're staying in Bliss?" Matt said.

She turned toward him. "Yes, I work at the Calico Café and rent a room overhead."

Hands fluttering like the plumes on her hat, Mrs. Cummings, the pastor's jovial wife, darted to them, then drew Miss Phillips into a one-armed hug. "In town only a week, and already Julia has volunteered to assist with Sunday school." She tugged the young woman against her ample frame. "You've blessed me more than I can say."

The pastor's wife gushed on to Miss Phillips as Hannah, Matt and Allie moved up the aisle, and spoke to the preacher and others. Matt and Allie headed for the buggy. Delayed by a member of the congregation who'd been ill when Papa died and wanted to offer his condolences, Hannah trailed behind.

She passed the newcomer. "Nice to meet you, Miss Phillips."

Miss Phillips bent close as if to give Hannah a friendly embrace. "I didn't expect you," she said in a harsh whisper against Hannah's cheek. "That complicates things."

Goose bumps rose on Hannah's arms. Before Hannah could react, the woman sashayed off. But the chill remained. Hannah might not understand what Miss Phillips meant, but she understood a threat when she heard it. The peace she'd sought and found in worship had been destroyed.

On the way to the ranch, Hannah ran the encounter with Julia Phillips through her mind. The way she'd focused on Matt and Allie, all but eating them up with her eyes. That puzzling remark she'd made in private.

"Matt, how do you know Julia Phillips?"

"We go way back. Went to high school together."

"She was a friend of Amy's?"

The question seemed to puzzle him. "I wouldn't say a friend. More like a classmate." He glanced at Allie sitting between them. "I'll explain. Later."

Allie crossed her arms, a scowl on her face. "Kids never get to hear the good stuff."

Matt tugged the ribbon on Allie's hair. "Is that right?" Over Allie's head, he and Hannah shared a smile. "Well, does this rate as good stuff? I'd like to take you, Jake and Hannah fishing this evening."

"Whoopee! I've never been fishing." The smile back in place, Allie chattered away.

Hannah didn't hear a word the little girl said. Like a stuck phonograph, Miss Phillips' words kept running through her mind. The woman spoke in riddles.

During a break in the conversation, Hannah said, "Any idea why Miss Phillips moved back to Bliss? Surely not to offer condolences."

"I'm certain something else brought her here."

"Like what?"

He shrugged. "Hard to say. A job for one."

Pastor Cummings's sermon popped into Hannah's mind. If she wasn't careful, she'd be slandering a woman she'd just met.

But one thing she knew, she'd go along when Matt made his next trip to town.

At Matt's invitation to go fishing, Jake had agreed, returning a few minutes later with a bait bucket, tackle box and pole. "Ain't put a hook in the water in ages."

On the way to the creek, Jake rode in the lead, Hannah followed on Star and Matt with Allie perched in front of him brought up the rear.

The beauty of the Texas landscape stretched before him as far as his eye could see. Bluebonnets and Indian paintbrush dotted the countryside. Overhead, filmy clouds brushed across the blue sky. A mockingbird sang on a fence post nearby. Parrish cattle grazed in the pasture. A few lifted their large heads to stare as they passed, then returned to their mindless munching.

Near the fence, mustang grapevines grew over scrubby bushes. In midsummer he'd return to pick the small ripe black-skinned grapes Ma made into jam. No, he'd pick the grapes for his wife, not his mother, though most likely Rosa would be the one making the jam. He grinned. A good thing, if Hannah's attempt at a pie was any indication.

At the pecan grove, they hitched the horses to low limbs, then carrying fishing equipment and a bag of cookies, they walked to the stream. Allie dipped and skipped along, a human bobber if Matt ever saw one.

Alongside the creek, they found a comfy spot. Jake set down his gear, then baited Allie's hook. With the line swinging between them, he handed her the wooden pole he'd whittled from a tree limb years before.

"Be careful of that hook, Allie girl. It's sharp."

Matt knelt beside her. "If the bobber goes under, that means you've got a bite." He showed her how to grip the pole. "If you do, jerk back on the pole like this," he said, demonstrating the technique. "That'll set the hook in the fish's mouth."

"Does the hook hurt the fish?" Brows furrowed, Allie gnawed on a fingertip.

With a sweep of his hand, Matt turned to Jake. About time Jake took his uncle role.

"Don't rightly know," Jake muttered. "Reckon not much. They survive it just fine."

What Jake didn't say—any fish they caught would turn up in the frying pan.

With Matt on one side, Jake on the other, Allie settled on her haunches, waiting for a strike.

"Largest fish I ever caught was nineteen inches," Matt said. "Still remember that day."

"Largest fish I ever caught would've fed a bunkhouse full of drovers," Jake said, eyes on the bobber.

Hannah arched a brow. "Aren't you exaggerating a bit?"

"Been a lot of years since I wet a line. Memory's bound to fail a feller."

Matt chuckled. "Doesn't matter, Allie. Big or small, they all taste good."

The bobber dipped. "I got a fish!" Allie scrambled to her feet as the bobber moved across the water. "Help me!"

"Pull up on the pole, Allie, like Matt showed you," Jake said. "That's the way."

But whatever was on the other end of the line had some fight in him. Jake grabbed hold and helped his great-niece pull in an eight-inch bass that flopped on the creek bank.

"He's big!" Allie's eyes shone as she reached down to touch the scales, peer into the round eyes.

Matt patted her head. "Sure is."

Jake clutched the wiggling fish and removed the hook from its mouth, then strung the bass on a line tethered at the water's edge.

Hannah put an arm around Allie's shoulders. "You did it, Allie. You caught your first fish."

"Uncle Jake helped." She sobered. "Next time, I want to do it by myself."

Matt chucked Allie under the chin. "Nothing wrong with getting some help."

He sat beside Hannah on the grass. "Don't know if you're rubbing off on Allie or if that stubborn independence of hers comes naturally," he said with a chuckle.

"Either way, she's just fine."

"Yes, she is." Their eyes met, Hannah's warm, proud almost as if she were Allie's mom. Odd how quickly that child had become part of their life.

"Uncle Jake," Allie said. "Is Grandma going to die?"

In the process of putting a worm on the hook, Jake dropped the wiggly bait. "Gertie's doing fine, Allie."

"She's old."

"Well, that's true."

"You are, too. What if Mama doesn't come back? Where will I live if you and Grandma die?"

"No point worrying about what could be a long ways off. Why, I'm too stubborn to die anytime soon."

Allie didn't look convinced.

Matt's throat knotted, his gaze locked with Hannah's. He read the question in hers, the same question in his. At his nod, Hannah nodded, too. They could no more turn away from Allie, than they could forsake this ranch.

"You can live here, Allie," Matt said.

"You'll always have a home with Matt and me."

The little girl turned to them, a smile as wide as the whole outdoors. "I can live here? Even if Uncle Jake doesn't?"

"We feel like we're your family, too."

"You're a fortunate little girl to have two homes and

lots of folks who care about you," Jake said, swiping at his eyes.

"Mama loves me, too," Allie said, in a tone that forbade anyone to disagree.

"She's your mama," Jake said. "How could she not?"

Matt hadn't lost a parent, not to death or desertion, but he knew the pain of a severed relationship. He suspected Hannah had felt as abandoned as Allie when Melanie Parrish had died.

He tucked Hannah close. "You'll always have me, too," he said.

She glanced away, as if their marriage of convenience didn't bring her comfort. Did she feel as he had with his father until recently, that their relationship of father and son was in name only? That possibility bothered him. Yet they were managing, walking that line, doing the best they could.

As Jake dug into the bait bucket in search of another worm, Matt rose and took Hannah's hand. "We'll watch from over here," he called, then led Hannah to a felled log near the water. "This should be far enough away we can't be overheard."

"You're going to tell me about Julia."

"Yes." He sighed. "It's not a pretty story. Julia got pregnant out of wedlock. Caused quite a stir in town."

"Who was the father?"

"Don't know. I suspect he left town and she didn't see the point in naming him. Some folks treated her badly. You know, walked passed her, didn't speak, as if she wasn't there. Her parents weren't much better. Amy and I would talk to her. Ask how she was feeling, stuff like that."

"She was appreciative."

"Yes. Not that we spent much time with her. She dropped out of school, but I'd see her in town now and again when I came for church, for school. To visit Amy."

At the mention of Amy's name, Hannah's eyes clouded. He suspected Hannah believed he still loved his wife. The truth would shock her.

She frowned. "What happened to her baby? Did she put it up for adoption?"

"The baby died a couple hours after birth."

"Oh, no."

"Losing that baby hit Julia hard. She was always crying. Her family moved away not long afterward, taking her with them. Said they wanted to start over. As I recall, they left town about a week before Amy and I got married."

"She must've been sorry to miss the ceremony."

Matt shrugged. "I don't think so. She avoided all the wedding talk. Not easy, when the wedding was Amy's prime topic of conversation. Probably reminded Julia of all she'd lost."

"That's sad. I feel sorry for her. But, she said the oddest thing to me at church."

"What?"

"She said, 'I didn't expect you. That complicates things.' Almost like she believed I interfered with her plan to have you."

He shook his head. "That's crazy talk. Are you sure you heard her right? The Julia I knew was never mean or conniving."

"I heard her right."

"Well, no telling what she meant. Hope she can find

some happiness here. Reckon with a town named Bliss, she should."

Not that he'd found any truth to the town's claim.

Still, across the way, Allie and Jake were having fun, no doubt reassured by the promise of a home for Allie. He and his pa were moving along the trail—perhaps a bumpy trail—toward accord. He and Hannah shared the goals on the ranch and affection for Allie. The future looked good.

Julia might be odd, but she wouldn't bring them harm.

Chapter Eighteen

On Monday morning, Hannah pulled up in front of the Montgomery house, then wound the reins around the hitching post. She'd promised Allie a visit with Leah's siblings. Allie was practically popping out of her skin with excitement. She clambered off the buggy seat, her upper lip beaded with perspiration, a smile wide on her face. Hannah welcomed a day away from responsibilities at the ranch, too.

Yet uncertainties niggled inside her. What if some section of barbed wire didn't hold? Or the windmill broke down? Or they didn't get the rain they desperately needed?

She tamped down all the qualms running through her mind, grabbed a handkerchief and patted her damp face. Ten o'clock and already the heat rolled in waves that took her breath away. The black buttoned-up mourning dress stuck to her skin and drew the sun's rays.

"Hello!" Leah motioned from the porch. "I've got lemonade waiting."

Within minutes, the five children downed their cold

drinks, then scampered around the shady yard in a game of hide-and-seek, oblivious to the sweltering temperature.

On the porch, Hannah removed her hat, then lolled in the wicker rocker, sipping from a tall glass, totally at ease as she and Leah watched the children and talked about the weather.

"So." Leah arched a brow, her eyes twinkling. "How's married life?"

Heat that had nothing to do with the temperature flooded her cheeks. Why hadn't she thought to bring her fan? "Uh, fine."

Leah chuckled. "That blush on your face tells me your marriage is better than fine. I'd say you're a happily married woman, Hannah Walker. Not that I expected anything else with that man you married." Leah grinned. "Wouldn't surprise me if you announced you're expecting."

Hannah choked on the lemonade she'd swallowed, then went into a fit of coughing.

"You okay?"

"Fine." Leah would faint dead away if she knew Matt and Hannah didn't share a room. Hadn't shared more than a few kisses.

Leah propped her chin in her hands. "Tell me. What's it like to be Mrs. Matt Walker? What's he like?"

"He's kind and ah, gentle."

Leah nodded once, twice, obviously wanting more.

"And, well…funny. He makes me feel safe. Special."

"Spoken like a woman in love." Leah sighed, then her smile faded. "I was afraid losing your father would make things difficult for you both."

"Matt's been very considerate." She'd appreciated the care he'd taken with her, the sympathy he'd extended. "He mourns Papa, too."

"He sounds wonderful."

Though the talk about wedded bliss had Hannah as edgy as an untamed horse being broken to saddle, she recalled the straggly bluebonnets Matt had brought her as a peace offering.

The way he'd tugged her to him after Papa died, insisting it was all right to cry.

His attempt to sweeten the mess she'd made of her first pie.

He'd perceived her needs and gave generously of himself, trying to meet them; unlike some men she'd witnessed who were long on orders and short on tenderness.

"I envy you, Hannah. No one in this town comes close to being suitable." She sighed. "I want what you have. A husband who makes me feel special."

Special.

Matt did make Hannah feel special, but always with the nagging reminder that they had married for business, not for love. Matt had made it clear he'd never love again.

That was fine. Just fine. She took a sip of lemonade, but the drink soured on her tongue.

"What about Zack?" she said, directing the conversation back to Leah.

Leah's lips turned down. "He's written me only twice. He came to Bliss for your wedding and your father's funeral, but never to see me." She sighed. "I felt a spark between us, but obviously that spark fizzled."

"His law practice may keep him too busy to come."

"Maybe. But, if you care for someone, nothing keeps you apart."

Hannah slid two fingers down her glass, wiping away the moisture in their path. How could she and Matt spend day after day together, as close as these two fingers, yet still be so far apart. Separated by something Hannah couldn't quite name.

Well, she no longer clung to the silly schoolgirl fantasy, but wouldn't ruin Leah's expectations for marriage.

"Anyway, let's talk about something else," Leah said. "Something fun like the kids. How's temporary motherhood?"

"Allie's a great little girl, but she resists bedtime. Most nights it takes us an hour or more to get her to settle down."

Leah chuckled. "Lots of children use one excuse after another to delay bedtime."

"You don't think anything's wrong? The first night she cried for her grandmother. Maybe she's afraid. Or feels deserted by her family."

"If she's not still upset, crying or having nightmares, I suspect she's got you and Matt wrapped around her pinkie," Leah said, wagging her little finger. "Have you tried giving her a glass of water, leaving on a kerosene night-light, then just leaving the room?"

"She clings to us for one more story, one more drink, one more hug."

"This is what we do with my brothers and sisters. After one story, one drink, one kiss, we say 'sleep tight' then leave. If Allie calls, ignore her. If she comes out, take her back to bed. Use a firm tone. Refuse to let her run the household."

After Hannah's mother died, Papa had stayed with her at bedtime until she'd fallen asleep. Was it cruel to expect more of Allie? To expect her to sleep in a strange house? Without her family?

"Thanks for the suggestions," Hannah said, then rose and hugged her friend.

"Yeah, all this wisdom about raising kids, yet I can't find a man who wants to spend his life with me and give me some."

"You will. You're pretty, smart, feminine as they come. And only nineteen." She clapped her hands together. "Oh, why don't you invite Zack to the Fourth of July picnic? It's the perfect occasion to see if there's still a spark."

Leah's face brightened. "You know, Hannah Walker, you may not know much about children, but you're shrewd about matters of the heart."

Hannah ran a finger around the high neck of her collar. If Leah realized the absurdity of her claim, she'd be aghast. "We'd better be going." She settled her straw hat in place, then slid her hatpin in the crown. "I promised Allie dinner at the café."

She called Allie's name, but getting the little girl to leave her new friends and into the buggy took ten minutes.

Leah leaned close to Hannah. "Yep, she has you wrapped tight. Nothing wrong with that, as long as she doesn't cut off your circulation. If you get my meaning," she said with a wink.

"What?"

Leah chuckled. "You're hopeless. By cut off your circulation, I mean with Matt, your time together. Don't let Allie keep you two apart."

If anything Allie brought them together when Hannah knew full well keeping them apart was a good thing. Keeping them from more of those confusing kisses. But Hannah merely gave Leah a nod, untied the reins, about to climb in the buggy.

Matt rode up on Thunder. "Hi, ladies." He tipped his hat to Leah, standing off to the side, watching their every move. Then swung down and strode toward the buggy. "You having fun, Allie?"

The smile on Allie's face said she was delighted to see him. Exactly what Leah would expect from Hannah, especially after everything she'd told Leah earlier. She would have to act lovey-dovey. A part she'd played before.

"Hi, Sweetheart," Hannah cooed, gazing at him with what she hoped were adoring eyes.

At her welcome, Matt jerked his head, ever so slightly, then gave a big smile and her arm a gentle squeeze. "Hello, wife."

"What a nice surprise. I didn't expect to see you in town."

"I promised Pastor Cummings I'd fix the railing on the church steps this afternoon. On my way through town, Martin's lawyer called to me. Wants you to stop in and sign a paper before you leave today."

"Thanks for bringing me the message."

"I'll see you at home," he said, his tone eager.

And grinding on every one of Hannah's nerves. "Do you want to join Allie and me for dinner at the café?"

"No time. You two have fun." He leaned down and kissed her cheek, staring into her eyes. "Don't stay away too long."

In a few strides, he swung into the saddle, tipped his hat to Leah, then rode off.

A dreamy look on her face, a sigh on her lips, Leah clasped her hands in front of her bosom. "Oh, you are the luckiest woman alive."

"I am." Hannah gave her brightest smile, then climbed into the buggy and flicked the reins.

Lucky hardly described her life. She'd come to town to give Allie friends to play with and forget her duties at the ranch. Forget Matt. Or try to. Instead his interruption had forced her into performing the second act in a three-act play. When would the curtain go down and expose the real Walker marriage?

On the square, the bench sitters were doing an admirable job of keeping their fingers on the town's pulse. Hannah ushered Allie to the gentlemen and introduced her.

"Howdy-do, young lady," Mr. Cooper said. "Nice to meet ya."

"Thank you."

"Ain't it a hot one for May? Hot enough to wither a fence post."

Mr. Brand nodded. "'Cept for our lips a'flapping, there ain't a puff of breeze."

Mr. Seller turned speculative eyes on Hannah. "Heard you was running the ranch yerself. One of your peeved cowpokes said he and yer foreman quit afore they'd work for a woman."

Mr. Cooper nodded. "Reckon ya got Matt to see everything gits done."

As if Hannah were merely a figurehead with no involvement in the operation of the ranch. She wouldn't grace the comment with a response. "We're off to the café."

"Git yerself a piece of the pecan pie. Nothin' better in that diner," Mr. Brand said. "Well, 'cept Miss Phillips. She's a real looker."

Hannah ushered Allie toward the Calico Café, steeling herself for an encounter with Julia. Inside she glimpsed the waitress out of the corner of her eye, and saw when Julia fixed her eyes on Allie.

"Come on, Allie. Let's take a table by the window," Hannah said, steering her across the room and into a seat. "Oh, look, at the pretty posies on the table. I love flowers, don't you?"

"Well, hello. Welcome to the Calico Café." Julia held out menus. "Here's one for you, Sweetie Pie."

"Hi." Allie took the menu in her hand. "I remember you."

"I could never forget *you*." Julia smiled down at Allie, who smiled right back. "Why, your smile is brighter than a sunbeam in summer."

Allie giggled, tucking her hair behind her ear, obviously delighted by the attention.

They ordered drinks. "Allie, did you look at the menu? See what you want?" Hannah said.

"Be right back for your order." Julia patted Allie on the head.

With Julia gone, Hannah folded her arms on the table

and leaned toward Allie. "Did you have fun with the Montgomery children?"

"We played hide-and-seek. Abe's nice. He saw me hiding behind a bush, but found me last." She giggled. "Anna's the boss of everybody, but she let me pick the first game." Allie inhaled. "Pete's speedy, runs like the wind." Her brow furrowed. "Susie's a crybaby. She's only six." Allie puffed out her chest as if a year made her far older. "Leah's pretty, but not as fun cause she's a grown-up."

After only a couple of hours in their company, Allie's descriptions were both accurate and amusing. "So grown-ups aren't much fun, huh?"

Julia returned with Allie's milk and Hannah's ice water. She plunked Hannah's drink in front of her, then bent toward Allie. "Here you go, Sweetie. Careful not to spill on your pretty dress."

"Thank you."

Julia crouched beside Allie, bringing herself to the child's level. "Aren't you a polite little girl. What grade are you in school?"

"Second," Allie said. "I can read good. Add and subtract."

"I loved to read when I was your age. What are your favorite stories?"

"I like books about animals." Allie's face lit. "We've got baby kittens at the ranch."

Hannah cleared her throat. "We probably should order." But Julia ignored the not so subtle hint.

"Oh, how sweet. What do the kittens look like?"

"Like tigers, only littler."

"Have you given them names?"

"I tried, but I keep getting them mixed up." Allie grinned. "So I call all of them Tiger."

"Aren't you smart. You won't get the name wrong."

Giggling, Allie leaned on her elbows, gazing up at Julia, obviously taken with the interloper. Hannah had looked forward to having a meal with only the two of them, expecting the outing would give her and Allie a chance to bond.

Instead Julia had commandeered the table the way a pirate seized a ship at sea, making Hannah the outsider. Or trying to.

"Do you have a special doll?" Julia asked.

"I like Ruth best. She's Hannah's doll. She sleeps with me cause she doesn't have a bed."

Hannah set her menu aside. "I'd like the special."

Julia didn't glance her way. "When I was little I loved dolls," she said. "Especially with open and close eyes."

"Julia, food's waiting to be served." Mrs. Shields stood at the kitchen door, a frown on her face.

"Oh, goodness." Julia smiled at Allie. "Be right back, Sweetie."

Throughout the meal, Julia hovered nearby, refilling Allie's glass of milk, praising Allie for her fine table manners, buying Allie a red lollipop from the stash for sale on the front counter.

Hannah wrung the napkin in her lap. Nothing wrong with all that attention, not really. Yet Julia had wheedled her way into what should've been Hannah's special time with Allie. Why, the woman might as well have taken a seat and joined them at the table.

Then she remembered Papa after Mama and the baby died. He'd stare at the empty cradle near the fireplace, then quickly look away with tears in his eyes. For three months that cradle stayed there, then one day the cradle was gone. Hannah knew Mama and the baby who should've filled the cradle were never far from Papa's mind. How could she resent a wounded woman for connecting with Allie?

But how could she trust Miss Phillips after that weird comment she made outside of church yesterday?

Finished with the meal, Hannah and Allie were leaving the restaurant when Julia met them near the door. "Come back and see me, Allie."

"Thank you for the lollipop, Miss Phillips."

"You're welcome, Sweetie." She touched the bow in Allie's shiny dark hair. "I feel like we're friends. Call me Julia."

"Okay," Allie said, "Bye, Julia."

"I'll have a lollipop waiting for you."

To ask Allie to call a virtual stranger by her first name tightened every muscle in Hannah's body. As she helped Allie into the buggy, she glanced back toward the café.

Julia stood at the door watching them. Then she called to Allie and waved.

With a flick of the reins, Hannah started the buggy for home. She couldn't get there fast enough.

Mrs. Shields was an excellent cook, but today, the food in Hannah's stomach churned. Why had Julia Phillips taken such a consuming interest in a child she didn't know?

Chapter Nineteen

Matt folded his arms across the top rail of the fence. "The way Allie went right to sleep last night, I'd say the day in town yesterday must've done her good."

With her desire to get back to work, to get back to normal, Hannah had shrugged off her worries about Julia Phillips. But Matt's comment brought the woman's strange behavior to mind. Her stomach rolled, and not from the noon meal they'd just eaten.

"Are you troubled about something?" Matt tipped back the brim of his hat to get a better look at her.

"No, just concerned about this cow."

From their side of the fence, Hannah and Matt inspected the cow and her calf. One of the heifer's corneas was cloudy, her eyeball red, inflamed and weepy. She swung her head, bellowed, obviously in a nasty mood.

Hannah couldn't blame her. "Pinkeye."

"Yep, she's losing weight. Probably not up to looking for feed and water. Should know in a month, maybe two, if she's on the mend or will lose her sight in that eye. Or worse."

"I've seen pinkeye before," Hannah said. "We'll need to be vigilant. Find and isolate infected cattle so this thing doesn't spread."

"The cow's other eye looks good. Something may have irritated that eyeball. If that's the case, this won't spread." He laid a hand over hers. "In the meantime, stay clear of her. Never seen a more cantankerous female."

With her elbow, she gave him a light teasing jab. "Keep giving orders if you want to see a doubly cantankerous female."

A lopsided grin on his face, he leaned close, studying her. "Better cantankerous than injured. Please, stay out of that pen. This gal's hurting and isn't partial to company."

With a noncommittal nod, Hannah turned away. When would Matt believe she could handle cattle? Even cantankerous cattle?

"Not much we can do for the cow. But if she doesn't eat well, her calf will suffer," she said.

"Once I'm back from greasing the windmill, we'll see that the calf gets nourishment."

Hannah had trained calves to drink milk from a bucket. Not hard to do.

A buggy drove under the Lazy P arch, interrupting the conversation. Visitors during the week were rare. Hannah watched the buggy's progress, trying to make out the driver's face.

"Oh, Julia Phillips," Matt said. "Wonder why she's here."

"Me, too," Hannah said. "Me, too."

Julia pulled into the barnyard. Matt crossed to the

buggy, spoke to Julia, then offered his hand, helping her down.

Hannah clenched her jaw so tight her teeth hurt. Julia had fawned over Allie at the café, now she was here at the Lazy P, touching Matt.

Dressed in ruffles and lace, a jaunty hat and gloves, feminine and beautiful, the woman could turn any man's head. But if that flirty smile she gave Matt meant anything, the only man's head she seemed intent on turning was Matt's.

Hannah's gaze dropped to her attire, smudged britches, rumpled shirt, dusty boots. She considered ducking into the barn. But wouldn't leave Julia alone with Matt. Hannah marched to the two of them.

Julia laid a dainty gloved hand on Matt's arm and gazed up at him with eyes filled with adoration. "Thank you, Matt. You're such a gentleman."

Matt's kindness to Julia all those years ago didn't explain this flirtatious behavior. With a married man.

Hers.

"What brings you here?" Hannah said.

Julia pressed a gloved hand to her nose. "Working hard today, Hannah?" Julia's smile held an edge, but then she turned to Matt. "Your wife defines helpmate to a T. You must be proud of her."

"I am."

Matt's tone was strong, his words certain. Still, he hadn't rebuked Julia for belittling Hannah, which was exactly what she was doing.

Inside Hannah, temptation reared its ugly head. She'd like to toss this woman, fancy finery and all, into a pile of manure. Even that fine perfume Julia swathed herself in wouldn't cover that stench.

To keep from doing that very thing, Hannah fixed a smile to her face. "You haven't said why you're here."

"Why, I've come to see Allie," Julia said, her voice filled with anticipation.

As if the child had heard her name, Allie raced out the barn door from a visit with the kittens, then skidded to a stop in front of Julia. "Hi!" Allie said, eyes aglow, obviously delighted to see the intruder.

"Hello, Sweet Girl." Julia bent down and patted Allie's cheek. "I brought you a gift."

She reached into the buggy and brought out a doll-sized four-poster mahogany bed with a lacy canopy and coverlet, much like Aunt Mary Esther's bed in Charleston. That fancy doll bed had to cost a considerable sum of money.

"I was passing the Dry Goods Store this morning and saw this in the window and thought of you. Ruth deserves her own special bed, don't you think?"

"The gift is too much," Hannah said. "Really, you didn't have to do that."

"I know I didn't." Julia turned to gaze at Matt. "But this little girl is so sweet I couldn't resist."

"Well, thank you, Julia," Matt said. "That's mighty kind."

"Want to meet Ruth, Julia?"

"Oh, yes, I'd love to."

Without hesitation, Allie took the hand Julia offered and they strolled toward the house.

Hannah folded her arms across her chest as she turned to Matt. "That woman infuriates me."

"She is a nuisance."

"Nuisance? She's trouble. She practically drools over you."

"If you believe Julia means something to me, you're dead wrong."

Hannah snorted. "Like you didn't notice her feminine curves and fancy clothes."

He wagged his brows. "Your clothes appeal to me more. Must be the woman wearing them."

Julia Phillips was everything Hannah wasn't. She held out her callused work-reddened hands. "Look at my hands. Have you seen Julia's? They're dainty, dimpled—"

"Your hands are capable of branding cattle, handling a horse, tucking a child into bed." He chuckled. "Even baking a pie."

"No doubt Julia Phillips wouldn't forget the sugar when she makes her perfect pie."

As if he found the conversation amusing, Matt merely grinned at her.

No wonder. Like an idiot she'd listed Julia's assets, as if he hadn't already noticed. Matt had attempted to ease her mind about that woman with all this silly banter. Not that the ploy worked. Julia set her teeth on edge, but when it came to seeing trouble of the female kind, men were gullible.

"Be on guard with Julia."

"You're overreacting. Julia's lonely. Lost a child. She's obviously smitten with Allie, but—"

"That doesn't concern you?"

"Who wouldn't be? Allie's a delight."

"No one else in town makes a huge fuss over Allie

like Julia does. She buys Allie gifts, comes for a visit. Uninvited. Compliments her for everything but breathing."

"I don't see the harm in that."

A hundred different possibilities for harm marched through Hannah's mind. Julia treated Matt and Allie as if she believed they belonged to her. Why couldn't Matt see Julia's behavior was odd? The bargain she and Matt had signed might one day be sealed with affection. But with Julia around, the possibility of fondness between them seemed doomed to failure.

"Well, that windmill won't grease itself. Jake's going with me to ride fence and save my hide if I fall."

"Don't you dare fall," she said.

With a chuckle, he leaned down and gave her a peck on the cheek.

"A kiss doesn't mask the truth, Matt Walker. Julia Phillips is up to no good."

He chucked her under the chin. "Jealous?"

"Don't be ridiculous. If you've changed your mind about our marriage and want Julia Phillips, be my guest." Even as she uttered the words her stomach lurched.

The gaze he turned on her exuded anger, hurt. "Those vows we took were for as long as we both shall live," he said, tone steely, eyes hardening into glittering coal.

She meant to keep those vows. Wanted him to keep them, too. Till death do us part. But she remained silent.

He trotted toward his horse. Long-legged, wide shouldered, brawny armed, one gorgeous work-honed package encasing a good heart, a committed will, a strong faith.

Hannah's jaw dropped. Was it possible? Was she starting to fall in love with her husband? Had feelings for Matt made her see a problem with Julia where none existed? Had jealousy distorted her perceptions as Matt had intimated?

Why not admit it? Matt was becoming the center of her world. Just by entering a room, he made her pulse race. He made her laugh. He made her feel safe.

Tears filled her eyes. She'd believed the worst thing imaginable was to marry a man she didn't love. Now she knew that caring about a man who'd never love her in return was far worse.

With every breath in her, she'd fight those unwanted feelings. From now on, she'd handle the work on the ranch and tiptoe around her husband.

She couldn't keep kissing him, couldn't keep walking into the circle of his arms, couldn't keep playing this newlywed game. A game she'd lose.

Just as she'd lost everyone she'd loved most.

Matt and Jake rode out to grease the windmill. Not that the job required two men, but Jake had suggested he go along and ride fence. Probably feared Matt would fall off that tower, something he had no intention of doing. Still Matt was glad for the company.

"I appreciate you and Hannah taking Allie in," Jake said.

"Allie's a great kid. We're both fond of her. Not sure how we'll manage when she goes back home."

"Thought you and Hannah might be eager to see her go, being newlyweds and all."

What did a man say to that? Better to keep his mouth nailed shut.

Jake sighed. "Gertie's losing steam. My sis and I are getting old."

"When we said Allie would have a home here, we meant it."

The cowpoke released a gust. "Not that I'm trying to play God. A feller don't know what the future holds." He motioned across the way to some buzzards circling overhead. "But I can't pretend otherwise. Dying is natural, part of living, the cycle of life we see every day on this ranch. Cows die. Calves are born. We ain't got a say in any of it."

"Do you believe stuff just happens?"

"Not sure what you mean."

"Do you think accidents just happen? Or is God numbering our days?"

"Can't rightly say, but God's got the power to change the outcome. He allows what He allows. Ain't gonna question His wisdom." Jake tugged at his frayed cuff. "Even if my sis lives to be old as Methuselah, not sure that little imp will be happy with Gertie after the excitement of the ranch. Not sure how much longer Gertie can keep up with a child."

Matt chuckled. "That's a job, for sure. We'd need to talk to the women first, of course. But, I'm guessing Hannah and Gertie will want Allie to stay where she'll be happier."

Jake smiled, deepening the lines in his craggy face. "Gotta say, Matt, you've relieved my mind."

Up ahead the windmill rose into the sky. Beside it, cattle waded in the earthen tank. Jake rode off to look for breaks in the barbed wire fence.

Matt swung down, grabbed the grease pot and climbed the forty-foot windmill tower. His gaze settled on the herd grazing in the distance. A mighty fine view. Not his favorite perch but nothing compared to the peril of getting close to his wife.

Why, earlier, Hannah had practically handed Julia Phillips over to him. Blast it all, they were married. Married meant unavailable. Period.

As much as Matt didn't trust his feelings, knew he dared not rely on his judgment, he couldn't keep his distance with Hannah. Couldn't stop wanting to hold her in his arms. Couldn't stop wanting to kiss her. Not that his feisty wife gave him many openings.

He hooked his arm around the metal, holding the bail of the pot in that hand, then put the mill out of gear and greased the mechanism.

Matt knew his way around a ranch. Knew his way around horses. Knew his way around cattle. Much about the land, the weather, the animals was unpredictable. But nowhere near as changeable as women.

Women were baffling puzzles. Not surprising when he'd grown up in a household of men. His sensible Ma hardly counted. With Ma, he didn't need to be a mind reader. She spoke freely in language a man understood.

If only he could interpret his wife's words and actions as easily. Even Allie played that game upon occasion. He had no idea how to soothe his wife.

He had even less idea how to decipher Julia's conduct. Hannah saw Julia as a threat. Julia had flirted with him, but how could the woman be a threat when he had no interest in her? Still, with Julia butting into their lives, the added strain could sever the fragile thread of his and Hannah's connection.

One thing he knew. He'd stay clear of Julia. Not that he found the woman attractive or a menace, but she might misread the slightest kindness for something more.

His hand slipped and he wobbled, then tightened his grip. Better keep his attention on the chore at hand and off his wife, lest he break his fool neck.

He put the windmill in gear, then climbed down the tower. On the ground, he gazed up at the mill spinning without a sound. With a nod of satisfaction, he untied Thunder and swung into the saddle.

Jake rode up. "Fence is solid in this section."

"Nice to hear." Matt glanced at Jake. Never married, but still a man with wisdom. "Jake, you understand women?"

Hooting like a barn owl, Jake slapped his knee. "Only thing more unpredictable than a longhorn is a woman. Reckon the reason I never got hitched." He grinned at Matt. "Still, who needs to understand something so pretty to look at?"

Matt chuckled. "You've got a point."

"If it's all right with you, I'll ride on to the south pasture. Check that fence while I'm at it."

"Good idea. See you back at the house," Matt said, then rode for home.

He would check on that heifer and calf he'd wrestled to the corral. And on his wife. He might not understand women, but he agreed with Jake. Just looking at his pretty wife was worth every bit of his confusion.

Chapter Twenty

An hour spent watching Julia rope Allie in with compliments and gifts had Hannah cranked tighter than an overwound clock. Not able to take it any longer, Hannah had walked out to the stables and cleaned tack. Finished with the chore, she found Julia's rig was gone. Finally, the woman had left. Left Hannah's mind churning with possibilities. Possibilities that threatened Hannah's wobbly world. Julia's obsession with Allie and Matt put the life Hannah had built in peril.

Hannah had to do something to work out all her pent-up frustration or she'd burst. She strode to the corral, turning her gaze on the calf. The poor thing was unsteady on his legs, clearly in need of more nourishment. To train a calf to drink from a bucket was a sloppy task, but hungry calves learned fast.

The only obstacle—his cantankerous mother.

The heifer stood in the far end of the corral, turned away from the bright rays of the sun, her backside to Hannah. She wasn't eating. Wasn't producing sufficient milk.

Across the way, the calf moseyed toward the barn door. Why, in a couple of minutes, Hannah could have that calf inside.

Matt had asked her to stay clear of the heifer, but that calf could die while Matt was forty feet in the air, greasing the windmill. Jake had ridden with him to check fence. If he found breaks in the fence, they would repair the barbed wire. No telling when they'd return.

With Allie in the house with Rosa, Hannah had an opportunity to save that calf.

She moved to the section of the fence nearest the barn and farthest from the heifer. If she descended the rails real easy like, then moved slow and steady, she could guide the calf into the barn before the cow knew what happened.

With her eyes on the heifer, Hannah eased over the top rail and lowered herself into the corral. The sick cow showed no awareness of Hannah's presence. Hannah edged toward the calf, was steps away. Soon she'd have him drinking from a pail.

A bellow. Hannah whipped toward the sound. The cow charged. She shouted, flinging out her arms, waving wildly. The heifer kept coming and coming fast.

Hannah dashed toward the fence. She slapped her hands on the top rail, rising up to leap the rail. Just then the cow plowed into her hip, loosening her grip on the wood. With a shriek, she tumbled back into the corral.

Roaring with rage, the cow lowered her head, slinging slobber. Hannah rolled to the edge of the fence, curled into a ball, throwing her arms over her head.

Lord, help me!

* * *

The eeriest sense of doom shook Matt to the core. Something was wrong. He kneed Thunder. Under him, the stallion shot off, racing for home. The barnyard came into view, nothing appeared amiss. No buggy. Julia was gone.

Near the barn, he pulled back on the reins, slowing his horse when a flash of blue tumbled into the corral with that heifer.

"Hannah!" *God, help her. Help me.*

Strength surged through him. He dismounted at a run, flung himself over the fence, screaming like a wild man, waving his hat. The enraged heifer whirled toward him.

Behind Matt, Hannah huddled, quiet. Was she hurt? His throat closed. Was she dead?

Red eye weeping, the heifer pawed the ground, shaking her head, eyeing him. Her calf bawled. The cow swung toward her offspring, then trotted to the calf's side.

Before that cow changed her mind, Matt scooped Hannah into his arms, plopped her over his shoulder and raced for the fence. A few feet more and they'd be safely on the other side.

The cow roared, hurtling after him, hooves flinging clods of muck. Matt tore open the gate and shot through, fastening it behind them just as the heifer's wide body crashed against the wood. The gate vibrated on its hinges, but held. The animal butted the frame once more, then again returned to the calf.

Matt knelt and lowered Hannah to the ground. "Are you okay?" he said.

"I'm fine." She jumped to her feet, dusted herself off, then rubbed her side. "The heifer barely grazed me with one of her hooves. Must not see well enough to take good aim."

She behaved as if nothing had happened. As if she hadn't put her life at risk. Matt's face flushed with anger. "You might not have been as fortunate with the next stomp!"

"Why are you so upset?"

"What if I hadn't arrived when I did? In a battle between you and that heifer, the heifer wins."

His throat closed. And he would bury another wife. *Thank God not today.*

"I'm grateful you did," Hannah said, then turned back to the corral as if nothing had happened.

A wave of helplessness crashed over him, washing away every pretense he'd clung to, revealing the ugly truth. Hannah would never turn to him for help. He'd never be an equal partner with a woman who couldn't trust. A woman who took terrible risks to prove she didn't need him.

How could he keep such a woman safe? Whether she recognized it or not, he'd saved her life today. But what about the next day? The day after that? He couldn't go on like this.

Hannah's side ached, but she had no difficulty breathing, which told her she had no broken ribs. She'd be sore for a few days. Bruised. But nothing to slow her down. Things could've been far worse. *Thank You, God, that Matt came along when he did.*

Across from her, her husband paced the room like an

angry bull about to charge. She'd upset him with what he saw as a reckless act. She'd apologize. Try to mend that fence standing between them.

"Please, sit. I'm fine," she said.

"You are not fine."

"Well, I will be fine. In a day or two."

Matt released a shuddering breath and halted in front of her. "Why did you enter the corral alone? What were you trying to prove?"

"Nothing. The calf needed nourishment. That's all. I'm a rancher, Matt. It's my job to take care of livestock."

"It's also your job to use common sense."

She shifted her position, trying to ease the ache in her side. "I thought I could handle it. I'm sorry."

Matt knelt. "You and I aren't in a contest to see who's the better cowboy, Hannah. If I hadn't shown up when I did, you could've been seriously injured, maybe... killed."

Had she been trying to prove something? "I'm grateful you did, Matt, more than I can say. I don't know what would've happened if you hadn't come along."

"Does that mean you'll think twice before taking such a risk?"

If she didn't keep her independence, she might start relying on him. Counting on him. A huge lump lodged in her throat. She'd rather face a crazed cow than make such a promise.

"I...I can't promise. You know ranching. Dangerous situations come up every day. Anyway," she said, smoothing a hand over her lap. "I'm fine now and the calf will be, too. Life can get back to normal."

He rose, crossed to the open window, putting his back to her, staring out at the vast pastures. The clock ticked on the wall. The notes of a song drifted in. Rosa must be working in the garden.

Matt released a long breath and turned toward her. "Any man worth his salt would protect a woman. I can't protect you."

Why *had* she taken that risk in the corral?

"You're a bullheaded woman, Hannah Parrish."

To hear her husband call her by her maiden name sent a chill slithering along her spine.

He gave a wan smile. "I like that about you. I really do. Still, I've lost one wife," he said so softly, she strained to hear him. "I can't lose another. I can't live like this."

"I promise," she said, putting up her right hand. "I'll ask for help before going in the corral like that again."

"That's not it." A shade dropped over his features, trapping the air in her lungs. "I've made a decision. I'm moving back to the Circle W in the morning."

His words ricocheted through her like a bullet, banging against her heart, her lungs, her very soul. "What? Why?"

"I'm giving you what you want. Your freedom. You no longer need my help to run your ranch. Well, you may need my help, but you'll never admit it. We're not partners, Hannah. You're a solo act."

Her throat knotted. "The ranch is *ours*."

"No, it's yours. You've proven yourself. The ranch hands understand they work for you now. Our deal has been fulfilled. It's time for me to leave."

The rigid set of his jaw, the stony look in his eyes

belonged to a man who'd had enough. Enough of this farce of a marriage. Enough of her.

On booted heel, he pivoted to go.

Stifling a groan, Hannah struggled to her feet. "Wait!"

Rosa appeared in the doorway, brow furrowed, hands knotted in her apron, blocking Matt's path. "Allie gone. I look in house. In barn. In stable. I no find her."

Hannah's gaze flew to Matt. "What? That's impossible."

When had she seen Allie last? With her injury and their argument, they hadn't checked on the child.

"When did you last see her, Rosa?" Matt asked, his tone steady, every muscle alert. He looked strong, capable, ready to take action.

Tears brimmed in Rosa's eyes. "She play dolly with Miss Julia. I weed garden, see Miss Julia leave in buggy. I come inside, Allie gone."

"She can't have gone far," Matt said. "I'll ask Jake and one of the Lazy P hands to search the ranch. We'll find her." He turned to Rosa. "Stay close to the house, in case Allie comes back." He met Hannah's gaze. "Any idea where she'd be?"

"The only place I can think of is the Montgomery's."

"That's an hour on foot, a long walk for a child." He plowed his hand through his hair. "Still, I can't think of anywhere else she'd go."

"Unless… Unless she went with Julia."

"Why would Allie do that?" Matt said.

Hannah's mind traveled back to that day at church, to the words Julia had spoken. Was Allie a lure? A lure to snare Matt? Hannah's heart hitched. "What if she didn't have a choice?" she said, forcing the words past the knot in her throat.

Hannah knew then that she couldn't handle this alone. Not without Matt, a man who cared about Allie as much as she, and not without God. "We need to pray." Tears welled in her eyes. "Will you? Please."

With a nod, Matt took her hands in his. In his grip, she felt a sense of calm, of togetherness. These might be their last moments as husband and wife, but at least they were joined in purpose—to find Allie.

Matt bowed his head. "Lord, show us where Allie is. Keep her safe until we find her. Amen."

"Amen."

They strode out the door toward the stable. Matt turned his gaze on Hannah. "Why do you think Julia's involved?"

"Something she said to me that day at church."

"What exactly did she say?"

Hannah shivered. "She said, 'I didn't expect you. You complicate things.'"

Matt's features flattened, contorted. He looked riled, even dangerous. "Let's ride for town."

Hannah and Matt rode hard into town. Outside the Calico Café, they drew their horses to a halt, kicking up dust. The town's bench sitters sat out front, eyeing them. Matt swung from the saddle, and then helped Hannah down.

The ache in her side a painful reminder that the risk she'd taken had driven Matt away. She'd deal with all that later. For now, all that mattered was Allie.

"Howdy-do, folks," Mr. Brand said then gave a wheezy cough. "Appears you're in a mighty big hurry."

"We're looking for Julia Phillips," Matt said, ushering Hannah toward the door.

"Miz Phillips sure took a shine to that little girl living at your place," Mr. Brand said. "Got her that fancy dolly bed."

Matt paused and turned around. "You knew about that?"

Mr. Seller nodded. "Yep, saw Miz Phillips leaving the store with it. Said she'd bought it for her little girl."

At his words, Hannah's veins iced. She worked her mouth until the words came out, "Did you just say *her* little girl?"

Mr. Sellers nodded. "Strange, ain't it?" He turned to Mr. Brand. "Must've been one of them there slips of the tongue."

"At my age, I have them slips all the time. Why, I…"

But Matt and Hannah didn't wait to hear the rest. They dashed inside the deserted café. The noon crowd had gone. Evening diners hadn't yet arrived.

Carolyn Shields stood at the front scrubbing the counter. Strands of her salt-and-pepper hair had pulled loose from her bun, giving the tidy woman a disheveled appearance. "What can I get you folks?"

"Is Julia Phillips here?" Hannah asked.

"This is Julia's day off." Mrs. Shields shrugged. "I don't know where she is."

"Mind if we knock on her door?" Matt said.

"Not at all. I'll show the way."

They clomped up the stairs, trailing the widow. Mrs.

Shields stopped in front of a door, slightly ajar. "Looks like she forgot to lock up."

They followed her inside. A breeze filtered in through the open windows. The fragrance Julia wore hung in the warm air. The room was tidy, the bed made.

"What on earth?" Mrs. Shields plopped fisted hands on her hips. "I didn't know Julia was getting married. An employee should tell me such things."

Hannah shot Matt a puzzled frown.

Matt shook his head. "Julia's not getting married."

"Then what's that for?" Mrs. Shields pointed toward the far wall.

A wedding dress and veil hung from a hook.

Fingers of fear settled around Hannah's heart and squeezed.

"Well, looky there," Mrs. Shields said. "Can't imagine what she'd do with all those little girl dresses."

On an upholstered chair in the corner, as if on display, small dresses had been fanned out across the seat and back. Dresses that would fit Allie. These clothes— were they bought to earn Allie's love? Or to clothe Allie after Julia abducted the child and fled town?

"This is scaring me."

Matt put an arm around Hannah's shoulders. "We'll get to the bottom of it."

Carolyn Shields walked to a writing table under the window, leaned over, perusing something. She turned toward them. "There's more. Take a look."

She and Matt joined her. Laid atop the desk was a lithographed wedding certificate with Esther and Naomi gathering wheat in the field, a pleased Boaz looking on.

Hannah's gaze moved up the document.

Matthew Aaron Walker and *Julia Katherine Phillips* joined together in Holy Matrimony on the—day in the month of *June,* in the year of our Lord *Eighteen hundred eighty-eight.*

To see her husband's and Julia's name on that wedding certificate with only the day of the week left blank chilled Hannah to the bone, left her shivering.

Matt stood behind her, rested a hand on Hannah's shoulder. "This is crazy. What's she thinking?"

"I'd say Julia Phillips has set her cap for you." Mrs. Shields frowned. "But, aren't you two already married?"

"Apparently that's a complication Julia didn't foresee," Matt said.

Hannah locked her gaze with Matt's. For the first time, in his eyes, Hannah saw fear. Her stomach tumbled. How far would Julia go to get what she wanted?

"We need to find Julia." Matt strode to the door. "Now."

"Where?"

"I have no idea. But God does."

As they headed out, Hannah whispered a frantic prayer, "Lord, help us find Julia."

The One who ruled the Universe, the One who overcame evil with good would intervene. For surely Julia Phillips was evil.

Chapter Twenty-One

Matt and Hannah strode to their horses. The overcast sky promised rain, something they needed badly, yet Matt hoped the rain would hold off until they found Allie. A storm would only hinder them, eat up valuable time.

Where would they search? Matt's mind traipsed back through the years, searching for clues to Julia's whereabouts. He hadn't gone three feet when a possibility hit him.

He reeled to Hannah. "I know where Julia has Allie."

"Where?"

"Years ago, Julia confided to Amy that she and the father of her baby rendezvoused in the line shack on the far edge of the Circle W. The shack's out of the way, could hold supplies. Has a path of sorts leading to it. A path a buggy could manage."

"Makes sense. We'll find her," Hannah said, her voice strong with resolve.

"Before we leave town, let's stop at the jail. Tell the

sheriff what's going on and give him the location of the line shack."

Within minutes they'd spoken to Sheriff Spencer and rode side by side for the Circle W, hoping they were wrong about Julia and would find Allie safe and sound inside the line shack.

A terrible heaviness pressed against Matt's lungs. Once again he'd failed the people in his care. He'd not taken Hannah's warnings about Julia seriously and put an innocent child at risk.

"We have to find her," he said. "I can't live with letting Allie down, too."

"What do you mean—*too?*"

Might as well reveal what kind of man she'd married. "I'm to blame for Amy's death. Me. Her husband." His shoulders slumped. "The man who should have protected her."

"Amy fell from her horse during a race. Why are you to blame?"

In one long shaky breath, Matt released some of the pent-up pain he'd carried since that day. "What you don't know is I challenged Amy to that race. She died before my eyes." His voice broke. "I've gone over and over that day a thousand times. If only I'd taken a different route, nowhere near the gopher colony. If only I'd suggested a walk along the creek, not a race. If only…"

He couldn't finish. Couldn't tell her all of it.

"Sometimes things just happen and there's nothing we can do." Hannah's eyes brimmed with tears. "Like Mama dying. Like Papa. Like Amy. We don't understand why, only God does. You shouldn't feel guilty."

"But I do." He tore his gaze away. He couldn't bear

to look at her. Couldn't bear to see her reaction to the truth. He sucked in a gulp of air. "Oh, Lord, forgive me, a part of me was…" He closed his eyes. "Grateful."

"Grateful?"

He forced the admission over the lump in his throat, "Her death released me from a difficult marriage."

"You and Amy weren't happy?" Hannah said, her tone, her expression bewildered.

"We loved each other, but things got complicated. She didn't like living at the ranch. Didn't like the long hours I spent away from her."

"She knew all that when she married you."

"Maybe she didn't know she'd hate ranch life. She withdrew more and more." He sighed. "Our love got lost in a battle we both were determined to win." Weary of the regrets eating away at him, he groaned. "I never had a chance to make things right."

"Oh, Matt, I understand regrets." She sighed. "The day before Mama died she tried to pull me into her lap. I don't remember why but I wiggled away." A sob escaped her lips.

He wanted to stop, to pull her into his arms, but they had to keep going. Had to find Allie.

"The next day…Mama was gone. I'd never have the chance to sit on her lap again. I wanted to relive that day. But I couldn't. All we can do is ask forgiveness, then let it go," she said, sweet forgiveness in her eyes. "I can see guilt holds you in chains. Prevents you from living. In a way, you're killing yourself, too. Amy would want you to be happy."

Could that be true? Moments ticked by. Matt thought

about all the years he'd carried that guilt. Guilt hadn't changed anything. Anything but him.

"I do want to be happy. Maybe I'll find contentment when I return to the Circle W."

She stiffened. "Alone."

"I have to, Hannah."

"No, you don't." She nailed him with her gaze. "Admit it. You're running."

"Maybe I am. But what do you expect me to do?" He scrubbed a hand over his face. "Living with you in the same house, a bedroom apart, is sheer torture. *That's* what's killing me." He leaned toward her. "You tell me to take a risk and find happiness. What will it take for you to do the same?"

Her gaze dropped away. Silence.

More evidence he'd made the right decision about leaving. He clicked to Thunder and shot ahead, leaving Hannah, his past, what he'd once thought was his future, behind.

What mattered was finding Allie.

Despite the pain carving her features, Hannah kept up the pace. To leave this strong, feisty woman would be hard. She was like no woman he'd ever known. Yet he'd release her from a marriage she no longer needed, having proved she could run her ranch without him as a buffer. She might want him at her side, but her silence earlier proved she didn't want a real marriage.

In the distance thunder rumbled, the sky grew dark, matching his dark concern for Allie and the dismal prospect of life without Hannah. The wind kicked up, setting the branches of the trees swaying. Overhead the ceiling of clouds turned turbulent.

As turbulent as the eyes Hannah turned on Matt. "Do you...do you think Allie's safe?"

"Yes, I do. The clothes Julia bought her, the belief that Allie's her child imply Julia won't bring Allie harm."

"What's stopping her from taking Allie and fleeing town? Getting far from Bliss? Someplace where we'd never find her?"

"And leave that wedding dress behind?"

"Don't you mean leave *you* behind?"

Was that jealousy in Hannah's voice?

"If Julia sees Allie and me as her family, she'll stay put. For now."

No matter what he'd just said to Hannah, Matt wasn't sure about Allie's safety. Julia's belief that Allie was her daughter, along with the evidence they'd found in her room—the little girl clothing, the wedding gown and veil, the marriage certificate filled out with his and Julia's names—not only implicated her in Allie's disappearance, but proved Julia wasn't in her right mind. Somehow she'd functioned rationally in Bliss, held a job, attended church, taught Sunday school. How she'd managed that he didn't know, but those delusions of hers made Julia dangerous.

If she harmed or frightened that child—

Matt couldn't allow himself to consider the possibility.

"The sheriff promised to check out the line shack once he'd finished processing the prisoner in his jail."

Not that Matt intended to wait for the law.

A drop of rain fell on his hand, then raindrops spattered, leaving craters in the dust. Matt spurred Thunder on. Beside him, Hannah did the same.

The line shack came into view. A horse hitched to a buggy stood at the rail out front, his tail swatting at the rain like this was an ordinary day.

"Looks like the rig Julia drove earlier," he said. "Reckon she's holed up inside with Allie."

"I'm praying she'll give Allie up without trouble."

"Me too. But with or without trouble, we'll be leaving with Allie."

The front door swung open. Julia stood in the entrance, wearing a confident smile and a fancy pink dress. "I've been expecting you," she said in a chirpy voice, as if they'd come to pay a social call.

"And here we are," Matt said, forcing his tone to remain light, when he wanted to push past her and see with his own eyes that Allie was unharmed.

The rain came, harder now. Before Hannah could dismount, Matt strode to her side. He helped her down, then took the reins from her hands and looked her straight in the eyes. "Trust me," he whispered.

She held his gaze for a moment, then nodded.

He gave her a parting smile, then flung the leather around the hitching post.

"Aren't you cute as a button, Hannah?" Julia said with a smirk. "Why, it's hard to tell if you're a man or a woman."

Matt recognized the spark of temper in Hannah's eyes and shot her a steely look, a warning not to raise Julia's ire.

Hannah gave the slightest nod, then smiled at Julia. "Pretty dress."

"I wore it just for this occasion." Julia flashed a flirty smile at Matt, then sashayed inside.

He and Hannah followed her in. Holding his smile firmly in place, he closed the door behind them, then scanned the room. A cozy spot if not for the cobwebs and the faint odor of rodent excrement barely discernible under the fresh scent of rain. A stove sat in the middle of the floor, obviously lit by the steam coming from a teakettle. Two cots lined the walls. One empty.

Matt's gaze darted to the bed beneath the single window. Covered with cobwebs and coursing with rain, the small pane let in meager light. Still, it was enough to see Allie curled on her side, asleep, her chest rising and falling. Matt released the breath he hadn't realized he'd been holding. Proof he'd been less certain about Allie's welfare than he'd let on to Hannah.

"You've made a cozy place here, Julia."

"I had to." She heaved a sigh. "Hannah can't keep an eye on the child."

"I can see that." He glanced toward Hannah, then back to Julia. "So did you and Allie make plans?"

"I invited Allie and she came willingly. Allie loves spending time with me."

Apparently, Allie had fallen for Julia's ploy. No doubt Julia had offered candy or a toy or some adventure.

With an eye on Julia, Hannah edged toward the cot, no doubt to position herself near Allie. He'd never been prouder of his wife.

"Leave my daughter be!" Her face contorted in anger, Julia slashed a hand at Hannah. "You're not responsible." She smiled up at Matt. "You can count on me. I'll never allow Allie out of my sight."

If the situation weren't so grave, Matt would've argued the point. Allie Solaro was not an easy child to corral.

"Hannah's not worthy of you, Matt. I'll be a good wife. Just wait and see," Julia said, then laid a hand on Matt's chest.

A hand Matt covered with his own. "You're a lovely woman, Julia. What man wouldn't appreciate a wife like you?"

Unable to tear her eyes away, Hannah watched as her husband cupped Julia's jaw with his hand, gazing down at the woman with admiration in his eyes.

Julia snuggled against him, laying her head against his broad chest, wrapping her arms around him. "I love you, Matthew. I've loved you for years."

A woman who would speak those words to a married man in front of his wife had a skewed view of reality. Hannah's hands fisted. *And* whether she knew it or not, took her life in her hands.

"That's mighty good to hear. I feel the same, Julia," Matt said wrapping her in his arms, murmuring endearments in her ear.

Hannah's heart tumbled in her chest. Matt had told her to trust him. She knew he was performing, pretending to adore Julia. But, to see him hold another woman in his arms, to hear him all but declare his love for her, slashed at every inch of Hannah like a serrated blade of a knife.

A desire rose up inside of her. To grab Julia by that fancy collar, snatch her from Matt's arms and toss her out the door and onto her backside in the mud. Exactly what the woman deserved.

Hannah's breath caught. She wasn't reacting like a woman content with a marriage of convenience. She was reacting like a woman in love with her husband. Who longed to hear words of love directed to her.

As if the floor shifted beneath her feet, Hannah fought for balance, for composure. Was it possible? Was it possible she had fallen in love with her husband?

Matt was mouthing make-believe endearments, performing like an actor in a play, a play with high stakes. Hannah knew no matter what he'd said, Matt felt nothing for Julia. Tears stung her eyes. And he felt nothing for her. He might want her, but he hadn't mentioned love. Every particle of her being wanted to run, to hide out, to wrap herself in that armor of fear. But she didn't have the luxury. They had Allie to protect.

As soon as they got the little girl safely home, Matt would move out as he'd planned, leaving behind the pretense of a marriage. Of love.

One glance at Allie curled on the cot, vulnerable, in need of protection, stiffened Hannah's spine. Twice before, Hannah had played a role. To protect Allie, she would play a part again. Only this time, instead of pretending to be the blissful bride, Hannah would pretend not to care, not to feel anything, while her husband held another woman in his arms.

"He's mine, Hannah." Julia cackled. "Not yours."

Had Julia read her mind? Hannah forced up the corners of her lips. Her face felt rigid, as if the effort to smile would crack her skin. "Matt and I married to save the ranch." Hannah's voice caught, but she forged on,

"To give my father peace before he died. We never had a real marriage."

Their marriage was a farce. Something she'd thought she wanted, had even proposed, but now that arrangement left her empty. Now that marriage cost her far more than she could give.

Julia chortled. "I have the man I love." Eyes glittering, she glanced at Allie. "I have my child."

The crazy conversation swirling around Allie hadn't disturbed the little girl. She slept soundly. *Too* soundly. Nothing looked amiss but Allie was a light sleeper. The only explanation was that Julia had drugged Allie with something.

Had she given her too much?

A maniacal expression in her eyes, Julia celebrated her victory with a chuckle. "I will soon be Mrs. Matthew Walker." She tilted her face to Matt. "As soon as I heard Amy died, I came." She pulled away, the frenzied glow in her eyes hardened into icy shards. "Why didn't you wait for me?"

"I didn't know where you were, Julia," Matt said, cupping her jaw in his palm. "I didn't know if you were married or single."

Tears flooded Julia's eyes. "If my baby girl had survived, you'd have married me. We'd have been happy, the three of us."

"I'm sorry your baby died. You've been through a hard time."

"I missed my chance. Then. Now I have a second chance. A second chance with you and Allie." She touched Matt's cheek. "We'll go to my room at the café. Pack Allie's and my things, then leave for Louisiana tomorrow."

"What if Allie doesn't want to go?" Hannah said.

"She'll go. A little laudanum and she'll sleep like a baby on the train."

For the briefest moment Matt's dark eyes blazed with rage, then as if donning a mask, his expression softened. "Whatever you say, Julia. You deserve to be happy."

Julia rose on tiptoe and kissed Matt's cheek. "We'll get married in my church. Live in a mansion surrounded by live oaks dripping Spanish moss. You and Allie will love living there."

"You have it all planned out," Matt said.

"I've thought of nothing else for weeks." She giggled. "Amy talked on and on about your wedding until I wanted to slap her senseless. Now I understand. I can't get the image of our wedding out of my mind."

Lightning flashed, illuminating the dingy shack. Thunder rumbled. Rain hammered the tin roof, the din almost deafening.

Julia's brow furrowed. "Except *she's* still your wife." She pivoted to Hannah. "Well, that's easy enough to fix." She chuckled, the sound devoid of humor.

As if on a Sunday stroll, she stepped to the stove, opened the door handle with her skirts, then grabbed the unlit end of a small log from the fire with both hands. She whirled toward Hannah, carrying the log upright like a torch. With each step Julia took, the burning end flamed brighter.

"It'll appear like an accident," she said softly.

Icy fingers danced along Hannah's spine. *God, save us!*

With quick, silent steps, Matt edged behind Julia, clasped her shoulders, stopping her in her tracks. "We don't want to hurt anyone," he said firmly. "Give me that log."

Julia spun toward him, waving the torch toward his torso. "You're a liar! You don't love me. All you want is Allie!"

The flames lapped at his sleeve, the cotton flared. Hannah shrieked. *God, help him.* Matt wrestled the wood from Julia's hands, then slapped at his shirt, losing his grip on the wood.

The log tumbled to the floor, blazing brighter as it rolled across the planks. Hannah jerked a blanket off the empty cot and dropped the wool over the flames and stomped them with booted feet, smothering the blaze.

Red-faced, Julia screeched, heading toward Hannah. "I can't let you live!"

Matt grabbed Julia's arms and dragged her kicking and screaming toward the door.

Away from Allie. Away from Hannah.

Julia's features contorted with hatred. "What are you doing?" She jerked against Matt's hold on her, lunging toward Hannah, flailing her arms. "You're hurting me!"

Matt lowered his face to hers. "Julia, you're in big trouble. Settle down."

"Let go of me!" Julia hissed. She twisted in his arms, raised cupped palms and scrapped her nails down his cheeks.

Blood oozed from the welts. *Oh, Matt.*

Breathing heavy, Matt rammed Julia against him, pinning her arms to her sides. She fought him, shrieking like a banshee, but wrapped in those strong arms, she didn't have a chance of escape.

The door banged open. Sheriff Spencer stood in the doorway, expression fierce, gun drawn, rain dripping from his hat, from his slicker. "What's going on here?"

Snarling like a vicious animal, Julia lunged against Matt's hands, kicked at his shins. "I hate you!"

"Appears the lady's not in the mood for reason. Still, won't be needing this." The sheriff holstered his gun, then whipped shackles from his belt and snapped the cuffs to Julia's wrists. "Sorry, ma'am, but I can't trust you to mind your manners," he said, then let his gaze scan the shack. "The child okay?"

"Julia gave her laudanum," Matt said. "Her breathing is regular. She should come around soon."

"You or the missus hurt?" He scowled. "Looks like you've got a burn."

"We're fine."

"Now," Hannah said. "I'll see to Matt's burn."

With a nod, the lawman led Julia toward the door.

"The rig belongs to the livery," Matt said.

"I'll drive it to town. Mind getting Miss Phillips inside the buggy while I tie my horse to the back?" he said, then turned Julia over to Matt.

On shaky limbs, Hannah stepped to the doorway. She wanted to fall into Matt's arms, to thank him for everything he'd done to protect them, including pretending to love Julia. One thing she knew. Matt would never knowingly put anyone in danger. Yet, he felt responsible for Amy's death and carried a load of guilt.

Matt lifted Julia onto the seat, then cuffed her hands to the rod supporting the roof. She slumped against the cushion, her hair already matted to her head by the deluge, never once taking her eyes off Matt.

Sheriff Spencer untied the reins, then clambered aboard. "Will need a statement soon as you can get to town."

Matt nodded. "Ask Doc Atkins to look at Julia. Maybe he'll know how to help her."

"I'll ask him to stop by the jail."

At the mention of jail, Julia swayed toward Matt. "Don't let him take me! You love me. Why are you pretending you don't?"

"I'm sorry, Julia." Matt took a step back. "Sorrier than I can say."

With a shake of his head, Sheriff Spencer clicked to the horse. The mare started forward with a weeping, wet and bedraggled Julia on board. Julia twisted back as far as the cuffs would allow, staring at Matt. As if he somehow held the answers.

He watched her go, solemn, resolved. Silent.

The nightmare was over. An icy dose of reality hit Hannah. As soon as they returned to the ranch, Matt would leave and return to his land. And she'd be left feeling as bereft as Julia.

How could she say goodbye to him? How could she let him go?

She loved him.

The truth swished through her, trapped the air in her lungs. She loved her husband. The way he teased her. The way he supported her. Oh, and the way he kissed her.

Tears stung her eyes. Too late. She was always too late.

Or was she? They had one last evening together. She had one last chance. One last chance to try again.

As disturbed and misguided as Julia had been, she'd gone after what she wanted.

Perhaps, just perhaps, Hannah would take the biggest risk of her life and fight for her marriage.

Would she fail as Julia had? If so, the pain she carried from that tussle with the heifer would be nothing compared to the pain in her heart.

Chapter Twenty-Two

Allie came first, before Hannah, before Matt, before this last chance to save their marriage. Hannah shifted her gaze to her little charge. Allie had come through the ordeal with Julia, without any lasting physical effects. Thank God.

Now tucked on the parlor sofa between Hannah and Matt, her thin arms wrapped around her bent knees, Allie chewed on her lower lip. Then, gazing up at Hannah, finally, the story unfurled, one quiet word at a time. "I cried to go home, but Julia said no. She said we would ride on a train, go far away. She said it would be fun, but…" Tears filled her eyes. "I didn't want to go. I want to stay here. With you and Matt and Star. So I ran outside. She ran faster and caught me. She held my nose. I had to drink yucky medicine." She wrinkled her nose at the memory. "I was scared, Hannah."

Over Allie's head, Hannah met Matt's dark stormy eyes. Hannah wanted to wring Julia's neck. Beside them Jake and Rosa's lips thinned, their nostrils flared. From the look on their faces, Hannah would have some help.

Matt tugged Allie close. She released her knees and curled against him with a sigh. "I'm sorry, Pumpkin," he said. "Julia shouldn't have done that."

"Why did she say, 'You're my little girl. You're my little girl?' Over and over. I'm not."

Hannah trailed her fingers through Allie's hair. "Julia's confused, that's all. Don't worry, Sweetie. You'll never see her again."

"Good. She's not nice." Allie held up a forearm with bruised spots where Julia's fingertips had pressed into her skin. "She hurt me."

"You were very brave, Allie," Matt said.

Jake's jaw tightened. He knelt beside the sofa. "Shame on her. Want me to kiss those spots?"

Allie giggled. "They don't hurt now, Uncle Jake. Unless I poke them."

Eyes luminous with unshed tears, Rosa bustled around the room, plumping the pillow behind Allie's head, giving her a blanket. "I sorry. I not see you go with Julia."

"Did Julia hide you?" Jake asked.

They'd all wondered how Julia managed to conceal Allie.

"Julia told me to hide on the buggy floor. She said it was a…game." Allie's face crumpled. "When I was on the floor under the blanket, I prayed. Really, really quiet." Allie smiled at Matt. "And God sent you and Hannah."

Tears of gratitude and praise slid down Hannah's cheeks. *Lord, please help this child recover from this trauma. Keep her safe for all her days. Help Julia find the help she needs. We're all wrung out.*

Allie yawned, proof the hour had gotten late. "Matt, will you read me a bedtime story?" Allie asked. "Please."

"Of course," Matt said. "Tonight I will."

The unspoken message—tomorrow Matt would be gone. The truth pressed against Hannah's lungs.

Allie chattered a while longer, then began to nod off.

"See you tomorrow, Allie," Jake said, then gave his great-niece a kiss on the forehead and trudged for the bunkhouse.

Rosa gave Allie a hug with a promise of fresh-baked cookies in the morning and anything Allie wanted for supper, then left for her quarters off the kitchen.

Matt hoisted the child into his arms. She nestled her head in the crook of his shoulder as Matt led the way toward her bedroom. Why, the three of them looked like a family. Allie could have been their daughter.

Up ahead, Hannah caught a glimpse of Matt's belongings stowed in a neat pile outside the door to his room. She realized then, tomorrow this perfect little bubble would burst. Matt was leaving. Her family, if she could call it that, was dissolving. Soon Allie would go to live with her grandmother. In the morning, Matt would be gone.

Inside Allie's room, Matt tucked the little girl in, then they sat on either side of her on the bed. Struggling to keep tears at bay, Hannah watched Matt read the story about a lost duckling finding the way home. She loved this little girl. How could she bear to lose her?

An answer gripped her, giving her the first ray of hope for the future. She'd invite Jake's sister to move here. Gertie, Allie and Jake would be Hannah's family.

Finished, Matt closed the book, got to his feet and kissed Allie good-night.

"Night." The little girl's mouth stretched wide in another yawn that ended with a hiccup.

"Sleep tight, Allie." Hannah leaned over and gave her a hug and kiss.

Matt helped Hannah to her feet. The solid warmth of his grip slid through her, felt right, like home. The soreness in Hannah's body from the tussle with the heifer had eased, but the ache inside her had grown until she felt like her heart would burst.

She bit her lip. That pain was partly her own doing. She'd stubbornly refused to seek Matt's help with the heifer, adding the last straw that had shoved him to quit their marriage.

As if by an unspoken agreement, she and Matt strolled to the porch, the place they'd spent many evenings, talking and studying the night sky. The thunderstorm earlier had ended the drought and moved on, leaving stars twinkling above and the earth with a fresh scent, washed clean, revived after an arid season.

Hannah had experienced the bleakness of an arid season and would know one again when the man she loved left. She needed the refreshment of God's gentle shower of blessings, the certainty of the direction God had for her. If Matt was her future, how could she plead with a man determined to go?

She'd need courage. Courage to fight for her marriage.

Lord, help me to take a different kind of risk. A risk with my heart.

Hannah dropped onto the settee, leaving room for

Matt. Instead of joining her, he took the chair across from her.

She forced a smile to her lips and worked a sentence to her throat. "How's the burn?"

That would hardly convince him to stay. Still, fear of rejection kept her mute.

"Doc gave me a salve that's helped ease the sting."

"What did he say about Julia?"

"He believes she's delusional. He says as long as she's in town, she's a threat to Allie, you, even me. Doc gave her a sedative and she's locked up in a cell. Unless we file a complaint, at some point, the sheriff will have to let her go."

"How long can they hold her?"

"The sheriff wired her brother. He can hold her until her brother arrives to take her home."

"That's good to hear. I promised Allie she'd never see Julia again."

"And she won't."

A lump knotted in Hannah's throat. Banalities. They were making small talk instead of discussing the real issue hanging between them like a dark ominous cloud.

"We've got a lot to be grateful for." Tears sprang to her eyes. "God protected that precious child. God answered our prayers to find her safe."

"I've thanked Him for that." Matt shook his head. "Never thought I'd be glad to see a child drugged but I'm grateful Allie slept through Julia's attack." His brow furrowed. "No matter what, I wouldn't have let you and Allie down."

"You've never let anyone down, Matt. Not my father. Not Allie. Not me."

"I'm not a man you should depend on, Hannah. Stop making me out to be something I'm not."

"Oh, Matt." She leaned forward. "Why can't you forgive yourself? What happened to Amy wasn't your fault."

He lurched to his feet. Tall, powerful, all cowboy. From his stance, he had his defenses firmly in place. "We can't change the past."

"Can't we?" Hannah rose, lifted a hand toward him.

"No, we can't. I didn't protect Amy. Just like I couldn't protect Allie from falling into Julia's clutches." He shook his head. "I'm not the man for you."

"You're the best kind of man," she said softly, laying a hand on his arm. She waited for him to meet her eyes. "You're a man who has loved and lost. Most of all, a man who risks everything he has for others." She cupped his cheek. "Risks everything that is, but his heart."

He didn't speak, but shifted his gaze to some spot over her shoulder. The drained expression on his face suggested he'd traveled a long, weary road. "I...I can't do that, Hannah. What if..." He let out a gust. "What if something happens? What if I'm not here when you need me?"

"And what if a tornado hits tomorrow? Or a nor'easter? Or the sky falls?" She sighed. "You can't live life worrying, Matt. All you can do is put your faith in God and let Him take the reins."

He harrumphed. "Says the woman who never lets anyone take the reins."

She grinned. "I'm good at giving advice, not necessarily good at taking it."

"Care to explain why you can't give up those reins?"

"I've learned to handle every aspect of my life on my own."

"You're a competent rancher. I should've trusted you more."

"I should've trusted myself less. And God more."

"Like you just told me to do," he said, arching a brow.

"Exactly. You know, for two risk takers, we're both running scared." She fiddled with his collar. "Take a chance, Matt. On us."

He took a step back. "It's getting late. You've had a rough day and need sleep. I need to finish packing."

"You're still leaving?"

"Has anything changed, Hannah?"

"I have."

"I can't—"

She put up a palm. "Hear me out. Seeing you with Julia today made me think. About a lot. Like why I can't give God the reins." She sighed. "When Mama died, I was too young to understand what happened. To me, she died because she was delicate like a rose, not suited for life on a Texas ranch. I needed to be sturdy like Indian paintbrush and bluebonnets that thrive here, like my papa. I had to take care of things. Take care of myself. Not rely on anyone."

"Losing your mother had to be hard on a little kid."

"I used that independence as armor to protect my heart. I see now that my need to handle everything myself, instead of relying on you, trusting you, comes from fear. Fear of needing another human being, of loving another human being. Then, losing him."

"You weren't the only one who wore that armor. I let what happened with Amy stand between us."

"And what good did that armor do? For either of us? I lost Papa anyway." She choked back a sob. "Now I'm losing you."

Matt shifted on his feet. "Hannah, we had a marriage of convenience. We both know that. I'm giving you what you wanted." His gaze softened. "Your independence."

"I want that independence. With you." Tears brimming in her eyes, she stepped closer until she was inches away. "When Papa was dying, God planted the idea in my mind to propose to you. I didn't trust His plan for my life. I didn't trust that God had given me a far better gift than a solution to my problem. He'd given me the man of my dreams."

He arched a brow. "Me?"

She laughed. "Who else could tame this filly?" She sobered. "If I could design a man especially for me, you would be that man. You love the land and the way of life I cherish. You have a work ethic that never stops and a heart as big as Texas. And kiss like...well..." Heat flooded her cheeks.

A smile curved his face. He touched her cheek with calloused fingers. "Ah, my strong-willed wife."

"Not strong when it comes to you, Matt Walker." She took a deep breath and swallowed hard. "I tried, oh, how I tried not to, but I've fallen in love with you. With all my heart. The question is—can you take a risk and love me?"

A grin quirked up Matt's face. "Love a woman who insists on carrying her own trunk? Love a woman who delivers a calf in jeopardy? Love a woman who races breakneck over Texas to save a little girl?" He tugged her to him. "Yes, Hannah Walker, I love you. I love every side of you. Debutante, filly, cowpoke, doesn't matter to me."

Hannah arched a brow and shot him a saucy grin. "Even if I can outwork, outride and outshoot you?"

"Even if."

"Then you'll stay?"

"Forever."

Life hadn't been easy for Hannah. Yet she never lost her strong faith. Her determination to save the Lazy P and her way of life. How could he have ever thought of leaving her? Feminine and fragile one minute, strong and capable the next, Hannah challenged him, made him want to be a better man, a better person, a better husband.

He brushed his lips across her cheek. "I love that cute way you have of raising your eyebrows when you're amused. That endearing habit of lowering your eyelashes when embarrassed. The way you can put me in my place with just a look."

She laughed. "Why, you're a romantic, Matt Walker. I love you lock, stock and barrel."

She curved into his arms, a perfect fit, and a perfect mate. Matt's heart filled with an almost painful bliss. After years of living with the guilt of Amy's heartrending loss, lonely even when surrounded by family and friends, he'd been given a second chance. A new beginning with the woman he loved. The woman who loved him in return. The sorrowing years were over. The joyful years just beginning.

He lifted his hands to her face and showed her that truth, the deepest feelings of his heart with his kiss. A long, tender kiss filled with certainty that God had brought them together for a real marriage.

"Mercy, this marriage of convenience is most definitely in trouble." She raised her face to his, an invitation in her eyes. "Trouble we both are prepared to handle."

"No trouble at all." He grinned, hugging her to him. "I'm not letting you go, wife."

"Well, in that case, how will we get the work done?"

"Maybe you should take life a little easy and let me carry the weight for a while."

She tilted her head, considering. "Okay, but only until my ribs are healed. Then I'll go back to carrying my own weight."

"I have no doubt that my feisty wife can handle the heavy things, the tough things, even the imperfect things." His dimple winked. "The reason she married me."

She snuggled closer until their hearts beat as one. "We'll hang a W beside the P and make the ranch ours."

"Our land," he said, "our home."

"Yes," she whispered as the night birds called and the moon caressed the landscape. "Forever."

* * * * *

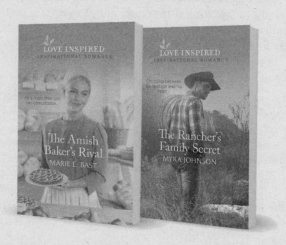

SPECIAL EXCERPT FROM

🌿

LOVE INSPIRED
INSPIRATIONAL ROMANCE

*What happens when a tough marine and a sweet dog
trainer don't see eye to eye?*

Read on for a sneak preview of
The Marine's Mission *by Deb Kastner.*

"Oscar will be perfect for your needs," Ruby assured Aaron,
reaching down to scratch the poodle's head.

"That froufrou dog? No way, ma'am. Not gonna happen."

"Excuse me?" She'd expected him to hesitate but not
downright reject her idea.

"Look, Ruby, if you like Oscar so much, then keep him
for yourself. I need a man's dog by my side, not some…
some…"

"Poodle?" Ruby suggested, her eyebrows disappearing
beneath her long ginger bangs.

"Right. Lead me to where you keep the German
shepherds, and I'll pick one out myself."

"Hmm," Ruby said, rubbing her chin as if considering his
request, although she really wasn't. "No."

"No?"

"No," she repeated firmly. "First off, we don't currently
have a German shepherd as part of our program."

"I'd even take a pit bull." He was beginning to sound
desperate.

"Look, Aaron. Either you're going to have to learn to
trust me or you may as well just leave now before we start.
This isn't going to work unless you're ready to listen to me
and do whatever I tell you to do."

His eyebrows furrowed. "I understand chain of command, ma'am. There were many times as a marine when I didn't exactly agree with my superiors, but I understood why it was important to follow orders."

"Okay. Let's go with that."

"For me," Aaron continued, "following orders is black-and-white. My marines' lives under my command often depended on it. But as you can see, I'm having difficulty making that transition in this situation. We're not talking people's lives here."

"I disagree. We're very much talking lives—*yours*. You may not yet have a clear vision of what you'll be able to do with Oscar, but a service dog can make all the difference."

"Yes, but you just insisted the best dog for me is a *poodle*. I'm sorry, but if you knew anything about me at all, you'd know the last dog in the world I'd choose would be a poodle."

"And yet I still believe I'm right," said Ruby with a wry smile. Somehow, she had to convince this man she knew what she was doing. "I carefully studied your file before you arrived, Aaron, and specially selected Oscar for you to work with. I'm the expert here. So how are we going to get over this hurdle?"

"I have orders to make this work. How will it look if I give up before I even start the process?" He shook his head. "No. Don't answer that. It will look as if I wasn't able to complete my mission. That's never going to happen. I'll *always* pull through, no matter what."

Don't miss
The Marine's Mission *by Deb Kastner,*
available July 2021 wherever
Love Inspired books and ebooks are sold.

LoveInspired.com

LIEXP0621

LOVE INSPIRED

INSPIRATIONAL ROMANCE

UPLIFTING STORIES OF FAITH, FORGIVENESS AND HOPE.

Join our social communities to connect with other readers who share your love!

Sign up for the Love Inspired newsletter at **LoveInspired.com** to be the first to find out about upcoming titles, special promotions and exclusive content.

HARLEQUIN

Heartfelt or thrilling, passionate or uplifting—Harlequin is more than just happily-ever-after.

With twelve different series to choose from and new books available every month, you are sure to find stories that will move you, uplift you, inspire and delight you.

HNEWS2021